INFOMOCRACY

INFOMOCRACY

MALKA OLDER

A TOM DOHERTY ASSOCIATES BOOK
NEW YORK

INFOMOCRACY

Copyright © 2016 by Malka Older

Edited by Carl Engle-Laird

A Tor.com Book
Published by Tom Doherty Associates, LLC
175 Fifth Avenue
New York, NY 10010

www.tor-forge.com

Tor® is a registered trademark of Tom Doherty Associates, LLC.

The Library of Congress Cataloging-in-Publication Data is available upon request.

ISBN 978-0-7653-8515-4 (hardcover)
ISBN 978-0-7653-8514-7 (e-book)

Our books may be purchased in bulk for promotional, educational, or business use. Please contact your local bookseller or the Macmillan Corporate and Premium Sales Department at 1-800-221-7945, extension 5442, or by e-mail at MacmillanSpecialMarkets@macmillan.com.

First Edition: June 2016

Printed in the United States of America

0 9 8 7 6 5 4 3 2 1

TO THE ONES I LOVE

ACKNOWLEDGMENTS

Thank you to my family: Lou, Calyx, Dora, Marc, and Daniel. I couldn't have done it without you. My mother, Dora Vázquez Older, read the initial drafts chapter by chapter, providing me with encouragement, soft deadlines, and invaluable suggestions. My brother, Daniel José Older, helped me navigate the complications of publishing.

Huge thanks to Carl Engle-Laird at Tor.com, who encouraged this book, believed in it, and bought it. He understood what I was trying to do from his first, very early reading of it, and his support, ideas, and close attention to language improved *Infomocracy* immeasurably, while his humor and respect made the editing process a pleasure. Many thanks also to everyone else at Tor.com and Tor Books who was involved.

I did a lot of writing before I got to this book, and the encouragement and feedback of many friends and family, including Professor David Gullette, Jessica Hammer, Rotimi Babatunde, Austin Grossman, Jim Jarvie, Barbara Parker, Julie Hackett, Chris Thorpe, Dora Vázquez Older, Marc Older, Daniel José Older, and Lou Valdez, among others, kept me writing. Thank you.

This is a global book, and I could not have written it without the people who have welcomed me all over the world. The following is a partial list, limited to the countries that appear in the book. Apologies to everyone I don't mention by name. You know who you are.

In Kagoshima, the Board of Education of Ei back when Ei was a town, and the musoshinden-ryu iai dojo that used to practice above the Tsubame Taxi Company. I also want to thank all my martial arts instructors outside Japan, especially Sensei Brian Ricci for sai technique, fighting strategy, and the anecdote about the katana cutting into a machine gun. In Kansai, Nazuki Konishi and her family. Also, Professors Mayumi Sakamoto and Aiko Sakurai, for separately introducing me to the great work of the Disaster Reduction and Human Renovation Institute, which does not deserve to have its beautifully designed facility attacked by anarchists. In Tohoku and Tokyo, the Peace Winds Japan team. Also in Tokyo, the Save the Children team, and Yoshi-haru Kimura. Felipe Ospina and Kaori Yamaki, for going beyond hospitality, often when I was too shattered to properly respond. Thank you.

In Argentina, Javier Otaka and his family. In Indonesia, the Mercy Corps team and Sheila Town and her family. In Singapore, Yibin Chu. In Peru, the Save the Children team and the Tierra de Niños team. In Addis Ababa, the Save the Children DRR working group, and Mohammed Ali, who invited me for coffee and chechebsa. In New York, Jessica Hammer, Chris Hall, and my brother, Daniel José Older. In Sri Lanka, the Sewa Lanka team and the Mercy Corps team, with special thanks to Dasan Stephen for his stories about the Maldives. I'll thank Jim Jarvie and Laurie Pierce in the Sri Lanka section as well, although their care, friendship, and insight have been as global as this list.

Thanks to all the strangers who made my visits to Naha and Beirut so fantastic. I've spent more time in the Doha airport than in Doha itself, so a shout-out to the Nepali staff there.

In Paris, Olivier Borraz, who is a profound, committed, and principled thesis advisor and writes brilliantly on risk and on local government, two important themes of this book. He went above and beyond to help me integrate into the city, and his kindness colored my experience of it. So did the warmth of Anne Macey Baverel and her family, and Anita Michel-Schieszler and Sedgwick Schieszler and their family, who welcomed me into their homes. The researchers and doctorcitos of the Centre de Sociologie des Organisations, who make it such a wonderful place to study: I am grateful for the opportunity to learn with and from you. Also, my former neighbors in the 14ème, for breaking every stereotype about rude and unfriendly Parisians.

I'm going to thank my family again, because thanking family is so obvious and so often done that it can be taken for granted. I have done many things in my life more or less alone, which made it easy to forget all the ways in which my family made it possible for me to do them. This book was not one of those things. I wrote the bulk of it while I was deeply and happily enmeshed in family, and the writing and editing took time and emotional effort that could have gone elsewhere. Thank you for giving me what I needed to work on this, for supporting me while I did, and for being there when I finished.

INFOMOCRACY

CHAPTER 1

The sign on the defunct pachinko parlor proclaims 21ST CENTURY, but the style—kanji in neon outlined in individual light bulbs? Who does that?—suggests it was named at a time when that was a bold look toward the future, not a statement of fact that has been accurate for more than sixty years. As Ken watches the sign draw closer and closer on his dashboard, he wonders whether the place closed as a consequence of gambling becoming illegal when that canton split off from what used to be Japan, or whether it was a function of its location on a nameless stretch of highway between two tiny towns, one of which no longer exists. He doesn't care enough to check. What is important is that it is closed, and likely to remain so, and unlikely to be watched.

He gets a shock as an old-fashioned bicycle toodles by the building on his display, the rider a cocoon of parkas and scarves. It's a live feed? Ken cares enough to check on that but is reassured to find that the camera has been focused there for almost three years, apparently in response to teenagers joyriding in search of ghosts. Ken shrugs mentally; he'll have to hope no one who knows enough to pay attention to him is watching. The odds are pretty good, given how many feeds there are out there and how few people know they should be interested in his actions.

After months of campaign research in dense potential domino centenals, the solitude out here is putting Ken on edge. It's a strange place to meet that happened to be convenient for both him and his contact. He took the ferry over from Korea to the west coast of Japan. The plan was just to pass through Akita on his way here, but he was able to get in a few quick lay-of-the-land surveys and shoot them up the hierarchy in case they either prove to be useful or get someone to notice his initiative and hustle. Akita felt so remote and unnoticed that he broke character a little and went beyond data gathering to do some actual campaigning, but he doubts it had any effect. The same reasons that made it safe made it useless: the people he talked to were callused old farmers and fishermen who believe the election is local and vote for whatever party co-opts their traditional leaders. He tried to suggest to them that the Supermajority was important, that it could be their centenal that decided it, but it wasn't even that they disbelieved him. They just didn't care.

In Akita, he rented a mini-motor and crossed Honshu to the eastern coast, following the old high-speed rail tracks that cut straight across the country until his maximum-utility path deviated from them and he had to pull off onto narrow, well-maintained roads in what was clearly the middle of nowhere.

Sure, it's not one of those centenals in the Gobi Desert or the Australian Outback where the hundred thousand citizens are scattered over hundreds of empty miles. There are towns here, tiny shrunken ones that show up as dots on his map projection, almost lost within the erratic, widely spaced centenal borders. Ken breezes through a couple on his way: white houses with grey slate roofs pitched to let the snow slide off, isolated shops with antiquated signs lit from within advertising Pocari Sweat or Boss coffee. Heavy grey clouds make the sky darker than the snowy ground, but it's still technically daytime, and most of the light in the towns comes from glowing Information hubs doubling as vending machines. He stops to get a can of coffee at one, his Information visuals projecting translations and explanations next to the product descriptions. Then he roars off, and from there it's just road and sharp slopes covered with trees. Even Information has little to say here.

Ken pulls his mini-motor off the road well outside camera range of the feed he was watching and walks the rest of the way. Bundled as he is against the winter's edge, he won't be recognizable on a feed of that resolution. If anyone happens to be watching they'll think he's some local farmer, stepping into the run-down building for a respite from the cold.

Not an undercover political operative slipping in for a meeting he doesn't want anyone to know about.

Despite not wanting to be visible any longer than necessary, Ken finds his steps slowing as he nears the pachinko parlor. Below the deadened pink neon of the sign, the building is a fading, windowless grey. The smoked-glass door was once automatic, and Ken has to struggle to edge it open. The scant light that makes it into the entrance hallway dies mired in the moldy plush carpet. The next door, only a few steps away, must once have swung open easily to welcome gamblers, but as Ken pushes it, his sleeve wrapped around his hand to avoid touching the crude and dusty alloy of the handle, it stutters along the floor before finally giving in with a screech.

Which is when Ken gets his second unpleasant surprise of the day. Despite his arrival a clean two hours early, his contact got there first.

· · ·

"You don't *vote*?" The girl's tone rises with the incredulity of someone who has sucked up every mag article and vidlet about this being the event of the decade, the election of the century, the most important vote yet, a chance to change the established order, blah blah blah blah blah. Her echo chamber of friends and rivals does not include non-voters. She's come to this supposed voter registration rally not only because it's the best party on tonight in the greater Río de la Plata area, but also because it feels like virtuous pleasure, an exciting civic duty with a built-in conversation starter. In sum: a semisentient being experiencing the first election she can vote in.

"Nah," Domaine says, taking a toke. "Why? Do you?"

Girl laughs. "Of course! I'm already registered. Why wouldn't you vote? I mean, in this election, we really have a chance to change things. Your vote could be the one to make the difference."

"How do you know whom I would vote for?" Domaine asks. "Your vote and my vote might cancel each other out."

She's still smiling, maybe because his voice has a way of making that sound like a sexy proposition, or maybe because of the alcohol and weed, the mild summer air of the dark night, and the sounds of the electric accordion from the stage. "Somehow, I don't think so," she giggles, which makes Domaine want to gag, but he keeps his game face on. "Anyway, the important thing is that you vote. It's all about participation."

Yes, it's all about participation. No matter who wins or loses, as long as everyone plays the game. Never mind that half of Buenos Aires belongs to Liberty and is likely to continue to, and the other half has its head up its denialist ass and consistently votes itself into what's left of the European Union. All this surrounded by a checkerboard of populist and regionalist governments in the provinces, few of them with any centenals outside the southern cone.

"How do you know whom to vote for?" Domaine asks. The girl's wearing an oil-slick dress, and it reflects the glow of the string of light bulbs swinging above the outdoor bar like fires on the water.

"That's what Information is for," she says, giggling again. Which is what Domaine has been waiting for.

"Really? And where do you get your—"

"An afro that big has *got* to say something about sexual potency."

Domaine snaps his head around, brushing the incipient ideologue with the edge of his 'do, to see an auburn-haired Asian woman at his right elbow.

"Mizzzzzz Mishima," he growls, feeling his pulse rate climb.

Mishima is also wearing black but in the thinnest of airy cottons, flowing around her body in a way that probably obscures a few concealed weapons. "Domaine. *Imagine* meeting you at this party."

Domaine is too busy imagining those weapons. He considers himself an eminently reconstructed male and is disturbed by how much those images arouse him. *Would you be turned on if she held a knife to your throat?* he asks himself. *Probably,* is the even more disturbing answer.

Voter girl is still talking. Domaine runs his right hand through his hair, giving it a subtle twitch by his ear. The magnet in his ring turns off his automatic interpreter, and her Lunfardo patter goes back to being unintelligible. He needs his mojo back. "Party?" he repeats, leaning toward Mishima. "Is that what this is?"

She smiles with dark-crimsoned lips, looks around. "Live music, decorative lights, various recreational drugs," nodding at the joint between Domaine's fingers. "Looks like a party to me."

"Ah," Domaine takes a long pull from his blunt, as though he had forgotten it was there. "I must have been misinformed. I thought it was a voter motivation drive."

"I suppose they might be multitasking," Mishima says. "You looking to sign up?"

"Baby, you can motivate me any time," Domaine rumbles. He pretends to think about it for a moment. "I wouldn't have to actually vote though, would I?"

"No, Domaine, you don't have to do anything at all," Mishima says, turning away into the crowd. She's gotten word in her earpiece: they checked him out and found nothing in a long-distance body scan or the records of his recent movements to suggest he's planning violence. Maybe it's her narrative disorder acting up again.

But before she can take a step a deep rushing noise builds over the notes of the alt-tango. Mishima swings back around. Domaine has turned too, although she doesn't realize it at first because his head is silhouetted in the glow of the huge flaming letters rising above the park, igniting one by one:

WP = DICTADOR.

Domaine laughs with glee and spins back to Mishima, but she has already propelled past him in the direction of the fiery libel.

· · ·

It is so dim inside the old pachinko parlor that it takes Ken several seconds to make out the gun. He edges past the sticky glass door, blinking at the dust and the rows of silent slot machines, which his Information is busy annotating with release date, model, and largest jackpot at this location. Fortunately, Ken is practiced at ignoring the scrawl projected onto his vision. He takes another cautious step, then stops short as more faint light creeps in from the entrance behind him, glinting off something just ahead.

The metal tip of an arrowhead. Ken raises his eyes to find the face behind it. And lets his breath out slowly. He's still not sure he isn't dead, but at least he knows the person who's aiming a spear gun at him.

"Amuru-san," Ken says, slowly and clearly. He raises his hands, also slowly, to unwrap the scarf and push back his hood. "At last we meet in person."

Amuru grunts but does not lower the gun. "You are early."

"Clearly not early enough," Ken answers, hands hovering around his collarbones. He feels like he should unzip his coat to allow for freer range of motion in case this does get physical, but the temperature in here is not much of an improvement over outside. "Can I provide you with some reassurance as to my identity?"

"No, that won't be necessary," Amuru says, but he waits an extra beat before sliding the spear away from Ken and setting the gun down on top of a long-obsolete change machine close at hand. "This is, after all, a friendly exchange of information. Two friends talking about politics from their respective viewpoints a few weeks before an election." Nothing in his face or tone changes to make it feel friendlier than a holdup.

"Indeed." Ken is impressed by the spear gun: an unorthodox weapon, sure, but both legal and lethal. That the person holding it is from Okinawa gives it additional credibility. He takes a cautious step forward. "Perhaps you could start by describing to me the situation as it stands in the Ryukyus?"

Amuru nods. He's wearing a dark blue parka, fur from the lined hood peeking around his collar, but now that Ken is closer he can see the man's large brown feet crossed by the black thongs of plastic flip-flops.

"It could be worse. As usual, we have a couple of centenals that are sure for your side, and others divided among the various corporates. 1China will not do well; the centenals that went with her last time are disappointed and somewhat open to new suggestions."

"We'll have a fairly open field there?"

"It is possible that the opportunity has gone unnoticed. But there may be others, like me, helping others, like you."

Ken nods. Obviously, there will be. Policy1st is hardly the first government to try to campaign without broadcasting its strategy. "You said you'd bring a breakdown of the key issues in these areas?"

Amuru casts a projection up with a detailed map of the islands and pulls out notes for each centenal, detailing their political, socioeconomic, and cultural characteristics as well as recent events or trends that might affect voting. It's professionally done, and Ken is pleased although not surprised. Policy1st tends to attract people with a grasp of the issues and of what's at stake. Every centenal, every collection of one hundred thousand neighbors, matters, whether it is spread over hundreds of miles in the tundra or crammed into a couple of overdeveloped blocks in Dhaka.

"And there on that coast, there's something going on with

the shoreline. They've had a lot of erosion there recently; I don't know what the cause is but it's a big concern for everyone. Also, that's where the American base was for decades. Even though it's been gone almost as long, they still remember it, so you have to be very careful with anything that suggests it even remotely, anything that reminds people about colonialism or militarism in any form."

Ken is listening, nodding, recording everything. He has his own detailed map of the Ryukyus open, the projection glowing brighter than usual in the dusty, dim air between them, and is adjusting the color coding on the centenals the Okinawan is mentioning and adding notes of his own.

"The thing you should know, though," Amuru goes on, "Liberty is making a serious push."

"Sou desu ka?"

"Yeah. Not so much with the 1China centenals; more with the Ryukyu nationalists. They've been telling people, quietly, that if enough of Okinawa's centenals go to them and they become the Supermajority, they'll annex what's left of Japan."

Ken's eyebrows shoot up. "They said that?"

Amuru nods slowly, then adds, "Peacefully. They always say 'annex peacefully.'"

What does that even mean, "annex peacefully"? Ken's grasp of twentieth-century history is dim, and he can't find an analogy. "Don't people realize they're not seriously going to do it?" he asks. "I mean, they *can't* be serious."

"Does that matter?" Amuru points out. "If they gain ground in Okinawa but do not become the Supermajority, no one will expect them to keep the promise, and you can be sure they will try to consolidate in the Ryukyus over the next decade."

"And if they do win the Supermajority?" Ken knows he shouldn't even suggest the possibility. Campaigning 101 includes never admitting that an opponent's victory is even conceivable, but he's off balance.

"Maybe they will do what they claim," Amuru says. His eyes drop from Ken's. "That promise, of annexing Japan and especially Satsuma—it is still very powerful for us."

"More powerful than micro-democracy? More powerful than peace?"

"Micro-democracy has brought winners and losers in the Ryukyus, like everywhere else," Amuru answers. "As for peace . . ." He shrugs, and fires off a four-character adage that Ken's not familiar with. It seems to suggest peace without justice isn't all it's cracked up to be. Or peace without vengeance. The phrasing is ambiguous.

"Has it been recorded? This—" threat? Promise? "—slogan?"

Amuru shrugs. "Wouldn't you know that better than I do?" Ken is too busy composing an urgent message in his head to answer, and Amuru presses his advantage. "Let's see your globe."

Ken expected that, expected it enough to prepare the globe he wants Amuru to see and store it in a special filepath as though it were the only one, but he's still surprised to be asked. He supposes, as he goes through the motions of opening the file under LATEST PROJECTIONS, that he expected more sophistication from someone who brought a spear gun to a data fight.

The globe he opens is purely speculative, and in most areas strategically optimistic, although their projections for mainland Japan are distinctly underplayed. The heavy spotting in China is possible but unlikely, and although Ken is hopeful for Java, it is still far too early and crowded there to be sure. As the globe spins, a darkened Middle East and Central Asia come into view, then a surprising amount of color through sub-Saharan Africa and—this much Ken feels is justified—large swathes of Europe, not just western. North America is its usual mostly bipolar patchwork, with isolated representation for Policy1st in some of the urban areas, and Latin America looks on this version like an intense battle-ground, pulsing dots in Caracas, Cartagena, Buenos Aires, and a dozen more cities showing voter events going on at that very moment.

Amuru must know that this can't all be true, or at least not verified. Maybe he wants to know what Ken, and the government he represents, want him to see. Or maybe he wants to see anything at this point, any intel about the way this contest is going, any hint that he can take back to share with others or keep close for secret reassurance. One thing Ken has learned in this job: people like to think they know things, even the unknowable.

Whatever he's looking for, Amuru grunts as if he's found it. "Ganbatte iru, ne," he comments, which Ken takes as a positive reaction. It would be tough to convince people to vote for them if they didn't think they were working hard. "It would help," Amuru goes on, "if you gave us a *person* to vote for. Ideally someone photogenic and smooth talking, like the others have."

It isn't the first time Ken has gotten this request. "We want people to understand that they're choosing a set of pol-icies and principles, a way of life, not a person. Of course," he adds as Amuru waves his hand, now alarmingly holding the spear gun, in annoyance, "we will have people represent-ing us at the debates. Attractive, well-spoken people."

"People?" Amuru asks suspiciously.

"We will have different representatives at each of the debates," Ken explains, rewrapping his scarf.

The older man, moving toward the door, leans close to Ken. "They have said that if they win, they will *peacefully* annex Japan. What do you think they will do to those centenals in Okinawa that belong to other governments, like yours?" His heavy eyes stare that idea into Ken's brain, and then he disappears into the cold. "Wait at least an hour before you follow me out!"

Ken shivers and finds a seat at a pachinko machine (a 2008 Evangelion Premium that once shelled out 28,830 yen to a lucky winner) to send off some heavily underlined messages and check the latest polls while he waits. At least he'll be out of here earlier than he expected. Sixteen days until the vote and one of the corporates is threatening war. There's a lot of work to do.

Mishima activates her crowdcutter and it springs from its microcrimped home in the clasps on her dress, a transparent vinyl shell shaped like a shark fin that lets her scythe through the mass of people glomming toward the sign.

"Jorge!" she yells into her earpiece mic. Her vinyl wedge is pushing aside clingy couples, shoulder-hugging friends, and, as she gets closer to the building with the fire-writing on top, a dense mass of openmouthed spectators. "I'm on my way. Have whoever gets there first cover any rear exits; everyone else, meet me on the roof. Mariana, prepare the rebuttal." She hates that word, *rebuttal*. If they had done their jobs right, the misinformation never would have gotten out in the first place. "It should be a projection the same size and

position as those letters. Georgina, keep eyes on Domaine . . .
That guy I was talking to . . . He's connected with radical
antielection movements—" She can't waste her breath on
this; she's about to run up who knows how many flights of
stairs. "Just look him up. And don't lose him!"

Another *whoosh*. Mishima glances over her shoulder long
enough to see the flames shooting off another rooftop but
doesn't pause to decipher the words. "Jorge?"

"I'm on it." Her interpreter gives her the words in Japanese but keeps Jorge's deep, calming tone. "We've got plenty
of people here. We're covered."

"Not covered enough," Mishima mutters.

The Avenida del Libertador that runs between the park
and the adjoining ForzaItalia centenal has been closed off to
ground vehicles for the rally, and Mishima skids across it
without slowing. She's already pinpointed the apartment
building, a pale façade latticed with minimal rectangular
balconies, awnings fluttering over them in the faint breeze.
She pulls the blueprints as she barrels into the lobby, projects them at eyeball level, and heads straight for the door
marked EMERGENCY EXIT.

The stairwell is cool after the heat of the crowds and lit
only by an illuminated banister zigzagging up into the dimness. Mishima dumps her crowdcutter at the bottom—it
won't refold and doesn't provide much protection—and
starts up the first flight.

WP stands for William Pressman, the nominal head of
the Heritage government. He's not a dictator, even though
Heritage has held the Supermajority since the election system started. Every second, as she pounds up and up, those
letters are there, burning for all to see, being recorded and
sent around the world. Even though the truth or at least all

the relevant Information is easily available, every second the words are up there sows more doubt and confusion. She can still hear the music from the rally; the alt-tango has given way to a fast-paced kora–steel drum duet, which only ratchets up the tension. Why couldn't the organizers have stuck with some rousing but low-tempo trova? Breathing heavily but still moving fast, Mishima risks a glance out a window on what is either the fifth or the sixth floor. The fire phrase on the other building shines clearly now: H=CHILABOR, a reference to a Heritage sweatshop scandal from a couple of years ago. Mostly false. That one is going to require a long and complicated rebuttal.

Mishima pauses at the top of the stairwell to steady her breath and draw her stiletto. There is a steady thrumming from the other side, through which she can make out the occasional crackle of flame. She doubts she'll find anyone on the roof: any half-decent plan would have the perpetrators far away by now. But the first rule of security is *Don't be stupid*. Mishima pushes the roof-access door open hard, keeping her body angled away, and checks the whole roof before settling down to examine the mechanism that's keeping those letters roaring two dozen feet above her head. It's a simple enough system: letter-shaped frames around the wicks, and a pump sending accelerant—kerosene, from the smell of it—from a barrel next to the access door. Mishima wants to slash the line, but spilling flammable liquid all over this roof is not worth even a few seconds' gain, so she settles for turning off the pump.

The fire-writing gutters and, letter by letter, blinks out, leaving the roof in retina-stinging darkness. Mishima darts back inside the stairwell to grab a fire extinguisher she saw a few floors down. By the time she gets back to the roof, the letters have blackened and shriveled, and are sinking slowly down. She douses the wicks as they land. Two security officers from Jorge's team show up while she's doing so, with their own portable extinguishers.

As they finish spraying, the nitrogen haze around them turns ruddy, and Mishima looks up to see the glow of a projection. Rubbing at the patina of sweat across her face, she walks to the parapet and twists around to see the rebuttal. Mariana followed the instructions: the letters look to be about the same size, and she's even added a sort of shimmery cast that approximates fire. But they are utterly lacking in menace and go on for a paragraph and a half, stretching far along the avenida and referencing, as far as she can tell from this angle, the official Academia Española definition of dictador.

She turns and looks out across the park in time to see the *o* and the *r* from the ChiLabor message wink out. A faint sigh comes up from the crowd: the excitement is over. The kora and steel drum duo—Mishima can see the stage from here—launch into another piece, this one more of a ballad. The projection detailing the accusations and counteraccusations related to the labor misconduct from two years ago appears at the other end of the park, but nobody is watching anymore.

"Jorge?" Mishima mutters. "Did we get anyone?"

"Negative."

"Georgina?"

"That guy hasn't moved. He's standing right where you left him. Seemed to enjoy the show, though."

Domaine has indeed enjoyed himself, alternating his gaze between the flaming subversion of Information and the pantomime of excited consternation, urgent documentation, and rapid, vapid commentary in the faces around him. He stayed put in part out of hope that Mishima would come back to finish their conversation, and his eyes scan and rescan the laughing, talking, drinking, smoking, swaying Buenos Aires elite for her figure, although he realizes it's a diminishing possibility. Finally, he swings around toward the group he was talking to when Mishima arrived. Voter girl gave up on him some time ago and has gone back to talking with her friends, glossy lips in unstopping motion, perfectly content to be part of this newsworthy, useless event.

"They're using you!" Domaine hisses, leaning in close to her, then sweeping his wide eyes around the circle of expertly made-up faces. "All of you!"

CHAPTER 2

Although he has twenty-three centenals scheduled for a South and Southeast Asia swing over the next five days, Ken mostly expects to get yanked into a meeting about what he learned from Amuru. No message comes during the night, and despite his fondness for certain familiar parts of the upcoming trip (the foot massage in the Singapore airport; a certain bar in Kemang; a thosai spot he's fond of in Chennai), he is grumpy as he sets out. It doesn't help that he has to fly cargo class. Even the thought of the equatorial warmth can't soothe him.

It's still dark when he drops off his rented mini-motor and checks in at the airport. His Information presets had very little to tell him during his rural detour, except the occasional comment about the type of tree sliding by or when the road was constructed, and the rush of exposition in the airport comes as a shock, especially on such little sleep. Ken quickly learns, and completely fails to absorb, a great deal about the politicking involved in the airport's initial construction and the decision on its location, as well as which airlines serve it and since when and to which connections, and its place in various ranking schemes (official associations, user-generated, statistically based), while bypassing reams on the sourcing of materials, the architecture firm, and the history of the land below it. Along the way, ads—flat and projected, still and animated—crowd his vision, all of them translated and most of them annotated by his Information: he learns that the company trying to sell him whiskey is a subsidiary of Coca-Cola (not surprising, since they are part of the corporate government that owns this airport) and sees the annual statement summary for a firm offering wealth management. Not having any wealth to speak of, he ignores both the ad and the background Information discrediting it.

As he walks past the large windows looking out on the runways, Information projects a split-screen view with old-school vids of exactly the same scene taken during the flooding of the 2011 tsunami. Because his tastes tend toward the political and cultural rather than the nutritional or ecological, during his brief lap through the gift shop his Information explains the projections of cows making rude faces at him with a discourse on the importance of beef tongue as a delicacy in the Sendai area. His gaze rests momentarily on an unidentifiable stuffed animal, a sort of curved triangle with bulging eyes and an unlikely smile, and he learns about shark hunting, long illegal but, his Information suggests, still practiced in some of the surrounding towns; the fluffy souvenir represents the fin.

He heads to one of the cafés and orders a concoction of caffeine, sugar, and artificial flavoring—Ken has blocked his handheld from giving him dietary breakdowns on anything he's ingesting, as long as it's not outright poisonous—from the superfluous, bright-eyed attendant. The attendant has allowed some of her Information to be public, and so while he waits for his beverage, Ken sees projected next to her cheerful face the high school she went to (Sendai Shougyou) and her favorite cartoon character (Hello Kitty in a frog suit). He takes the silicon mug to the gate, its animated map showing the recycling bin closest to his current location auto-updating as he moves. He glances at the polls, then watches the deicing going on outside the window (he has also forbidden his feeds from giving him any data about the age or airworthiness of the planes he's about to board) while he tries to talk himself out of his funk.

It's normal that they might not want to include him on strategy discussions, even if those discussions are based on his intel. He's young, after all, and has shot up the ranks at Policy1st fast, and via an unlikely path. Ken is reminding himself that he's in it for the right reasons, for the policy, not for the excitement, when Suzuki Todry sits down next to him, a similar silicon mug in hand.

"Interesting stuff," Suzuki says.

"Surprising," Ken ventures, trying to keep his tone as neutral as his mentor's.

Suzuki shrugs. "Not necessarily."

"Threatening war?" There's no one within three meters of them, but Ken keeps his voice down anyway.

"It might be just that," Suzuki says amiably. "A threat. Posturing. Remember, if this statement hasn't been recorded, not only can we not attack them for it before the election, but no one can hold them to it if they do win. Maybe they're betting that they can win Okinawa this way, but not the Supermajority, so they won't have to make good on the promise."

"Liberty's trying to go all the way," Ken says.

"But it's not at all sure they will."

"Either way. This is extreme. This is exactly what the system was created to prevent."

Suzuki nods. "We have people in Okinawa trying to get vid of this promise. We're also thinking of running an ad or two ourselves." He holds out his screen. "What do you think?"

The soundtrack goes straight into Ken's ear amplifiers, and he sets the projection to play in stereo at the closest possible points to his eyes, tiny and two-dimensional so no one else can watch, although his brain stitches together a full-sized, full-depth result.

It's your standard election ad, inspiring music over scenes of happy, sunlit, productive people of different races, interspersed with graphics that suggest, without ever showing the full picture, prediction maps of a Policy1st landslide. The narrative is in Okinawan, but there are subtitles in English, Japanese, and Chinese for people who don't have translators.

Twenty years ago, the people of the world came together in an unprecedented step to form a new international order. Since the first global election, war among participating jurisdictions has been eradicated, and prosperity and trade have spread.

Policy1st believes in the principles of the elections. We offer you a clear, honest expression of our policy positions, and seek peace and economic growth in all our centenals. Visit one of our centenals, check us out on your comparison sheets, and use your Information to see what Policy1st can do for you.

It ends with the Policy1st campaign slogan for this election, drawn in expertly calligraphed characters in their signature colors, bold yellow on a fresh, sky blue background.

The best policies, the best results.

"Pretty good," Ken says, impressed at the subtlety and at how quickly they put it together. It never mentioned war, annexation, or Japan but would draw a clear counterpoint for anyone who had gotten Liberty's message. "But you know, anyone excited by the idea of . . . you know, *war*, I mean . . . this is not going to change their minds."

"If we find something concrete, we can get more aggressive with our advertising and at the same time launch a complaint to the election board."

"It's amazing, with all the Information collectors out there now"—Ken shakes his head—"how many things still slip through."

"Amazing," Suzuki sighs, "but true. There's a lot that gets past Information analysis. You should know that better than anyone," he adds, glowering at Ken from under his eyebrows. Ken wonders if Suzuki has already checked whether yesterday's rendezvous showed up anywhere. "We can't depend on them to protect the fairness of this election. I want you to keep an ear out on this trip. See if Liberty has been making similar promises elsewhere."

Ken runs through his destinations in his mind. "Hard to sell in Java, although they might scrape a centenal or two together on that basis. But Liberty's pretty weak there; PhilipMorris is the big corporate to worry about. Singapore and Taiwan—yeah, an anti-Japan message could still resonate. But war?"

"Be alert," Suzuki says. "It might take other forms. Try to record anything relevant you find."

Ken nods, feeling a pulse of excitement. "They won't make that easy."

"Buy whatever recording devices you think will help. Check out the latest generation of recorder disks; they're amazingly small. Plenty of places where you can do that in Singapore—or Jakarta, for that matter. Try the centenals belonging to Asia's Return—they have particularly lax controls on pirating electronics."

Better and better.

"And keep your own head down—this does not supersede

our overall strategy. We don't want them to know where we're playing." A second of hesitation. "Keep your head down, and watch your back."

Mishima stretches in her travel bed, checks the time. Late. The Buenos Aires voter motivation party rocked until well past dawn. Mishima knows these events are important, and maybe once she would have enjoyed them, but now she finds they leave her feeling drained. Not tired so much as empty, annoyed at all the hullabaloo for people who barely even think about their votes. Officially, she was there to collect as much data as possible and send it up for analysis, like any other Information employee, but her secret purview is far wider. Last night, in addition to supervising the organization of the gig and coordinating with the local security team, she was keeping an eye out for the kind of campaigning that governments do at voter rallies, which are supposed to be apolitical. Usually it is much more subtle than unsubstantiated allegations spelled out in giant burning letters.

She rolls over and checks the status of the libel case. Jorge and the local team are focused on RosarioPrimero, the only government competing directly with Heritage in the immediate surroundings, but Mishima is not so sure. Heritage may not be in many close races in the Río de la Plata area, but the big governments are thinking about the Supermajority, and any loss for Heritage will increase their chances. Besides, those images were recorded and shared so quickly, they could influence voters anywhere; it might well be a global play rather than a local one. A team is working on cleaning it up, but the changing patterns of the flames is making it hard to efficiently search for the shots. A bit sophisticated for RosarioPrimero, Mishima thinks, checking out their Information: only two centenals, one of which they're probably about to lose to Heritage. She told Jorge to look bigger, Liberty or PhilipMorris or, possibly, 1China, who have been making inroads in the southern cone lately. She doesn't think he's going to, and toys with the idea of taking a quick scan herself, but she knows she can't solve every campaign infraction she comes across. She's supposed to be looking at the bigger picture now.

The encounter with Domaine still bothers her. Was he involved in the libel plot? It didn't look like it, but what else would he be doing there, in person and apparently alone and unarmed? Disillusioning voters one at a time? She spent the rest of the party on edge, called in half a dozen potential threats. None of them turned out to be armed, but she wants to review the vid footage anyway.

First, though, she calls up her Information. Like most people, Mishima has a couple of favorite feeds, sources that she's found to be fast and reliable, although she's probably both pickier and a better judge of "reliable" than most people. She has her screen set up to automatically calculate and source the most popular feeds globally and locally, so that at any given moment, she knows what most people are learning. She includes the major news compilers, regardless of how many people are paying attention to them, broken down to the continent level and sometimes further. Besides that, her algorithm adds in a couple of random streams that flick between various compilers, opinionators, and virtual plazas without regard for size or relevance. It's a tactic that reminds her, every time she uses it, of the panels from *Watchmen* where Ozymandias watches multiple TVs tuned to different channels to reach a composite view of society and make predictions, both financial and political. Not for the first time, Mishima wishes that her world had as few channels as his.

As usual during the keyed-up election season, she is faintly disappointed by the lack of anything earthshaking in the results. There is the standard slew of local news—minor floods in Bangladesh, a daring jewel theft in Paris, an indiscretion by a music star—none of which raises serious pings on her Radar. A significant smattering of stories about the mantle-tunnel approval process, which doesn't look like it will make it through before the election. (Mishima wonders briefly whether Heritage has delayed it on purpose, but decides the issue is too divisive for that.) Everything—the floods, the music star, obviously the mantle tunnel—is tied to the elections by this point in the cycle. All of the major feeds are dedicating resources to the campaigns, and most of them strive to have at least some coverage every day, but Mishima finds nothing surprising there, either. She skims a few of the longer features, hoping they will enhance her worldview or lead to an epiphany: "Who are the least-campaigned voters?"; "Pivot centenals across Southeast Asia"; "Most effective campaign vids." Mishima remembers similar titles from a decade ago and learns little new.

Finally, she checks up on a few races and aggregates she is following closely. With nearly a hundred thousand centenals, it can be hard to pick favorites, but part of Mishima's job is looking for trendsetters and possible dominos, as well as places that might represent interesting global dynamics. Some of this, of course, is subjective, like the centenal in Tokyo where Mishima used to live. While it was solidly Sony-Mitsubishi back then, shifts in employment and a couple of minor bureaucratic scandals have left it open to contestation, and both Heritage and Liberty are advertising heavily there. The latest polls show Liberty slightly ahead, but it looks like Sony-Mitsubishi has finally caught on to the gravity of the threat and is trotting out some new job-training programs, so it may shift again. This story—aggressive plays against weakened incumbents that are slow to respond but often effective when they do—is a key pattern for this election cycle and seems to justify Mishima's belief in subjectivity, even if not all of her supervisors agree. She also looks at the distribution in the greater Mumbai area, a seething anthill of demographic diversity and cutthroat competition, and notes Policy1st's continuing progress across Eastern Europe. Not much change since the last time she checked, twenty-two hours ago, but the data is still trending upward.

Still in bed, she checks her schedule—and, while she's at it, her location. Mishima's crow is not large, and it's not fancy, but it's almost hers. Which is to say, it belongs to Information, but it's hers to use. The fact that Mishima convinced Information that it made more sense to loan her a personal crow than to continue paying for commercial travel and hotels makes her feel additionally proprietary toward it, as a good which she has not paid for but won with her wits. (It has also given her a certain cachet among the few other Information employees who have heard about this and made her a hero to the even smaller number who were able to work out the same deal.) The best part is getting several hours alone whenever she has to travel. The best part is being able to work in bed. The best part is being able to move whenever and wherever she wants.

She's almost halfway across the Pacific, slightly delayed by inclement weather that diverted her from the optimal path. She has a few meetings to project into over the next couple of hours, and then a brainstorming session on the name-recognition problem tomorrow. In the meantime, drafts of the weekly comparison sheets, compiled by lower-level operatives, have come through for her review, so she decides to go through them before the meetings. The comparison sheets are formatted as a grid, with important topics across the top and governments down the side. There are pull-out sections for local issues at various levels—centenal, municipality, microclimate, island, time zone, language group. Each square offers the stated position of the government, an explanation of what that was calculated to mean in practice, and, if applicable, the deviation from that stated position indicated either by previous performance or current rhetoric. Citizens can even see a personalized grid with specific outcomes of each government for them: how much they would pay in taxes, for example, or changes in the funding projected to go to their kids' schools, or the probability that their local bar will be shut down.

It's a popular tool, and surveys last decade showed that a plurality of citizens used it to decide their vote. Mishima is checking for anything that she can add based on her exposure in the field, as well as scanning for questionable items, hints to campaign strategies, and possible trickery. Part of her brain is looking at it in a more personal way too: she's also an undecided voter trying to get a full picture of the options.

Halfway down the grid, as she's running her finger along the row assigned to LIBERTY, Mishima sits up in bed fast. She adjusts her vision settings, opens more feeds, tries to read five articles and watch two vids at the same time, then stops herself. She only has a couple of hours. Where should she look? She might as well start with where she's headed. Mishima begins pulling up Information from Asia.

CHAPTER 3

Domaine sees himself as being like one of those campaign workers, or a high-level Information agent like Mishima (Mishima! He wonders if it's her first or last name). He's working himself to a thread, traveling constantly, playing the geopolitical Great Game. He's just doing it for a different cause.

"Yeah, just like them. Except you hate everything they stand for," says Shamus.

Shamus is a second-generation Irishman whose maternal and paternal grandparents were, respectively, from Zambia and Gambia. "Really," Shamus says. "Imagine the limericks."

Domaine tries. "What was the fifth-line rhyme?"

"Usually Namibia. If you have enough of a brogue, you can make it work."

"You must have had fantastic geography courses," Domaine says. "Most kids where I grew up couldn't have named one country in Africa, let alone three. Hell, most of them thought Africa *was* a country."

"And where did you grow up, then?" asks Shamus. "Not Africa, I take it."

Domaine ignores him, glances up at the massive three-dimensional football game projection above the bar. They are sitting in a pub in Addis Ababa, Domaine's second port of call since the Buenos Aires party. Shamus is a graphic designer and self-described "advid concept man extraordinaire." In point of fact, Domaine can't afford the best. In the past, though, he's been happy with both Shamus's creative output and his prices, happy enough to have a beer with the man.

Ideologically, they're on opposite poles, would probably be at each other's throats if Shamus cared enough about it, which makes the beers more interesting.

Shamus moved to Addis after the first global election, during the now-traditional period of loosened immigration controls. The whole point of micro-democracy was to allow people to choose their government wherever they were, but plenty of people didn't agree with their 99,999 geographically closest friends. Some areas—Ireland being one classic example, vast zones of what used to be the United States another—had been polarized so deeply and so long that your choices if you stayed were pretty much A or B.

"Or maybe I was looking for a better climate, didja ever think of that?" Shamus points out.

Opening the borders (such borders as remained, anyway) allowed the new governments to pull in more like-minded people, consolidating their holds on their centenals for the next election and stretching into neighboring ones as populations surged. Some journalist two decades ago dubbed the process mandergerrying, although it is also known as reverse osmosis, because it results in greater concentrations of like-minded—and, on occasion, racially or ethnically alike—constituents.

"And that's exactly what's wrong with the system," Domaine says, thumping the bar.

"The system's treated me all right, mate," Shamus says. "Plus, the immigration bit isn't even part of the system—

that's something governments choose to do, and not even all of them, mind. It's a by-product."

"Systems include their by-products; it all comes from the pattern of incentives they create. It's how they make people *think,* how they make people *behave.*"

Manchester United scores, and the crowd goes wild, drawing both of them to look up at the projection hovering above the bar. Most of Manchester, including the team, now belongs to Heritage, and when the broadcast projection shifts to a graphic representation of celebratory comments and memes related to the goal, it glosses pretty closely to a map of Heritage centenals, liberally splattered around the globe. Shamus, who's rooting for the Black Stars, shakes his head and taps in an order for another Guinness.

"Look, mate," Shamus says. "Seventy years ago, do you think my grandparents, may they rest in peace, chose Ireland? Do you think they, in Zambia and Gambia, went, 'Let's see, which of the developed countries will give our kids the best chance of making it good, i.e. letting us live out our old age in the lap of luxury? Which combination of welfare state and promotion of free enterprise will get them there?' Do you think they said, 'We want our grandkids brought up Catholics and football fanatics with Gaelic names in English spelling?' 'Yeah, we wanna be rained on all the bleedin' time?' D'ya think they made an informed bloody decision?"

"Don't get me started on Information," Domaine growls.

"They didn't! They made it to Morocco lugging everything they still owned and met someone who knew someone who had the connect in Cork to slip them through, and that was that."

Shamus getting worked up actually calms Domaine

down. "They could have reformed immigration without re-doing the whole global system."

"Apparently they couldn't, could they? Besides, why should people have to move halfway across the world—well, okay, a quarter or so in my grandparents' cases, perhaps more in yours—to have a decent government? And not for nothing, mate, but you should shave off that fro, at least while you're here. Look like one of those white Rasta pretenders."

Domaine runs a hand through his pouf absently. "I agree that loosened immigration is often better. Economically, it usually is. The problem is the concentration of ideologies—and, in some cases, ethnicities." He doesn't bother to look pointedly at Shamus.

"Where people want to live isn't an ideology," Shamus says. "How they want to live. Whom they want to live with. It's only an ideology when they try to tell other governments to do the same thing."

"It doesn't have to be." Domaine says. "But the election makes it that way."

"The fact that you're antielection just tells us that wher-ever you lived before it started, you were privileged. Don't you remember what it was like? Except for that global few for whom borders didn't matter, you were affiliated with where you were from. Kids born in Cuba were labeled com-munists, kids from the US imperialists, black kids from Ire-land immigrants and opportunists. It didn't matter if you disagreed or voted for the opposition. Your fate was ruled by the majority or the powerful minority, no matter how large."

"The fact that you can still accuse me of being from some-where privileged shows that the election hasn't changed any-thing," Domaine says.

"All right," says Shamus, standing up and slapping some money on the bar. "I'm in for the night. I'll get you some product shortly—how long are you in town for?"

Domaine shakes his head. "Out early tomorrow morning."

"To?"

"Saudi."

Shamus stares. "You don't need to convince *them* not to vote—they don't!"

"Exactly."

Policy1st doesn't have a full-time operative in the Ryukyus. It's a small archipelago with minimal domino potential, so only local governments and the biggest, best-funded players keep permanent staff there. But after hearing the rumor Ken passed on from Amuru, Suzuki (who is one of those people who always knows someone everywhere) gets in touch with a contact. At fifty-one, Yoriko is old enough to have a Japanese name instead of the more Okinawan versions that became popular since elections started.

"That's not how you say it," she corrects the salaryman in the back of her taxi. "This name didn't exist in Okinawan."

Offended, he doesn't tip her.

Yoriko absentmindedly curses him out through the windshield. The conversation they had on the way downtown (Yoriko suspects him of heading for a love hotel) gave her plenty of information to pass on to Suzuki. And while taxi driving pays the bills, being Suzuki-san's Naha Irregular is far more interesting. She's getting paid to gossip. She pulls over into an alley and opens a comms feed.

Suzuki is not impressed.

"That's very good work, Yoriko-chan," he begins. Suzuki is the kind of manager who starts everything with positive reinforcement—maybe it's the non-Japanese part of him—but she can tell that he's not happy. That there will be a "but."

"But we know all that. We know there are still people in Okinawa who hate Japan and would vote to go to war. We know 'vote for us and we will smite your enemies' works; it has worked since the Old Testament. What we need to know now is who is propagating the message, and ideally some proof."

"Of course," Yoriko says, trying to look intrepid.

"And I suppose," Suzuki adds to himself, "it would be good to know whether they mean it or not."

Yoriko bows again. She already has an idea for how to proceed. She has no idea how dangerous it will be.

CHAPTER 4

JaBoDeTaBekBan, the urban conglomeration with Jakarta at its heart, has more than four hundred centenals within the administrative limits, and perhaps another three hundred in its sprawl. Ken is now in one of the densest, most diverse places on the planet. In half an hour, he can walk through upscale enclaves where the intellectual rich have voted for tranquility and gardens, keeping out anyone who doesn't belong with guard-enforced no-trespassing laws; squalid centenals where the whole hundred thousand seem to be packed on top of each other, sustained by subsidized drugs and cigarettes and probably subsidizing some far away coconstituents through cheap labor; neocommunist areas with massive canteens and service economies; governments where pork is illegal; where beef is illegal; where any meat at all is illegal, along with advertisements, soda, and material possessions. Of the two thousand, two hundred and seven registered governments, nearly one hundred and fifty hold at least one centenal in the northwest tip of Java.

The demographics of so many competing and overlapping identities could not be easily divided into hundred-thousand-person chunks, so many of the centenals have the potential to shift allegiance. Even more importantly, there are still strong links between the urban center, the spreading peri-urban borderlands, and the countryside and small villages beyond, raising hopes for swinging multiple far-flung centenals through some intensive work in the city. Convince one centenal to vote for you, and its citizens will tell their friends and relatives and business contacts, hopefully bumping you up in the Supermajority race by several counts without your actually having to go out to the sticks to campaign. Some people say the phrase "domino centenal" was coined here.

Information estimates that the population of the megalopolis goes up by a tenth of a percent in the weeks before voting, and it's already full of election workers of all different stripes, not to mention PR people, vid producers, and various subsets of Information workers: the whole ecosystem generated by the massive undertaking that is an election. Sophisticated polls and predictive calculations are being run hourly at this point. Ken can see the results reflected in the intensity of the projections playing in the humid air, the layers of posters plastered on the pylons from the long-unused monorail (which Ken's Information tells him was largely funded by the Japanese and ran from 2018 until its untimely demise in 2032), the sediment of stickers on every three-wheeler, every wagon, every fence. There are centenals at play here, and it is massively competitive.

Not that Ken would know it from the informants he spends all day talking to, each of whom tells him that Policy1st doesn't stand a chance with their particular demographic. They don't say so directly; Ken's job is to get that intel (depressing as it is) without letting them know that he's looking for it. To that end, he presents himself as an annoying grad student. This is not entirely untrue; since it's extremely difficult to lie in your public Information, Policy1st enrolled him in a cheap PhD program. He can put up more or less legitimate credentials and mute the rest of his public

Information, as is common in professional settings. Unfortunately, this also means the informants treat him as an annoying grad student, and he spends much of his time begging for meetings, waiting for appointments, and stuck in traffic.

While sitting bumper-to-bumper on Jalan Antasari, he checks the polls. This far out, the predictions are still highly unreliable, a fact that some genius at Information has decided to represent by making the numbers literally fuzzy, so blurry that they have to be sixteen-point before anyone can read them. Even given the uncertainty, it's not heartening. Heritage, the Supermajority government, has a modest lead over the next clump of governments, which are too closely matched right now to be cleanly ordered. Last time he looked PhilipMorris was in second place; now 888 has edged them, with Sony-Mitsubishi, Liberty, and several other corporates, trendy technogovernments, and 1China also in the mix. Policy1st needs another five hundred centenals to even be in the same weight class as those governments. Five hundred, from anywhere in the world. A hundred on every continent. Or all four hundred and ninety-nine here in Indonesia, plus one from Tuvalu, or the Faroes, or the City of London. Policy1st has around three thousand campaign staff globally, not including volunteers and government staff who occasionally lend a hand. If one out of every six staffers can eke out one additional centenal, they'll be in the running for Supermajority.

Ken would like to be able to chalk up at least ten to his name, but so far it's not looking likely. His assignment is to feel out possibilities in unlikely centenals, and while it sounds exciting on paper, Ken has found that unlikely centenals are unlikely for a reason. Most of them seem all but impossible, and in his lower moments, he wonders whether this is a sham job that Suzuki made up to keep him busy and out of the way. "We have a special task that only someone like you can do, impeccably loyal but not publicly connected to us . . ."

Anyway, he's not giving up yet. He has more interviews tomorrow, and in the meantime he can catch up with one of his friends from the office here, siphon off some of his frustration, and cross-ref to get a better feel for how things stand. He messages the strategy director for the Policy1st office, and an hour and a half later (Jakarta traffic), he's sitting in his favorite bar in Kemang, telling her about that day's interviews.

"'Why don't they have actual people representing them?'" he mimics to Tanty, between swallows of a strong and spicy cocktail. "Every single one of them said that, and for most it was their first reaction when I asked about Policy1st. That's what we come down to: no people. No pretty airbrushed faces, no glib speeches straight from the heart via the teleprompter."

Tanty is not surprised. "It's depressing, ya? I mean, what part of 'policy *first*' do they not understand?"

Ken, who's on his third drink at this point, shakes his head. "Is it better to be popular or to be right?" he asks rhetorically, and then attempts to look on the bright side. "At least I didn't hear anything about Liberty trying to start a war."

"Liberty?" Tanty laughs. "Not much chance there. As far as corporates go, PhilipMorris has this place sewn up. That's why these are so cheap." She flicks the ash of her kretek cigarette. "And why I can still smoke them in here."

"Better to be right," Ken decides, waving away the clove-scented smoke.

Tanty laughs again. "Not in a democracy, Pak."

Ken drinks. "This is a *micro*-democracy," he says. "A vast improvement. Any chance of edging them somewhere?"

"I thought that's what you were here to figure out."

"Just curious about your perspective," Ken says, surprised.

"Come by the office tomorrow?" Tanty suggests.

"I'll be there, but I doubt your boss will make the atmosphere conducive."

They've shared their frustration with Agus in the past, but this time Tanty doesn't laugh. "Short answer is, unlikely. Besides the tobacco, PhilipMorris subsidizes jobs, sometimes even cars. People don't care that it's unsustainable; for the moment, they're doing better than their neighbors in other governments. They feel like the smart ones. Meanwhile, their compatriots in PhilipMorris centenals in Papua and Maluku are making it all possible, working their asses off for little money and no infrastructure. You should be looking there."

She glares at Ken, who shrugs somewhat shamefacedly; no one has the time to go campaign personally on an isolated island where the people are fully indoctrinated to their bum deal. "We're running advids," he offers, knowing it's weak.

"In Jakarta, then?" Tanty lifts her tumbler, swirls it, digs out a strawberry with the swizzle stick. "There are a couple of outliers, but I don't want to talk about it here."

"Here?" Ken asks, raising his eyebrows and glancing around. They chose this bar not only for its powerful swills but also for the level of noise and the general lack of interest from the patrons in anything other than their own latest-model projectors. Most of the clientele look like young professionals, educated (maybe even foreign-educated) and chic (some of them retro chic). "First of all, this looks like our demographic, or at least more us than a corporate. And secondly, do they even care?" He sighs and drinks. "Which is exactly the problem with our demographic."

"It's not that clear-cut. These kids all look cool, right?" Tanty flicks some more ash, trying to look cool herself. "Most of them are probably living with their parents. And their parents are definitely not our demographic. Some of them PhilipMorris, maybe one of the moderate Islamic governments, a couple in YouGov or Oranje or SecureNation. But that's normal; that's not the problem. The problem is Philip-Morris has been making noise about other governments 'spying' on them."

"Spying?" Ken feels his face slowly going red, although it's probably invisible against the alcohol flush. "This is normal! It's called campaign research. All the governments do it. Hell, you should see some of the things PhilipMorris does to get intel."

"Yeah, but here they don't have to." Tanty shakes her head as she stubs out her kretek. "You would think, with all the access to Information, that people would pay more attention to what their governments do in other centenals, but you know what they say: you can give a voter Information, but you can't make him think."

"Why didn't you tell Suzuki-san about the spying accusations here before he sent me?" Ken asks, trying to shake the feeling of having done something stupid.

Tanty rolls her eyes at him. "You think Suzuki asked my opinion? Or even told Agus? First we knew of it, you were already on the flight. It's true Agus is an asshole, but in this case he has a point. Nothing personal."

Ken has no answer to that. No wonder Tanty didn't want

to talk. He wonders how much griping about Suzuki goes on behind his back.

"It's not that bad," Tanty softens. "We do need the intel, it's just . . . things are sensitive this time."

"You said it," Ken mumbles into the bar.

"What was that about starting a war?" Tanty asks, but Ken waves her off, asking for the bill. He shouldn't have said anything, he thinks as he takes the stairs down to street level with exaggerated care. Though it is late, the road in front of the bar is still alight with the brake lights of a startling range of vehicles, of which only the motorcycles and unicycles are moving. Ken decides to stumble back to his hotel room, a kilometer and a half away over uneven sidewalks.

As he turns a corner, his antennae twitch. They are literal antennae, microfilaments that run from his earpiece, hooking over his ear and following his hair to the nape of his neck. Their wake-up twitch is designed to raise the hairs on the back of his neck to mimic, physiologically, the feeling of being watched, in case the wearer is too drunk to remember the significance of the twitch.

Ken remembers. But it doesn't necessarily mean he has to worry. The antennae keep an eye out behind him and alert him in case of abnormality, but that abnormality could be anything from a person's face appearing too many times in the crowd to a microscopic feed camera turning minutely to follow his path. He'll have to review the vid later to see what triggered them. For the moment he doesn't look back, but attempts to heighten his own alcohol-dulled senses.

It's dark where he's walking, and he's aware of an ever-so-slight rhythmic tilting below his feet. This part of the city floats; the crowded, crazy-quilt neighborhoods are built on huge barges, sometimes made from recycled tires, sometimes illicitly made from the tires themselves, tied together in massive rafts. The seams tend to fall along the roads, and in the crevice bordering this narrow street Ken can see the glint of seawater, or floodwater, or (judging by the smell) sewage. The neighborhood is dark but not empty. There is a tented warung up ahead on the left, the bare light bulbs illuminating a woman as she ladles sop buntut from a vat, and four men crouched against a garden wall smoking next to it. Ken blinks twice to bring up the map of his location at eyeball projection level. He knows how to get to the hotel from here, but he wants to see if there are any likely ambush sites ahead and check what centenal he's in. As Tanty could have predicted, it's PhilipMorris. Ken might not agree with their public health policies, but they have a pretty good reputation for security. He's unlikely to have to deal with a random mugging.

But what if it's not random? He enjoys the taste of fear in his mouth, and it feels too soon when he arrives safely at the hotel. He's tempted to walk around the block, see if he can draw out whoever's tailing him, but his antennae haven't twitched since that first time. It was probably nothing. Besides, he's tired and drunk. Spying!

The Information hub in Singapore is one of the oldest and best-developed in Asia, located in an unmarked but subtly imposing building not far from Bugis Junction. Mishima knows it well. She passes under the digitally engraved quote about a well-informed public, flashes her badge, and walks past the vast translators' bay. The glass-fronted elevator gives her a view of floor after floor of endless cubicles as it rises, like cross-sections of a hive: the mindful drones of Information collecting, processing, and compiling records of every bit of human action or interpretation they can get their feeds on. She has sometimes wondered if this is why people hate Information; whether the idea of all those people working for an enormous bureaucracy, supposedly sapped of their individual identities, spurs some primal fear in people. Or guilt that unimaginable masses of workers have to sort through vids and grind out commentary nonstop to provide the extraordinarily individualized Information that almost everyone on Earth now feels entitled to. She usually concludes that it has nothing to do with the structure of the organization. The power it wields is enough to make people hate it.

Why the corporates hate Information is clearer and just as evident in the structure of this building. Like much of the other hardware involved in the effort to keep people well-informed, the Singapore hub was funded by the massive settlement accorded after *People vs. Coca-Cola et al.*, the civil action when Americans realized that diet soda was depriving them of their right to be thin. Further support was provided by the subsequent lawsuit, building on that precedent, which led directly to the cable news collapse.

Mishima goes straight to the office of the director of analysis and tries to explain what she's looking for: "It's what they used to call a dog whistle. But they've gotten much better at it these days." Mishima can already feel her vowels and rhythms molding themselves to Singlish speech patterns, and hopes no one will think she's making fun of them. It's not something she does on purpose, and it doesn't help that she hasn't slept in several time zones.

"Yeah, I know what that is," Tabby answers. "So, you think Liberty is sending messages to extremists about what they'll do if they get the Supermajority, messages that don't register with anyone who's not looking for them?"

Mishima nods.

Tabby frowns. "It would be a bit—strange, no? What would they be signaling that they wouldn't want to say directly?"

"War."

"Really?" There's a pulse of excitement in Tabby's voice behind her incredulity.

"Or dismantling the election system. Something like that."

"Yikes," Tabby says, digesting it. Dismantling the election system, unlike war, leaves her out of a job. "How did you find this?"

"It's more of a hunch than anything else," but Mishima is pretty sure. She knows these bastards. "Look." She projects the comparison sheets and highlights the Liberty line.

Tabby picks up on it almost immediately. "Restoration, retribution . . . that's not the usual rhetoric for a corporate."

"And look at this one," Mishima says, highlighting. "Not under the IF ELECTED TO SUPERMAJORITY line, under WITHIN CENTENALS THAT SELECT. 'Aggressive land tenure reform.'"

Tabby enlarges the explanation provided by the Information worker who glossed this: WILL WORK TO CLARIFY AND/OR REALIGN LAND OWNERSHIP. "They took it at face value," she says, pushing the tail of her sari back off her shoulder. "But you're right. That doesn't make any sense in the context of the positions Liberty's been putting out for the past two years. They're all about protecting private property, especially land."

"Unless they're not talking about private property but about neighboring centenals."

"And people will understand this?" Tabby asks.

"The right people will." Mishima pulls up comparison sheets from the previous weeks. "What's most impressive is how the rhetoric rises subtly over time. Look."

Tabby nods. "Still fairly recent, though."

"There could be a mistake somewhere," Mishima says. "Or this might not have been fully vetted, might have been put out by someone who has gone rogue. It's a huge organization."

"They might have changed leadership," Tabby says. They both know she is not talking about Johnny Fabré, the glossy good-looker who has been the public face of Liberty for over a decade. "Changed direction."

"Four weeks before the election?" Mishima asks.

"Or . . ." Tabby says.

"Or they could have been planning this all along."

"Laying the groundwork."

"Establishing their credibility as a major, legitimate corporate government, committed to micro-democracy, while making sure that the people they want to reach would hear the dog whistle."

"Making sure those people want war."

Every hypothesis seems scarier than the last.

"Do they have a chance at the Supermajority?" Tabby asks finally.

Mishima shrugs. "A chance? Yes. They are the fifth-largest government now, and you know the margins are tight at the top. How much of a chance?" She leaves the question hanging. Information employs hundreds of thousands of people worldwide, with an unprecedented technological infrastructure, and still their projections of election results are little more than guesses. Mishima's intuition is one of the reasons she's so valuable to them, but she's still not ready to predict the Supermajority winner, not two weeks out.

"So?" Tabby says, impatiently. "Did you find anything?"

Mishima opens a sheaf of files on the projector. "It's all small stuff—very circumstantial. They're being careful."

"But why . . ." Tabby stands back, shakes her head. "There are plenty of governments that want to change the system."

"But they're all fringe governments. Liberty is huge. They might take the Supermajority—they could make this happen if they win. And if it breaks too soon, they lose their chance. Look at this one." Mishima opens an advid playing in eastern sections of Europe. The images are innocuous: the usual peace and prosperity, shot through with corporate icons. Mishima isolates the soundtrack. "So, this means nothing to anyone who didn't grow up hearing . . . this." She pulls up an ancient advid, a television ad. "This was ubiquitous in those areas of Europe forty to fifty years ago." It's for the digital upgrade of the game Risk, and the same jingle plays through it over videos of children advancing their avatars across a map of the world.

"Wow," Tabby says. "That's . . . subtle. Are you sure it would get across to anyone?"

Mishima shrugs. "If it were only that one, I'd say maybe it was a coincidence, but take a look."

Tabby flips through Mishima's projection, scanning the documents as they hang in the air in front of her eyes. All the search terms are so oblique as to be almost counterintuitive, a reminder, if Tabby needed one, of how good Mishima is at her job. "You were being careful," she says.

"I think they're going to be looking for someone looking for them."

Yoriko is looking for them. She starts by using Information, reading everything Liberty has put out in Okinawa over the past three months. Not unaware of the danger (although she tells herself it's silly, this isn't a spy vid, nothing dramatic is going to happen), she hopes her searches will look like those of a potential new voter practicing due diligence. She finds it hard to imagine anyone doing this much background research for voting, though; most of her friends don't even talk about the election except to say how annoying all the advids are.

The searches don't turn up much. The adwriters for Liberty have been careful (if there is anything to be careful about). They stick close to their tagline of *Freedom*, and attach it to everything. *Economic Freedom*, *Family Freedom*, *Educational Freedom*, *Consumer Freedom*. Mostly *Economic Freedom*, the headline accompanied by sharply animated 3-D vids explaining wordlessly how lack of regulation leads to economic growth. Yoriko's seen it all before, during the last two election cycles and lots of times this one, but even so, she finds herself sliding closer to the almost-convinced voter she's pretending to be. Wouldn't it be great to have a whole house for her family? To take vacations somewhere far away? She wonders how much Suzuki will pay her if she gets him what he needs.

There are a few places that make her pause the vid to

rewatch. One explanation of economic growth shows Liberty's centenals, colored an attractive aquamarine on a stylized map, spreading toward an island that looks vaguely like Kyushu. This wouldn't mean much, standard campaign "yes, we will be the Supermajority" sort of signaling, except that Yoriko notices that particular vid was only shown in Okinawa. Feeling slightly squeamish, she pulls up Liberty vids from other parts of the world, vids that were only shown in limited regions. It takes some looking, since they weren't released on the same day, but she eventually finds a counterpart for Aceh, with an undefined archipelago being threatened; a release for Malaysia, showing the tip of a peninsula being surged by light turquoise color; and a version for China, with Liberty swamping an island that's shaped more like Taiwan. She doesn't bother to look beyond Asia.

Spooked, Yoriko closes her feeds—then worries that she closed them too suddenly. She reopens to watch as many more Liberty vids as she can stomach. When she has calmed down—after a bath, a short nap, and a couple of innocuous fares in her taxi—she begins to think it's less significant. It's a campaign, and there's always posturing. Not every government is going to be like Policy1st, so principled they won't even use spokespeople. Yoriko shakes her head. When she finishes her shift, she's going to start checking through Liberty's public appearances in Okinawa. Maybe she'll even go to one.

CHAPTER 5

Ken's first stop the next morning is at the Policy1st office. He's undercover, but with all the election activity in Jakarta, he thinks it's safe enough, and at this point in the cycle, he wants the latest data, to the nanosecond. Plus, he wants to see if he can learn anything about Liberty's possible malfeasance. Looking through the office's existing files will save him specific Information searches that might alert others to what he's on to. He didn't want to make the office an obvious home base, though; rather than the slightly squalid, windowless place around the corner from the Policy1st office that the travel coordinator suggested, the hotel Ken chose is a little farther away and significantly more pleasant.

It makes for an entertaining walk to work. Jakarta is hot and smells of durian. It's in season, apparently; Ken sees thorny slabs of it laid out on rough wooden tables along the road. He abstains until he reaches a centenal governed by UNICEF, which is supposed to have better food hygiene standards, and buys some rujak from a pushcart. The vendor hands him a small paper envelope of typhoid inoculation with his purchase, which Ken rips open and sprinkles over his fruit with the chili-peanut sauce; so much for hygiene. He uses an elongated toothpick to eat the pieces of papaya, starfruit, mango, and pineapple while he walks, but has to rush to finish before crossing the all-but-invisible border to the next centenal, warned by dancing public service pop-ups along the walls that not only street-vending but also street-eating is illegal there. He considers going around that territory, but a glance at a map projection tells him it sits squarely in the middle of the shortest route to the office. He's already running late, and he's almost done with the rujak anyway. Besides, strolling through that uptight centenal has its own pleasures: the tropical gardens are well tended, their fragrances painting the humid air, and the street-vending prohibition doesn't extend to musicians, who seem to be encouraged. Ken does note that most of them are cleaner than average. Maybe a government program rather than free-flowing capitalism, although he doesn't bother to check.

Policy1st's offices are, as usual, in a Policy1st centenal (Ken has argued to Suzuki that they should open satellites in the territory of any government that will allow them to, at least during this last month). Ken is pleased to see that their policies have been adapted to the local context. The accountability board, available for immediate projection as always, has also been painted in appealing colors and fonts on a wall by one of the main streets. When he examines the demographics of the centenal on Information, he sees that levels of education and handheld penetration are in fact quite high, which tracks with most Policy1st demographics. Maybe the mural's not strictly necessary, but it's still a nice touch.

As he turns onto the side street where the Policy1st office is located, a pop-up catches his eye. He's not sure why, something about the particular degree of sparkle on the jet-black coloring, or the font, which is somewhat reminiscent of the KISS band logo, or the rhythm of its bounce in the air; something about it says "cooler than all the other advids," and his eyes stick for the briefest microsecond as they slide past. The sophisticated sensors in the ad projector notice, and the ad immediately flies to the forefront of his vision.

IGNORANCE, it says, in that sharp-edged script, humming in place.

The word flies away and is replaced by another.

IS
BLISS

And then it's gone in a scintillating starburst. No feed address, no Information link, no explanation of what they're selling. Hurrying on with his eyes firmly fixed on the door of the office, Ken wonders if he was wrong and rather than an ad, it's some attempt at street art. Either way, he finds anything that flies in his face too annoying to appreciate.

His irritation only grows as he walks into the office. Given how dynamic and competitive the city is, Ken finds it surprising that the Policy1st office in Jakarta isn't more impressive. Not physically; Policy1st's aesthetic tends to be understated and geeky, representing its positioning as the wonk that cares about substance rather than flash. No, what Ken finds unimpressive is the management. Agus, the office head, keeps Ken waiting for ten minutes and then talks at him from behind his desk, twiddling a pen while blandly refusing to be of any help whatsoever.

"Liberty? I wouldn't have much on them beyond what you can find in Information."

Ken always reacts badly to Agus's particular brand of obfuscation, and based on his chat with Tanty last night, he's starting to suspect that Agus knows this and is doing it on purpose. "I am asking you instead of searching Information myself, because I don't want people to be able to figure out what I'm looking for."

"What *are* you looking for?" Agus asks, but it was probably just provocation, because he doesn't wait for an answer. "I'm asking because you'll be exposing me and this office by going through us, so I think I have a right to know."

"As the campaign office here, it makes sense for you to have a file on the main competitors." Ken says. "In fact, you don't have to do any new searches. Just show me what you have already."

Agus doesn't seem to like that much, probably because he hasn't been doing his job properly and doesn't have much opposition research to show. "Well," he drawls, leaning back in his chair and swiveling it, "we don't consider Liberty one of our main competitors for the Supermajority. I mean," he adds to Ken's raised eyebrows, "obviously they're a competitor, but we don't think that we've got a lot of overlap with them in terms of potential voters. On the global scale, we're focusing much more on SavePlanet and Economix, for example."

Ken happens to know—no, he doesn't *happen* to know; he did his homework before coming, that's how he knows—that SavePlanet doesn't have a single centenal in JaBoDeTa-BekBan. "I thought your job was to win centenals in Jakarta, not to worry about the Supermajority."

"I thought your job was to get Suzuki where he's going and then wait for him in the car," Agus shoots back. "What are you doing here, anyway? Some supersecret errand for the big man, huh? Don't start checking up on me, son. Leave the real work to the experts."

Ken thinks about hitting him, can actually see it play out. Leaning over the desk, knuckles connecting with jaw. Not very hard, because he's leaning so far, but then it wouldn't take much to tip that chair over. That stupid pen flying across the room, Agus scrambling up from the floor, calling security . . . Ken cuts it off there. He's not worried about his job. Suzuki appreciates a man of action and has bailed him out from worse scrapes than this would be. But Ken doesn't like to call in favors from his boss, since he's aware there might not be a bottomless supply. More importantly, he's unlikely to get the intel he wants that way. They're fourteen days out, the first debate is in thirty hours, and some wack shit is going on. He doesn't have time for fisticuffs.

"Yes, it is a job for Suzuki, and your boss works for him too. Why don't you give me whatever you have so that he doesn't come asking for it himself?"

Agus shrugs and with a few motions, sends a file to Ken's workspace. "Here," he says, tossing in a few others. "So you can see what campaigning looks like."

"Great, thanks," Ken says, pretty sure that they won't be helpful anyway. "See you later."

He heads for the door.

"Where are you going?" Agus asks.

"To talk to some informants," Ken says, backing out the door. "You know—real campaigning."

Ken's antennae jiggle frantically as he walks away from the building, but he figures that's Agus staring daggers at him from the window and ignores it. He's got to get his over-eager grad student vibe on.

Domaine does get rid of his fro for the meeting in Saudi, but only by braiding it up tight. It's a style that has come into fashion in the Gulf states recently, but no one will know he's following it unless he takes off his keffiya. The important thing is that he now looks not far off from Arab.

The meeting is with a sheikh he has connected with through the intercession of a music star who prefers to remain anonymous, but who is willing to put both money and social networks (a publicly traded commodity) to the cause of reforming (or "overturning," as she put it in an overenthusiastic message) the election system.

And now Domaine is here, shifting uneasily in his robes in the thick air conditioning, rare as bananas these days. He wants to get self-righteous about it, but after briefly experiencing the heat outside, he can understand, if not condone, why they still use it.

It's not his first time meeting an Arab prince. Back in his private-sector days—before he saw the dark—he was in and out of Dubai all the time. He knows the drill: the trappings of multinational politeness, the echoes of tribal customs made infinitely more comfortable. He's looking forward to the tea, rather less to the small talk. And he can't deny his nerves, those intimately measured connections trembling just below his skin. He assumes they have body-stat monitors here, and can only hope that they take his anxiety as a compliment. Saudi, even what's left of it, is not Dubai, and he's not sure how much leeway he has here.

The sheikh enters, preceded and followed by the cloud of his entourage. Tea is poured, small things ("The weather? Ah, still hot.") discussed.

But the sheikh, also a multitrillionaire CEO, does not have a lot of time to waste on formalities. "It is election time again, I understand," he says, as if it were something he happened to notice at the bottom of one of his feeds, as if just because Saudi doesn't participate in the election system, the outcome wouldn't affect his multiple business interests in thousands of ways.

"It is indeed," Domaine replies. "Trillions of bits being spent in six months of global pageantry."

"We, as you know, are not involved," the sheikh says, although what Domaine does know is that he has personally donated billions to not one but several of the major governments that he thinks will be favorable for his investments and corporations. Domaine tries to swallow the disgust rising in him.

"Given that perspective," he says, "we hope that you can support our opposition to the system."

The sheikh is practiced at this and merely plasters a sage expression on his face, but Domaine notices that some of his henchmen are smiling. "We do not get involved in the sovereign affairs of other governments," the prince proclaims, another statement Domaine knows to be false. "If the other peoples of the world wish to hold these events, that is their affair. We choose not to do so here."

"The peoples of the world didn't choose it, though," Domaine says. "Did they? I mean, the system was dreamt up and pushed through by some soon-to-be-ex-UN officials who grew a pair, and ratified by governments under duress or false promises, not all of whom even called themselves democratic."

"I am not," the sheikh says, "the most ardent believer in democracy, so this perspective is not exactly troubling to me." It's the only true thing Domaine has heard him say since they agreed that the weather was hot.

"Which is exactly why we should work together," Domaine says.

The sheikh deigns to raise his eyebrows. "You, who believe

the system is not democratic enough, and I, who believe it is far too democratic?"

"Exactly," Domaine says, making his voice vibrate with urgency. "We form a coalition. Now is the time, before a new government takes over the Supermajority and starts to cement its power."

The sheikh shows interest for the first time. "You believe that Heritage will lose the Supermajority?"

"Our Information makes that look like a serious possibility," Domaine says. He twists his wrist, and in a nice bit of coding showmanship, a globe projection leaps out and slowly revolves. It shows what Domaine believes the sheikh would like to see, to the extent that Domaine thinks the sheikh will credit it: the major governments, corporates and traditionals, splintering the vote until the domination of Heritage is in doubt. "Of course, there is still time, and the debates, so nothing is certain."

He doesn't bite. "Regardless, I am not interested in changing a system that I do not participate in."

Seems unlikely. "It is a shame that Information is constantly attempting to influence the minds of your people, claiming that the election system is the answer to all their problems."

"Information does not enter here," the sheikh answers. "We provide our subjects with all the news and entertainment that they need."

"But still." Domaine leans forward. "The election system, flawed as it is, is constantly held up as a paragon of democracy, peace, consumer choice. It exerts an insidious appeal on nonvoters, no less dangerous for being false."

The sheikh is silent for a moment. Most of his entourage are suddenly busy with their handhelds, perhaps rechecking

Domaine's background and reassessing the discussion. Domaine presses on. "Surely you would prefer for the election system not to exist? We are working to eliminate it, or at the very least make it more realistic . . ."

The open question breaks the tension, and the sheikh laughs. "Why would we want to change it? There is nothing that suits us more than most of the world believing that their will is being carried out by governments that do exactly as they please."

There is little else to say, and eventually Domaine is graciously removed from the room.

Ken's antennae jump again as he's leaving his fourth interview, and he jumps too. His first thought is that he's glad he invested in the antennae, because he's so hyped from the conversation he just had that he probably wouldn't notice anything without them. His second thought is: because of that conversation, this must be the real thing.

Maybe it was a trap to begin with. The centenal secretary seemed eager to give it to him. Or maybe the overworked woman wanted someone besides her clients to see it. Maybe whoever it is has been watching her office, just in case. Or maybe they've been following him for a while. They've figured out who he is, or they don't care who he is but they don't want anyone to know what he heard. Or what he has.

It is nightfall, the sky a luminous blue above the city glow, and the centenal he's moving through now is a poor one with few streetlights, darkening fast. He glances at windows as he passes, but in the glare of the pop-ups, tuk-tuk headlights, and vendor sparklers, he can't make out anything in the shifting space behind him. Without stopping, Ken rubs his eyes as though tired, adjusting his antennae to broadcast video into the corner of his vision. He doesn't catch anything immediately.

Policy1st's transportation policy includes only environmentally neutral vehicles. Ken got here on a Sunway borrowed from the office, solar-powered and with a top speed of a slow jog. It seemed perfect for the Jakarta traffic, which rarely gets above a slow jog anyway, and after the transport frustrations of the previous day, Ken thought it was necessary. It's also about as inconspicuous as elephant coitus, which is not unheard of in these streets but still draws a crowd. As he gets back on, he notices a small switch labeled AUXILIARY SPEED—EMERGENCY USE ONLY.

He proceeds with caution at first. His mind is processing a million different things at once: the map of this and the surrounding centenals, superimposed over his vision; the small vid of the space behind him; not hitting anyone with the snail's-pace Sunway; and, most importantly, trying to figure out what to do with the intel he just received.

His initial impulse is to send it to Suzuki right away; he even half-composes a message muttered under his breath. Then he remembers that this is not the type of data that can be transmitted that way. Ken curses, accidentally leaving a trail of profanity in his message draft, then closes it. He's not used to carrying heavy stacks of physical paper; he didn't even bring a bag. The Sunway has a small storage trunk on the back, but it would be too easy for someone to swipe from. Ken was holding the packet close to his ribs when he left the meeting, and he doesn't see any option other than to keep doing so. He shoves it into his waistband to free his hands and tucks his shirt over it. He considers sending a message hinting at what he's found. If he doesn't make it back, Agus can follow the trail. He discards that idea, too. If, and (glancing at the rearview vid) it seems more and more unlikely, there are people following him because of what he's just learned, they'll be expecting him to transmit it somehow. They might be able to snag it off Information before it reaches its destination, use the transmission point to find him if they haven't already. Besides, Agus would be sure to mess it up.

Just as he's starting to think the antennae were overreacting, triggered by a random repeat passerby or innocent stares, he passes under a rare bank of solar-powered streetlights, and a few seconds later he sees something in the vid: the glimmer of the lights passing over the carapace of a vehicle, a large vehicle. That in itself is not strange; what is odd is that the behemoth is not nudging people, donkeys, motorcycles, three-wheelers, and Sunways out of the way to pass. Ken risks a glance over his shoulder, and the headlights of the massive all-terrainer seem to wink at him. It is hanging back, maintaining a distance, inexplicable in this cutthroat traffic culture unless there is some other motive.

His heart speeds up, adrenaline spurts. He has to think, though. There's no way he can outrun them. Ken maneuvers his Sunway around a donkey cart, then stays between it and a three-wheeler for a couple of seconds. When the slow pace of traffic gets him near enough to the corner, he swings the Sunway up on to the sidewalk, slides it around the corner onto a dark, almost-empty side street, and flips the auxiliary speed switch. The platform below him hums, then vibrates. He hears honking from the street behind him as the SUV tries to make it to the corner. Then his head jerks back in a gush of smoggy air as the Sunway takes off, bouncing along the imperfectly paved road.

Ken gets a momentary thrill, although it's a little

muffled by the effort he has to make not to get jounced off the thing. Then he's thrown against the handrail hard. He chokes, staring down at the dimness of unlit pavement. His ribs hurt, although the package did cushion the impact some. He pushes himself back up to standing and hits the accelerator, and the Sunway gives a plaintive whine, shudders, and completely shuts down. Coughing, Ken glances behind him. He's only about three hundred meters from the main road, where he can make out large, high-set headlights lurching around the corner toward him.

He gives the Sunway one last shake, and when it doesn't react, he jumps off and runs.

The street that Ken is running down is what is known in Jakarta as a jalan tikus, a mouse road. It is lit only by the faint luminescence coming from house windows and a few outdated, immobile advids. He starts to turn down a cross street, aiming back toward the main road he came off of, but when he notices on his map projection that it's actually blocked off by some kind of commercial complex he has to duck back out again, dodging past two guards playing chess in front of a gate. The SUV's headlights are about a block behind him. He asks Information how common plastic guns are in Jakarta, hoping that the answer will be reassuringly lower than he expects. In fact, this is a major underground trade point for them. He runs faster.

Ken's map is helpfully calculating the quickest and most direct routes to his hotel, and he tells it to stop and use the centenal filter instead. He wants to find a government nearby with better law-and-order stats, or at least more streetlights. There are some alleyways that look too narrow for the SUV, but most of them only have one egress, and it's a pretty sure bet that whoever is trying to follow him is looking at the same map he is. Ken gets so caught up in checking the parameters of a neighboring centenal that he almost steps in an open sewer. Blinking away the afterimage of the map, he glances back at the headlights (gaining) and sprints toward the next turn, where the street jogs left.

He dodges a motorcycle coming the opposite way and swings around the curve, blowing past a tiny kiosk, its only sign a red-and-white ad for PhilipMorris products, glowing in the night and clouded with mosquitoes. A line of tuk-tuks sits beside it. Their drivers cluster in the light of the kiosk, most of them sporting examples of its merchandise between lips or dangling from their fingers. Ken ducks behind the tuk-tuks but he's too scared to stop running, so he keeps sprinting forward in a crouch until the headlights of the SUV swing toward him. He hunkers down behind the black canvas hatch of the last tuk-tuk and holds his breath. In the white flash of the headlights he can see the torn leather on the seat of the three-wheeler, the rusted lock clamped on the fuel tank. Then he's in darkness again, and the huge vehicle is sliding down the road beyond him. Ken waits until it passes the next turn . . . ten meters past . . . they're slowing. They must have figured out he's not ahead of them. Before they can turn, he bolts.

As soon as Ken breaks his cover he sees the red reflection of the brake lights. They don't even try to turn around on the narrow road, just reverse hard over the potholes. Ken makes it to the turn first, skids around it, and takes off down the street as the SUV backs past the junction, stops, and lurches forward around the corner after him.

But Ken has already crossed the border into the next centenal. The laws, which Ken already knows from his map, are posted in illuminated signs at the junction. Ken wonders whether his pursuers will read them or just plow through. He doesn't dare stop to find out. Then he hears the series of sharp bangs. He ducks and glances back over his shoulder.

But it's just the tires exploding on the antivehicle protection in the street. This centenal belongs to a green-party government that runs in Jakarta on a radical antitraffic platform, and is pedestrian only. In the dimness (the eco-government of the centenal is experimenting with wind-powered streetlights, and they are on the faint side) the SUV settles, like one of those beetles that gets eaten from the inside out. Then a door opens.

Ken turns back around and concentrates on running. Whoever's in that SUV has legs too. But now he has a head start, and the darkness is in his favor. He loses himself in the side streets, using his eye-level map to avoid dead ends. What he wants to do is to lie low until they've given up or until daylight, but he doesn't have anywhere safe to go. He's tempted by a late-night warung whose patrons are slurping bowls of noodle soup (vegan, according to Information). As he's hovering in the shadows across the street, indecisive, a man significantly larger than Ken runs up, pauses, and darts inside the warung, glancing at faces. Ken turns and walks quickly in the direction the man came from, heart pounding.

They know what he looks like. Without slowing, he plots a way back to his hotel on his map, prioritizing busy and well-lit streets. Following it, he comes out of the centenal at an exit right on Sudirman Avenue. Vehicles dart by on the six-lane road, and along the middle of it the monorail tracks loom like the spine of some huge, useless, and long-dead animal. Ken considers hailing a public transportation crow, but in

Jakarta these are few and overcrowded, with out-of-date algorithms. Besides, if they're tracing his comms, they could find him that way. He's got an old-fashioned cargo; he might as well get home the old-fashioned way. He flags a cab and disappears into the anonymous crawl of Jakarta traffic.

CHAPTER 6

I don't understand," Agus says for the third time. First it was disbelief that Ken had been followed, and possibly threatened, by PhilipMorris goons. ("We don't know they were from PhilipMorris," Ken warned. "Just seems the most likely candidate.") Then it was reluctance to admit that Ken might have gotten some valuable intel with his unorthodox methods. Now Agus is hung up on the technical details. "How did they take the poll without it coming up in Information?"

Suzuki, conferencing in from Budapest, doesn't bother to hide his irritation. "They used pen and paper, kid!"

The flash of pique from his boss lets Ken take the high road. "It's amazing," he says. "I can't imagine how many people they used or how long it took. But they wanted to have this intel without anyone else knowing."

"And what does it tell us?" Suzuki asks.

Ken laughs and shakes his head. "Look," he says. "This was done by hand, and it has to be analyzed by hand." He picks up the slab of papers and drops them on his hotel desk for emphasis. "Before we can say we know anything, we should verify it ourselves from the data. But what my informant told me, when she handed these over, was that in several of these centenals"—Ken blinks to bring up his notes—"3539082, 3539091, and 3539080 are the most promising—there are significant grassroots opposition movements, and PhilipMorris is doing everything it can to downplay them in Information. Then there's data on the biggest issues for the populations, possible angles to approach them. Like here"—he flips through to a summary page he found for one of the sections. "Listen to this: in 3539091, a lot of concerns were raised about the education system in the mid-cycle governor's election. So, PhilipMorris funded five new, latest-model school buildings for the new governor. All that should be on Information, I guess, for us to check. But according to this poll, people are angrier than ever, because there aren't enough teachers and the curriculum is, according to Stania, mother of three, 'stupid.'" Ken looks up. "I would say that's an opportunity, with the new education plan the policy department is so excited about. I'm sure they'd tailor something for this centenal if we ask them."

"Maybe," grunts Suzuki. "They're pretty busy with the debate prep, but it's true they are very hyped about the new education initiatives. I can try to push it along. Agus?"

Agus, woken in the middle of the night and conferencing in pajamas from his living room, blinks rapidly, no doubt going through maps and pulling up cheat sheets. Ken almost feels sorry for him. "Yeah, we're working hard on 082," he says. "The other two, according to our analysis, they're not in play. But, um, I like the idea of education . . ."

"Look," Ken says. "You have to go through the data. There's some good qualitative stuff here, but I don't know if it's enough to get us there. That's your department."

"Agus, get your people on that analysis right away," Suzuki barks. Ken spares a thought to hope that it's not Tanty who gets stuck with the grunt work. She's far too valuable for it, but Agus might be that bad a manager.

"I will as soon as I get the physical data," Agus grumps.

"I'll swing by with it in the morning," Ken says. "And I'm photographing it already, in case . . ." In case they come after him again.

"And don't just analyze, Agus. Act!" Suzuki throws in.

Duly chastened, Agus signs off, but Ken hesitates. Suzuki sighs, rubs his face, then looks up. "So," he says. "What's our play?"

Ken wasn't ready for that question. "Well, we use the data, right? And we turn it in to Information, expose what Philip-Morris has been hiding, maybe get them a penalty."

"Do we," Suzuki muses, "do we."

It's not a question, but Ken answers anyway. "We have to," he says. "Or we could get sanctioned for keeping it."

"The issue," Suzuki says, "is whether we benefit more from keeping it or sharing it. A slap on the wrist from Information, at this stage in the game, isn't going to have much effect on the voting. If we give the data to Information, on the other hand, everyone gets to use it. The edge we get from this vanishes."

"Well," Ken says uncertainly, "if we analyze the data fast, we can still get a jump on the rest of them."

Suzuki shrugs. "True, but we are investing our own time and energy in analyzing it. Everyone else gets the numbers crunched for free by Information."

"We could take the time to analyze it before we give it to them," Ken says, knowing he is falling into the trap.

"And once we take that time, why not take a little more?" Suzuki asks. "It becomes a question of degree." He laughs at Ken's discomfort. "Don't worry, son. I'll turn it over to Information. We want to win this the right way. Now you get some rest. You did good work today. Exactly what we hired you for." And he cuts the connection before Ken can figure out what expression to put on.

The Merita hotel chain offers rooms at a steep discount to people whose Information shows that they are interesting: as cocktail-chatter counterparts, as connections for entrepreneurs, as potential romantic partners. It's a strategy to convince wealthier, duller clientele to pay a premium in order to share some sparkling conversation, or in the hopes that they will be able to pass for one of the glintelligentsia themselves. Most Information drones do not remotely qualify, but even if Mishima's particular job at Information weren't deeply interesting to the power brokers of the world, she would have no trouble getting in. When she was six and watching television (the opiate of choice at the time) her mother once asked her, vaguely, "When you watch TV, do you ever feel guilty about wasting your life?" a question that probably had far more effect than an admonition would have. It had even more impact when her mother died shortly thereafter. Ever since, Mishima has taken pains not to waste her life, and her Information reflects it.

She doesn't take advantage of the Merita deal very often; sometimes, the stress of staying at a deluxe hotel can outweigh the relaxation. But after the long night of research, and given that the public lot she found to moor her crow is both bumpy and loud, she decides she needs it.

The room is a luxuriously spacious eighteen square meters and immaculate. Mishima stretches and meditates, then gets in some long-overdue wushu practice until her empty stomach reminds her of one of the disadvantages of Merita.

They have excellent restaurants, but since part of the point is that the fascinating people mingle with those who merely pay, there is no room service or takeaway, and they are generally located in neighborhoods without decent streetfood or other easy options.

Mishima goes to the restaurant and selects a common-table seat that is, at least for the moment, neighborless. She takes a look at the menu and checks her body stats. The endive-prosciutto salad mostly closely matches her nutritional needs, but that's hardly portable. Mishima decides to splurge on the peanut butter–banana-honey sandwich instead, a true luxury given the rarity of both bananas and honey. When it arrives, she waits until the waiter walks away, then wraps the sandwich in the linen napkin and heads back to her room. She doesn't feel like making small talk with anyone right now, and they should understand. It's election season.

Mishima eats the sandwich slowly in front of her feeds. Nothing surprising, although she notes a slight increase in what is usually labeled "unrest" in a number of closely fought centenals; that has been consistent in the run-up to every election so far, but it still puts her on edge. She finishes eating and takes a long bath. The tub is wrapped in mirrors (whose idea was that?) and she ends up looking at her own face as she lolls. Even in the dim light (romantic?), she can see the hints of softening, the beginning of furrows. Before crawling into bed, she applies antiwrinkle electrodes to her forehead, coaxing the skin into folding at a different place the next time she frowns in concentration. Mishima is not vain, but she remembers how smooth her mother's skin was. Her own flaws seem to represent everything that is wrong with her life: too much work, not enough sleep, too much stress, no love interest, no home. Of course after thinking all that she can't sleep anyway, so she grabs her handheld from the nightstand and gets back to work.

She checks the most recent data correlating voter interests and Information usage, basically whether people are looking up what they should. It isn't promising. In the first election, Information leadership was naïve and idealistic (Mishima's read not only of the broadcast speeches but the internal memos). They thought that providing data about each candidate government would be enough for people to make informed, more-or-less-sensible choices.

That did not work out so well. The new Heritage coalition of wealthy, experienced global corporates ignored the accessibility of Information, produced their standard glossy misinformation, and not only took the Supermajority but won centenals where, analysts agreed, it was demonstrably not in the interests of the people living there to vote for them.

The lesson was learned too well. In the second elections, Information spent billions of bits on slick presentation of their data. This failed as well; people continued to vote in ways that were highly irrational from any standpoint. Some blamed the incumbency problem, claiming that Heritage had accrued certain advantages, including of course name recognition. There was also significant evidence of a backlash, voters sneering at Information's wealth and power. The corporates—many additional conglomerate governments had sprung into being after Heritage's success—played their hand well, Mishima thinks, flipping back through the vids from the time; they insinuated that these expensive productions showed an unlimited, unmonitored budget and made Information the enemy.

Mishima shakes her head. She has her own theory: Information workers, with their ingrained culture prioritizing rigorous truth, struggled to slap motivational music or abstract video of stunning views and happy faces onto their datasets, and it showed.

This cycle, there are strict budget equivalency rules: no Information campaign can be more expensive than the campaign of the governments it is evaluating. Mishima suspects that when the dust settles, they'll find a lot of government vid budgets were larger than reported, but beyond that technical problem is a larger one. Information is still reacting, and the corporates—and the other major governments, by this point—are far too smart to play that way. She has been pushing a viral strategy combined with increased efforts at communicating transparency, but it's hard to get the point across. Two decades into its existence, Information is now full of decision-makers who always seem to want something flashy and expensive.

Moving on, Mishima rereads the notes from the session on the name-recognition problem. There was a study done with minimally educated voters who, given a hypothetical ballot, picked the names of famous serial killers over randomly generated names as well as over those of actual, less well-known politicians. Most of the discussion among the Information workers was about how to increase the name recognition of the politicians and governments in this election, or whether there's any way to evaluate the exact degrees of name recognition different actors have or even—and here the conversation gets very tentative and hypothetical—weight the voting accordingly. In the resulting unease, someone extended the conversation to face recognition, a consistent problem for governments like Policy1st or Economix that either don't have official spokespeople or select boring and/or unattractive ones. At that point, Mishima started to tune out. What worries her, and what nobody at Information seems to want to talk about, is how the name recognition problem could be used as an argument against the whole system.

That reminds her of that encounter with Domaine in—what city was that?—and she checks up on him.

Saudi? What's he doing there? Since the country is closed to Information, there's not much she can find out. But there's no one to convince not to vote. Is he looking for funding? She checks in with some of her informants, but they can't give her anything beyond his itinerary, which she already knows.

Her intuition is tingling, although Mishima tries to talk herself out of it. Because she's been painstakingly looking for evidence of war plans and clandestine coalitions all day, her mind jumps there as soon as she sees an unexplained fact, knitting together an unsubstantiated narrative with its usual skill. When she reviews the dossier, there's no sign that Domaine has ever worked for a corporate; he's more the underdog type. But then, what is he doing in Saudi? Maybe he would align himself with anyone to overthrow the election system. Very, very carefully, she begins to search Information for intersections between Domaine and Liberty.

K en climbs into the climate-controlled bed in his narrow hotel room. He's going to have a lot of follow-up to do tomorrow while keeping his antennae flexed in case those goons find him again, and he wants to be fully alert for the debate in the afternoon. Of course he can't sleep; it was a ridiculous idea to try. This is not the first time he's been of use to the campaign—there was last month's scoop about the wavering governor of a SecureNation centenal in Austin, and of course the intel from Amuru—but it is certainly the most dramatic. He relives briefly the moment crouched behind the three-wheeler, the glare from the headlights splashing over him. *So* worth documenting.

He sits up in bed, pulls over his handheld, and starts looking for vidfeeds that might show him in that moment. Removed from all context, it could be a cool avatar. By the time he's gone through the two feeds near that kiosk, he's realized, belatedly, that they (PhilipMorris heavies? Local rent-a-goons? Centenal-level security?) might be trying to identify him this way, and then he has to check through the feeds along his entire route that night. It's humbling to look at it on a map: the drama felt like it took hours and involved a mile or two of road, but the stretch he sees traced on his locator is tiny.

As he's doing this, he has his other feeds on, as usual. Ken doesn't go on Information these days without opening a minimum of two real-time poll sites (one is generally considered to be slightly Heritage-biased; the other is an indie site with less carefully validated data and is a little more daring in its conclusions), at least one news compiler for each continent, and Policy1st's campaign stream. His Information automatically prioritizes the feeds in order of most recent update, so as he's watching the vids from along his route, they are interrupted every few seconds by one of the other feeds jumping into the foreground with a new headline or a minuscule poll shift. He falls asleep without dimming them, and the feeds keep leaping into place to compete for his attention until his handheld realizes nobody is watching and autoextinguishes.

CHAPTER 7

ANNOUNCER: Welcome to the first debate for the third global election! We welcome representatives of the thirty-three governments that meet the official cutoff to be candidates for the Supermajority position, according to the latest round of official Information polling. Each of the candidates will now present a brief opening statement, followed by questions from the moderators.

HERITAGE: Thank you, and we are very pleased to participate for a third time in this inspiring and historic process of global democracy! We are also thrilled to celebrate with you, with our constituents all over the world, and with everyone who is participating in this wonderful exercise of citizenship and empowerment! *You* are the ones who make micro-democracy great—we couldn't do it without you! And so, before we even begin, I want to thank you for giving us the opportunity not only to govern our centenals but also to guide this amazing effort toward peace and prosperity as the Supermajority for the past twenty years!

Ken shakes his head and takes another swig of his beer. William Pressman is so smug and obnoxious. If he were on the Heritage team—not that he ever would be!—he'd advise them to cool it with that. He doesn't think their attitude helps them with undecideds. Although considering their record, he could be wrong about that.

Despite the unpleasant ambiance at the Policy1st office, he stayed in Jakarta to watch the debate. He's managed to find a centenal where alcohol and marijuana are legal but tobacco and pop-out advertisements are not. As Ken waited for the debate to start, he checked out this government's broader policies. They're called Free2B, which sounds like they might promulgate that kind of individualism that gets annoying quickly once your neighbor starts playing gronkytonk at top volume at five a.m. or refuses to donate to the volunteer fire department until their house is burning down, but when he scans their policies, he sees they're reasonably socially conscious. If they've got anything in a more temperate climate, he's seriously considering moving there once the election is over.

The bar is unfinished blond wood with light fixtures made of old-fashioned glass beer bottles and lots of ceiling fans powered, according to a sign in the bathroom, by an anaerobic reactor. They have a wide range of drink and drug offerings and some good early '20s music playing through the ambience. It's too bad he has to get on a plane tomorrow; there's a World Cup elimination match he wants to see, Hokkaido versus Greater Bolivia, and this would be a great place to watch it.

The Heritage spokesperson is complaining about why there are thirty-three governments included in the debate. Since Policy1st is currently thirteenth in Information's ranking of Supermajority candidates, Ken would very much like for there to be exactly thirteen parties up there. Or maybe fourteen or fifteen, so his isn't dead last. Thirty-three does seem like a lot—even with simulquestions, this is going to take forever. But Heritage wants to cut it down to five. Naturally, the fewer governments people take seriously, the better chance Heritage has to hold on to what they've got. Having looked at the numbers recently, Ken knows that the text and animations that the moderator is superimposing over Heritage's long-winded statement are accurate: there's a huge gulf between number thirty-three and number thirty-four on the list, so it's the most sensible place to make the cut.

Whether the ranking criteria are valid is a whole separate set of questions, though, and one that no one but the big muckamucks at Information is likely to get a chance to ask.

HERITAGE: You will see many advids from our opponents, and particularly from Information, claiming that we have not kept every single one of our campaign promises. But we would like to remind you that, as the only Supermajority holder in history, we are the only ones who have been tested in this way. It is easy for the others to claim they will keep all their promises if elected.

This argument makes Ken grind his teeth. Dodgy as it is for Heritage to admit they haven't kept all their campaign promises—in fact, he thinks, they've barely kept any—this is a very clever way for them to do it. All of the governments on that platform have several thousand centenals and therefore plenty of data about how well they've held to campaign promises, even if not as the Supermajority. By accusing the reliable scapegoat Information of bias, Heritage can defend itself and point out the failings of its competitors at the same time. Indeed, as Ken watches, some jerk at Information takes the bait and starts scrolling down the screen a table with all the data they've accumulated on broken promises by other governments. Ken waits, trying not to cringe, until Policy1st's turn and internally refutes every accusation:

Campaign Promise	Result	Ken's response
Greater transparency in decision-making and administration	Legislative processes made public and external agencies contracted to provide technical explanations; executive and bureaucratic branches still excessively protected	*We tried, but some things take longer to explain and clarify. Data management isn't easy, especially in places with low education. And we were blocked in some centenals by agreements to respect previous policies to protect existing bureaucrats. We're just starting to work our way out of some of those traps now.*
Data-based policies	Greater explanation of data basis, but still notable politicization in the way data is selected	*It's impossible to be completely neutral, but we have commissioned external experts in almost every case and tried to open up broad fields of questioning. See above about low levels of education.*
Removal of unsupported tariffs	47% of pre-existing tariffs still in place	*Our trade partners wouldn't cooperate! Unilateral removal of tariffs would have been economic suicide. But still, we got most of them.*
Focus on long-term over short-term policies	Unclear	*On this . . . there have been some trade-offs.*

Noticing that absinthe is also legal here, Ken decides to move on from beer.

LIBERTY: . . . and we welcome the chance to set forth our ideas for world government as we celebrate another decade of freedom and economic growth in our centenals!

Yoriko finds herself nodding along with the people around her. She is watching the debate at a Liberty campaign event: a huge projection set up on the beach, with cows turning on spits and, of course, lots of free Coke and Dasani, Gauloises cigarettes, Degree antiperspirant and Unilever soap, and Nestlé breast-milk substitute. There's a play area set up for small children, which Yoriko appreciates (she couldn't get a sitter) almost as much as she is surprised by it. She thinks of Liberty as being uncaring and not exactly family oriented.

STARLIGHT: We'd also like to protest the refusal of Information to broadcast vid as well as sound. We feel that the public has the right to see as well as hear their candidates. Studies have shown that nonverbal language is a key element of trust and decision-making.

Mishima doesn't move, but inside she's somewhere between rolling her eyes and cursing. She can't believe Star-Light is among the contenders, if toward the bottom of the pack, and she *really* can't believe they're dragging this argument out again. They better be out by the next debate. As she watches, whoever's working the debate starts scrolling text down the screen about why debates are sound only. It's a stupid, process-oriented point to even be having a discussion about, but Mishima knows that all over the nonelection world—in Saudi Arabia, in Switzerland, in holdouts of the former USA and PRC and USSR, people are watching the debate for its entertainment value and loving every dig at Information.

She can't show her indignation, because having stayed an additional night at the Merita hotel, she's watching the debate in the bar. She would prefer to be alone or with like-minded colleagues, but she considers it a professional responsibility to check reactions. The Merita has thrown an actual party for the debate, with reduced-price drinks and free snacks, and a lot of people have shown up. Unfortunately for Mishima's purposes, more of them seem more interested in the drinks and snacks (and each other) than in the massive and multilinked projection of the debate. Mishima can barely hear through all the meaningless chatter, and she has unobtrusively turned on her earpiece and linked it in to her own feed.

POLICY1ST: . . . we welcome the audio-only format of the debates, as well as the simulquestions and the comparison sheets. These elections should be about policy, not presentation, and not even people. Our government officials are all chosen for their qualifications and capacity, not for their looks.

Ken catches himself wincing, or maybe it's the alcohol. Not that he disagrees; of course not. He just wishes Vera Kubugli hadn't let herself get pulled into such a silly issue, and without excuse of a direct question. Something about it sounds smug and self-righteous, which is a bigger risk for Policy1st than for Heritage.

Still, he is guiltily glad that it's Vera representing them in this debate, rather than Suzuki, who has an even greater tendency to let his tones get sententious. Vera is warmer, or at least comes across that way—Ken's only met her briefly.

Also, she's female and not remotely white. Ken has gotten the sense that she's one part of the government that Suzuki can't micromanage.

Wow, absinthe really works fast. And well. Ken admires the empty cup, then punches in the order for another.

MODERATOR: Thank you all for your opening statements. We will now move on to the questions. As you all know, due to the high number of participants, we will be taking answers in groups simultaneously. The audience can select which voice to hear while the other answers are transcribed on the screen; we do encourage you, however, to listen to the recorded answers of all the respondents later, to get the full effect of all of their statements.

Mishima orders a bourbon, pleased that she is no longer in the Information trenches. When her drink comes, she raises a silent toast to all the grunts who are poised at their interfaces right now, fingertips and neurons twitching. There are two groups of Information workers on a debate: the A team, which does the simultaneous fact-checking and context-setting that viewers see on their screens, and a second set of less-senior but also well-regarded staffers who collect data from the listeners and integrate it into analysis and projections. One of the first Information datasets to come out of a debate is which government got the most listeners. Some argue that it's not a great determinant of the way the polls will move next, on the theory that people listen for entertainment value and vote out of self-interest, but Mishima has been with Information long enough to be cynical: most people's interest *is* entertainment. From the icon in the corner of the big projection, she can see that this Merita hotel is tuning into Heritage, which now that she thinks about it, is not particularly surprising even if they are sitting in an 888 centenal. She brushes her hair back, casually adjusting the feed in her earpiece to listen to Liberty.

MODERATOR: Let's move right into something that some of you have mentioned in your opening statements: law and order. Suppose that an individual commits a violent crime in the jurisdiction of some other government and then flees into one of your centenals. Will you extradite that individual, subject him or her to a judicial process under your government, or ignore this circumstance unless the crime affects your citizens?

In Addis Ababa, in the same bar where he met Domaine (what a nutter!), Shamus rolls his eyes. They always haul out this question, or something like it, for the debates. For all of Information's bullshit about transparency and clarity and highlighting differences, they live off of people using their communications and reference systems, and they love questions that get people talking. Extradition policies are all clearly posted in the comparison sheets, but people still get excited about crime, even if there's nothing new in the answers. He keeps an eye on the debate projection in the bar but switches his personal feed back to football replays, and curses Information again for not allowing any live matches during the debates.

HERITAGE: . . . in addition, we would like to take the opportunity to decry the incidents of violence that have been occurring in far too many centenals in the run-up to the election. It is deeply unfortunate that the micro-democratic process causes so much strife, and we earnestly hope that someday we will always be able to govern the way we do between elections: peacefully and prosperously.

Subtext: skip the elections and let us rule forever, Mishima thinks, slugging back the rest of her bourbon. It's enough to make her wish she hadn't shut down that WP=DICTADOR fire-writing in Buenos Aires quite so quickly. She orders another, willfully oblivious to the solicitous expressions on the faces of various high-paying guests hovering in her vicinity.

POLICY1ST: Our extradition agreements vary from government to government. We would never extradite someone to a government with cruel or unusual forms of punishment; however, we would likewise never let a violent criminal wander our centenals unpunished and unrestrained. So, while the precise answer will vary according to the case, you can be sure that such an individual would be subject to a process of justice, either under our laws or under those of the centenal where the crime was committed.

Ken nods, satisfied. He hopes that a lot of people were listening to Policy1st, because Vera nailed it: not only the words, but also the firm yet compassionate tone. As much as he agrees in principle with Information's embargo on video during the campaign, he wishes people could see her open, earnest face as she's speaking.

He listens to her on his earpiece, but with the volume low enough so that he can hear the soundtrack playing in the bar, too. They are taking votes among the patrons to decide which feed to listen to for each question (seriously,

Ken loves this government—maybe it's just the bar, but surely an enabling environment has something to do with their easy participatory approach) and so he hears a bit of PhilipMorris's answer, which everyone wanted to listen to because they are famous for their continued defense of the death penalty. At the same time, he scans the transcribed answers crawling up the projection, with some extra attention to Liberty's. Nothing surprising leaps out at him. Everyone knows the extradition policies anyway; this is a pure crowd-pleaser.

MODERATOR: Thank you. The next question is on foreign policy. Now, we are all aware of the legal issues concerning centenal sovereignty, but there are grey areas staked out by treaties and intercentenal coordination, and cross-border concerns have raised new models of how centenals may interact. The question is: are there any circumstances under which you would attempt to influence a centenal belonging to another government?

In the bar in Jakarta, in the hotel in Singapore, and on the beach outside of Naha, Ken, Mishima, and Yoriko lean forward simultaneously. Ken switches his earpiece, then registers that he is hearing the same thing from both ears; the bar has voted to listen to Liberty. He wonders whether the rumors are out while loyally switching his own feed back to Policy1st; every listener helps build their buzz.

LIBERTY: Of course, we respect the integrity and political independence of all governments. We also respect the rights of our own citizens, their needs, economic fulfillment, and pursuit of happiness. And especially, of course, their freedoms. And we will defend that.

Mishima stands up, drains her third glass, and heads for her room, ignoring the gestures of the well-dressed man sitting next to her, who's been trying to buy her a drink for half an hour. Ken slumps back in his chair and wishes he were more (or less) sober. Yoriko, sitting on the warm sand and listening to the warm voice of Johnny Fabré boom through excellent acoustics into the night around her, wishes suddenly and urgently to be somewhere else.

Domaine, still in Saudi, misses the debate entirely.

CHAPTER 8

After the debate Mishima checks out quickly, annoyed with herself for indulging in the Merita longer than she had to, and gets back to the relative privacy of her crow, where she can deploy her superpowers. Which is to say, her high-level clearance and sophisticated analytical software, not to mention her brain. As soon as she's comfortably settled, she sets up a private connection to Information that doesn't go through the Merita line. After a moment of reflection, she goes further and unmoors, disconnecting physically as well as virtually. She sets a course for Tokyo, since she's pretty sure she'll have to talk to people with significant authority about whatever she finds, and probably urgently. Tokyo's both the closest power hub and the one where she has the most connections. Or, to put it differently, home.

She opens feeds to the latest real-time polls, using her Information biometrics pass to get the raw data as well as the crunched and cleaned-up results. The first thing she sees makes her punch up the speed to get to Tokyo earlier: Liberty has jumped a full four points. Mishima yanks the data onto her closed system so she can play with regressions and slice it up in different ways without anyone using Information to guess what she's looking for.

Now that she's locked off for at least seven hours—seven and a half, she sees, glancing at the ETA—she takes her time. Clicks in an order for tea, arranges her feeds the way she likes them. She would hesitate to admit it to anyone because it sounds so antisocial, but she enjoys the long hours of travel in this job, knowing that every couple of days, week at most, she's guaranteed at least a few hours where, even if people can reach her, she never has to be in the same room with them.

A few advids slide in along with her feeds, reminding Mishima that she should refresh her security filters. There's one from AllFor1, a middle-tier government that has been trying aggressively to move up in the ranks this time. The vid is a close-up on the face of a woman—not too young, not too old, some kind of Asian-Caucasian cross: a trendier, cleaner version of Mishima herself.

"Tired of getting treated like a statistic? We know you're more than just part of a group. You're an *individual.* Help your centenal join the government that works hard to treat you like one."

Mishima has to smile. The phrasing is supposed to remind you that AllFor1 has one of the lowest unemployment rates on the planet. The rumor is that they guarantee all their citizens jobs in the extensive government bureaucracy needed to treat every case individually. Mishima, along with anyone else who bothers to look at the Information crib sheets, knows this isn't true, but even the 63 percent government employment rate is high. And questionable in terms of viability, especially if they grow significantly this cycle, as it looks like they might. With that much government, they don't actually produce very much. They fund most of that employment through high taxes; you pay your own salary, in a way. One of the most common debates in the Information staff virtual plaza is whether they will be able to swing it somehow, maybe by contracting services out to other governments.

The AllForl logo comes up, and Mishima notes that they've changed it. In the last election, when they were targeting mainly European and American markets, the supposedly individualistic cultures that some cubicle analyst thought would be a better demographic for them, they were All4One. This cycle, having realized that Asians like personalized attention too, they're trying to go global, and that meant adjusting their numerology.

The advid ends and another catches her eye: it's the word INFORMATION, and something about it—the rich red hue, the ornate script—tells her that whatever this ad wants to sell her, it has nothing good to say about her employer. She wonders what went wrong with their targeting software. Although she has to keep quiet about her precise functions, she makes no secret of her affiliation with the organization. Then she notices another ad-word that she thought was separate, IGNORANCE, in a far sharper font and sparkling black fill, swinging closer to and now orbiting the other. The two words spin faster and faster, finally resolving into a version of the yin-yang, curled around each other. It's nicely done but evaporates without any explanation or address, and Mishima gets back to work.

She needs to prepare a presentation to convince her superiors that the potential problem with Liberty is worth putting resources toward, and that the first resource should be Mishima herself. It's not going to be an easy sell. The Information bureaucracy, vast as it is, is stretched tight with the election: tracking all campaign actions, official and unofficial; mediating disputes; managing the delicate, highly technical process of voting itself; promoting voter registration; helping smaller governments fulfill their transparency obligations. Hypothetical threats are low on their list at the moment. And her evidence is very thin. It seems so unlikely. People have gotten lulled into security over the last twenty years of relative peace.

Ken is pumped after the debate—well, once he's sobered up by watching replays of that Liberty answer a few dozen times, while in his other feeds their polls soar. He wants to do battle. He's ready to be sent straight to their headquarters to take them to task. Or better still, to the news compilers, to explain exactly what's *wrong* with this kind of rhetoric, or maybe more than rhetoric, at this point in civilization. It doesn't help that it's Agus who tells him he's been called home.

"Tokyo. Of course," Ken says, nodding as though he had expected it. "That is, after the debate last night . . ."

"Vera did pretty well, huh?" Agus says, almost like they're buddies who can enjoy the moment together. "Our polls have been tracking up."

Ken abstains from calling him an idiot. Yes, their polls have shifted slightly upward in absolute terms (insofar as there is any absolute in the baseless game of electioneering). But the leaders, the top three and several of the next eight, have moved up more steeply, widening the gap between Policy1st and the Supermajority. At this point Ken just hopes they'll make it into the second debate. But right now should be all about optimism.

"Wait till Suzuki gets at 'em in the next debate," he promises.

By that point there are no flights that will get him in before evening. He has the choice of rushing to Tokyo to cool his heels or taking an overnight and going into the meeting eyes raw and mind wandering. As he's looking at the options, though, playing with connections in Rangoon or Ulaanbaatar, he switches his calendar to Tokyo and notices an event notation: an invitation to a party that very night. Done! He punches in for the earliest arrival he can find, and heads for the airport.

here are you going?" The man in the backseat taps on the divider. "Ma'am? Go straight here!"

Yoriko catches his eye in the rearview monitor, nods, and flips off her turn signal. She wasn't trying to increase the tab, although that wouldn't be an unwelcome side effect. Ever since the debate, she's found herself avoiding Liberty centenals.

Not that her work is done. As Suzuki didn't have to point out, everyone saw the debate. Yoriko learned nothing special by being at the event. Or, at least, almost nothing.

"Wait," Suzuki had said as she described the beach barbecue. "What did you say they were giving away? Nestlé breast-milk substitute?"

Yoriko squints to remember. Yes, she can see again the baby-blue logo.

Silence. In her projection, Suzuki is frowning slightly. "So, Nestlé is in bed with Liberty," he says finally. "Odd."

"Maybe it's a new treaty," Yoriko suggests. "There were Shiseido products as well." She had refrained from mentioning those earlier, because she's embarrassed how many sample packs she took.

"Well, aside from that." Suzuki pauses, and she can hear him muttering under his breath as he notes it down for follow-up. "Any other strange behavior?"

Yoriko swallows. "I'll keep looking."

And she will. There's a rally tomorrow night she's planning on going to. She's both sorry and relieved that they are unlikely to show any sensitive material in an open meeting.

Tokyo is almost as dense as Jakarta, but not nearly as diverse in terms of governments—or, really, in any terms Ken can think of. A lot of it has belonged to the technocratic Sony-Mitsubishi merger since the first election, with a few centenals going to Japanese nationalist governments instead and the usual outposts of the top players: Liberty, Heritage, PhilipMorris, SecureNation around the military bases, and yes, Policy1st, which holds the centenal where Ken lives, along with a few others. The hot-button trend this year is the few local "progressive" governments focused on legal and economic systems that try to enable young entrepreneurs. Despite that story having been told in every generation since the first election, they still haven't swept away the old guard of entrenched corporates, and the safe money is that they never will.

Tokyo was one of the first cities to form a municipal coalition government, and it shows. The public transportation system is subsidized and therefore cheaper than most, although inhabitants, Ken included, complain every time the prices rise. Ken prefers the municipality initiatives that contribute to the flavor of the city, as when they reimagined the crisscrossing tracks of the old public transportation system—metro, commuter rail, monorail—as urban art gallery and sustainable street lighting. Tourists cluster around the old pillars of the elevated trains, examining an exhibit on historical, ink-on-paper advertising, and drunken salarymen stumble in the steady, colored lighting from the fluoron ropes looping the city.

Another effect of this is that, at least at night, you know immediately when you step into a centenal that is not part of the coalition, because the hulking tracks are dark. It is in one of these areas, under the ancient arch of a railway bridge, that Ken finds himself that evening, his brown engineered-leather boots splashing through puddles of groundwater. It's a grim-looking place, the unmarked rusted-steel door under a sign, unlit, for a long-closed metro station. But Ken pushes without hesitation, and the interior is warm, light, clean-lined, as swanky as the penthouse of any high-rise. He slips off his boots before taking the two steps up onto the hard-wood floor, raised almost a meter above ground level to pro-tect against flooding. The air inside is fresh; and the lighting is pseudo sunlight. The long rooms are just on this side of crowded, and all the people are beautiful and beautifully dressed.

Ken shuffles off his coat at the coat check, and with it his work life. He runs a hand through his hair, throws his shoul-ders back, takes a cosmo off a tray, and sidles through the crowd. A quartet is playing twentieth-century jazz in one room, a DJ mangling more recent lounge beats in another. Peering through a half-open door, Ken sees a small group clustered around a projection of that World Cup elimination he wanted to watch. He's tempted, but is feeling too social for that right now, and goes on to check out the rest of the party. Eventually, Ken spots the host, Eichi, his old high school roommate, who now works for a flash sustainable ur-ban architecture firm—hence the digs. He angles through the guests—some of whom are now swaying in time with the music—till he reaches his friend, and clinks glasses with him.

"Hey!" Eichi says. "I didn't expect you to make it."

Ken winks, appreciating his status as a man of urgent international tasks, maybe with a whiff of mystery and importance. "Lucky scheduling coincidence. How are you?"

They catch up. Eichi's lovely wife, a doctor, slinks over to greet him. The kids are in bed. An energy consultant and a rising-star newscaster drift into their discussion. The proposed mantle tunnel comes up, which was pretty much guaranteed, since the first trial is planned to be a Tokyo-Taipei link. The newscaster is ebullient about it; the energy consultant sees some benefits. Ken, whose personal take is not far from the official Policy1st position that drilling through the earth's crust for faster and supposedly safer medium-haul transportation is inviting an environmental catastrophe, if not the apocalypse, limits himself to a few clever but noncommittal remarks.

"Of course, Heritage will monopolize it," the energy consultant says. Ken pegs him for a Sony-Mitsubishi stalwart.

"Well, naturally, it will run to and from Heritage centenals, but they've promised it will be accessible to all at the same price," the newscaster answers. "Besides, other governments are free to build their own."

"If they can raise the funds," Eichi puts in. "But aren't they going to put a limit on the number and density of the tunnels? We don't want to turn the earth into Swiss cheese."

"It's only a tiny fraction of the crust," the energy consultant says.

To Ken's relief, the conversation eventually wanders on to Tokyo's canals and waterways (cleanliness of, alternative uses for, risks of) and from there to a new blood glitter that subtly highlights the veins beneath the skin, apparently the latest craze of the überrich. Ken gets to expound on his theory that hair care has taken a disproportionate role in perception of public figures since the turn of the century, but unfortunately that turns the conversation toward the campaign. Johnny Fabré's mane is justly famous, and in any case at this stage of the game, the election is never far from the surface of any sparkling conversation. A mayoral aide (not from this centenal; slumming like the rest of them) joins the group, and Ken's attention wanders away. Not that he isn't endlessly fascinated by the campaign, but right at this moment there's too much he can't say, especially with the newscaster's eyes lighting up. All of their gossip is at least a day old, anyway.

It is perhaps because of the earlier conversation that he notices the auburn-haired woman, although she is striking enough—smooth face, smooth figure draped in a dress of shining copper cords loosely woven enough to show the occasional glimpse of smooth skin—that he thinks he would have noticed her anyway. An almost-visible energy trembles in the angle of the wrist holding her champagne flute. Maybe she noticed him first, because as soon as he really looks at her, her eyes meet his. Her personal Information is completely mute, an opaque absence of facts and figures in the air next to her face. Ken pivots away from his group, gently enough not to disrupt their conversation.

Mishima has had a rough day. Walking out of the Information offices into the chilly Tokyo twilight, she'd thought about going back to her crow and getting some sleep, but she doubted sleep would come. Her fingers were twitching like a pianist's and she kept looking back over her shoulder as she walked along the narrow streets of Marunouchi. She had broken down the numbers for them in the glossy three-dimensional charts that people always seem impressed by, although at this point Mishima can generate them without effort. The percentage of voters who, according to their best Information, would vote to change the entire system, or to threaten it by going to war. It's a small but not insignificant coalition of haves who think they deserve to be have-mores; nationalists who consider some aspect of identity (ethnicity, religion, place of birth) more important than the government one chooses; and all-out cranks and contrarians. Maybe six to eight percent, although she warned them that it's possible that they are underestimating. There are likely to be some who would support this but, not believing they have a chance, vote on more mundane concerns that will matter if the system continues to function. The danger is if Liberty can succeed in attracting these voters without losing their more mainstream constituency, they might actually be able to win the Supermajority. If this is actually why they want to win it, they could then throw the entire system, the hard-bought peaceful cacophony of the past two decades, into violence and chaos.

The bosses didn't buy it. Mishima can still hear LaForge, who, as the Director for Strategic Election Analysis, is her boss's boss: "These aren't even campaign infractions."

Mishima had explained patiently (hopefully it didn't show that she was being patient) that they are being subtle because this is not about mass campaigning, but about signaling.

"Really?" LaForge had raised his eyebrows. "Is there any indication that this signaling, if it even exists, is more than a campaign ploy? Troop movements, perhaps? Weapon purchases?"

If there was, Mishima didn't have it. "We haven't even looked," she pointed out.

The atmosphere had remained disapproving. Mishima's own supervisor, Malakal, was projecting in from Juba, and had been quietly supportive but not particularly enthusiastic about the idea of her taking time off from her other duties. She can understand that: he got stuck overseeing the centenal mapping when what used to be Sudan finally accepted micro-democracy a few months ago, and he's swamped. Everyone else in the room had seemed bored at best, hostile at worst. It makes no sense, but . . . Mishima wishes she had more confidence in the organization she works for.

Her crow was moored in Shinbashi, a couple of kilometers away. Without thinking, she turned away from the spilling lights of a public transport crow hovering near her and kept walking, ignoring the pop-up advids and peering at the tiny slices of Tokyo life visible through windows, open doorways, among the drunks laughing red-faced outside of bars. When she reached her crow, she found she was still not tired enough to sleep.

It is that same nervous heartbeat that sends her to the party. That and the new dress she hasn't worn yet, which fits perfectly when she slides it on back in the crow. Maybe a night off is exactly what she needs. She punches in the coordinates of the party and finds a mooring spot above a hotel nearby.

When she spots Ken, she's already on her fifth glass of champagne. She's seen him somewhere before; that's why her eyes stick on him the first time, and linger as she's trying to place him. *Not an Information drone, please.* She sips. But he must be connected to the campaign; she hasn't seen anyone not related to it in months, and the tingle of recognition feels more recent than that. Was he in the Singapore hub? Or maybe at the Merita, at that stupid debate party? No . . . By the time she's figured it out, *It was an event, not sure where, he works for a campaign, not one of the awful ones, which though?* he's noticed her, and now he's turning, smiling. The smile doesn't say he knows her but that he'd like to. She prepares to stomp whatever line he's come up with.

"Please," he says. "I need to talk about anything but the election."

Mishima can't help smiling back. "Me, too." They are speaking Japanese; Mishima clicks off her translator to be sure. "What topic were you thinking?"

"Well . . ." Ken had been about to suggest hair, because of his earlier conversation, but the unusual color of hers makes him self-conscious. "Well."

"What did you do before working on the campaign?" She's supposed to be taking the night off, but at this point, Mishima doesn't even think about her leading questions.

"Actually, I'm in school," Ken says. "Postgrad. And before that, working."

The smile is easy, no manufactured charm, and his tone is confident. She lets him slide on the school thing even though she's more and more certain he's connected with a government campaign somehow.

"Working on?"

"Tech," he says, and leaves it there. "And you?"

Mishima briefly considers her previous careers—security specialist, spy, financial trader, farmer—and decides not to reveal any of them, retreating instead to her usual ploy. "I work at Information," she says.

His gaze almost immediately skates past her face, scanning the party, and Mishima worries for a second that she's underplayed, that he's lost interest. She barely has time to be surprised that she cares whether he's lost interest before she realizes he was looking for another topic. The idea of the massive bureaucracy of Information tends to make people want to talk about something, anything, else.

"Where are you from?" Ken asks.

Another tough one. "All over," Mishima glosses, twinkling. "You?"

"Here, more or less," Ken says. "Do you live here now?"

"I don't live anywhere." It's not the way she usually tells it, but she's decided she wants to hold his interest. He's cute enough and so far has avoided saying anything incredibly stupid. And she needs a night off.

"You don't have a place?" Ken's wondering how badly Information pays its employees, and whether her lack of an apartment is enough to convince her to come to his. Although now that he thinks of it, his place isn't in much of a state to receive visitors.

"I travel too much," Mishima says.

"What do you do, stay in hotels?"

"Sometimes," she says. And then, as if she's just remembered, "I do have a crow."

"A crow? Your own crow?"

"Sure," Mishima says, and gives him one more long, appraising look. "Wanna see?"

As she told him on their way up, it's not a luxury crow. It's utilitarian. And decidedly neater than his apartment, Ken thinks, looking around. There's not much more than a spotless workspace—a small fridge, a food-cooker, and a good-sized printer with five different material nozzles. Behind that is a tiny bedroom, the futon folded into a couch. Mishima pulls some beers—real ones, Ken notices—out of the fridge and turns on the music. They stand chatting by the table for a while, the brassy braided strap slipping off her slim shoulder driving Ken batty. They listen to the music, some kind of West African soul, he would guess, and drink another pair of beers, and finally they slide into the bedroom. He kisses her earlobe, her neck, and she growls low in her throat and pulls him against her. Ken is just sober enough to remember to display his birth control (enabled) and inoculation status (up to date) on his personal Information to avoid any awkward pauses later on. He doesn't usually sleep with girls he's just met, but this one—Mishima, she told him her name is—is irresistible. And it's election season.

CHAPTER 9

Domaine leaves Riyadh on a flight to Almaty, thirsty and desperate for news of the election. Fortunately, they serve alcohol on the flight, but they block all feeds other than their own for the duration, and the hours of repeated segments about Kazakh tourism and special haj deals drive him to drink more than he should. He asks for a digital newspaper, and the flight attendant smiles inscrutably at him and keeps pushing the drink cart up and down the aisle, up and down the aisle.

As soon as they touch down, Domaine tries to link in to Information from his earpiece, but the connection is maddeningly slow. Once he's off the plane, he whips out his handheld and starts opening feeds while he walks, but even before he can get any news, he starts to notice it: the pitch of the background buzz, the number of tablets people are staring at, the raised eyebrows, covered mouths. Something has happened.

Ken wakes up naked and can't remember why. Unconcerned, he lets his gaze wander the small room, round-cornered and compact. It's not until his eyes light on the shiny bronze coils piled the floor that he has a kinetic memory, his hands sliding that coppery netting down a muscular back. He turns his head and finds a pair of brown eyes looking straight into his own.

"Good morning," she says. In the pale light from the frosted window, Ken thinks her more beautiful than the night before, her dark red hair even more dramatic. "Ocha?"

Ken nods as she delicately crosses over his body to step, naked, out of bed. She pulls a robe from somewhere and eases into it, indigo with flowing silver flowers.

"Did you sleep well?" Ken asks, unable to think of any other way to make conversation. He's trying to remember what exactly they did last night after removing their clothes, but all he gets is a haze of alcohol and a few indistinct sensations. A moan? His or hers? A curve under his palm, definitely hers, but which? Most of all, he's trying to remember her name.

"I slept *beautifully,*" she says, unfurling her arms into a stretching yawn before going back to the neat movements of preparing the tea—the old-fashioned way. Ken approves of teapots, but he wonders what kind of energy this crow runs on, what it's using to heat the water. Everyone says nuclear energy is totally safe, but Ken still doesn't completely trust nuclear-powered water heaters and food-cookers.

"I don't know about you," the woman goes on, giving him an absolutely killer-cute look over one shoulder, "but these days—during the campaign, I mean—I don't sleep well at all. It's crazy, I'm so tired all the time, and yet when I get a chance to nap . . ." She shrugs, the silk sliding with her movement.

"Oh, I'm the same way," Ken nods. "Every time I lie down, my mind thinks of a million more things I should be doing. All the different time zones don't help."

"Where did you say you work, again?" She brings over the teapot and two cups, white Satsuma pottery that grants him a flashback of the skin over her ribs, and hands him one cup so she can pour.

He hesitates for a second, then goes ahead. "Policy1st." He's not sure whether he told her the night before, but it's not so much of a secret. Particularly for someone who works at Information, as he now remembers she does.

"Oh," she says, looking thoughtful. It could be worse than Policy1st, for sure. Where has she seen him, then? On the campaign, and he speaks Japanese, so . . . "You work with Suzuki-san?"

"That's right," Ken says. "He's my boss. Do you know him?"

"A little." She's met him briefly a couple of times, but—like all the major operators of the major government campaigns—she has enough Information about him at her fingertips to have formed an opinion. "Suzuki Todry."

The mention of his mentor reminds Ken that he has a meeting with him today, this morning in fact, an important one. He's trying to figure out how to check the time without looking like he wants to leave. He wishes he weren't in a hurry (or, quite possibly, already late); sitting in a crow over the city of Tokyo drinking green tea with a gorgeous woman sounds like a pretty good plan for a hungover day. Maybe she can give him a ride. He doesn't even remember what part of town they are hovering over.

"So, what do you do for Policy1st?"

Ken looks down at his cup, wondering how much he should say. His hand is trembling slightly; his hangover must be worse than he thought. His handheld beeps; must be Suzuki calling to ask why he's late. As he reaches for it he hears a skittering: the woman's earpiece, which she must have taken off at some point the night before, is vibrating its way across the shelf. It occurs to him that the sound his handheld is making is not the call alert.

Hot liquid sloshes onto his hand. Looking down he realizes that no, his hand isn't trembling; it's the whole cabin that's swaying. The woman jumps up, hurries into the other room. The crow tilts from side to side, then starts to thud up and down as though it's being dragged down a flight of stairs, like turbulence except they're in a *crow*, not a plane. Ken puts his cup down, stupidly, and it immediately falls over, the steaming liquid disappearing into the stain-absorbent floor.

"What's going on?" he asks, trying not to sound panicked. Stumbling on the jerking floor, he follows his voice into the next room, where she is leaning over a control panel.

"I don't know," she says. "I—we're still moored . . ." She raises her eyes, and they both get it at the same time, their imaginations following the long anchor line down from the ship to the supposedly stable building it's linked to.

"Jishin da," Ken whispers, the fear in his tone so elemental that the interpreter doesn't even bother. "It's the earthquake."

The crow is yanked earthward.

The early warning alerts go off as far away as Okinawa, where Yoriko pulls over her taxi and waits for a tremor that she barely feels.

In Almaty, Domaine gets on to Information perhaps half an hour after the quake. It is clearly too soon to have much data, especially since—and this is not a good sign—most of the live feeds in Tokyo and the surrounding area have been disrupted. He opens ten or twelve feeds at once, all of them scrolling frantically. The numbers range from two thousand to one hundred thousand dead, so he feels comfortable discounting all of them and assuming that for the moment nobody has the slightest idea. He tries to think if he knows anyone in Tokyo but doesn't come up with any names. Highly organized and strongly democratic, the Kantō area has never been a target for him.

He scrolls farther. The little footage that has gotten out already, of wavering buildings and dust-covered, stunned inhabitants, is disturbing, so he doesn't watch too much of it and tries to think practically instead.

What will this mean for the election? Cold as it seems, Domaine is not the first person to ask that. All of the governments with hopes of a Supermajority send their top representatives to Honshu before the ground stops shaking. Some of them were already there; one of the questions flooding feeds is what losses were sustained, both personal and material, that might affect the outcome of the race.

A major earthquake had been predicted for the Kantō area for decades, the meme resurfacing in morbid feeds and (correctly) alarmist commentary every couple of years. As usual, however, Ken finds himself without a flashlight, spare solar charger, or alternative communications option. Not to mention naked. Fortunately, their sharp fall didn't stop with them hitting ground, but with a sharp deceleration that left them both sprawling, cushioned by the crow's airbags. As the bouncing slows, Ken scrambles to his feet and, finding himself more or less unharmed, stumbles back into the bedroom to pull some pants on. He considers going into the bathroom to throw up on the way but isn't quite enlightened enough to be able to do that in front of this woman he's just slept with. More rationally, he's not sure he should be dumping any underutilized calories right now. He may need them later.

His hands might not have been trembling before, but they're shaking now.

As he's getting dressed the woman comes in, gives him a shaky grin, and pulls on a pair of cargo pants under her robe. "Do you have people in the city?" she asks.

Ken shakes his head. "My family . . ." He rarely tells people about his family, but right now he can't spare enough brain function to think of a reason not to. "My family's in Brazil." What family he has. She nods. "Friends, though, some." He thinks of the architect from the night before, wonders if the old elevated subway held. It should have; it's held for years, through other earthquakes before this. This must have been a big one, though. "You?"

She gives a half-nod. "Work colleagues, mostly." She frowns, remembering the frustrating meeting the day before. It no longer seems so bad that she is not tasked with chasing down the lies of a particularly devious rogue government. "Where are you headed? I mean, not to kick you out. You're welcome to stay. Really." She puts her hand on his arm, and Ken feels a tingle like an electric shock, but maybe it's the adrenaline of the moment. "Staying here might be the safest thing . . ."

He's already shaking his head. "I have to go check on some people. Actually"—he glances at the time on his handheld with an uncertain laugh—"I had a work meeting half an hour from now."

She nods and then pulls out her handheld and transfers him her details using line-of-sight. "If you want to come back here," she says, then shakes her head. "I don't know if the network's working or will be . . ."

"We'll figure it out," he says, happy to see her name. Mishima. That's right. "I'll be back, if not tonight then . . . once . . ."

She nods too.

Domaine has to tear himself away from the disaster feeds to board his next flight. The casualty numbers are still unstable, no one knows what industrial horrors may have been released, and at least a dozen governments with bases in or around Tokyo are completely offline, opening the potential for anarchy in their centenals around the world. Domaine actually considers ditching his flight to keep watching but decides there won't be any concrete information for the next six hours anyway, and goes on to Istanbul as he had planned.

After that dramatic farewell, it takes them a while to separate. First, it takes each of them some time to convince themselves that they won't be able to access Information. Mishima spends fifteen minutes adjusting configurations and logging in to various high-security portals. Ken, who has long since given up on getting anything other than error messages, wonders again exactly what it is she does. The longer they stay, the harder it is to leave, especially after feeling the gentle sway of the pendulum start up again during three separate aftershocks. Each time, their eyes meet as soon as they sense it; each time leaves them feeling sweaty and knotted.

But once it is clear that they cannot only do nothing but also know nothing while in the crow's protective cocoon, staying is unbearable. Disembarking, however, turns out to be nontrivial. Mishima hesitantly points out that the sharp fall at the height of the earthquake was probably the building they're moored to crumbling, and suggests that they try to find a safer landing spot. She realizes as she says this that she will have to navigate manually, since all Information links are cut. Fortunately, she's done that before and, although not in many years, in almost as dire circumstances. Ken agrees, remembering how he had wondered if she might give him a ride to work, although that seems like it was in a completely different world.

But the anchor won't disengage.

"Something must have . . . caught it," Mishima says, from the control panel. They share a look, and without words, she starts reeling them in, closer to whatever destruction lies below. In her eagerness to get on Information, Mishima had forgotten about the outboard cameras; now she flicks a switch that turns them on, and swivels them down.

Her first glance at the city, as the cameras pan past the horizon on their way to a bird's-eye view, is not as bad as she expects. But then, Mishima generally expects the worst. She sees most of a skyline, the uneven pattern of tall buildings breaking up the sky. Something still stands. The pale roof of the hotel comes into view below them in time to see a broad crack across it before they settle gingerly to a landing.

"Do you think it—do you think it's completely collapsed?" Ken asks.

Mishima tilts her head slowly, eyes wide. "I don't know."

Leaving the crow seems like a terrible idea. She wishes they could put on spacesuits to venture out into that hostile environment.

"I'll go," Ken says. "You stay here, in case you need to fly the crow."

"Are you crazy?"

"It makes more sense than both of us risking it," Ken says. He's only partly trying to impress her; he's also itching to see what's happened.

Mishima starts pulling on a pair of cracked rubber boots. "I'm going." She manages to leave the rest unsaid: *What you do is up to you.*

The roof, white concrete gridded with faint lines from its prefab mold, is more stable than she expected, although slightly angled. It's disconcertingly hard to tell how high they are off the ground; some of the buildings around them are still standing, but she can't tell what floors' windows she is looking at, and her gaze keeps catching on the upside-down red triangles that mark emergency exits. She can't catch a glimpse of ground in the cityscape around them.

Ken steps uneasily over the crack in the roof, tests the other side. It doesn't wobble, and he picks his way toward the edge. Standing well away from it, he leans forward just enough to get a sense of height. They are still far off the ground, maybe forty or fifty feet. Below him he can see a small crowd of people, some of them sitting on the pavement. He shivers, then turns back around as Mishima calls to him. "The anchor's over here."

As he starts toward her, he feels the vibration in his feet and sprints the few steps of roof to grab the anchor line, the foot of the crow, anything.

The tremor subsides after a moment, and he grins sheepishly at Mishima, although he sees she's also gripping the line. "Here," she says, pointing to where the line disappears into a jumble of debris, in which Ken makes out a doorknob, the rest of the door buried. It must have been the top of the stairway to the roof, or maybe a small utility room. They start moving fragments of concrete and brick, hand over hand, the dust staining their fingers and their clothes. Some of the pieces are heavy enough that they have to work together to lift them, Mishima thinking how we forget the physical weight of all the things we've built up around us. She can't wait to get back on the crow and off this unsteady ground. She's sweating as she and Ken grip different sides of the door and angle it off the roof, dislodging more crumbles of concrete that tumble to the roof with a raucous clatter. In the sliding of those smaller pieces they almost miss the new rumbling below them.

"Here's the anchor," Ken says, breathing hard. The newly excavated mechanical hand still grasps a piece of metal railing, and Ken grabs it, tugging at the tines. The roof shakes and then drops, a sudden violent jolt. Ken catches the anchor line, hangs on as his legs try to keep him upright on the pitching building. He looks back to see Mishima scrambling to her feet.

"We've got to go!" Mishima yells, taking his arm.

They sprint for the door of the crow. The roof is pounding, and what should have been three running steps becomes five or six uncertain footfalls. Ken dives through the opening headfirst, Mishima leaps so she can dash for the controls. She pushes them up in the air, away from the rocking ground, and orders the anchor to unlatch as they rise. It opens, and she exhales, retracting the mooring line. As they lift, she stares down through the camera. The crack in the roof widens, yawns, opens, and then the view is obscured by a cloud of dust. Ken hopes the people in the street below got out of the way in time.

They are silent for a moment, watching the dust settle in on itself.

"Are you sure you want to stay in Tokyo?" Mishima asks. "I could take you somewhere else. It's going to be pretty messy down there."

The pull to be in the middle of the action is too strong. "I have some things to take care of," he says, which sounds annoyingly arch but is also true. "What about you?"

Mishima tries to grin. "Messy is what I do," she says, glibly irritating Ken even more than he irritated her.

"As close as you can get me to the Policy1st building is fine," he says. "It's in Ichigaya."

"Perfect," she says. As expected, the auto system won't take coordinates, so she points them to the northeast and steers manually. Out of habit more than conscious respect, she avoids the airspace over the emperor's palace, weaving along major arteries as she normally would. They are peering down at the crowd of people in Hibiya Park, pale faces turning up to follow their path, when the pattern of light changes. Mishima glances up and sees a wall of windows looming toward them, so close she can make out the pale blur of a face, its shocked expression matching hers as it hurtles toward them. She swerves hard, throwing Ken against the wall and almost losing the controls.

"Sorry," she says, righting the crow as the skyscraper that nearly clipped them sways back in the other direction like a sapling in a strong wind. Crows normally don't fly very high, but Mishima decides to add some altitude, and they cruise the rest of the way well above the tops of the buildings.

CHAPTER 10

Suzuki is bleeding—still, slightly—from a cut on his forehead. It must be a kind of magic, Ken thinks; even when he's thrown against the edge of a desk in the middle of a massive earthquake, he manages to come out with a perfectly photogenic injury. No black eyes, no squashed fingertips, just a heroic-looking streak of blood in exactly the right place for the cameras. Which, thankfully, haven't arrived yet.

The Policy1st offices, in an appropriately nondescript, unextravagant five-story building, remain standing, although people are still picking up furniture, wall hangings, tablets, broken teacups.

One man who Ken knows slightly, Hirano-san, was burned when the water heater shattered. "Koike-san took him to the hospital," Suzuki says. "Although who knows what kind of treatment he'll be able to get in this mess."

Ken feels like he should ask if Suzuki's family is okay, but he's not sure if he has one or if they're in Tokyo. He's almost positive Suzuki's not a native, but he does spend a lot of time in the greater metropolitan area to be completely alone.

Suzuki spares him the quandary by not having time for further pleasantries. Even as he's giving Ken his trademark special-occasions bear hug, in this case for being alive, minions are hovering nearby with tablets to be signed and decisions to be made.

"Ready to work?" Suzuki asks him.

"That's why I'm here," Ken says.

"I'm glad you made it," Suzuki says. "I was worried you might be stuck on the public transportation—it's apparently gone haywire since all the maps are down." Ken keeps his mouth shut, and Suzuki goes on. "Do you have your tablet?"

Feeling suddenly naked, Ken shakes his head. "Just my handheld."

"Here." Suzuki shoves one (Koike's? Hirano's?) into his hands. "The intranet's up, even if we don't have access to Information. Log on. We've got work to do."

As she redirects the crow toward the Information offices, Mishima is already sorry she was so short with Ken. It doesn't bother her long; she knows that as soon as she can connect, she'll be glad he's gone so she can work. All she wants to do right now is work. Someone has to fix this.

The Information hub in Tokyo is, not by accident, a long, low, earthquake-resistant building constructed in space made available by the last missile strikes during the fall of North Korea. The building is virtually undamaged, and Mishima is able to moor easily to the roof and disembark at the crow passenger access door. She tries not to think too much about her entrance the day before, that time from the ground floor, full of purpose and energized to take on Liberty. It still stings that they wouldn't authorize her to pursue it, but for the moment, the issue is moot.

On the first floor, Mishima finds Rachchivandrum, who, by happy chance, is both one of the colleagues she likes reasonably well and the person who seems to have taken charge. "What can I do?" she asks as soon as there's a pause in the flurry long enough for her to get his attention.

"We've only got three uplinks going," Rachchivandrum says, barely looking up. "And I don't know if anyone else in the city is connected at all. Go over there and give Korbin a hand—she's synthesizing reports as they come in, trying to upload concise bulletins and build a disaster map at the same time."

Tamping down her disappointment at not being able to connect immediately, Mishima joins Korbin at a workspace projecting five different small screens and a billiard table–sized map of Tokyo. Korbin, who oversees Heritage campaign coverage in East Asia, was silent and unhelpful on the Liberty question yesterday. Now, though, her eyes are half-closed in concentration and her hands are moving faster than Mishima's ever seen.

"Take these," she says without any other greeting, and waves a bunch of projected files into Mishima's workspace. "I haven't started on them. Triage, see if there's anything urgent that we can help with, and then consolidate as much as possible—the uplinks are ridiculously slow."

Mishima digs in with an uneasy satisfaction but keeps half an eye on Korbin.

"What do we know?" she asks ten minutes later when she sees her colleague's concentration relax momentarily.

Korbin's pale water-colored eyes meet hers. "Not many details. Massive infrastructure damage. Obviously, communications are almost entirely out—so much for resilient networking."

"We knew there were vulnerabilities," Mishima says, but even she can hear how futilely know-it-all it sounds. Korbin ignores her.

"Because of the comms problems, public transport is down. We're working with the municipal government to reprogram the shuttles to run standard routes, but because we're not sure what's standing and what's not, it's been tricky to identify optimal landing points. Similar issues for restocking private businesses—grocery stores, pharmacies—we're going to be looking at shortages pretty soon."

"Are we working with the private sector?" Mishima asks. Since it's Japan, the tea station is still working and she walks over to get a cup for each of them, brewing it bitter and strong.

"Domo," Korbin says gratefully, accepting hers. "Yes, 'we' in the sense of Information outside of the affected area. They're sourcing and staging as well as they can, and doing pinpoint coordination with anyone they can talk to. It's still going to be slow, though."

"So, we have to get Information connections back up."

"I'm going to switch over to that team pretty soon—I used to work on network regeneration. Can you take over here?"

Mishima nods. She swirls her tea, waits for what hasn't been said. Finally, she asks, "And?"

Korbin knows what she means. "No solid casualty numbers yet—there's stuff being floated online, but none of it comes from us. They must all be algorithms or straight-up guesses, because I'm pretty sure no one has better info than we do and we're lost."

"Order of magnitude?"

"At a guess? Nanmannin, tens of thousands," Korbin says. "But nothing to back that up. Could be way higher, or even lower. At the time it hit, many people would have been on their commute rather than in a building, which should help. But there's a lot of damage."

"Emergency services?"

"Deployed and responding. Some better than others, of course." Korbin rolls her eyes. "Sony-Mitsubishi teams are all over the place and seem to know their stuff. Hello Kitty, not so much." She's talking not about the corporate conglomerate that includes Sanrio, but about ChouKawaii, a single-centenal government specializing in fanfic and cute characters. Economically they do pretty well, but apparently they haven't been investing much of the revenue in disaster preparedness.

"Any big civil disturbances?" Mishima asks. She knows compiling assessments is one of the most valuable things she can do right now, but she can't help itching to get out on the street.

"Not that we've heard. *But* all the major party reps are nose-diving in, naturally, so if you consider that disturbing the peace . . ."

Mishima wishes that she were in one of the places where spitting on the floor would be an acceptable response. But there was something else she wanted to ask. "What about shelter? It's cold out there."

Korbin shrugs and it turns into a shiver. "We've heard reports of gatherings in the usual places: parks, community centers, high school gyms. The museums. There are a lot of people in Ueno, and we've even heard of congregations in the park around the Imperial Palace."

"Okay." Mishima goes back to her files. "I'll have these done in a few." She is constructing a table of the intel, with casualty and injury projections, types of damage, commodities needed, and specific problems, and at the same time adding it to the map. Most of the incident reports are text-only, and Mishima feels herself detaching, slipping into a state in which her mind bypasses emotion and narrative and gets the job done. It helps that she can't plot any intrigue around this; deus ex machina, Mishima notes grimly, seems to be good for her concentration. When she's finished the batch, they upload a brief bulletin with the Information they've gleaned and do another. By the time Korbin switches to uplink recovery, the map of Tokyo glowing in front of them is starting to look like the new, devastated reality.

Ken spends most of the day collating data about the needs in the Policy1st shelters. Runners—high school–age interns, mostly—show up at the office from one of the eight shelters in Policy1st's three centenals, transmit a chunk of numbers and one-word questionnaire answers using line-of-sight, and head back out. Ken's itching to get out there himself, but Suzuki pointed out that none of those kids could do his job, and they know the neighborhoods better than he does. Besides, the numbers are coming in almost nonstop, and another two shelters have opened. Ken focuses on his spreads, trying to keep his eyes away from the workspace next to him: Mizuno is working on a missing-persons database, and projected above his desk is a growing gallery of pictures brought in by terrified relatives and friends. Every once in a while, one gets shifted to the LOCATED file, but new photographs are coming in far faster. Whenever Ken catches a glimpse of one of those faces, he feels the sorrow and anger clogged up inside him. Instead he zooms in on the numbers: heated blankets, diaper sizes, bags of rice. Soon, Suzuki told him, the offers of assistance will begin pouring in, and then they'll need to be able to match them with the needs as quickly as possible.

When Suzuki finally tells him that he should go check on his apartment, some fourteen hours after he started working, it takes Ken almost an hour to get there. Public transportation, which normally works by compiling all requests and calibrating the optimal route, is completely down because of the Information disruption. Ken thinks about hitching, but the faces he sees in driver's seats are uniformly pinched with worry.

Even on foot, it shouldn't have taken him that long, but he keeps stopping, stunned by the sight of another building toppled, a pile of wreckage from some landmark, and, once, an arm protruding from under a slab of concrete. His antennae twitch so many times that he turns them off. Twice, he stops for aftershocks, darting in a panic into the middle of the street along with everyone else as the buildings around them tilt vertiginously.

He notices the differences in the centenals he passes. Heritage has obviously thrown much of its considerable weight into Tokyo; a helicopter is hovering over their centenal in Shinjuku. In Liberty's territory, government staff with manual loudspeakers are announcing the locations of shelters and food distributions. Emergency crews are running through Ken's own centenal, and he feels a spike of pride in Policy1st. Boots on the ground are better than expensive giveaways or large machinery any day.

He's dully surprised to find his own building still standing, and immediately starts calculating the possibility of a hot shower—not good, he decides, trying to keep his hopes low. When he gets closer, he can tell that something's not right. Rounding the corner, he sees a long vertical crack running up the building next to the exterior staircase, which is blocked off by a string of tape (again, points to Policy1st for addressing structural instabilities so quickly!). Ken hesitates by the entrance, wondering whether there's anything in there worth risking a quick run in. The ground vibrates, and he backs away.

He considers going back to the office to sleep, as any loyal worker should, but all day, as he sobered up, he's been having flashbacks to the night before. Her hair against his face, her arms pulling him close. Before she let him off in the morning, Mishima told him that she was going to try to moor above the Information offices. It's not far. Besides, given the option, he'd rather sleep off the unsteady ground tonight.

It takes him twice as long as he thought it would to walk there. He has to detour twice around pieces of skyscrapers that are now effective roadblocks, and the aftershocks continue almost regularly; Ken finds himself treading as if the ground were shaking even when it's not. As the night deepens, the cold presses against him. His jacket has heating, but Ken forgot to recharge it last night, didn't even think about it during the day, and now it's running low. He turns the optimal temperature down a couple of degrees, hoping it will last longer, and hunches his shoulders, thinking of all the people who ran outdoors this morning—yesterday—with no coat and watched their belongings disappear into a dust-filled mound of crumbled concrete. When his stomach rumbles, it occurs to him that he has barely eaten all day. He can remember at least two raids on the Policy1st office cache of teatime snacks, but no actual meals. Now he can't stop thinking about how hungry he is and, more disturbingly, whether he'll be able to get any food.

Three arduous blocks and one terrifying highway overpass later, he sees the dancing blue animation of a Lawson sign. The convenience store is tucked into the ground-floor arcade of an office building, at least six stories, but after an uneasy glance up, Ken decides to risk it. The empty spaces on the convenience store shelves contradict the rules of daily life in Tokyo and shake him as much as the grander scenes of destruction. It is more believable that skyscrapers crumble than that he can't get an onigiri at three in the morning. He stares at the few items left on the ramen shelf for a long moment, waiting for his Information to pop up with the ratings rundown, then remembers that they're not going to appear. He grabs a couple of bags of senbei, a handful of chocolate bars, and five cans of coffee, but stops short halfway up the aisle when he realizes that without an Information connection, there is no way to pay. He cautiously approaches the autoclerk and finds a handwritten note—thank goodness his visual translator doesn't require a live connection. The reader has been reconfigured to accept details via line-of-sight, and will bill him later. It is something of an honor system, since the antitheft had to be turned off, and Ken is grateful for it. He zaps in his details, adds a small "thank you!" to the others scrawled in various languages at the bottom of the note, and continues on his way.

By the time he sees the low Information building, it is long after midnight. The city is dire cold and nearly unlit, and Ken is equally exhausted and afraid to sleep. He thinks he can make out the grey blur of a crow or two hovering above the building but can't be sure.

Amazingly, there is someone at reception, and when he asks for Mishima, she directs him to the roof without further questions. Through his fog, Ken wonders at the lax security but decides that they are trying to make it easy for friends and relatives. When he gets to the roof, he immediately sees the crow's anchor, familiar now. The line extends up at an angle, trembling with another small aftershock. He freezes until the vibration stops, then tries to call Mishima. Only after listening to the silence for almost a minute does he remember that comms are out.

Ken stares up at the indistinct bulk of the crow. So close but so impossible to reach. He considers sleeping on the roof, but it's far too cold, or trying to shimmy up the rope, but that is obviously impossible, especially in his current shaky condition. The best option seems to be going back inside and finding an unoccupied corner, but he finds himself reluctant to be under a roof, even if this building has survived so far.

Bending down, he finds some small stones and tosses them, almost hopelessly, at the crow. One of them pings off it, then another. Ken waits, then scrabbles on the ground to find more. He looks up to see the anchor line vibrate, not with the ground this time but as the ship retracts it, pulling its way down toward the roof.

CHAPTER 11

Yoriko isn't sure whether she's at the Liberty "mutual assistance drive" as part of her spy work or because she wants to help, and Liberty's adverts have been the first, fastest, and most frequent. Hell, she's not even sure this assignment is still a priority, or running at all, or even if Suzuki is . . . In any case, she felt she had to be here. There is roughly the same assortment of products that they were giving away at the debate party, with a few sensible extras like blankets and bottles of water (mostly Coca-Cola's Dasani brand, with a sprinkling of Nestlé). Yoriko is welcomed by a wide-smiling greeter and joins other volunteers packing the goods into boxes and taping them shut. In the middle of the room—the "citizens' center" of the Liberty centenal—they are running a projection with photos and vids from the disaster. It shifts occasionally to show a map displaying the route the boxes will take to Tokyo, by sea since the lack of Information connections is making air travel around the affected area very dangerous. There have already been reports of one collision. There are also maps of the Tokyo area indicating in red where the goods will be going—all Liberty centenals, of course. But that's normal, right? Governments help their own people. And at some point, one of the cute young female welcomers comes around and offers to take Yoriko's contact information. The boxes are being tracked, she says proudly, so Yoriko can get a thank-you vid from the people who receive the goods she packed.

At that, Yoriko panics and stutters no thanks, she would rather, she's not doing it for the thanks, that is, she doesn't need a thank-you from those poor people who are already going through so much. After the taken-aback young woman moves on, Yoriko worries that maybe it looks suspicious not to put her name in. She is so unsettled that she leaves shortly after, and the more she thinks about the whole exercise, the dirtier she feels, especially listening to all the news reports about the disaster and how cold it is in Tokyo and how many people are crowded together in the shelters. Finally, even though she should get home to see her kids, she finds another volunteer station, this one run by the Red Cross. Their maps show not centenals but evacuation centers, and when Yoriko timidly asks, they tell her that they target by most vulnerable.

It is then that the surveillance starts.

Ken is disappointed when a washed-out blond woman in her forties opens the door of the crow, her shell-shocked expression a distorted reflection of his own, but Mishima is right behind her, and she takes his arm.

"Come on in," she says in a whisper. "But careful where you step." The limited floor space in the working area is covered with sleeping forms, barely visible in the low lighting. Ken follows the two women into the cabin, where Mishima makes another cup of green tea to accompany the two half-drunk ones already sitting on the floor. Pleased to have something to offer, Ken tosses down the remaining bag of rice crackers and the chocolate bars, and settles himself on the floor next to the blonde, who introduces herself as Yelinka.

Ken had nothing more in mind than falling asleep next to a warm-smelling body, but he finds that sitting and sharing intel in low voices with these two sharp-eyed women fulfills another need that he hadn't noticed. They have a lot to say.

"At least we have power."

"Yeah, the networked grid worked well."

They exchange a muted high five and Ken wonders what role these two women played in setting up Tokyo's power grid. He always imagined working for Information as long hours in a cubicle cataloguing the world's most boring videos, but it sounds like there's a lot more to it than that.

"Still, though, the public transport . . ."

"I know; that's a major problem."

A pause.

"The Iimashita building went down."

"What? Those bastards, they must not have built to code."

"I don't know . . . nothing is completely earthquake-proof; the energy could have hit it at the wrong angle . . ."

"The Tokyo Eye is down," Ken puts in, glad to be able to add something.

"Oh, really?"

"What did it look like?"

"Pieces."

"Big pieces?"

"Pretty big."

A pause.

"Does anyone know about the . . . the Imperial Palace?"

Silence.

Ken catches the flashing along Yelinka's eye that tells him her projection is updating. "Confirmed that all the bridges are down," she says. "I mean the small ones, along the river."

"Who can we get to put barges in place?"

"Some of the governments are already working on that . . ." Ken crossed one, in a Sony-Mitsubishi centenal, he thinks, although his walks through the city are already starting to blur.

"Food deliveries?"

"The Kansai coalition has said they'll make a major shipment, and I guess that other governments will do the same. Still, logistically . . ."

"How long do you think it will take to fix the Information connections?" That from Mishima.

Nobody answers.

The plane to Istanbul also blocked Information access, but Domaine gets on as soon as they touch down and lets himself read everything disaster-related he can find—still not very much—on the public transport into the city. Casualty figures vary drastically from one feed to another, but there are more photos and video now, and already a bit of analysis. He dives into the latter thirstily, multitasking only a little as he tries to decide where to stay. There's a hotel he likes in a Turkish nationalist centenal not far from Istiklal, where he can reliably overhear old men in tea shops complaining about elections, but he wonders if a centenal with a large Tokyo presence might offer additional sources of intel. And, possibly, be cheaper.

Indeed, he finds that 平和亜紀, a superficially pan-Asian, peace-loving government with a semi-covert Japanese ex-

pansionist agenda, has managed to claw out a single centenal. It's on the outskirts of the city, but Domaine decides
it's worth it; he's only going into town for the one rally later
that night, and he's starting to wonder whether it will be canceled because of the earthquake.

The hotel itself is nice enough, and it has a Japanese-style
bathtub in the room, which Domaine appreciates, as well as
a hamam off the lobby. Definitely the makings for a pleasant
stay. But the mood is somber. There are projections in the
lobby tuned to nonstop coverage, and a pair of elderly Japanese men in winter-grade suits sitting there watching. They
have resisted universal outlets, and when Domaine asks at
the desk for a converter to the old Japanese style, the clerk
shrugs and tells him they only have converters going the other
way, from Japanese plugs to standard outlets. Let them go out
to the world, Domaine thinks grimly as he walks out to find
a hardware store. No need for anyone else to come in.

He had expected to find the centenal full of the Japanese
who must have moved there in droves to tip the voting, but
perhaps they're all holed up in front of their projections or
trying to get through on nonexistent comms, because he sees
very few. The hardware store he finds is manned by a guy
who looks Turkish. On the other hand, all the products are
Japanese and the prices commensurately high. They have to
do something to subsidize their world domination, he guesses;
nationalist governments tend to have trade difficulties.

They started out sitting, but they all end up sprawled on
the floor, still sputtering odd phrases as they try to keep
their eyes open. When the blond woman, Yelinka, falls
asleep curled on her side on the floor, Mishima takes Ken's

hand and tugs his willing body into her futon. Ken isn't sure he wants or can manage sex at that point of exhaustion, but she wraps herself around him and seems to fall asleep. He does the same. At some point, he wakes and finds that he's shaking, and then he realizes it's not him but her, and he runs his hands up and down her back, strokes her hair, shushes soothingly in her ear until her crying trails off.

Once appropriately kitted, Domaine jerry-rigs a moderately secure connection, banking on the hope that at this particular moment in history, no one is going to be interested enough in him to break his weak firewall, and calls his people. He uses voice only since, thanks to enterprising scammers, some governments require both audio and visual for positive identification of digital communications.

"Shamus."

"Domaine! Oh, man, glad to hear you're okay. What a thing to happen."

Domaine can hear it immediately, the self-importance of being alive and aware at the time of an international tragedy. "We need to put out an ad," he says.

"Uh, what d'you mean? They're all out and running."

"A new one," Domaine says. "But you've got to get it out fast—I'll pay extra."

Silence. Domaine knows what's coming and waits for it.

"Uh . . . do you think now is the right time? I mean, no one will be paying any attention to the election."

"No?"

"Domaine, there's just been a huge disaster. The second debate is canceled. They're talking about postponing the election!"

"So?"

"So? All anyone wants to hear about is the earthquake. It would be in bad taste to advertise."

"Tell me, Shamus, where are *all* the major party representatives now?"

Shamus pauses before saying, "In or on their way to Tokyo."

"Or as far away as they can be while still claiming Tokyo as their location," Domaine corrects him.

"Okay, okay, it is a political event. But still. Everyone's focused on fundraising. I'm just telling you, as an advertising expert, that now is not the most effective time."

Domaine sighs, runs his hand through his fro. "Shamus, it's great that they're raising all this money for those poor rich people in Japan. I mean that. Those people need help, and they should get it. But they're getting help, probably more than they need, because of the election. Because it looks good. Because these damn governments are competing with each other to help the most. Meanwhile, is anyone raising money for . . . I don't know, the two million people in Central Asia who will die of starvation or exposure this winter? The millions of homeless kids in centenals all over the world? The children and women being trafficked across continents? No. The world ignores those problems. Governments don't want to talk about it, and the international community can hide behind these shitty elections as though so-called micro-democracy makes everything okay."

Silence.

"It's all part of the system," Domaine says. "You don't have to agree with me personally, but I do hope I can count on your professionalism."

"Okay," Shamus says. "What do you want to say?"

CHAPTER 12

It takes fifty-eight hours for communications to come back online for the greater Tokyo area. When signal is reestablished in the Information hub, a couple of hours earlier, Mishima hears the soft whoosh of air that is hundreds of staff letting out their breath at once. Mishima would have expected a whoop, but she herself makes no more noise than that whisper of relief. She then immediately wonders how soon she can remove herself from this mass of people, working almost silently together for the common good, and shut herself away again in her crow. She casts sideways glances around the room, waiting for the collectivity to dissipate. Knowing that her desire for isolation is unusual has made her sensitive to the social acceptability of acting on it.

Over at Policy1st, they start kicking people out pretty much as soon as comms come up and they can once again do the same job anywhere in the world. Tokyo has become dangerous, grubby, and most of all expensive, given how much of the real estate has suddenly evaporated. Ken lasts a day or two longer than most, since he's based in Tokyo anyway and isn't racking up huge hotel bills or crowding the office floor (he's not sure whether Suzuki knows that his apartment isn't habitable or where he has been spending his nights). But as crisis experts flood in from all over the world, Ken is told to get back to campaigning. He's not displeased; it feels like ages since he's seen the polls. When he finally squeezes some time away from relief work to look at them (feeling shallow for doing so), they've shifted in thrilling ways. Heritage has fallen significantly, although they're still in the lead; governments with no centenals in the Kantō area have also dropped, from lack of press coverage; Policy1st has moved up a rank in most predictions and hovers around eleventh. He hopes the election doesn't get delayed long enough for the bump to evaporate—or, worse, canceled.

"They're not going to cancel it," Suzuki says. "I doubt they'll even postpone it. Tokyo should be set up to vote within the next week, easy, and that's all that really matters. Time for us to get back in the game—without, of course, letting up here."

"So . . ." Ken says.

"Same assignment as before. Check the temperature, quietly, in key areas. I don't need to tell you where—start in Istanbul or Lima maybe; work from there. And keep an eye out for that Liberty stuff. I don't think they'll give up on total world domination out of sympathy for the unfortunate victims of a natural disaster." He claps Ken on the shoulder. "We'll talk about your next role after the election."

Ken is bubbling on the glow of that for the next hour. This is exactly how he has risen up the ranks at Policy1st so fast. Suzuki-san sees that he is something special. Now he can add emergency response to his resume. Not that he has to add it, because Suzuki knows it's there. The thing is, he's never doubted Ken. And what will this new position be? Ken had been hoping for something new after the election. He's proven himself again in this campaign, worked harder and longer than anyone else. He's shown he's smart. And the campaign job is about to evaporate anyway, so he will need to go on to something new, something bigger and better. But how much better? What if Policy1st should rise in the ranks unexpectedly too, what if Policy1st should—he doesn't even want to let himself think it, but it's not impossible—what if Policy1st should win the Supermajority? What kind of roles might that open for him?

He decides not to get his hopes up.

And just like that, his mood plummets. After all, isn't this how it's always worked? Suzuki praises him, dangles approval in front of him, throws him a raise or a new title. It's usually less than he secretly expected, and he always waits, knowing that it takes time, that he's come so far already. But maybe they're squeezing him, getting as much for as little as they can. He wonders if the Policy1st powers that be have already discounted the Liberty threat and are putting him on it to keep him busy. He discards that idea almost immediately; it's the end of election season, and they need every ten fingers and functioning brain they can get put to good use.

Before he leaves, he invites Mishima out for a coffee. Even a day or two before, that would have been impossible, but walking from the Information hub to the Policy1st offices that morning he had noticed the lights on in the place on the corner, a middle-aged man wearing a germ filter sweeping up the dust inside. On his way back, now alert, he sees two other places with motion inside, and the place on the corner has a blackboard with an encouraging がんばろう！written above the available offerings (coffee, tea, and hot water). Mishima is at first reluctant to leave the crow—he's not sure she's gone outside since comms came back up—but since he's about to ditch town, she agrees.

"Plus," she says, as they go down the stairs of the Information hub, "we have to support the local economy."

The man who runs the coffee shop is certainly happy to see them. He comes up and pulls out their chairs, and then tells them about his experience in the earthquake until they hear the water boil (he is using an old-fashioned kettle to save energy). He startles and rushes to it, the back of one large hand at the corner of his eye. There is a minor rumble, but it dies away almost immediately.

Ken glances at Mishima. Her eyes are darting around the room, and he wonders if she's avoiding his gaze or still spooked by that tremor. But then she shifts her chair and leans toward him at an odd angle and he realizes that she must have been figuring out feed cameras. She takes his hand, spreads the palm, and scribbles something with the tickling rounded stub of a worn pencil. Ken looks. Nine alphanumerics. He raises his eyes to Mishima's waiting stare and nods. She spits neatly into his hand and rubs it discreetly, so that by the time the man comes back with their coffees (no milk yet, but the sugar is unrefined brown straight from Okinawa via an aid shipment), the numbers are long gone and it looks like they're affectionately holding hands. Ken finds he is close to tears himself but shakes it off to hold up his side of a lively discussion about reconstruction politics. She leaves first. He, feeling more adult than he ever has (secret affair! With an important, mysterious woman!) takes a long last look before twitching at the lapels of his jacket and stepping into the cold.

"Good luck," he calls to the shopkeeper from the door.

. . .

After the first few days, when no one talked of anything but the earthquake, Okinawa is returning to normal. Yoriko can finally pick up a fare without immediately receiving an onslaught of earthquake commentary and engaging in mutual head-shaking and concern. She has spoken to Suzuki, and not only is he still alive but the disaster holiday is over; time to get back to work.

The campaigns have gotten back to work too. When Yoriko returns to the volunteer aid-packaging place, it is still running, but the only people there are a few grandmothers who seem more interested in chatting with each other than boxing relief goods, and one of the formerly smiling greeters drinking the free coffee in the corner. Yoriko wavers. She came to the volunteer site because it felt less intense than the campaign events, but with no one around, it's almost scarier. She starts to retreat, but too late: the greeter has seen her (or, possibly, been alerted by Liberty's security team).

"Yes?" she says, hurrying over with the smile clawing its way back over her face. She's aggressively cute, and Yoriko feels both old and unexpectedly angry. "Can I help you? Did you come to volunteer?"

"It doesn't look like you need more volunteers here," Yoriko says as coldly as she can, nodding at the gossiping obaasan, and turns to leave.

"No, wait," the girl calls, following her toward the lot where her taxi is stored. "You were here before, weren't you?"

Yoriko hesitates again. "Yes, I came by after the earthquake because I wanted to help."

"You're not a Liberty citizen, are you?" The greeter's smile has shrunk to a more normal size, but Yoriko warily notes the continuing shine in her eyes. She could break back into full manga mode at any second.

"No," Yoriko says. "Not at the moment. But I'm still undecided for the election . . ."

That's all it takes. The girl busts out in uncontrollable bubbliness.

"Oh, isn't it exciting? Let me show you around! We're doing such marvelous things for the people affected by the—"

"I saw it when I was here a few days ago," Yoriko says. She knows that she should want this, that she should be trying to see everything she can, but she also feels a rising panic.

"Come on," the girl says, sounding almost whiny through the glare of her enthusiasm. "It'll be fun! If you don't want to see the earthquake relief section, I can show you the campaign area?"

"Well," Yoriko says. She glances at the door one more time. "Okay, fine, but I have to leave soon."

CHAPTER 13

In a "tribute" to the earthquake victims (unbeknownst to either of them, Mishima and Domaine share a desire to retch every time they hear that phrase), the election committee decides to hold the second, and now last, debate in Kansai. Since Mishima is already in the area, her boss asks her to join the team covering it, doubled up as intelligence and security. Mishima isn't thrilled with the assignment. She wants to keep working on the earthquake response. They've barely done anything yet. It's true that the pace has slowed, and that reinforcements have finally arrived: Information drones by the dozens, showing up by boat at first and now by air. They came in clean and eager, and Rachchivandrum has parceled them off, seconding them to help centenal governments that were badly hit or putting them on more standard tasks: intel sorting or analysis or broadcasting.

Mishima thinks they're all too happy and excitable, not properly steeped in the horror of what happened, but she knows that's probably not true, or not important, or maybe both. She's more concerned that nobody is thinking about the big picture, the longer-term solutions. She can feel the difficult problems of reconstruction sticking their thorns into the pretty postdisaster unity of the first couple of days. Already, Heritage is under attack for being too slow to respond; people seem to think that being the Supermajority makes them a superpower. The Tokyo municipal coalition is wobbling as members squabble over relief funds. Sure, there are permanent staff members in Tokyo who will be dealing with these issues, but Mishima doesn't want to leave all of this for a front-row seat to politicians sniping at each other.

She also suspects the move is partly to keep her off the Liberty follow-up. Yelinka Korbin, who has softened considerably since they shared the floor of her crow, tells her that they thought she was exaggerating the threat. "They don't believe it's anything more than an empty campaign promise. And here's the thing." Korbin glances around. Senior analyst though she is, she doesn't merit an office in the open-plan third floor of the Information hub, and they brought their tea out to the external staircase. The weather is raw and there is nowhere to sit, but there is no one else outside to overhear them.

"Look, this is my interpretation," Korbin goes on. "Nobody said this to me directly. But there's a lot of concern over the possibility of Heritage winning again."

Mishima nods. She's heard that undercurrent too: each term of incumbency, the thinking goes, makes it harder to topple the Supermajority. One or two more cycles with Heritage on top, and nobody will bother holding elections. Mishima thinks that's a bit extreme, but she can understand the concerns, and William Pressman hasn't helped with his comments at the last debate.

"They don't want to put extra scrutiny on Liberty, because they're among the top contenders to beat Heritage this time around."

Mishima scuffs her boot on the landing. A lone cigarette butt has been crushed into the corner; illegal in this centenal, she remembers. "That's ridiculous," she finally says, letting disgust thicken her voice. "Either it's democracy or it isn't."

Korbin laughs. "You know better than that. Anyway, it's mainly because they don't take it seriously. Harassing Liberty over a bogus threat is as bad as not harassing them over a real one."

Korbin doesn't buy it either, Mishima realizes. Remembering how much easier it was to convince Tabby in Singapore, she wonders if the Information upper echelon is completely out of touch. "What would I need to convince them?" Mishima wonders out loud.

"Let me know if there's anything I can do to help." Korbin tips back the last of her tea and turns to go inside. "But with the earthquake response, they're going to be even less interested."

After that discussion, Mishima tries to look on the bright side of the debate assignment. Attending in person, she can watch for any discrepancies that might be smoothed out in the broadcast, and she'll have a broad enough mandate to report them. Looking presentable is part of the job, but Mishima doesn't feel like wearing the braided dress again so soon, and she doesn't have anything else fancy enough with her, so she skims Information images until she finds something she likes: tight along the bodice with plenty of flow in the long sleeves and skirt, with miniscule cutouts in the shape of stars tracing a tiny galaxy under the navel and up the ribs. She picks out an indigo shade with a subtle sparkle, buys it, prints it out, and sews some minor alterations by hand. The dress turns out well, but studying herself in the mirror, Mishima is struck by the pallor of her face, the shadows under her eyes. The earthquake, shimmering like a mirage. She has pushed it out of her thoughts so effectively that she hasn't even dreamed about it yet, but she knows that she will.

Mishima decides that a facial massage and an elaborate

coif are what she needs to lift her appearance, and perhaps her spirits too, to their usual exceptional level. She noodles around on Information till she finds a photo of the interlocking braided look she wants, then shoots it off to the stylists within a reasonable range of the debate site. When the bids come in, she cross-references with reviews, picks one with a midrange price and reviews that include "relaxing," "informal," "pampering without posh."

Yoriko does not get to leave soon.

The overenthusiastic greeter does not take her to the campaign area. In retrospect, and Yoriko has plenty of time to think about this as she waits in an empty room for what she can only assume will be an interrogation, it was silly to imagine that Liberty would show an outsider their campaign office, or that it would be in the citizen's center. She supposes she imagined a campaign volunteer area or something; that seems more plausible. Instead, she was led down a long corridor, and when at one point she looked back over her shoulder, there was a large man walking behind them.

Maybe she should have tried to run then. But he could have been a staffer going from one room to another, and even if he wasn't, Yoriko doubts she could have outrun him. They stopped at a door with another large man standing outside of it. He nodded to the greeter, who cheerfully told Yoriko, "I'll leave you here," and did. The man who had been following them took her place, and Yoriko was ushered into the room, which was empty except for racks of Liberty promotional material lining one wall. She turned around and the man who had been waiting in front of the door said: "Please wait here for the head of security." He said it very politely, using all the most honorable forms, but then he shut the door and, she imagined, went on standing right outside it.

There's no signal for her handheld and nothing to do but read the pamphlets or watch the animated advids. Yoriko refuses on principle to look at the propaganda, and instead spends the first hour combing through the existing data on her handheld to see if she can find anything helpful.

Nothing.

If she could only connect to Information, she could call up the plans for this building, see who the head of security for this centenal is (or did they mean for all of Liberty on the island? In the region? She could look them up, too), review some self-defense techniques, check on her legal standing, both in this centenal and in her own. If she could connect to Information, she could call the police, or her centenal's emergency support team, or at least Suzuki-san.

She doesn't even have maps stored on her handheld, which now that she thinks about it is pretty stupid for a taxi driver. What if there was a disaster here that knocked out communications, like the earthquake did in Tokyo? Downloading hard maps will be the first thing she does when she gets out of here.

If she gets out of here.

To calm herself, she starts trying to build a map of the immediate surroundings in her head. She's driven through this centenal often enough, and she finds that she can come up with a pretty good, if idiosyncratic, rendering. She doesn't know which streets she doesn't know about, but at least she could find her way home. She has plotted eight different routes before the door opens.

The man who enters is not as large as the two thugs, but to Yoriko's eye, practiced from assessing clients, he looks hard. The skin on his face is worn like a thick seashell, and she notes that the first two knuckles on both hands are heavily calloused. He doesn't touch the door; the big guy outside opened it for him and closes it behind him.

"Now," says the head of security, "it seems we have a problem." His tone is less menacing than bored. "From what I understand, you've been spying on us." He raises a placating hand as Yoriko starts to protest. "Please. We are quite sure; we have excellent surveillance." He starts to pace; there are no chairs in the room, not even tatami. "Spying on the government is a felony according to Liberty legal code, section 9, paragraph 118. In the six months prior to an election, the offense is aggravated."

"I didn't—I don't—" starts Yoriko.

Again, the hand, palm out, pleading with her not to bore him further by dragging this out. "I know. You didn't actually find anything useful." Not only do they know she's a spy, they know she's not a good one. "That doesn't mitigate the penalty according to the law, but we do have some leeway, and we prefer to use it when we can. So. Do us all a favor here. Let us know who you're working for. You'll be prohibited from entering Liberty centenals for a period of twelve years—tough luck for a taxi driver—unless, of course, you manage to become a citizen."

Yoriko wants to ask what will happen if she doesn't tell them, but she doesn't trust her voice not to shake, so she waits. After a pause, he gives her the rest of it.

"The offense carries a sentence of five to seven years normally, ten to fifteen in the election period." He's rattling all this off like a tour guide who's been on the same route too long. It makes Yoriko wonder how many of these he has to do a week. "Now, as I said, we have plenty of evidence and

I have no doubt about a conviction, but that does take time. With the election in under a week, we'd like to know who sent you sooner rather than later. We'll keep you here until we can convince you." A pause to let that sink in. "Or you take the sweetheart deal and collect your taxi right now. You won't have to look at the inside of another Liberty centenal until after the next election."

Then he stops and waits.

Ken has barely landed in Dubai to change planes when he gets a message from Suzuki. Apparently, one of the promo vids taken of Policy1st staff hard at work for their constituents after the earthquake caught Ken in the background.

"At my desk, hard at work for our constituents," Ken says.

"I'm sorry," Suzuki says. "They should have checked more carefully. Usually they do, but with the emergency . . ."

It's an excuse Ken is starting to get tired of, from himself as well as from others. "So?"

"Look, go ahead, same assignment, but in the open now. Tell people you work for us."

Ken scratches his head. "Do you think they'll talk to me if they know I'm from a government? Can't we say I was volunteering or something?"

"Nah," Suzuki says. "Too risky. Better to have you declare yourself than to have someone else sniff it out and catch you in an omission. Pick your targets carefully and try to keep it quiet, get as much intel as you can. Besides, the campaign's almost over; we'll have you working higher profile soon enough," he adds, setting Ken on another of his self-esteem rollercoaster rides.

. . .

Yoriko does not want to get beat up or to be a prisoner for even a few days. In an hour, she's going to be late to pick up her children from school, and while her friend Yua can usually help out for an afternoon, the thought of asking her to raise her children while Yoriko rots in jail makes Yoriko's eyes water. Besides, Liberty seems to know everything already. Would it do any harm to tell them? If she hesitates, it is mostly to wonder whether they will let her go so easily. All she has to do is say the name of the government that hired her and she can leave? If that's true, it means they really want to know.

Which means they don't know yet.

The head of security clears his throat, or maybe he's stifling a yawn, and glances at the time on his handheld. He starts to roll up his sleeves.

"Okay!" says Yoriko, almost yelling in her anxiousness to cooperate. "I'll tell you. It was 平和亜紀. They paid me to hang around you guys and see what I could find out."

The security chief's eyebrows go up, then come down again in a puzzled frown. "Those Japanese nationalists?" he says. "They're not even competing for centenals here."

"They heard you were, um, showing some aggression toward the mainland," Yoriko says. "They wanted to know more. They asked me to find solid intel so they could plan something preemptive."

His face hardens again. "And did you?"

"Nothing more than hints," Yoriko says, hanging her head as though ashamed.

"Where'd they hear about it in the first place?" he asks.

"Not from me!" Yoriko says quickly. "They only contacted me once they were already suspicious."

"And why you?"

"I don't know. Some Japanese guy gets in my cab, asks if I want to make some extra money." She lets the tears that have been pressing on her eyes seep out. "I never thought it would be this dangerous!"

When she gets to Kobe, Mishima does a walk-through of the debate venue. Some genius in the events section decided to hold it in the glass-paneled building housing the Disaster Reduction and Human Innovation Institute, established after the Hanshin-Awaji quake at the end of the last century. In theory, the globally broadcast debate doesn't require a lot of space; in practice, Information raises considerable revenue by selling tickets to the extremely wealthy, so they try to get large auditoriums. This time, they've upped the prices for seats inside the moderately sized conference hall, then removed some interior walls and sold additional tickets for people to watch from outside the glass walls, hovering in private or rented crows.

It's a security nightmare, but they've got a streamlined peacekeeper crow and six prototype scooter-sized tsubame to cover it. Thankfully, Mishima will be stationed inside the hall, so it's not her problem. She's not super happy with the setup there, either. They've put the stage in the center of the auditorium rather than at one end, both to allow for more of the expensive front-row seats and to avoid seating-arrangement conflicts among the debaters as much as possible. That leaves a lot more angles of attack to cover, so they've doubled the standard security complement. While she's checking emergency exits, she hears a buzz: the walls vibrating with a minor aftershock. Mishima scowls. Why anyone would construct a glass building in an earthquake zone is beyond her.

Despite all the vulnerabilities and the lack of prep time, the enlarged security team knows their stuff and seems to have things well under control; she's not sure why she couldn't have stayed in Tokyo. Since she's there, though, she might as well take advantage. Mishima flies to Osaka for an early dinner at an okonomiyaki place Korbin recommended, and then heads to Arima to spend the evening soaking in the hot springs. Immersed to her neck in steaming water, she can admit that time off from emergency duty might not be so bad.

Yoriko scurries to her taxi, amazed that they let her go. They must have been convinced by her lie about her employer and her truthful lack of success. Maybe she's right about how routine this kind of spying is. They didn't even bother to search her. She has it all worked out in her mind: the route that gets her out of this centenal quickest and goes nowhere near the other Liberty centenal in Naha on her way home. There's a red light on the first corner, and Yoriko stops for it, her hands shaking when she takes them off the wheel. Traffic lights only turn red when something is coming from the other side, and she shuttles her eyes between the rearview mirror and the cross street. What if the head of security has changed his mind? Is he trying to stop her from getting out? A Sunway finally dawdles by and the light switches back to green. She feels her shoulders slump as soon as she leaves the centenal, although she's not completely safe yet: she has to look up which governments have extradition agreements with Liberty.

At least she knows Policy1st doesn't, and as soon as she crosses the border into their territory, she wants to call Suzuki. She hesitates, though; everyone says that it's easy for people, or governments, to snoop on calls. She pulls over in a Royal Host family restaurant parking lot and finds the nearest 平和亜紀 office, which is in some small town outside of Fukuoka.

"Hello, Peaceful Asian Era, humbly at your service," says the extremely polite Japanese voice on the other end. Yoriko drags her eyes from the rearview to glance at her hand-held and sees an impassive office-girl face framed by neat hair and some kind of blouse with a big bow under her chin. She's glad she doesn't have her own vid turned on; she must look like a vagrant or a psychopath or a crank caller. The receptionist would click off immediately.

"Hello, hello," she stutters. "I was wondering . . . what is your policy on Okinawa?"

The receptionist is silent, off-railed from her canned answers by a question that hasn't made any sense since before she was born. "We don't have any centenals in Okinawa," she says finally.

"But if you did?" Yoriko presses, her eyes still skittering around, hitting the rearview, coming back to the cars around her.

"All of our policies are available on our Information," the woman says primly, and clicks off. Yoriko hopes it was long enough to seem credible. She pulls out into traffic again and drives slowly home. She calls Suzuki while packing.

CHAPTER 14

Ken walks into the waiting room of a small office in a low apartment building in Miraflores where he has an appointment. He is still trying to figure out how he can present himself now that he's not undercover. On the other hand, he feels better about the way he's working with local offices now.

He called Natalia at the Policy1st office in Lima before he got on his second plane. She sounded harried but reasonably pleased to hear he was coming in.

"I can't give you much time," she said in what he assumes was polite understatement. "What do you need?"

"What do *you* need?" Ken asked. "I'm sure you're campaigning flat out in the centenals you've targeted. My mandate is to look at any other centenals—maybe that you think are borderline, maybe that you haven't had time to fully assess—and see if there are any quick fixes, or anything worth calling in extra troops for."

"Okay, cool," Natalia said. "That would be good. You'll have a list of priorities by the time you land."

Miraflores is at the top of the list, which surprises Ken; he thought the pleasant beachfront centenal would be reliably Heritage. He guesses that Natalia, like Agus, can't help looking beyond winning local centenals and is strategizing for the Supermajority. If Policy1st can't win it, the least they can do is help knock out Heritage, open the race up for next time.

The door opens and a neat little woman nods Ken into her office. He settles himself into the offered chair, hoping the sweat isn't showing under the arms of his recently purchased guayabera. It's nice to be back in summertime, but he's starting to wonder if this climatic ping-pong can be healthy.

"So, what can I do for you?" she asks.

"I'm a researcher for Policy1st," Ken says. He's decided that "researcher" is still the best way to describe his work; it distances him from campaigning. He pulls a small notebook and a pen from his bag, a trick he's stealing from those Luddite pollsters in Jakarta.

It works amazingly well. The small woman, an ex-politician and catedrática, stares at him, chuckles, and immediately opens up. "I'm so glad to see paper coming back into fashion among you young people," she clucks. "Naturally, one worries about the forests, but as long as we use it in moderation . . ."

Ken twists his question to be as indirect as possible. "You've noticed a lot of people using pen and paper recently?"

"Well, certainly among you pollsters," she says. "That nice young lady who was here the other day was doing the same, although she had a much larger file."

"Where was she from?" Ken asks, wondering if the answer can be trusted.

"Oh, one of the corporates."

Ken swallows his eagerness, keeps his smile on. "Is that so? Which one was it?"

She hesitates a long moment, perhaps hoping that he'll let it go, and then digs her handheld out of her pocket with a light grunt. "Let me see; it should be in my appointments calendar. Ah, yes, Liberty. She didn't want to say so at first, but eventually she had to mention it. Nice young lady. All sorts of questions, but very polite."

Ken is wondering how he can very politely ask what his counterpart discussed with this dapper, inoffensive woman who is the power broker for at least three centenals, but before he can find a formula that doesn't sound entirely unethical, she has moved on.

"So, I suppose you want to know what Policy1st needs to do to win here?"

Maybe she is answering his unasked question after all.

"Of course we want to know how we can better serve the people of this area," he says as smoothly as he can, "but I'm a researcher, not a campaigner, so I'd most like to hear about the issues here, what people are concerned about. Whatever you can tell me."

She has barely drawn her breath to answer when Ken jumps to his feet and sprints for the door, getting halfway there before he realizes the profesora hasn't moved. At first, he thinks she hasn't reacted at all, but with adrenaline-sharpened sight, he sees her beringed fingers clutching the arm of her chair like talons before they relax. She smiles at him. "Just a little tremor," she says. "We have them frequently here, although that one was a bit larger than usual. Nothing to worry about."

Muttering an apology, Ken edges back into his seat.

Sitting back in the salon chair while the stylist blow-dries, Mishima's fingers tingle with the urge to access Ken's Information. Normally, Mishima would have known everything about him long before they slept together, even if she had to scan his file at eyeball level while in the bathroom between the main course and dessert. She can admit it's a little unfair; in addition to her hyperconnected, high-speed brain, she has easy access to almost any Information, even most protected data, through her job. If he looks her up, he will find very, very little and most of it misdirection (unless she's underestimated him). But it's only sensible to check up on someone, especially during the election season. For now, she leaves it. The election will be over in a week, and she's unlikely to see him before then, anyway.

Instead, she decides to feed her narrative disorder. Mishima doesn't have to check her biometrics to know that her brain could use some downtime. She scrolls through her favorite feeds to a Korean soap, the nth-generation descendant of *Boys Over Flowers*, leans back, and watches the antics of spoiled, implausibly attractive rich kids while the woman massages her hair.

"You know that content was compiled by underpaid children in Bangladesh."

Mishima has a brief flashback to her visit to one of those content-creation sweatshops. The teenagers, mostly girls, manipulating names and images and chunks of text on endless digital storyboards. Their smiles as they crowded around her. Without moving from under the easy fingers of the masseuse, she slides her hand under the smock to touch the handle of her stiletto, and shifts her gaze to the seat next to her, where Domaine is having his 'fro spritzed.

"Teenagers in Armenia, actually. That was one of my first jobs for Information." She'd been careless about covering her tracks; the salon bids were neither encrypted nor protected. It must have been easy for him to find her.

"What?"

"Checking out corporate claims. Something like what you were doing in Saudi, perhaps?"

Domaine chuckles, low and rumbling. He's having a pedicure done along with his hair, toes already fanned out in the bamboo separator, and his laugh sounds like he's enjoying the foot rub a little too much. "Yes, similar." He reaches into his pocket and flips something shiny at her. Mishima catches it in the air with a satisfying smack, ready to toss it back if it gives any indication of exploding, but when she looks, it's just a small disk.

"Take a look," Domaine says. "No viruses, I promise."

It's almost a joke—Information antispyware and virus-blockers are legendary—but Mishima doesn't laugh. She looks, not at the disk, but at him. She has to admit, something about Domaine makes her libido twitch. There's that fanatical devotion to his ideals, the edge of danger, and his combined underdog/lone-wolf thing. Mishima is happy to have reached an age where she doesn't need to give in to every urge.

"What's on it?"

"See for yourself," he says, settling back into his salon chair and closing his eyes. "I'll wait."

Her handheld scans it and finds nothing suspicious, only a few seconds of aud/vid. Still suspicious, Mishima has it play, but with sound on mono and the images translucent, so she can keep an eye on Domaine at the same time.

It's a montage of world undesirables—a Saudi minister, the leader of a band of violent Sahelian rebels, a religious autocrat in the former United States—each identified with subtitles, each lauding the micro-democratic election system, which allows them to pursue their decidedly undemocratic ends. Or, as the sheikh puts it: "There is nothing that suits us more than most of the world believing that their will is being carried out by governments that do exactly as they please."

"Tell me something I don't know," Mishima says when it's finished. *So, that's what Domaine was doing in Saudi,* she thinks. No wonder she didn't find any connections between him and Liberty.

"You're fine with being part of the problem?" Domaine asks, eyes still closed.

Mishima doesn't deign to answer.

"Most people don't know, or never think about it," Domaine goes on, finally looking up. "The fact that the election system enables the atrocities of its so-called enemies? It's going to make a compelling anticampaign ad."

Most people don't care, Mishima thinks. "It doesn't look like these people were filmed with permission."

"As if that matters," sneers Domaine.

Mishima laughs. "It would be suicide to use that," she tells him, tossing the disc back.

Domaine's mouth twitches oddly as he tosses the disk in his palm like a coin. "Why, Mishima," he says. "I didn't know you cared."

"Was there anything else?" The stylist has started the braiding, and Mishima would like to relax and enjoy it.

"What do you think you're fighting for, anyway?" Domaine hisses. "Democracy? Hardly. The system is creaking already. You're one or two Heritage wins from a de facto dictatorship. A dynasty." Domaine nods at his pedicurist, who starts the hairdryer on silent mode and runs it over his newly gilded toenails. He leans over the arm of Mishima's lounger. "I know you agree with me."

Mishima doesn't look away from her own eyes in the mirror, yawns.

Domaine glances down at his widespread feet, laughs a little, then leans back in toward Mishima. "Whatever you think of me, I believe you have good intentions," he whispers. "Which is why I'm going to tell you: be careful of your friends. Not everyone you work with is on your team."

"What, you've got moles in Information?" Mishima asks, dubious but intrigued.

"I didn't say Information. And I didn't say they were mine." Domaine leans forward to check his toenails, then slips on sandals and flip-flops away.

Mishima motions to her stylist and requests that they move into a private room. She's not going to be able to think, much less relax, expecting him to return at any moment. Before she forgets, she mutters a quick message to the security team leader with Domaine's description and history to alert him that he's in the area, then sets her handheld to run a complete scrub. It's a good use for the enforced downtime of the braiding.

So," Ken says, speaking slowly and deliberately as he tries furiously to catch up in his notebook, "you're saying that some governments are threatening war?"

"More promising than threatening," the profesora reflects. "They're quite open about it, too. And it's not doing them any harm, as far as I've been able to learn. Talk about going after Bolivia or Chile still resonates, even though Bolivia and Chile don't exist in the old territorial sense."

"Fascinating," Ken says, scribbling away. "Why doesn't

anyone report them to Information or the election commission?"

"Like I said, many people view this favorably. And the ones who don't probably don't take it seriously. After all, what could they actually do?"

"Declare war, say it was democratically justified, and use illicit weapons and physical force to draw the region into a self-destructive conflict?" Ken suggests.

"I suppose," the profesora agrees with a desultory wave of her hand. "But it seems so unlikely, doesn't it?"

"Does it?"

"Listen, I'll tell you what I told that other young lady." Ken's not sure whether to be thrilled or annoyed that he's getting exactly the same data as a Liberty spy/researcher. "For most of the people here, it doesn't matter. If Liberty wants to win this centenal from Heritage, for example, they'll have to do it using well-respected members of the community. The people who have a role now. And, in gratitude, Liberty will allow them to keep that role. Oh, there may be some shuffling, but these are petty issues. There's no need for *war*. And in the end very little would change."

Ken bites his lip so as not to point out that electing Policy1st—or Economix, or even YouGov—would change a great deal. "What about the Supermajority?" he asks instead.

"If we were to change governments, or if Heritage were to lose the Supermajority, then there would be some changes," the profesora admits. "There are benefits to being in a centenal belonging to the Supermajority, as I'm sure you've realized," *in your quixotic quest to defeat the incumbent,* Ken finishes for her in his head.

"So, when the Supermajority is at risk, does it lead to tension as elites try to predict who will win?"

"Do you believe the Supermajority could change?" she asks, looking at him with curiosity, as though the answer would tell her more about him than about the status of the election.

Ken pulls out the latest tailor-made globe. "As you can see—" He motions, but she waves it away rather rudely.

"Come, come, I'm asking you. Not your Information falsification team."

A month ago, Ken would have bristled, made some wild claim about the high truth standards of Policy1st staff, but he doesn't feel quite as confident in that anymore. Even if he did, he's learned that nobody else is going to believe it. He makes himself smile. "I made this one myself, so any errors are mine," he manages, feeling suave. She only smirks, and he gives in to irritation. "Look, you don't have to believe it, but this is what we're seeing: Heritage stock is dropping in megalopolises and other disaster-prone areas because of disappointment over handling of the earthquake. That's compounded in Japan and the rest of East Asia by repercussions around the mantle-tunnel decision."

After the earthquake, the plan to make the Tokyo-Taipei route the first tunnel was quickly jettisoned, and the talk is now Paris-Dakar. Half of East Asia is pissed off that they lost the tunnel, and the rest are using the debacle to claim it was too dangerous in the first place. "The other corporates, smelling blood, have taken out their knives. Have you seen this one?" He extinguishes the globe projection and throws up an ad that the Policy1st office in Bosnia recorded and sent around.

The voiceover and subtitles say, "Who do you trust to protect you when things fall apart?" over a video clip of a Heritage worker in an elaborate emergency vest, drinking a cup of coffee while a line of shivering citizens is visible through the plate glass doors. The vid cuts to a Heritage warehouse filled with tents, a reminder of the accusations that they were slow to distribute goods that they had stock-piled nearby.

When Ken watches this, he always feels a twinge of sympathy for the poor sap in the emergency vest. He himself drank plenty of coffee while he was working on the response. On the other hand, if Heritage did hold blankets they were ready to distribute until new vid feeds could be set up, like people are saying, he hopes they get nailed for it.

"Let's say the Supermajority changes," the profesora says. She really sounds like an academic now, as though he were a bright but naïve undergraduate and she were using the Socratic method to show him the error of his ways (Ken's experience of such things is entirely book-, vid-, and game-based, and might be somewhat idealistic). "What difference will it make?"

"If it's another corporate, probably not much in the grand scheme," Ken says. "The incentives will shift toward another collection of consumer products. Possibly a very similar collection, depending on which corporate won."

"But?" the profesora prods. She is still smiling, although he thinks this is where he goes off her tracks.

"But if it's not a corporate, if it's a policy-based government like Policy1st, an environmentally focused government like Earth1st, or even an individualist government like YouGov—then things will change."

"Perhaps," the profesora says. "But there will still be winners, and there will still be losers."

Ken tries not to grind his teeth. What did the Liberty spy promise her to convince her she would be one of the winners? "Of course," he says through as much of a smile as he can manage.

"Our impression," she goes on, "is that Policy1st is too transparent to have very many winners. But perhaps we are wrong?" She raises her eyebrows, daring him.

Ken wonders if the paper and pen have made her incautious about being recorded, or if she's accustomed to impunity. Either way, he gives up on this woman. "Oh, on the contrary," he says. "With transparency there are the most winners of all. Everyone in the centenal gains."

The profesora bursts out laughing. "Well done, joven," she says, and actually stands up to slap him on the shoulder. "That woman from Liberty took me out to lunch and offered me, and I quote, 'Everything Heritage gives you, with a little something extra for your retirement.'" She grimaces. "As *if* I was anywhere near retiring! Well, tell me more about your policies. Don't"—admonitory finger raised—"get your hopes up; I meant what I said about there being benefits to being in the Supermajority. I wasn't talking about personal benefits but for the centenal as a whole. So, I doubt we will change. But why don't you give it a try?"

CHAPTER 15

Participation in the final debate has been cut down to the top nine, a drastic choice reflecting the compression of the process, and of morale, after the earthquake. Information and the election commission are providing a questionnaire to the next seven and will make their answers public as well, but that requires potential voters to search those answers out and read them. The conventional wisdom is the any government that didn't make the debate can forget about the Supermajority.

Suzuki is in the greenroom, piling powder on top of his sweat (although video won't be broadcast, it doesn't do to leave any detail of appearance uncurated). Policy1st has squeaked in at ninth place, in part because of surprisingly high polling in certain centenals of Jakarta and a late surge in urban areas of Latin America. The biggest factor, however, was the unconsidered comments of Reginald Baste, a representative of YouGov. The popular technogovernment was in fifth place until Baste suggested that the earthquake, though tragic, was causing disproportionate disruption in the election process and that "we should all move on." The bit of vid was made much of by the other frontrunners, who pointed out that YouGov didn't have a single centenal in the greater Tokyo area.

Despite this callousness being eminently rational (in fact, as Mishima well knows, a majority of voters agree with the statement "My government should prioritize the needs of its citizens over those of noncitizens"), YouGov fell fast in the polls. More surprising was that the collateral damage included a small but significant fraction of voters from Your-Story, which fell from ninth to tenth (*The name misrecognition problem*, thinks Mishima, wondering which of the governments will rebrand first).

Policy1st is the only issues-based government in the top nine. All the others are corporates, except for 1China, which employs nationalist rhetoric among the huge vestigial population of the PRC and its carefully cultivated colonies, and offers aid and trade support elsewhere. Suzuki normally thrives on public speaking opportunities, his chest expanding with the sound of his measured, reasonable voice and occasional wry quips. But tonight, he's aware that he's representing more than himself, more even than his government. Oh, it's extremely doubtful that Policy1st will win the Supermajority—he would say impossible, but elections are rife with unexpected events—but this is a chance to get more people to take issues-based campaigning seriously. If he is boring, his cause will be dismissed as pedantic and elitist; if he is too aggressive, the others will gang up on him; but if he can strike the right tone, they might reach new listeners. Multitasking as usual, he considers the modulations of humor and gravity that are required while making arrangements to relocate Yoriko and her family. They are moving to Amami Ōshima, an island whose sole centenal, while not, unfortunately, Policy1st, has no extradition treaty with Liberty. He's about to listen to Yoriko's recording of her brief interrogation one more time, to psych himself up, when he gets an urgent message from Veena Rasmussen. Even with so little time before the debate starts, Suzuki doesn't hesitate to accept the call. Rasmussen is executive director of Earth1st, a government that spun off from Policy1st in the previous election when they realized there was enough environmental concern out there to merit a separate platform.

Although Information has stood firm on the audio-only policy for the debates, bootleg videos are always a problem, and one of Mishima's lower-level duties is to prevent clandestine recordings. She's gently but firmly removing a handheld from a dignitary in the third row when Suzuki, in the Policy1st opening statement, makes his big announcement.

"I'm thrilled to be able to say," he says, managing with difficulty to balance on the fine line between pleased and smug, "that, as of tonight, Policy1st will be reuniting with its sister government, Earth1st."

Mishima manages not to look up from her work, but her mind is tracing a dozen possible branches of causes and consequences as she passes the handheld back to the overdressed old woman, vid deleted and recorder temporarily disabled. She is so edgy that for a moment, she wonders if this could be what Domaine was talking about, if by "friends" he meant Ken, and if "not on your team" meant that Policy1st was not what it seemed to be. Could Ken have somehow gotten illicit information from her? Mishima tries to tamp down the fear of having slipped up, missed a trick, given the enemy what they needed. Is Policy1st using her to rig the election?

But of course this is not true, not possible, has not happened. This announcement isn't a betrayal. It's not even a problem. Once Mishima calms down, it sounds like the best news she has heard in weeks.

She moves back along the aisle, keeping an eye out for more vid recording as she goes. The intricate curls of fluoron that cover the ceiling like a thicket of baroque chandeliers provide a strong, even lighting, and when Mishima looks at the glass walls she sees the reflection of the bright, densely packed auditorium. Glancing up, she can make out the dark shadows of the crows outside, floating and silent as sharks. She turns her back to the wall and continues scanning the crowd while she considers the merger.

Election guidelines are fairly strict on coalitions. They do not affect the count to the Supermajority unless the two governments fully merge—identical policies, complete subsuming of one into the other. Policy1st and Earth1st form one of the rare pairs that can pull it off, mainly because they used to be a single party. The Earth1st spinoff was a matter of emphasis rather than difference, a savvy marketing stunt that had produced significant gains. Sort of the opposite of synergy, the sum of the parts greater than the whole.

Reuniting at this particular moment should up their stock again. Policy1st and Earth1st combined do not take the lead for the Supermajority, but it might get them into fourth or fifth place. That should get them momentum, credibility to draw in those cynics (Mishima among them) who believe a government based on good governance will never convince the majority of the voters to elect them. Some of those people (and Mishima is not among *them*) choose to vote instead for what they see as the least of the possible evils; this merger could inspire them to actually support a government they like. Maybe.

. . .

In a bar in Manila, Ken's jaw drops, and then he is biting his lip to keep from jumping up, whooping, and pumping his fist in the air. Suzuki is a *genius*! Why didn't they think of this earlier? Had he been strategically holding it back to get the momentum now? When they need it, when it might be enough—no, he can't even let himself dream. Not yet. He starts frantically refreshing polling sites.

The flight from Lima to Manila was almost enough to convince Ken that the mantle tunnels would be worth it. By the time he's three drinks deep on debate night, however (and wanting to be in the right time zone for the event might have been a small part of the reason he's back in Asia), he's happy to hear Suzuki railing against it.

"Time and again, we've heard large corporations urging a risky new technology on us, one that they say is totally safe and entirely necessary. Policy1st is not against progress, or against the economy, or against high-speed transportation. But we are in favor of knowing the dangers before we commit ourselves to expensive, disastrous projects that will benefit a tiny few. And we are against drilling holes through the planet so the rich can shave a few hours off their vacation commute!"

It's stronger rhetoric than usual. Policy1st's spokespeople are not supposed to vilify anyone, not even the rich, and Ken thrills to the knowledge that it's go-for-broke time. He twitches the volume up on his earpiece; although most of the clients in the bar are focused on the debate, a small but noisy contingent is belting karaoke in the back.

"Our esteemed colleague"—it is the spokesperson for 888, a China-based corporate government, who speaks after Suzuki—"worries much about the risks he does not know but says nothing about the risks that have already been confirmed. Excessive plane travel is choking our planet and strangling our economies. Mantle tunnels will use a combination of gravitational forces and sophisticated engineering for clean and sustainable long-haul travel. 888 is committed to continuing our efforts to fully leverage this great advance in technology."

Ken frowns. You would think Earth1st would have the environmental angle sewn up. Maybe this unification thing was last minute and they didn't have time to brief Suzuki.

The next three spokespeople each take up different counterarguments, as neatly as if they had planned it together. They are piling on Suzuki, and to cheer himself up, Ken starts planning out his next few days. He sent Suzuki the intel from the profesora in Lima, and there's been no answer yet. Debate prep must have been all encompassing, but Ken's starting to feel antsy. He figures he should get confirmation from additional sources here, but he's not sure there's much point. He's not going to get anyone to say it more clearly than the profesora did. If that didn't get a reaction, what will?

An idea that has been lurking in the back of his mind filters its way to the front: he could send the recording of the interview directly to Mishima. His noncommittal searches haven't uncovered what her job at Information is, but she's obviously influential. Mishima would know what to do about Liberty.

He hasn't heard from her since Tokyo, which might be because she's busy, but might also be because she's forgotten all about him. Deciding that it's at least partly business, that he won't look like a lovesick idiot if he sends her a casual message, he whispers, "Hey! How's it going?" into his composer and sends it. He tries not to wait for an answer, which gets more difficult in proportion to the time that passes and the beers drunk, but then he remembers that the debate must be a heavy work night for her, and resolves not to think about it until the morning.

Mishima doesn't see Ken's message; she's locked down unsecured communications while she's working. Even if she hadn't, her eyes are focused on the debate stage, flicking between the speakers, the subtitles, and the annotation from her Information. Suzuki's surprise move has put the corporates on the defensive, which for most of them means the offensive; she's waiting for one of them to go off script.

The debaters sit around a conference table. The vid broadcasting ban means they're able to stay linked in to their Information, and Mishima can see the occasional flash over someone's eye as they receive messages from aides or update their feeds. Not Johnny Fabré; except for occasional glances around the table at his rivals, his eyes stay trained on his lap, where, Mishima guesses, he's positioned his handheld. Still not comfortable with eyeball-level projections, apparently. She wonders how old he is. His well-tanned skin does look a little leathery, but it's hard to judge with all the foundation piled on.

"My friends," he begins, and Mishima has to marvel at how he can sound so warm and engaged while reading off a screen. If she closes her eyes, it feels as though he's making eye contact with her. When she opens them, he's just a handsome, strange-looking man talking to his handheld. "We live in a time of upheaval and change. But at Liberty we cling to core principles, principles which have guided governments for centuries. Our freedom . . ."

He goes on like that for at least five minutes; Mishima loses focus and has to wander slowly around the room as if she were on patrol to stay awake. It's clearly a canned speech: he hasn't made any reference to the Policy1st-Earth1st merger. She can't even remember what question he was supposed to be answering.

Then she catches it. "We believe in righting historical wrongs, because the boundaries of this modern system do not always leave room for justice." That's enough for her, but he goes on. "Certainly, as we continue to work for freedom and prosperity for all, every system must be refreshed from time to time with revolution, revolutionary ideas and bold policies."

Mishima looks around the audience, expecting outcry or nervous glances or at least expressions of surprise. Nothing. It wasn't an applause line (applause isn't allowed in the debate hall, but many of the performers leave brief gaps for those who might cheer at the broadcasts), and he's still talking. She scans the crowd again. One couple whispering, but it looks more amorous than political. A woman coughs slightly into a germ filter, the light shimmering over the veins in her temples as she sits back again. Mishima looks at her handheld, checks the transcript and the annotations. The transcript skips "revolution," assuming that he stumbled before finishing "revolutionary" and then corrected himself. Just to be sure, Mishima listens to the recording from a few seconds earlier: yes, she heard it correctly. The notes are brief, since the sentence is basically gibberish: *Liberty's definition of "for all" is suspect; they do not work for freedom or prosperity for those outside of their centenals. They concentrate more on continued stability than on revolutionary ideas or bold policies.* She whispers a furious message to the analyst bureau, asking them to take another look at that section. The seconds pass and nothing changes. It's right there! How can they not see it? The voters, her bosses, how can they ignore this?

Mishima is so puzzled by this willful obliviousness that she almost misses it. The instant the low persistent buzz makes its way to her awareness, she knows, with a sting of compunction, that it's been going on for some time: thirty seconds? A minute? She glances left and right, looking for a small automated device that could produce such a sound: a recorder? A weapon? Maybe the lights are vibrating. She looks up, but the fluoron loops hang unchanged over the hall. Then she shifts her eyes to the wall above her.

"Takeda," she murmurs into her earpiece. On the stage, Fabré is still talking. "There's a crow way too close to the wall. South side, up by the roof." She has turned slightly to keep her eyes fixed on that point above her head.

The head of outdoor security responds immediately. "Hosono, get over there. Kumagai, back him up! I'll be there as soon as I can." Something Mishima doesn't catch, maybe a muttered curse. "I'm stuck on the opposite side dealing with a minor spectator collision." Under his breath but audible: "Could be a setup."

She sees it then: a tiny flicker. The crow is cutting into the glass wall with a laser. "Oh-five, oh-five!" As she calls the evacuation code, she sees the quick swoop of a tsubame closing in on the crow.

This time, she hears Takeda swear. "Don't you want to wait and see if Hosono can manage it?" he snaps. But the control station has already decided, after a moment of doubt (or maybe it was reaction time), to trust Mishima's instincts.

Evacuation sirens blare into the quiet hall, steamrolling Johnny Fabré's speech. A gravelly rush of startled voices rises to a crescendo of alarm. This soon after the earthquake, everyone knows where the exits are, and despite the noise, the initial rush to the exits is orderly, although Mishima registers some dramatic indignation from the stage.

Her attention is pulled away almost immediately; another tsubame is arcing up toward the crow, but at the same time, there's a dull pop, loud enough for people inside the room to look up and see the explosion. The walls tremble, and something tsubame-sized falls through the darkness on the other side of the glass.

At that point, the evacuation starts to unravel. Voices rise hysterically and the movement of the crowd turns jerky and dangerous. Mishima wishes for her crow, but it's parked two blocks away. "Can we get a tsubame or two on the inside?" she asks her earpiece, and without waiting for an answer, activates her crowdcutter and pushes her way along the wall toward the glass ladder in the corner. On stage, the candidates have mostly stopped arguing and are either staring at the blast site or leaping off the platform only to get mired in the crowd. She spots Suzuki under the conference table and sees a knot of bodyguards that probably hides Fabré at its center, but she doesn't have time to look more closely.

She reaches the access ladder, sheds the crowdcutter, and pulls herself toward the catwalk as fast as she can. This is why she wears only flats when she's working; her shoes are light and flexible, with grips that cling to each rung. Her coif is holding up well so far; it probably doesn't look as sleek as it did a few minutes ago, but her hair is out of her face and her vision is clear. The dress is another story, but it's not tight enough to restrict her climbing. It will do for now.

Outside, Kumagai in the remaining tsubame has shifted to combat tactics, diving and swooping to strafe the miscreant crow with brief flashes from its high-intensity flamethrower. The crow lobs another grenade, but Kumagai dodges easily, and the projectile explodes at ground level, six stories or so below. The walls rattle again. As she gets higher, Mishima can make out more clearly the damage the crow's laser has done. There's a fissure in the wall, a clean line describing more than half of a circle. It's not big enough for the crow to get through, and with a physical thump of fear, Mishima sees what they are doing: they must be cutting an entrance slot for a bomb.

She wastes a glance down at the politicians stuck in the middle of the room at the point farthest from every clogged exit. There's no way the candidates are getting out in under three minutes, six or more to get out of the building; far too long to get out of blast range if they have something bigger than those grenades. Assassinating the front people for every Supermajority candidate government, crippling the nine largest governments simultaneously—Mishima stops thinking about consequences and focuses on her target. She's on a small platform just under the lights in the corner of the hall; the blue flicker of the laser in the glass is less than twenty feet down the wall. She reaches up for a chandelier branch. "Cut the lights!" she yells into her earpiece.

This time, the reaction is instantaneous. The hall goes dark, triggering another collective wail from below. The crow outside is suddenly distinct and menacing beyond the glass: a small model, like Mishima's, agile and unmarked. As Mishima watches, a blur of motion diagonals up and slams into it, knocking it upward: Takeda's crow.

Another salvo of explosions. Mishima grabs the rail of the

platform. At least the aftershocks have gotten her acclimated to shaking. What's more worrying is that the laser-cut circle in the glass is almost complete. "Control! Do we have anything we can use to seal that or block it somehow?"

"We're working on it!" The urgency is tinged with annoyance; obviously, they've also figured out what's going on. It doesn't sound like they've got a solution. Mishima hopes Takeda can manage this one, because she has no idea what she's going to do to stop the crow from in here, armed as she is with five shuriken and a stiletto. Even so, she can't just stand here and watch. Mishima grabs a cool tube of fluoron, smooth as an antler and the perfect circumference for a comfortable grip. She inhales, steps over the platform rail, and lets her legs swing forward, reaching ahead to seize another loop with her other hand.

When she looks up again, a few seconds later and halfway to the circle, Takeda's crow, emblazoned with the green and white of Kobe, is hovering protectively between the attacker and the almost-complete incision in the glass panel. She watches as the enemy crow launches a grenade, but Takeda only has to bob slightly to dodge it. The tsubame weaves around the mystery crow. The flamethrower mounted on its nose hasn't had much effect, but Kumagai is trying to hamper the crow's movements as much as he can.

Mishima keeps swinging forward, more cautiously now. There is a pause in the explosions, and she wonders if the attackers are out of ammo. She hasn't looked down at the dimness below her dangling feet, but the hall must be emptying out by now. She wonders when they will decide the attack is no longer worth it, that it's time to cut their losses. Then she sees a sudden jet of motion and hears a bang: the attackers have adjusted their timing, and this grenade hits Takeda's crow straight on. Mishima thinks she hears Takeda grunting as he tries to compensate, but she's not sure because of the rushing in her ears as she pulls her legs back and swings her body forward with as much momentum as she can gather. The green-and-white crow is propelled backward by the explosion, lightly tapping the center of the circle before Takeda can pull away; a nanosecond later, Mishima's feet hit the wall from the inside with a jolting smack that she feels all the way into her shoulders. Glass squeaks against glass. Swinging back, her arms tingling with fatigue, Mishima sees a couple of centimeters of laser-cut glass exposed where the circle has been pushed inward, but it's holding for now. Through it, Mishima sees Takeda's crow sink.

The throb in her palms and her forearms is starting to block out everything else when she feels something under her limp feet. Scrabbling for purchase, she looks down: a tsubame is hovering right below her, hatch open. The top, where her feet are balanced, is transparent, gently curved and about the size of a pool chair. Mishima has to remind herself not to close her eyes as she yells, "Stay there!" and lets go of the lights. The pilot has a steady hand, and she lands in a crouch, fingertips pressed to the tsubame top, without so much as a waver. From there it is only slightly scarier to swing herself in through the open hatch. As she does, she catches the flash of another tsubame swooping up from the darkness inside the hall.

"Thanks," she says as the hatch closes behind her. Tsubame are designed to carry two people if necessary, but it's a tight fit. "Is there a plan?" Mishima asks.

"Keep that glass in place and capture the perps if possible," the pilot answers without taking his eyes off the circle in the wall. "Nice kick."

Mishima believes in taking compliments, but she's not sure she earned this one. "Thank Takeda for pulling back as fast as he did."

Takeda's crow takes another hit. Mishima can't see the cockpit, and she hopes he's okay in there. It's a good sign that his crow is still battling to stay in the air, but it's already drifted below the level of the circle and will soon be out of the fight entirely. As she watches, the enemy crow approaches, nosing up to the wall.

"It's empty!" the pilot grunts in surprise. Mishima doesn't follow at first. Peering over his shoulder, she looks through three layers of glass straight into the crow's cockpit: there's nobody there.

"It's a remote!" she exclaims. As they watch, the hull door on the right side opens. The front of the crow presses forward against the newly cut circular panel. The two tsubame inside the hall bump up against the glass to push back, but they are no match for the thrust of a full-size crow. With a slow, painful screeching, the heavy disc of glass is forced inward until it wrenches free and disappears below them, the clatter of it hitting the floor obscured by the rush of air and noise. The crow has backed off and is turning to align its open hull door with the hole, but Kumagai on the outside is hampering it as much as it can, darting in and around and attacking its air pressurizers.

Mishima thumps her pilot on the shoulder. "Take us through!" she yells, and he nods, inching them forward until they are outside, between the crow and the building. The crow has turned enough so that Mishima can see the lone piece of cargo through the open hull door: a large plastic cube, dully reflective. "It's a remote," she says again to herself, and then to the pilot, "Open the hatch! Take me closer!"

He catches on immediately, and as the vertical door slides up and frigid outside air rushes in, he flies forward, positioning them above the crow's open hull, so that all Mishima has to do is step down from one to the other.

She expects the crow to try to dump her out as soon as her feet touch its floor, but it continues rotating toward the building with occasional weaves to avoid the tsubames. Whoever's controlling it must not have vid of the inside. Which is fortunate, because if they did, they probably would have detonated by now. She looks the cube over quickly. "Dark grey plastic, a few blinking lights—" She runs her hands over the outside, looking for a seal of some kind.

"Just get it out of there!" someone yells over the earpiece.

"There's no visible timer; I'm guessing it's set up to detonate on impact," Mishima warns. They are all yelling now, and the crow jolts as one of the tsubame tries to knock it back from the building, Mishima's hands involuntarily gripping the sides of the bomb.

"Slide it out; we'll manage it with the air pressurizers," her pilot says.

"It could be rigged to blow up as soon as it leaves the crow!"

"No choice! Get it out of there; you don't have much time!"

The cube looks heavy and Mishima sets up to put her weight into shoving it, but it moves easily, sliding too quickly down the short gangplank ramp. She skids after to make sure it doesn't shoot off the end into the building, and manages to deflect it to one side, where there is just enough space between the crow and the glass wall for the bomb to slide through. She catches a glimpse of the two tsubame whirling around it, but before she can see what happens, the crow is tilting sharply. Mishima, already off-balance, has no chance to grab hold of anything. She is tipped out through the opening like the bomb would have been.

"Lights!" she yells with what breath she has left. She pushes off from the gangplank as her feet skitter down it, a bad jump but with enough lift to catch one of those comforting, perfectly curved loops as the fluoron coils leap into visibility. She dangles there for a moment. The hall twenty feet below her is a mess of overturned chairs and abandoned belongings, empty except for the security personnel, most of whom are staring up at her. Mishima twists to look back over her shoulder, which is how she knows that the first explosion isn't the bomb going off but the crow self-destructing.

The feed from the debate was cut when the sirens started, but Ken missed the turmoil completely. A few minutes into Johnny Fabré's speech, a fight broke out among the karaoke singers. When one of them pulled an illegal plastic gun, Ken hit the floor and, in the same motion, muted his earpiece to give his full attention to his surroundings. He can listen to the recording later.

The centenal he's in belongs to a local, Manila-only government, which has contracted police as well as military services out to SecureNation, and when the security personnel show up a minute or two after the first shot is fired, Ken keeps his cheek pressed to the beer-sticky floor. On the off chance that this gets picked up by any local news compilers, he wants his face to be visible in as few of the feeds as possible. The SecureNation guys get him up to take his statement, but they are polite and efficient, and even let the bar reopen, minus the karaoke. As much as that improves the atmosphere, he decides he's done for the night. His hotel is right around the corner, and it's not until he's lying on the hard single bed that he flicks the debate coverage back on. He's planning to flash back to the point where he stopped, which is why he doesn't open any simultaneous feeds; he would rather not get the analysis before he hears the actual statements. He would like to know whether that scuffle in the bar made the news compilers; he has just decided to open a tiny projection for a local site when the debate audio comes on. "*. . . sugar-coated oppression. Elections are sugar-coated oppression. Elections are sugar-coated oppression.*"

Ken sits up fast, the anti-stain coating on the mattress crackling. Who the hell is that? As he's trying to place the voice among the nine debate participants, his brain informs him that it is obviously distorted. Besides which, no sane person would repeat the same sentence over and over again in a debate. He spreads his projection out large and switches from local to top news, opening three more feeds at the same time.

The miniscule room is humid and warm as a sun-baked cement block, but as Ken sees the initial images of the debate hall, he feels the sweat congealing on his back. The monotonous refrain is cut off in the middle of the word "sugar." There is dead air for a moment, and then a shaky but undeniably human voice: "We humbly apologize for the, ah, disruption." A moment of hesitation and indrawn breath: the instinct is to spin or smooth, but the facts, such as are known, are already available for anyone to see. In the last two seconds, Ken has learned about the autocrow, the evacuation, and the explosions. "There has been an attack on the debate facility and a simultaneous appropriation of our broadcast." Another pause, and Ken switches the audio off—he can read much faster. One free-swinging news compiler is reporting a claim of responsibility from Anarchy, the radical antielection group. Apparently, not everyone at Information is in shock, because someone has already annotated the story to say that no physical evidence has yet been analyzed to confirm or disprove the claim.

Watching and rewatching the tiny splice of video that someone grabbed before the lights went out, Ken calls Suzuki, but no answer. That's to be expected, he tells himself: he must be in the middle of a cyclone now, probably getting checked by emergency services and fielding interview requests and trying to figure out what to do next, not to mention receiving a million other attempted calls at the same time. The casualty figures are low and nobody has mentioned any of the candidates being hurt, which would be big news. Suzuki's fine, almost certainly. His eyes on the repeating clip of video, Ken suddenly leans forward and enlarges it. There's a glittering dark figure climbing the back wall, and something about the way it moves . . . but what would Mishima be doing there? She does work for Information, so it's not impossible. The face is turned away, and the quality of the image is poor. Ken can't be sure. He is about to try calling her when he remembers he already sent her a message that night, and decides to wait. Play it cool, he tells himself. Whether she was there or not, anyone working for Information is going to be pretty busy right now.

The debrief takes an hour and a half. Mishima has to detail minutely the moments leading up to her evacuation call and her actions on the crow. After her report, she stands in the back, watching the projector replays of the air fight and listening as the discussion about their massive security gaps heats up. The event manager is complaining about the short timeframe for rearranging the debate after the earthquake, and the regional operations chief is muttering about political pressure to use that venue and provide more seating. The deputy head of security is sidelined next to Mishima, his face locked in a worried frown. Hosono's in the hospital with three fractured ribs and a snapped ulna after one of the tsubame's airbags malfunctioned, and Takeda's in intensive care for burns and shrapnel from the grenade bursting his windshield. The bomb was successfully dumped over the ocean and went off on impact with the surface. Considering the circumstances, damage was minimal, although Mishima wouldn't have liked to be on one of the tsubames that took it out there: both the pilots have popped eardrums and probable concussions.

Even the safe disposal of the bomb is a cause for complaint. "If we had recovered the explosive device, we might have found valuable clues about how this was planned and by whom," barks someone from the investigative team. Mishima wonders when she can leave. The obligatory scan showed that she didn't need any medical care aside from some antiseptic for a few scratches, but the draining adrenaline has left her headachy and tired.

When she finally gets back to her crow, though, sleep will not come. She flies to Kyoto to get away from the commotion at the debate site, finds a mooring lot by the river, goes for a walk. It is well past midnight, and this part of town is quiet: little shops bamboo-barricaded against the darkness. She keeps thinking about Domaine and his warning. Was he involved in this? It seems extreme compared to his record. She flashes back to the moment when she looked down on the politicians scrambling to get off the platform, how helpless they were, and imagines again the blood and fragments of an explosion. She rubs her forehead. It didn't happen. It didn't happen. She needs to think about something else.

As she's climbing back into her crow, she remembers Johnny Fabré's statement. That gives her something to work on. She sends a message to Tabby in Singapore, asking if she's found anything and attaching the clip. A reply doesn't come right away (it's that kind of night), and while she waits, she decides it's time, past time, to throw a wider net. Mishima has been traveling for Information for two years now, and beyond what her official position offers, she has an extensive, if idiosyncratic, network of people she's worked with one way or another. She spends some time composing a message that will alert people to what she's looking for but not trigger panic, paranoia, or false positives, asking for any indications that high-ranking governments might be suggesting armed territorial aggression as a clandestine part of their platforms. Waiting for replies, she falls asleep.

The next morning, she's woken by an urgent message to call her boss's boss.

LaForge, a tall, frosted Westerner who looks like he was born in his suit, is seated behind his desk when his secretary lets Mishima project in. He gets right to the point, no small talk, no thanks for her efforts the night before. "I thought we were clear last week about not wasting resources on these unlikely suspicions you have about Liberty." He softens from there: she is a huge asset, but with the intense stress of the election, the narrative disorder that he sees listed in her file seems to be affecting her work.

"It always affects my work. Seeing these patterns before anyone else does is exactly what you pay me to do." Mishima has learned by experience that, in matters of mental health, offense is the best defense.

LaForge clears his throat. "Records show that at the debate, you accessed replays and transcripts and requested annotation rewrites while on duty." A moment to let her see where he's headed. "It seems that this conspiracy theory is affecting your ability to see other patterns, including those directly endangering you and those around you."

Mishima swallows two separate defensive answers before she opens her mouth. "I wish I had heard the laser cutter earlier," she says. "But I'm certainly glad I heard it in time." Her forearms ache, but she doesn't want to rub them in case it's taken as a sign of nervousness.

"Indeed. Your actions last night were . . . *heroic*." The tone makes it sound like a bad thing, as though she had been showing off. "But I think you can see the point. We've looked at this problem you cited. We—your peers and"— pointedly—"your supervisors—have come to the decision that it is not an efficient use of our resources—resources that include your abilities. Until the election, we are paying you to focus that expertise on the standard, so to speak, types of misinformation and fraud associated with campaigning. There is more than enough of that to go around. And, as a reminder, giving orders to regional offices on how to use their resources is not part of your purview."

"They weren't orders, just suggestions," Mishima says, but she knows it sounds argumentative, and she manages to keep her mouth shut while the high muckamuck gives her a brief review of chain of command and then unceremoniously dismisses her.

At least she knows she's still too valuable to fire.

CHAPTER 16

B y the time Suzuki gets back to him, Ken's already in Chennai.

"No, no, I'm fine," he says, brushing off Ken's concern. "Really, Information security did a great job. So, down to business! I've been meaning to tell you what excellent work that was in Lima."

Ken refrains from mentioning that Lima was a continent and a half ago.

"It was so clear," Ken agrees. "What more could we want?"

"Our person in Okinawa got some damning recordings of Liberty too; at this point, we have everything we need on them. The thing is," Suzuki goes on, after a brief pause, "after the debate, we have to be careful."

"What do you mean?" asks Ken, although Suzuki's tone tells him he's not going to like it.

"The way the debate worked out, it was us against the corporates. And then with the attack, people are going to be very focused on antielection violence. If we bring out these conspiracy theories about a participating government now . . ."

"They're not theories," Ken says. "I mean, I'm not sure we have legal proof, but we have very convincing intel."

"That's not the point," Suzuki says. "No matter how

convincing it is, at this point in the game, it simply wouldn't look right. We'd lose as many votes as we gain."

Ken doesn't buy it, but he tries another tack. "If you don't want to use it, why not pass it to Information? They can sanction Liberty, or . . . or do something about it, anyway." He's not sure what Information can do to stop war from breaking out.

"We don't think that's the play right now," Suzuki says. "It would be public Information that it came from us, and it could get very complicated very fast. This close to the election, we can't risk it."

Ken doesn't say anything, and after a pause in which he was probably hoping for agreement, Suzuki goes on. "We'll bring it up after the election, try to get something done."

"What if they win?" Ken says. "What if they start a war?"

"They won't," Suzuki says. "Have you seen the latest polling data?"

Ken has, and he flicks the polls open again. Heritage is ahead by 2,309 centenals, but that's well within the normal swing range. The last time he looked, Liberty was in third behind PhilipMorris, but now they're in second, in front of 888. Those three are bunched too closely to call. He suspects that Suzuki's referring to the Policy1st trend: a sharp bump with the merger and the debate, and a slower but continued rise since then. Fifth place, but pretty far behind that top group.

"So, what do I do now?" Ken asks.

"Where are you? Look, go to the nearest office and see what you can do to help out for the last few days of campaigning. Wherever it is, I'm sure you'll be a huge asset. We'll talk in Tokyo once this is over."

"I understand," Ken says, trying to sound more enthusiastic than resigned.

"Oh, and Ken?" Suzuki lets the pause hang in the cyberspace for a moment. "You have to stop seeing that woman. At least until after the election."

Mishima's first impulse, after that meeting, is to vent to someone (*Can you believe what he said to me? And the day after I . . .*). Maybe uncover some similar stories, document evidence of a pattern of mismanagement or discrimination, bring a formal complaint, topple the hierarchy. But right now, nobody has time for that, not even Mishima. Whoever's not working on the attack investigation is frantically cross-referencing the wild claims and overblown assertions of the frenetic last days of campaigning, which is exactly what she should be doing. LaForge was right about one thing: there is plenty of "standard" preelection work to do. Mishima throws herself into it for a few hours. She points her crow south and immerses herself in the backlog of questionable statements until the concentrated effort has cleared some of the frustration from her brain.

When she pauses for a tea break, she lowers her security a few notches to check her feeds. An advid slips in, rendering a beautifully detailed jar the size of the workspace, packed with uncountable jellybeans and glowing with color. Guess how many, reads the text, briefly. By the time the answer comes up, Mishima sees where this is going. They say your vote counts, but if the contents of this jar represented eligible voters, you wouldn't even be a jellybean. You'd be a grain of sugar. Use your resources where they can do some good. The projection morphs rapidly through scenes of hungry children, homeless elderly, smiling women ladling food in soup kitchens, a teenager helping a child with her homework. Civic duty is more than voting. Mishima rolls her eyes. Then she sees the message from Ken from the night before.

When an advid inexplicably worms its way in through all his firewalls, Ken is annoyed, but then it unrolls in his palm, and his pulse quickens as he sees nine blank slots. He whispers Mishima's code into his hand.

The strip of text, the size and appearance of a fortune-cookie fortune, flips over. Ken stares at the message for a long time. Although his spoken Japanese can be mistaken for native, his reading is rudimentary at best. He finds it less a disadvantage than a pleasure to occasionally wander Tokyo without his visual translator activated. Each character is so decisive, so clearly pointing at a specific meaning that is invisible to him. It's soothing to be so aware of so much Information, all around, incomprehensible to him but transparent to everyone else.

This time, he wishes he could read the message without mediation. He stares at the characters, as if concentrating hard enough will make them give up their secrets. He knows enough to see that the message is informal, or maybe familiar is a better word. Intimate, even? He wonders if Mishima drew the characters herself, an improbably romantic but not impossible scenario.

Finally, he turns on his visual translator, and the message resolves: Nothing to do on Preelection Day. Wanna go on vacation?

The answer is obvious. The only reason he pauses at all is to consider the best response: skip the question, step to the next level. Where should they go? Some place democratic but with as little election drama as possible, and easy to get to. He has no idea where she is right now, so the latter applies only to him. *How about the Adapted Maldives?* he suggests, checking the spelling and then writing it out in his kindergarten kana.

M ishima was being somewhat disingenuous when she said she had nothing to do on Preelection Day. The campaign ban in the twenty-four hours before the election is almost impossible to enforce, and Information will take all the help it can get on monitoring and evaluating infractions. But the work is obvious, petty, and mechanical, and she has so much vacation saved up, they can't say no. She decides to take Election Day off, too. There are plenty of Information grunts who can observe poll behavior, spot-check identification verification software, and crunch the numbers as they come in. Mishima prefers, whenever possible, to do work no one else can do. Besides, she has sore muscles and blisters on her palms, and her organizational loyalty is at a low ebb.

She likes Ken's proposed destination. Like some other small islands and archipelagos, the Adapted Maldives—along with Resilient Tuvalu, they changed their name as a political statement once the last natural land in their archipelago was underwater—have a dispensation giving them centenal status even though their population is fewer than one hundred thousand people. They're democratic, so she doesn't have to feel guilty about spending money there, but not hotly contested, so there shouldn't be much stress, ads, or shenanigans in the air. She does some quick cross-referencing and finds a place to stay, sends the location to

Ken with a question mark and the offer to pick him up on her way out. She can use her crow for nonbusiness travel as long as she pays for the energy use at a reasonable per-kilometer rate.

He gets back to her a few minutes later with a thumbs-up for the hotel but tells her he's already close and he'll meet her there. Ken likes boats and can get a cheap and convenient one, and getting picked up seems an awkward beginning for a romantic getaway, especially with the memories already floating around her crow. ETA 5.5 hours after close of campaigning, he writes, and gets back to work.

Domaine is under no restriction from campaigning during the day before the election, and he plans to enjoy it. He is making sure to get the last advid out to as many markets as possible that day. Shamus refused to touch it, especially after Domaine admitted that most of the quotes were recorded without the knowledge of the dictator in question. "Come on," Domaine had argued. "You can't exist today, much less be a dodgy, widely hated world leader, and not assume that your every action is being documented."

"Assuming it is one thing," Shamus replied, "and not killing people for doing it is another." He agreed, grudgingly ("I'd drop your account altogether if I knew what was good for me"), to run the jellybean spot he'd already put together, but Domaine had to find another, less reputable agency for the recordings.

Ken initially considered Suzuki's ad hoc order to go to any random Policy1st campaign office and chip in borderline insulting, but within three hours of signing on, he realizes that this is the most satisfying experience he's had since campaigning began. In part, this is because of the Chennai campaign manager, Xavier, who not only has every centenal within a fifty-mile radius painstakingly mapped but also shows an impressive intuitive grasp of his top targets. He quickly sizes Ken up. "Go with Keerthy to the university; we've got a twenty-four-hour booth there—no, no, no, no more new advids; everything should be person-to-person from now on." He raises a finger to Ken, indicating that this last was for his earpiece. "See if you can get one of the priests to come with you. Yes, use my name. Okay." He comes back to Ken with a head waggle. "There are a lot of foreign students there; you can work on them for wherever they're voting from, but keep an eye out for professors; they are mainly local and have influence. You want to emphasize how forward-looking we are, touch on science but especially the importance of policy in a rapidly growing city, smart traffic and electrical grids, you know. We have some chance in that centenal, so every vote counts. Oh, and if you see the PhilipMorris paan cart, take as many free samples as you can. I'm hoping they'll run out." Xavier grins, not very optimistically. "I'll send you data as it comes in. If you have any other ideas for what we can do, let me know."

Ken is partway out the door when Xavier calls to him from a flurry of signature requests, newly crunched polls, and volunteer organizers. "I almost forgot—there's a group of off-brand Liberty supporters that's been making trouble near the docks; be sure to steer clear of them."

Ken hovers. "Trouble?"

"I don't know," Xavier says, waving his hand. "Somehow, they've gotten the idea that if they win, they'll be invading

Sri Lanka, and they're going around yelling about it. Crackpots. Best to stay out of their way."

Mishima is doing as she was told, scanning the latest set of comparison sheets, albeit with somewhat less verve than usual, when she gets a message from Tabitha Sung in Singapore. SORRY IT TOOK SO LONG TO GET BACK TO YOU, SO BUSY WE CAN BARELY CROSS-REF HERE, it starts, and Mishima realizes it's about Liberty. So, LaForge didn't publicize his edict against following up on Liberty. Either he believes it's so ludicrous that no one else would bother, or he's avoiding scrutiny. She goes back to the message. GLAD YOU WROTE THOUGH, BECAUSE I'VE BEEN KEEPING A CLOSE EYE ON WHAT WE TALKED ABOUT. NOTHING DEFINITIVE, BUT I DID FIND SOME UNUSUAL PATTERNS. NO IDEA IF THEY MEAN ANYTHING, BUT THEY'RE REPEATED OUTSIDE THE REGION. CALL ME IF YOU NEED MORE—LET'S TALK AFTER THE ELECTION MADNESS!

Mishima checks the attached data: purchase records, but not for weapons. Mostly comms stuff, but fairly generic. The strange thing, as Tabby noted, was how uniform the purchases are across Liberty centenals. The invoice notes state that the gear is for postelection citizen-relations initiatives. Mishima makes a note to cross-reference and see if she can find any plans or promises matching that description, but she doesn't see an immediate threat and time is short, so she goes back to the comparison sheets. Heritage looks increasingly desperate, bringing up security issues at every opportunity. Mishima remembers Domaine's warning. It's true, Heritage winning again has risks for the system, but what if they are unwilling to lose? People like to think micro-democracy is stable, safe, unbreakable, because there have been two successful elections with plenty of power shifts at the centenal level. It's too easy to forget the system hasn't seen a peaceful Supermajority transition yet.

Campaigning in Chennai closes at 5 p.m.—midnight on the international date line. Ken is deep in conversation with an undecided voter outside a grocery store, and Keerthy has to nudge him a couple of times before he drops off with a regretful "Well, think about it." They've been campaigning nonstop for the past two and a half days, taking turns to drop for a couple of hours of sleep on a cot in the tiny booth. They held conversations like these with whoever stopped by, talked to any news compilers they could find, and conducted intermittent data analysis to see where an extra door-to-door push might give them the votes they need to stretch over the top. The idea for the last six hours has been to try to raise discussions that people will continue among themselves over the next day while campaigning is prohibited; Ken was the one who suggested targeting grocers, barbers, and other social dominos. He feels like he hasn't stopped talking in weeks.

Keerthy grins in sympathy as he massages his jaw, and invites him to come back to the office for the postcampaign party. Ken wavers, but only for a moment. If the election started now, he would want to stay and watch the results with these people he's worked so hard with, but being here for the enforced idleness that is Preelection Day sounds awful. Relaxing at a remote ocean resort with Mishima sounds pretty good. He thanks Keerthy for her help, tells her to stay in touch, and heads for the port, detouring only briefly to grab a quick bite at his favorite thosai bar.

CHAPTER 17

Ken's speedboat, a colorfully striped fifteen-foot sloop with large high-efficiency engines hanging off the back, is less than an hour out of Chennai when he gets a call from Xavier.

"Hey, I wanted to thank you for all your help," Xavier says. His face looks slightly different over the feed, and Ken realizes it's because the man has actually relaxed. His jaw has loosened enough to allow a breath or two between sentences, and the earpiece is gone. His default expression is a hazy smile. The Preelection Day campaign ban is a wonderful institution. "We appreciate you coming out. It was good to have fresh eyes, and I know you put a lot of effort in when you must have been exhausted."

"No problem," Ken says. How nice of this guy to call. He guesses, though, that relaxed though he may be, Xavier's probably still too amped up to sleep. "It was my pleasure, really. You did a great job."

Xavier laughs shyly at the praise. "Well, let's wait for the results. Oh, and by the way, congratulations." Ken perks up. "I hear Suzuki's going to make you his personal assistant in the new government."

Ken can't speak for a moment, and Xavier, sensing a faux pas, coughs. "Well, that may have been only a rumor . . . Anyway, I'll be sure to tell him how impressed I was with your work here."

Ken mutters his thanks and clicks off while still parsing his reaction. Yes, he's disappointed. What did he expect, exactly? A real job, he tells himself, disgusted. Something official, in the government. Obviously not a ministry, obviously not a centenal governorship; he's far too junior for that. He thought he'd be sent to some remote centenal for one of those jobs that seems boring, but you know that later you're going to see how much you learned from it, ground-up stuff. It would be rough for a couple of years, but he would know that Suzuki was investing in him. If he had been given his choice, he would have picked something at the government level that would keep him bouncing around like he's doing now. Well, as Suzuki's personal assistant, he'll be bouncing around all right. But before, when he was nominally a driver, wasn't he doing everything a personal assistant would? This is a promotion in name only.

If he takes it.

But what else can he do? This is the problem with not having a real job; when you want to look for another one, nobody knows what you've done. His only currency is in the people who interacted with him directly.

Maybe he can ask for a centenal-level job with Xavier or Natalia.

Maybe Mishima can help.

If nothing else, it makes him feel justified in blowing off Preelection Day. And not letting Suzuki tell him whom he can and can't see.

The boat speeds out of the Palk Strait, the lights of Colombo gleaming and then fading off to the left. In the open sea, the swells climb higher, and the prow slams down on them, sending spray up into Ken's face, slapping him out of his thoughts. Good. He's on vacation.

. . .

Shamus wouldn't have taken Domaine's suicide-mission job in any case, but it helps that he's already working on another contract. Another one based on illicit recordings, in fact, although of people who are less likely to seek retribution. Suzuki hired him to leak Yoriko's recording of the Liberty head of security in a way that will get a lot of press but will be untraceable—"minimally traceable," Shamus corrected him; "nothing is one hundred percent untraceable"—to Policy1st. It's a sketchy job, especially because Suzuki wants it to run through Preelection Day, a clear violation if it comes from the Policy1st campaign office.

"Look," Suzuki said when they were working out the deal. Suzuki had come to Addis in person; he didn't want to discuss this over a comms link. "This is data that needs to be out there before the election. It would be wrong to hide it. But because of . . . of politics, you understand, because of perceptions, we can't do it ourselves. And Information, you know . . . first of all, they'd attribute it to us, and secondly, it would get lost in the morass."

"You don't have to justify yourself to me," Shamus answered. "Just pay me."

That's not strictly true, but Shamus likes projecting a tough-guy, in-it-for-the-money vibe, especially to fallen idealists, which is definitely how he reads this nutter. Also, he has no love for Liberty or its component multinationals, most of which have at one time or another created an advid that offended Shamus's African pride, professional standards, or both. "Fucking colonialists," he mutters while prepping the audio recording, even though Suzuki hasn't given him the background.

He listens through it a couple of times. This is a bit more of a challenge than he expected. The interrogator was careful not to suggest anything illegal, and without video, it's hard to get a sense for how threatening he's being. Still, Shamus decides he can put the viewer—because of course he'll add images—in the place of the poor sucker the guy is harassing, and play up the contrast between the title "Liberty" and the emphasis on incarceration. While he's editing, he slaps up a geographic strategy based on Suzuki's budget and the latest projection globe he's seen.

Mishima times it perfectly, gets in right before Ken does, and is still having her welcome drink (fresh jackfruit–passion fruit juice, with a cluster of rambutan glowing red in a bowl to accompany it) in the resort lobby when Ken stumbles up from the dock. He looks like she feels, with the addition of five hours on a speedboat. "Hey," she says, and then, because he seems so worn, she puts her arms around him and holds him for a couple of long breaths. She feels as though she should ask how it went but decides not to. She doesn't want to hear anything about the election, not for the next eighteen hours, anyway. "Let's go to the room."

Each suite in the resort used to be on its own island; now each is elevated on pylons on its former island, with one to three meters of clear aquamarine water between sand and flooring. A bellboy takes them out in a small launch and starts to explain the system of flag signaling they have for ordering room service and so on. Mishima cuts him off, tells him they'll read the manual, gives him a huge tip, and sends him away. Ken wanders the airy rooms, trying to feel happy to be there. But it's almost midnight, the night here is as dark as any he's ever seen, and all he can feel is tired.

"Ooh, there's an airbed," Mishima calls. "Come check it out."

Ken drops his bag and walks into the bedroom, which has the expected thin linen curtains and turquoise ceramic touches in all the right places. Mishima is hovering above the mattress, fiddling with a handheld control screen.

"Try it; it's great!" she says. "There are separate controls for your side of the bed."

Ken, who has never heard of an airbed, finds that the phrase "your side of the bed" sticks in his mind in an interesting way. He sits down gingerly on the cushion of air.

"Lie back," Mishima says. "Let it calibrate."

He leans back. The sensors get to work, and suddenly he feels—well, like he's floating. The air pressure adjusts to his body, aligning his spine and allowing every muscle to relax, and then it feels as if every individual part of his body is floating separately and in harmony.

"It's true; it's amazing," he murmurs.

"Try the massage," Mishima encourages him. She's hoping it will serve as subtle fore-foreplay, but when she glances over, he's already asleep. As bad as Information is before an election, working on a campaign must be even worse. She brushes the hair off his forehead and lets her disappointment slide into exhaustion. She punches in a gentle rocking pattern for her side of the bed and curls up with her face against his shoulder.

On Preelection Day, with his last advid already taking advantage of the air empty of government-sponsored pollution, Domaine is free to enjoy his work and amuse himself needling idealistic voters. Despite a frigid wind, he wanders through New York City with a swing to his step. Most of the population of the formerly United States continues to vote in automatic swathes of Democrat or Republican, and every election season produces some variation of a political cartoon in which blinkered Statesers examine a narrow choice of governments while congratulating themselves on their democratic traditions. It's an exaggeration, of course; there are numerous shady governments branching to the left and the right of both venerable trunks. SecureNation always gets a fair amount of votes, and owns most of the centenals on military bases; LaRaza and ElNuevoPRI battle over wide areas; and StarLight tends to do well. Still, the stereotype has some truth, and most governments don't bother campaigning in the heartland.

New York City, on the other hand, has fully embraced the micro-democracy concept. In a way, it's the perfect place for it: a city already divided into boroughs and then neighborhoods of tightly knotted communities, each as different from the next as two countries half a world apart.

Unfortunately—and Domaine can't help snickering about this—these communities rarely divide cleanly into that magical number of one hundred thousand people. The result is a set of centenals nearly as angst-ridden with internal conflict as Asia Minor after Sykes-Picot. Centenals that split their vote between RastaGov and Chabad; between (the retro-ironically titled) HipstaLand and the Universalist Church; between OrgulloDominicano and 888 and Académe. For the most part, these rivalries are low violence, although there are always a few threatening to teeter into open warfare every election season. The city is full of rancor and complaints, especially before an election, and Domaine feels right at home.

There are several submunicipal coalitions, and they've even managed to keep the old subway system running, skipping the stops in the centenals that don't tax in to pay for it. There is a relatively strong movement for shifting to a true municipality-wide system, but it's never made much headway, because it's not so much a movement as movements, a collection of poorly organized and ineffectual advocates who can't even agree on where the municipal limits are or should be. Still, Domaine applauds their efforts. He spoke at one of their events a month ago and considered meeting with them again, but decided it wouldn't be worth the aggravation, although he tips his flat cap in solidarity whenever he sees one of their picketers.

He's enjoying himself so much that it takes most of the morning (a leisurely brunch with kumquat mimosas and runny quail eggs dripping with hollandaise, then a long walk in Manhattan) before he can pinpoint his unease. He keeps checking over his shoulder, which is not how he likes it; Domaine prefers to be the pursuer. Once he thinks about it, he knows what's bothering him. He's already seen his "people you love to hate loving to hate elections" ad twice, and the ex-US might not have been the best place to be when it dropped. The American theocrat in the ad had the most to lose from being outed as antielection, and even if New York City isn't exactly his turf, there are no oceans between them. Not that any of the other strongmen will react well to being used for publicity. Domaine begins to consider investing in a pair of antennae, or maybe a radar attachment.

They sleep late and spend most of the day having sex, swimming, diving, and eating. Despite the archaic system of ordering, the service is speedy and the food is luscious. There are brief moments when Ken thinks he never wants to leave. But neither of them gets too distracted to notice when four thirty hits and voting starts.

"We won't know anything for a while," Mishima says.

"It's way too soon," Ken agrees.

The voting day is twenty-four hours worldwide, midnight to midnight on the international date line. Few centenals register enough votes to be sure of the winner before the last six hours of the election, and many can't be called until voting closes.

"I'm going to vote now, though," Mishima says. "To get it out of the way."

"It's a good idea," Ken agrees. "Just in case."

Out of tradition, rather than necessity, they split up to vote, Mishima in the bedroom, Ken out on the dock, swinging his bare feet above the waves. When he's done, he leans into the front room to leave his handheld there and slips into the water. Mishima joins him a few minutes later.

Neither of them thinks they'll be able to sleep that night, and they climb into bed late after a last dark dip in the rising sea. The combination of residual exhaustion, a day of sun and swimming, and the excellent sea-skate curry proves them wrong. Ken falls asleep first, but even Mishima, with her chronic insomnia, is out before she hears his snores.

Suzuki shipped Yoriko's taxi to Amami for her. She is using it as a personal car, because she's not sure she can be a taxi driver in a completely new city. Once she sees how small it is, she realizes it won't take her very long to learn. Only 250 kilometers north of Okinawa, Amami Ōshima is familiar enough in terms of climate, island culture, and food. Yoriko imagines that Naha itself might not have looked much different at some time in its troubled history: a harbor edged by a cluster of pale multistory buildings, windows darkened against the sun. But Amami is much smaller. Yoriko has never been in a place where the human environment is so overwhelmed by nature; most of Okinawa is thickly populated, and even on the beach, you can feel city looming behind you. Amami feels like nothing more than an outpost against the green of the jungle.

She was worried that her kids would hate it—only one outmoded projection arcade, barely a downtown to speak of, none of the buzz of Naha. She almost chose Kagoshima City instead, but she was nearly as spooked to be in Satsuma territory as she was to be around Liberty centenals. And so far the kids seem happy. They still think they're on vacation. The house here is much nicer and larger than what she could afford in Okinawa, even outside of the capital. She takes her children to the beach. It's not much, compared to Okinawa, but she's trying to embrace idleness while she decides what to do here.

She's watching them splash and trying not to sniff at the lack of banana boat and Jet Ski options when she hears a bored voice: "The offense carries a sentence of five to seven years normally, ten to fifteen in the election period." She jumps out of her lounger and spins around, pulse pounding. After a long moment in which the beach seems no firmer than the surf, she finds the advid, projected among a stream of others by the seawall. The bored drawl of the interrogator is replaced by a deep, threatening voice, overlaid on an animation of a barred door slamming shut: "They're known as Liberty, but their arbitrary laws will strip away your freedom."

Shaking, Yoriko collects her things, shrieks at her children until they come in from the waves, gathers them up into her erstwhile taxi, and takes them back to their unfamiliar house. With the kids ensconced in front of their favorite projections, she paces back and forth. She gave the recording to Suzuki to use against Liberty, yes, but she thought he would use it privately somehow. Send it to the election commission or make an obscure complaint to Information. She didn't expect to hear it, to have everyone else hear it, too! And what were they doing advertising in Amami, anyway? (Shamus's tech outsourcer made a typo in the projection address.)

In a fit of pique, she opens her voting application. She had wanted to forget it was Election Day; now she wants to take her revenge, however pointless (it's not like her vote matters in this centenal) on all of them, Suzuki, Liberty, even the stupid 平和亜紀. She clicks defiantly on 1China, knowing that hers will almost certainly be the only vote on all of Amami Ōshima for that government and probably won't even show up in the postelection data breakdowns except as a tiny sliver marked OTHER. Still, she closes her handheld with a feeling of vague satisfaction. She's not ruling out the possibility that Suzuki or that creep from Liberty could, by illegal means, find out how she voted, and if they do, that will show them.

Mishima wakes up and stretches on her air cushion. Her first impulse is to reach for her handheld, check the time and—the election standings!—but although her hand jerks, she calms herself. From the angle of the shadows, she can see it's still before noon. Yes, Information will be overflowing with numbers and analysis, but she knows as well as anyone that little of it will mean anything yet. She reaches for Ken and tickles him awake. They've already discovered that the airbed is terrible for sex. It adjusts too slowly for rapid changes in position and misinterprets rhythmic bouncing. Mishima hits the button to shut it off and drops them down to the mattress, but turns it back on afterward. It is perfect for afterglow.

"Do you know how they invented this?" Mishima asks, drifting on her cushion of warm air.

Ken shakes his head. As he strokes her hair, he notices a few strands of grey. It's surprising, because he assumed her dark red hair was a genetic modification, and most people who do that get the grey taken out at the same time. He wonders absently if she might be both Japanese and foreign, like he is.

"It was when the emperor was dying—Emperor Suisanmono. They did everything they could to prolong her life. Eventually, they tried to disassociate her from the physical world while keeping her in it. They devised the most gentle and nourishing of gasses to ease into her lungs. They experimented with creating a vacuum around her—that didn't go well—and wrapped her in cushions of different kinds—milk, honey, air—to reduce friction on her skin cells."

"Of course it didn't work."

"Of course it didn't work. Well, not forever. Whether it kept her alive a few seconds, hours, days, or years longer than she would have survived otherwise, I don't know. Either way, it gave us this small piece of wonderful technology."

Mishima is telling a fairy tale about protection from the

abrasiveness of the world; Ken hears a cautionary story about the excessive privilege of the irrationally adored. "Never would have happened in a Policy1st centenal."

"Almost makes me sorry I voted for them," Mishima replies.

It's meant to be tart, zinging him for his lack of imagination, but Ken doesn't even process her tone. He sees Mishima not as an idealist but as a pragmatist. Above all, he sees her as someone with her finger on the pulse. If *she* voted for Policy1st, they must actually have a chance. He squirms. "Do you mind if I just . . ."

She glances up at his face and is instantly infected. "Yeah, I think we've held out long enough," she says, already diving for her handheld. They lie next to each other on the airbed, each fiddling independently.

Ken is first to break the silence. "I can't get in," he says. "I wonder if something's wrong with the signal out here. We should go to the restaurant for lunch; they should be projecting—"

"Wait a sec." Mishima puts her right hand out, touches his forearm while her left continues to tap and sweep. On her handheld screen is an alert from five hours ago, an alert that she did not hear. She finally manages to connect to the Information intranet, and what she sees there is the virtual equivalent of a sudden blackout in a crowded room: shock, yelling, panic.

Information is down.

"What?" Ken asks when a minute has passed. He thought he was holding up well by staying away from Information yesterday and especially last night, but voluntarily, virtuously taking a vacation is entirely different from being exiled. His foot is tapping, his mouth dry. He's going into withdrawal. "If it's not working here, we should go uplink from . . ."

Mishima's mind flies through a barely hypothetical chain of events. She hooked up with Ken at that party; she was incautious after the earthquake and he figured out she was influential; Domaine got to him somehow, used him to distract her . . . or maybe not Domaine; he could be working for—Suzuki! He said he was working for Suzuki; could Policy1st be in on it? Or is Suzuki going rogue? How could she let herself get taken out of the game at the crucial moment? And what will happen now? If Ken is supposed to distract her until the election is over, what will he do when he realizes she's on to him?

Ken is struggling to keep his frustration under control. So, maybe there's been a transitory connection glitch in this country that doesn't really exist. It's still early; no results will be up yet, except for those rare centenals where all hundred thousand inhabitants have voted already. They'll be connected before it matters. He's been looking forward to watching the results with Mishima, as if she could bring him luck somehow. And she's knowledgeable and passionate about it, like he is. They'll find a way to get connected. Worst case, they can get back on her crow; extreme worst case, they can take it back to the tip of India. Connection failures happen, even with today's technology, Ken's spent enough time in remote locations to accept that.

"Maybe we're better off without it," Ken says, stretching his arms and getting ready to swing himself off the bed. He means, *We're in a landless paradise and it's too early to find out anything anyway, so we might as well enjoy the moment instead of being tethered to our handhelds.*

That is not what Mishima hears.

She jams her palm into the airbed controller, dropping them both down to the mattress, absorbs the shock into a roll toward her side of the bed and reaches into her pile of clothes, her fingers finding the narrow, lightweight haft immediately. In the same motion, she swings back toward the center of the bed and juts her stiletto into Ken's still-bare thigh.

CHAPTER 18

Shamus is in no hurry to vote. His centenal in Addis is reliably AfricanUnity (a somewhat optimistic name, which the government is nowhere near achieving), and while he still enjoys voting for it as a form of private self-expression, there's no urgency. Still, he doesn't want to forget. He wakes up early on voting day. It feels like a holiday to him, after the crush of preelection work and before the self-congratulatory postelection run of advids starts, and he takes his time, going to a hotel down the street to drink freshly roasted coffee on their pleasantly shady terrace. After a plate of chechebsa, he rinses his hands and pulls out his handheld to vote. Nothing works, though; he can't get in. He looks for the manager of the restaurant, a balding Ethiopian man Shamus has known for years. The man catches his eye and shrugs. Not working for anyone. Shamus registers that the bar's normal projection of football replays and Ethiopian music videos, which plays at low intensity even over breakfast, is missing. He starts to have a sinking feeling about the postelection celebration contracts he was hoping for.

If it were up to Suzuki, he would set his handheld to autovote the nanosecond he was eligible to do so, get it over with quickly and efficiently. It's not like he's going to get talked into changing his mind halfway through Election Day. He guffaws at the thought. But, for better or for worse, he is one of the public faces of Policy1st, and public voting is an important part of political theater.

He's in Paris for the election, a highly symbolic choice. Policy1st was dreamed up at the Institute of Political Studies in the seventh arrondissement, and yet until this year, they had never won a centenal in the city. Now buoyed by a coalition of anti–mantle tunnel preservationists, poli-sci geeks, and young parents convinced by the education plan, Policy1st's victory in the centenal that covers most of the fourteenth arrondissement is all but certain. The plan is for Suzuki to vote there, standing in the park in front of the old Mairie building with a cheering group of volunteers.

Policy1st has sponsored a street festival that carefully conforms to the no-campaigning regulations for expenditures and events on Preelection and Election Days: the government's name and logo do not appear anywhere on the booths offering music and free food, the bouncy castle in the shape of the Eiffel Tower, or the giant steampunk-themed carrousel. There is no grand speech, but the music all winds simultaneously to a close and the food vendors are all refreshing their stock as the volunteers swirl into an attention-drawing crowd around Suzuki and he pulls out his handheld with a flamboyant flourish. There is no doubt that this moment will be picked up by the news compilers.

The only problem is, he can't seem to vote. Holding an absorbed smile on his face—part of his professional skill set—Suzuki taps and taps, even whispers to his handheld, but nothing works. Finally, he raises the handheld above his head, fingers strategically blocking the screen from even the most high-def camera, and waves it back and forth, wearing the same triumphant smile as he would if he had managed to vote. The volunteers cheer, as they're supposed to, but it doesn't sound as loud as it should. Suzuki notes that some of them are fiddling with their tablets or handhelds too. He wonders which techie is to blame for this screwup and how to make sure that person never works for Policy1st again.

B oth of them stare at the pointed steel. Ken is starting to drastically reassess the situation, their relationship, everything he thinks he knows about her.

"What—what kind of an Information worker are you?" Ken finally asks. He can't seem to take the stiletto seriously. It happened too fast, he likes her too much, they were getting along too well. It barely hurts, as though she had thumped him in the thigh with her fist. It's a joke, such a funny joke he almost starts to laugh before he catches himself. Instead, he squirms upward toward a sitting position, his left leg still outstretched with that hilarious knife sticking out of it.

"I think I should be asking who you are," Mishima says in a conversational tone. "Who sent you?"

"Who sent me? What are you talking about?" Ken is thinking about Suzuki, about Suzuki telling him not to see her anymore. Did he know something about her Ken doesn't? The burn is stinging and spreading and he reaches for the handle of the knife, but Mishima grabs his wrist with a grip like a magnet, and Ken drags his eyes away from the blade in his leg to meet hers.

"Who are you working for? Anarchy? Domaine? Or is it Policy1st? Are they the ones behind—"

"What the—who? You know I work for Policy1st! Behind what?"

Does she know, though? Mishima is trying to remember if she's ever had any independent corroboration of that. Ken makes another grab for the knife, but she deflects him easily. "Why here? Was the idea to get me as far away as possible?"

"As far away from *what*? We're on vacation! This was your idea!"

It was, in fact, her idea. Reluctantly, Mishima does her own reassessing. "If you're trying to . . ." But the shock is wearing off, the pain is ratcheting up, and Ken is losing it.

"Get this thing out of me!" He kicks and wriggles until he frees his hands briefly, and Mishima has to use one arm to pin his upper body to the headboard.

"Hang on." She gets his wrist again, made easier by the fact that it's none too steady. "Wait—just *wait* a second, and I'll fix it." She gets his eyes focused on hers. "You're not—behind this, you're not with whoever's behind this?"

"What are you talking about? What is going on?" Ken yells.

Mishima bounces off the bed again, this time grabbing something from her bag on the floor. She's back before he can move, swiftly extracting the knife with her left hand—the skin tenting around it briefly before it pops out—and slapping something—a poultice? a balm? a patch?—over the wound with her right. And holding it there. The whole top of his thigh goes cold-numb, but what does that mean? Is that thing healing him or just deadening the pain? Ken is a little afraid to ask, partly because he's not sure he wants the answer, but mostly because Mishima's still holding the stiletto.

"In an hour or two, you won't even know it happened," she assures him, a little too breezily. Mishima is feeling somewhat ashamed of herself.

Ken shakes his head. "Who the hell are you?"

Mishima shifts, disappearing the knife somewhere and grabbing her handheld instead. She holds her screen out to him. "All communications are down," she manages to say. "Information is down."

Ken stares at her, and it, blankly. "You stabbed me because this hotel has a lousy Information connection?"

"No, not only here," Mishima snaps, her control failing again. "Everywhere! Look!" She shakes the screen in front of him. "That's the Information intranet. No one can do anything. No one can find out anything. They don't know what's going on. All. Information. Is. Down."

Ken gapes. "It's election sabotage."

"It's war."

CHAPTER 19

I have to go." Mishima still feels guilty about the knife wound in Ken's thigh. It was only a surface puncture, but she may have overstated slightly the effectiveness of the healing pad she slapped on him; while it's rebuilding muscle as they speak, and he shouldn't notice any decrease in mobility or strength, there probably will be a tiny little scar. She hears the brusqueness in her tone and modulates. "I mean, I have to get back to work. This is a mess, and they're going to need me. Do you want to stay? Should I drop you somewhere?"

Ken considers his options. He's calm again, and he wonders if that patch on his leg might include a sedative. Even artificial calm is better than panicking, he tells himself. "Where are you going?" It occurs to him that if he lets her go now, with this uncomfortable sputter of violence between them, he will never see her again, or at least they will never see each other in the same way. Which might be for the best, if she treats all her lovers this way.

Mishima is also thinking. Her instinct is to go to Tokyo, but it's far, and every hour of travel is an hour that efforts and initiatives and solutions are being made without her. If the intranet is up, it doesn't matter which office she's in, as long as they have the massive hardware of a hub. And, as much as she hates to admit it, people. She wants to be around people, other people who are freaking out and working frantically, even if she knows that feeling won't last long once she gets there.

"Doha," she says.

Ken nods, as though it's what he expected. "That works for me."

The resort's anachronistic semaphore system turns out to be extremely fortuitous; despite the complete collapse of digital communications, the launch comes for them almost as soon as they raise the flag. Fortunately, the suite was paid in advance, because as they sweep through the lobby, Mishima sees a gaggle of confused customers in front of a sweating manager. She considers stopping to tell them that it's not a local technical failure that prevents them from paying their bills, but a global attack on all transactions and interactions—on humanity, basically—but they are already past, and she suspects it wouldn't help, anyway. They clamber into the crow, she sets the best course she can manage using hard maps, and they take off.

Mishima stays at the controls far longer than she has to. Every time she looks at Ken, she sees his shocked face as he yelled, "Get this thing out of me!" and every time she feels worse about it. Instead of looking at him, she wants to curl up with *Jane Eyre*, or a highly compressed season of *The Wire*, or *Crow Wars V*, but she can't because she's too polite (or embarrassed) to use content in front of a guest. She wishes she hadn't let him come along for the ride.

What she can do without guilt is work, so she throws herself into that. Normally, this would work almost as well as a great narrative, but the patchy intranet connection is frustrating and disconcerting, and she can't immerse.

As she picks away at the gaps, testing an uplink in Goa, a route around a corrupted server in Prague, a cache in Alexandria, she starts to sense a pattern in the metadata. She configures her handheld to visualize it: a partial, shifting map of what she can and can't access. When she can't deal with resetting one more broken connection, she sits back and looks at it. Far more satisfying as a puzzle. She spins it around, looks from different angles. Information isn't down. She tests this, calls up some random data: last year's top-grossing song, the date the subcontinental highway was completed, the number of high schools in the nearest centenal. Only the last one gives her any trouble, and as soon as she modifies to look for older data—six months ago instead of this minute—she finds it. Information is still there; it's new Information that she can't get. News. Updates and annotations, which are designed to provide up-to-the-second Information, don't happen; since a lot of protocols are designed around updating to the nanosecond, that's thrown off some processes and led to global delays and errors. Communications are completely knocked out as far as she can tell. And anything relating to the election is particularly complicated.

That seems to confirm their initial assessment. (She remembers Ken saying "It's election sabotage" and sneaks a glance at his corner of the room. He's focused on his own handheld, and she wonders what he can possibly be doing.) This isn't a sweeping attack on infrastructure but a strike aimed specifically at blacking out the election.

That is helpful, but it doesn't make her feel much better. Even if this is an attack on the election, that doesn't mean it won't have broader repercussions. What is going on out there in the world? Has someone initiated a coup? Are close-fought centenals rioting? Are governments unilaterally declaring themselves the winner in individual jurisdictions? Do citizens even know that their votes are lost? Has war, as she suggested so grandiosely, actually started, or are the pieces still falling into place?

Mishima decides she doesn't care about being polite anymore. It's her damn crow. She goes into the cabin and shuts the door behind her.

Instead of diving into some form of narrative content, though, she goes back to work, reading through what her colleagues are saying on the intranet. She's been keeping an eye out for Yelinka Korbin, mostly because of the working rhythm they developed during the last crisis, but also because Korbin works on Heritage. Mishima would love to know what the Supermajority holder is saying about all of this, and what they were saying and doing right before it. Korbin isn't logged on, though, hasn't logged on since the intranet got back up six hours ago (only twenty-eight minutes down. Not bad, Mishima thinks). On a hunch, she checks log-ins by location. No one has logged on from the Tokyo office. They aren't connected to the intranet yet.

Or maybe they've been attacked.

Mishima glances at their (calculated, not updated) location on the map, grabbed by an urge to reroute for Tokyo after all. But she stops herself. If the office isn't back online yet, she won't be able to do much from there, and in the very unlikely (she tells herself) event that they've been attacked in the physical world, it would all be over by the time she arrived. A bleak thought.

She runs a quick check: Tokyo is not the only office that has not checked in. Seoul, San José, Budapest, Glasgow. A number of other smaller ones. No pattern that she can make out, at least not yet. Why can't she just *know* what's happening on the other side of the world? She feels blind.

Her stomach gurgles uncomfortably. She—they—didn't eat that morning, haven't eaten since last night's curry. And of course the food-cooker is in the other cabin. She considers restricting herself to the emergency snacks she keeps in the storage compartment in the bathroom, then tells herself to grow up and goes back into the work area.

"Do you want something to eat?"

Ken looks up from his handheld, starts to shake his head, then changes his mind. "Seems like a good idea," he says.

Mishima goes to program the food-cooker. Her scalp prickles and she adjusts her angle so that she can see Ken in her peripheral vision, but he hasn't moved. Just her damn overactive narrative drive again.

"How's your leg?" she asks.

"It's fine," Ken says. He bends and stretches experimentally. The numbness has faded and there's no pain. "Totally fine. How long should I leave this thing on it?"

"No harm in keeping it there a little longer." It can be removed as soon as symptoms have subsided, but Mishima would rather be on the safe side. "I don't think I said"—she brings over two bowls of rice with nutrition sprinkles—"that I'm sorry."

Ken resists the urge to snap back, *Are you? Are you saying it now?* and arranges the rice bowl and chopsticks while he looks for a response. She hasn't started eating yet.

"Thank you," he says finally. After that, they eat in silence.

· · ·

Mishima's eyes only flash with one update during the meal, and it isn't a useful one. Another person sending out a ream of urgent questions on the intranet.

"They targeted the election," Ken says.

Mishima's eyes refocus on him.

"It's not general Information. A lot of old stuff is still available. It's the election."

She refrains from saying "Obviously" or even "I know," because she can't trust her tone not to be biting, bitter, or rude. And how did he figure that out so quickly, anyway?

"Who stands to lose?" he wonders aloud, this time not looking at her.

Mishima has been asking herself that question, but the answers are inconclusive. "It could be Heritage," she says, "if they suspected they were going to lose the Supermajority. Or one of their competitors, if they thought they were going to be close but not close enough."

Ken hesitates, but the tug to reknit their rapport is too strong. "Before this happened, we were following some . . . hints. That Liberty might be planning a war."

Mishima reassesses him again. How does he know about that? "We were looking into something along those lines too," she says, thinking through it. "But it looked like they were going to try to justify it electorally. What would they gain by knocking out the system without waiting to see if they could win the Supermajority legitimately? They were certainly in the running for it."

Ken is reluctant to give up on Liberty as the bad guys. "What if it's a fake-out? They knock out the election to show that they can—no, not that *they* can but that it can happen. It comes back online in a few hours, or a day—long enough so that everyone notices. But Liberty has shown they can handle it. For all we know, Information is up in Liberty centenals right now!"

Mishima checks, routing a connection through a server in a nearby Liberty centenal. "It's not."

"Or a distraction? This way, no one will know if they're taking over neighboring centenals until it's too late."

"If that's the case," Mishima says grimly, "there's not much we can do about it."

Back in the cabin, Mishima does what she should have done a long time ago: check Ken's Information. Everything that's publicly available and everything else that she can scrounge access to. His public profile is smooth and deceptive: student in a doctoral program at some utterly unreputed university, with the recent addition that he's working with Policy1st on his research. Misleading, yes, but transparently so; most of the large governments have semiofficial people working for them to suss out missed chances without alerting their competitors.

That gives her the idea to set her Information to compile a list of suspected clandestine operators for the major governments and their last known movements. It fails almost immediately. She sets the timeframe farther and farther back until it will run, but she doubts the outdated intel will do her much good. She leaves it building in the background while she delves deeper into Ken's life.

His most immediate job before becoming a fake graduate student was two years earlier and apparently unrelated: as a supervisor in a Sony-Mitsubishi projector factory, having worked his way up from foreman. She correlates his movements over those two intervening years with Suzuki's, and with a little more digging, she is able to turn up a temporary ID photo from a SecureNation garage fifteen months ago that identifies him as a Policy1st driver. Did he have any political leanings before that? She does a targeted search and finds that though he has no college degree, he did take classes at a junior college while he was working at the factory: political science, economics, and something called Shifting Conceptualities of Social Justice. Media Literacy and a follow-up, Media Management. Did he choose those, or was that already Suzuki? Or someone else?

His personal history, though not readily available, is easier to find: born in a Sony-Mitsubishi centenal in São Paolo, to issei. Seven years younger than she is, but she had suspected as much. Orphaned at twelve. High school in Japan. Moderate Sony-Mitsubishi scholarships to support him through that, but no follow-up for university. Instead, that just-above-menial-level job at one of their plants. She wonders how he met Suzuki. Surely the data is there, if she had the time to search for it, combing vids and feeds and visitor logs in the months before his job ended.

Mishima leans back against the wall. This hasn't been as helpful as she hoped. She can read this as the story of an underprivileged kid, interested in politics, who found an influential mentor in one of the most powerful policy-based governments in the world, and has been doing mildly dodgy but not outright illegal work to help that government gain power. Excitement, intrigue, world travel, the promise of a government job at the end of it, something that will give him the status he's never had.

But then again, she can read it as the story of a man who has lied about almost everything and has every reason to keep doing so. Maybe even this is a cover story, one she could crack if she had the time. Maybe he was a Sony-Mitsubishi mole at Policy1st. Maybe he's spying for them right now. He's very self-assured for a driver and factory worker. Then again, Mishima herself didn't graduate from university, so she can understand bootstrapping.

She's either going to have to trust him or not. The one thing this exercise has made clear to her is how much she wants to.

CHAPTER 20

Qatar, though it's no longer officially called that, is one of those vestigial countries that have managed to both participate in elections and survive as something approximating the nation-state it used to be. Its AlThani government has even managed to expand, winning centenals on territory that formerly belonged to Bahrain and along the western edge of Abu Dhabi. Foreign nationals vote in their home centenals, regardless of how long they have lived or worked on the peninsula, and AlThani regularly polls above 90 percent among its citizens.

They're gaming the system, and Mishima doesn't like it, but she's learned to live with it. AlThani offers Information low-rent offices and tax breaks on high-tech infrastructure, so the compound there is well-appointed and frequently hosts those conferences and meets that the hierarchy deems worthy of physical face-to-face. Mishima knows Doha well enough to have a favorite Persian restaurant and Lebanese pastry shop, and a place she's been a couple of times for projector tune-ups. Even with the navigation data still on the fritz, she's easily able to pilot to the Information hub.

"Are you going to get a flight somewhere?" Mishima is not sure whether she cares; she's very successful in sounding like she doesn't.

Ken hesitates. Even if Mishima wants nothing more to do with him—and she's the one who stabbed him, so he's not sure what *her* problem is—she's still his best chance to be involved in whatever's going on. He could go to the nearest Policy1st office—he's not even sure where that would be. Maybe Tehran? Or Amman?—and offer his services, but if he was going to do that, he should have gone back to Chennai. He could try to find Suzuki and act like the personal assistant that he's apparently destined to be, but he's still upset about being passed over. He's not sure he wants to work for Suzuki anymore. Plus, from what he's seen of Mishima and her friends back in Tokyo, Information isn't the boring hidebound bureaucracy everyone says it is. It's way closer to the heart of things than Policy1st, and that's where he wants to be.

"Um, do you think they need any help? I figure I'll do at least as much good here as at Policy1st."

Mishima looks like she's about to tell him to get lost, but then she wavers, and Ken feels a surge of pride. If she hates him for whatever mixed-up personal reasons, then any help she gives him now must be because she thinks he's worth it.

"Come on," she says. "Let's see what the situation is."

From the state of the intranet, she'd half-expected to walk into a tornado, people screaming impossible orders, tablets and chairs flying through overlapping projections. Instead, the Doha Information hub occupies a state of controlled chaos: quiet, fast-moving, dense. There are far more people than usual, and nobody is laughing; Mishima sees tight mouths, gripped fists, and urgent, low-voiced side conversations. She catches a glimpse of Roz hunched over a workstation and pauses. From her gestures and posture, Mishima can see she is sorting through a hunk of data.

"Try her," she says to Ken, nodding her head at Roz. He looks, nods, moves. "Good luck," Mishima says to his back, thinking she might not see him again.

Ken glances back at her. "You too," he says. "Call me when you can." And he turns away before she can react.

She stares after him, amazed that he still wants to talk to her. Well, sending him to Roz might change his mind about that. Not that Roz is awful; given the events of the last eight hours, Roz should be a far more pleasant companion than Mishima herself. But she is very good at painstakingly sorting input, and Mishima's not sure how Ken feels about essential, thankless work.

"Mishima!"

She looks up to see Stanislaw the statistician hurrying her way.

"Mishima, what are you doing here? I'm so glad to see you!" He throws his arms around her briefly. "We thought you were in Tokyo."

"What happened in Tokyo?"

"Sorry, sorry." Stanislaw raises his hands. "We don't know anything. Mishima! We don't know, okay? They're probably fine. We just haven't been able to get through to them."

"No contact?" she asks. They are walking together along the wide, fan-lined corridor toward the strategy department.

He shakes his head.

"Are they the only ones? I thought I saw a few more."

"Tokyo's the biggest one that hasn't checked in yet. We're still missing . . ." He blinks and glances quickly back and forth, checking the latest at eyeball level. "Glasgow, Kiev, and San José, as well as a few smaller offices, but Tokyo's the only one we'd expect to be back on already."

"Can't we call someone else in the area and ask them to walk over there?"

"We've asked Kansai and Sendai to send people, but everything's so disrupted . . ."

"How can there possibly be no comms?" Mishima asks. "Can't we . . . voice-call them or something?" Of course they can't. "Or send a—" Then she stops so suddenly that Stanislaw goes on a few paces before he realizes she's not beside him.

"What?" he asks, turning back toward her.

"A telegram. We can send a telegram! Remember? Like three security chiefs ago, oh, what was his name, the one who sent me that idiotic message during the summit . . ."

"Qasim," Stanislaw almost laughs. "He wanted to take you to his desert tent and grill kebabs for you on the bonfire! Oh, good times."

"Right, right! Remember, he was all about redundancy? He had telegraphs installed in all the major offices."

"Oh, yeah! He convinced them the cost was negligible compared to the benefit—"

"—in moments like these," Mishima finishes. "Where's ours? Does it still work? Who would know?"

"Roman, the infotech." Before he finishes speaking, they are running toward his office.

It turns out that the telegraph machine does work, although it's turned off and nobody knows how to use it. The director of the Doha office, Yasmin, power walks over while Roman, having finally found a converter for the power plug, speed-reads the manual.

"This could work?" she asks.

"Te-ó-ricamente," Roman says.

"Odds that the Tokyo machine is turned off?" Mishima mutters to Stanislaw.

There's a hum, and then a glow. Qasim the ex-security director believed in redundancy but not regression, and the telegraph has a digital terminal. Although it is connected to the original submarine line, it translates typed text automatically into code.

"How do we send to Tokyo?" Yasmin asks.

Roman is still skimming the manual at eyeball level. "There's no addressing and no operators. This is an emergency system, so it's designed to blast the message to all Information hubs on the loop."

"So potentially anyone else with a connected telegraph could overhear it?" Yasmin asks.

Roman shrugs. "Does anyone else *have* a connected telegraph?"

Mishima tries to look up the answer on Information, but even connected to Doha's giant uplink, it's slow and stuttery.

"We can send a nonproprietary message, like 'Tokyo, please respond with condition,'" Roman is suggesting, when the machine lights up and beeps. They all jump.

"What was that?" Yasmin asks.

"We're receiving," Roman says.

The first line reads TOKYO. The rest of the message needs no translation: SOS. SOS. SOS. SOS.

Mishima is moving. "Send whatever security you can spare to meet me at my crow, on the roof, ten minutes," she calls to Yasmin. "And contact the teams from Kansai and Sendai; tell them to be ready for trouble!"

CHAPTER 21

Ken's not sure that Roz has noticed he's not Information staff. As soon as his faltering self-introduction got to the point of offering help, she threw him a huge set of files and explained what she needed, and neither of them has come up for air since. At some point, Roz comes over and puts a mug of tea (red, not green, and very sweet) by his arm; at another point, somebody else refills it.

Finally, Roz taps his arm, as if he were deaf. Ken wonders if she's already said something he didn't hear. "I'm taking a break," she says. "There's free food in the canteen." Ken nods and follows her, too dazed for polite conversation. He checks the time on his handheld. They've been working for six hours straight.

The canteen is three floors down, large but sectioned off into smaller dining areas to seem less cavernous, with sand-colored walls and a casual, techie feel. There's a payscreen, but it's turned off. Free food for the duration, Ken guesses, helping himself from the heaping pot of seasoned rice mixed with okra and bits of what he thinks is lamb. He looks around for Roz and, not wanting her to think he's trying to weasel out of the work, sits down next to her at an otherwise empty table. She stops shuffling the food into her mouth long enough to ask, "You okay?" and then, "Who did you say you are, again?"

Ken shrugs, hoping to answer both questions that way. It

has occurred to him that Mishima might have suggested this work to get rid of him. He shouldn't be surprised; she's been trying to get rid of him ever since the comms fell apart. He rubs his thigh absently. "Um, Mishima brought me," he says.

"Ah," Roz says, nodding as if that explains everything. Ken guesses she's about Mishima's age, maybe a little older. Dark brown skin, black hair twisted along both sides of her head into a curl in the back. Turquoise-and-navy salwar kameez, probably what she wore to work a day and a half ago for what should have been a normal, insane Election Day. "Where are you based?"

Ken isn't sure how to answer. He remembers asking Mishima something similar and wants to say *nowhere* like she did, but doubts he can pull it off. He settles on "Tokyo," and Roz looks stricken and puts a hand on his arm.

"Sorry," she says, which Ken takes to be about the earthquake. He shrugs again and looks for a change of subject, but she has already gone back to guzzling her rice, as if she had made a faux pas and wanted to give him time to recover. He takes the opportunity to look around. If he's honest, he's hoping to spot Mishima, but in the divided, cellular dining hall, it's hard to see anyone for more than a passing moment.

"I guess the work is good for you, then?" Roz is asking. She is pinching the last grains of rice between her fingers, the rest of the plate streaked clean already. Ken is impressed.

"It's good," he says. "It's exactly what I want to do right now."

"Great," she says. "I'll see you back up there when you're ready." She nods and gets up, taking her plate with her to some recycling spot.

Ken doesn't like the work; it's painful and exhausting.

They are sorting records by hand, millions of them, and it is boring and exacting at the same time. But it is true that it's exactly what Ken wants to do, because about an hour and a half into it, he realized that the records they are sorting are the votes that came in before the system crashed.

Roz showed him how to check each record for key data points and what forgery indicators to look for, certain data fields that should look a certain way, a string of digits that he has to verify each time using a program she's rigged up. "Or anything else that looks strange," she said. He supposes they're looking for a clue, something to tell them what went wrong, what triggered the failure, or who might have done it. Maybe they want to have a partial count done by hand, since they can't trust their computer systems now. If that's the case, he doesn't understand why anyone would trust him and Roz to do it better (but then, he doesn't know Roz's reputation). It doesn't matter. He's sorting ballots, holding them in his workspace and in his head. It's almost better that they're ballots invalidated by the circumstances: no one else will ever see them or know the result that might have been.

When he realized what he was looking at, Ken's first thought was that he might learn something to help Policy1st, as though this were an incredibly realistic poll. He spent the next two hours debating whether or not it was ethical, given that he had volunteered his time and been accepted on the recommendation of a friend (or whatever Mishima was) and at the same time trying to figure out an angle that would be useful. Then he realized he didn't care. He is seeing the underskin of the election, the tiny teeth on the gears that make the machine work. He just wants to watch. What buoys him through the last stretch of his exhaustion is the knowledge that he is now a completely verifiable election geek.

· · ·

Even at top speeds, it takes Mishima's crow more than ten hours to reach Tokyo, which is plenty of time for her to decide she's made a mistake. The Sendai and Kansai teams will get there long before she does. By the time she arrives, whatever is going on will be over; she will have wasted more time traveling, and if Tokyo comms aren't up she won't be able to contribute for the rest of the crisis. In the meantime, she is staring at the intranet, where Roman has set up a dedicated space for them to stay in touch whenever the still-shaky connection allows. Most of the time, he has nothing new to tell her except that they are working on diagnostics to figure out what the hell happened to the carefully designed, presumably vault-locked voting system.

Trying to find something to do, Mishima scans through the results from the search she ran earlier on clandestine government campaigners. Ken comes up in it, which she supposes should give her confidence that he is who he says he is, but that doesn't seem to help. She looks down the rest of the list. Three PhilipMorris operatives across the globe; that Lebanese woman who works for Liberty, and another Liberty agent who Mishima doesn't know, active mostly in southern and eastern Africa; a couple of people she recognizes from 888; and a raft of stringers for 1China.

Unfortunately, there's no recent data. Everything she sees for Ken, for example, is from before she met him. Mishima cross-refs and crunches what she's got, but the patterns don't resolve. The problem, she decides, is that she's tired of working at eyeball level. She needs her privacy. Most of the seven-person security team is asleep on the floor anyway; it's not like she needs to keep them entertained. She wishes she could sleep like them. That's how you can tell they're pros. She retreats into the bedroom and shuts the door.

She is sitting on the futon, staring at movement plots, when Stanislaw pings her on the intranet.

"Hey," he says. "Can you hear me?"

"Yeah, for now it's good," she says. "What's up?"

"The Kansai team turned back. They got our message before losing connection and decided they weren't well-equipped enough to go into a security situation. We suggested they try to find some security support on the way in, cops or SecureNation personnel or something, but they didn't feel it was feasible given the total lack of Information."

"And Sendai?"

"They never left. The office decided they couldn't spare the team."

"Okay," Mishima says. "Any word on what knocked down comms?"

Stanislaw hesitates. "I'm not privy to the top-level discussions," he says.

"But?"

"But Maryam and the other techies keep saying it couldn't be done, because the system is so decentralized. It's easy to knock out, physically I mean, a server in one centenal. But everything else can be routed around it. Knock out one centenal and the system doesn't even notice. Not even the people in the affected centenal would know."

"What about a virus?"

"They say it's unlikely. Well, they say it's impossible, but I'm revising that down to unlikely, given that *something* happened. Essentially, everyone's saying it couldn't be done."

"Couldn't be done without . . ."

"Either an army of hackers or . . . someone on the inside."

With a chill, Mishima remembers Domaine's menacing hint. "Has anyone—" She stops. There's nothing she can suggest that they're not already trying. Besides, this channel isn't secure. "Stay in touch."

"As long as I can," he says.

From there on her insomnia takes a more dramatic tinge, as she imagines what they might find. A building completely empty, or full of the dead, or blown to pieces? The office she remembers humming along, making do without Information like they did after the earthquake, everyone amazed that she would come that far, with a security team no less, when they're all fine? She imagines hand-to-hand combat and stealthy file extraction, piecing together the motives of mystery assailants. She sees herself rescuing LaForge from desperate straits, her boss's boss, the one who told her to stop following the Liberty trail. In the fantasy, he falls on his knees to thank her and admits through his sobs that he was wrong. Although she still thinks that this doesn't look much like Liberty.

She closes her eyes and remembers the time after the earthquake, everyone working together in silence and frustration. She goes through the layout of the building from memory, even though blueprints and walk-throughs are available in Information archives. The vending machine corner, which fueled so many late nights. The tea stations on every floor. The unisex bathrooms, the low-ceilinged canteen, the roof access. The street outside. The café where she gave Ken her cryptokey.

Ken expects Suzuki to call him at any minute, asking where he is—no, he wouldn't do that. Suzuki never asks. He would tell Ken that there's a lot to do, time to get started.

Ken avoids looking at his messages or even checking where Suzuki is, on the superstitious grounds that it might somehow draw the man's attention. Then he remembers that Suzuki can't call him, and he can't check where Suzuki is, because Information is down.

This happens three times. In his defense, he hasn't gotten much sleep.

They're still plowing through the existing ballots. In some places, quite a high percentage of votes were cast, most of these in time zones where the first six hours of voting corresponded with the afternoon and evening hours. So far they haven't come across a single centenal where every vote has been reported; there might be a few where a high-enough percentage is in to calculate the winner without a doubt, but they haven't tried doing that, so he's not sure.

Ken is starting to get a sense for the magnitude of the problem. At first, he was thinking only in terms of winning: where Policy1st stood in the votes that had been counted, what they could do to make sure this disruption, whatever caused it, did not affect their chances. Now, though, he understands that this is not an attack on *this* vote so much as an attack on micro-democracy as a system. That idea is so scary he doesn't want to think about it.

He has gathered by now that Mishima is no longer in the building, or the country. No one told him directly, but he's overheard enough in the canteen and by the coffee machine, and from people walking by his workstation or coming to chat with Roz (a small number; she works relentlessly and doesn't encourage small talk), to be pretty sure she's on some desperate mission, probably in danger.

After that, the extra time his mind has between sorting and verifying votes is entirely devoted to intense fictional scenarios in which he comes to her rescue. She has been captured by the mastermind responsible for this election fiasco, and he bursts in with a flamethrower to release her from her chains. She's held hostage in high-level negotiations for the future of the planet, and he appears and distracts her captor long enough for her to escape. Her crow crashes, and he's the one who finds it and drags her out of the wreckage. . . . He shakes his head. This is stupid. Not only because he is sitting in an Information hub doing the most bureaucratic of Information tasks (and liking it!) and unlikely to get anywhere near whatever glamorous assignment she's on, but also because she stabbed him in the leg.

Why did she do that? He tries to put himself in her place. This enormous thing had happened. She thought he might have something to do with it. And her reaction was to stab him? Clearly, they are very different people. Granted, it was a minor wound, and she healed it afterward, but that doesn't change the fact that her reaction was mistrust and violence. What would he have done? Maybe ask her. Or try to trap her into admitting something. Not stab her.

He can't stop thinking about her.

CHAPTER 22

Information going down only worsens Domaine's suspicions. He can't check up on the people he's worried about, can't trace the movements of certain assassins and enforcers he's aware of, or check for suspicious money flows in the hours after his advid went live. He can't even get out of New York City, with four out of every five flights canceled. So, despite his worries (probably paranoid, he tells himself), he heads to one of the events that brought him here in the first place. Initially planned as a meeting of a select group of antielection organizations to discuss strategy after the election results, Domaine guesses it will now be a poorly attended klatsch of gossip, speculation, and accusations. Perhaps he'll learn something, although he suspects this election interruption has nothing to do with the people who want to interrupt elections and everything to do with those who want to win them.

The meeting is in the old Museo del Barrio, now a center for transcentenal community work that is forgiving toward antielection activists. Unfortunately, the Upper East Side neighborhood Domaine is walking through to get there is not the most salubrious. The pitiless buildings designed for the rich have been subdivided into bolt-holes for the desperate, and rats and cockroaches scuttle among the trash blown around by the stiff breeze. Normally, none of this would worry Domaine, but he is jumpy and convinced that the streets are too empty. He looks around for a public transportation crow, but of course with no Information, they are not running, or if they are they're avoiding this neighborhood, and he has no way to summon one. He is still glaring at his useless handheld when he hears the hum of an engine. A vehicle pulls up beside him. Domaine looks over. A Secure-Nation patrol scooter.

"How we doing?" the cop, or soldier, asks, leaning out the window. He's set the scooter to keep pace with Domaine's distracted walk, and it purrs with restrained power.

"Fine, officer; how are you?" Domaine responds, putting on a smile. He's trying to remember if this government subcontracts to SecureNation or not. In all honesty, he's not even sure which government jurisdiction he's under at the moment.

"Just fine," the man drawls. They continue in silence, Domaine speeding his stride and the scooter hovering beside him like a storm cloud. "Thing is," the cop goes on, "you're wanted."

"You must be mistaken," Domaine says, with utter confidence. He can't be wanted—he has an alert that tells him if any government is officially after him. His hand twitches for his handheld before he remembers that he can't prove it, not without Information.

"Reaching for something?" the cop asks, and when Domaine looks back he's holding a small plastic gun.

"Just my handheld," Domaine says, showing his empty palms. "Forgot about Information being out. So inconvenient." He manages a laugh. The plastic gun is a nonstandard weapon for SecureNation, a very bad sign. He's wondering: is this random harassment or a targeted attack? Which of the dictators, warlords, and autocrats he met with would use SecureNation to get at him?

At this point, it may not matter.

"Oh, it's not that bad," the cop says. "Not if you still remember how to operate without it."

"I remember you need an arrest warrant," Domaine says, keeping his voice light. He's not at all sure that's true in this centenal, but he wants to stall this out as long as he can.

"Thing is, I'm not on duty right now," the cop says. "Got lucky, I guess. How about we go for a ride?" The hatch for the sectioned-off rear of the scooter glides open, and the plastic gun sways suggestively toward it.

Lazy scum-searcher. "Sure," Domaine says, leaning back as if to climb in. As he lifts his leg toward the running board, he slips a small grenade out of his satchel and underhands it onto the floor of the scooter. As it hits the anti-stain cover, he pushes off the running board and sprints in the opposite direction.

The cop lets out an angry laugh. "You're only making it harder for yourself!" he yells out the open window as he closes the hatch and pulls a tight one-eighty. He's barely had time to accelerate after Domaine when the bomb explodes. The partition in SecureNation scooters is designed with precisely that sort of maneuver in mind, and Domaine knows without looking back that the cop—or mercenary, or whatever he is—will survive, but the scooter is done for. With any luck, the driver should be shaken, disoriented, maybe even concussed. Domaine turns down a side street and heads for the park, hoping to get lost in its anarchist wilderness before his pursuer can recover.

Ken sleeps under his desk, or passes out there. When he wakes up, Roz is already back to work (did she even sleep?), but when he stumbles back from the bathroom to join her, she holds up a hand. "I have something else for you," she says.

She projects a screen from her handheld so he can see it. It's a page from the intranet:

- Bogotá
  Minor unrest in outlying areas; scattered power outages
- Zurich
  Rioting over locked supermarkets
- Eldoret
  Mostly calm; growing concern
- Bologna
  Demonstrations in piazzas, tent cities starting
- Saïda
  Fisheries affected by lack of weather data, disruptions in transportation. Population calm.

The list of cities continues, scrolling down the page.

"There's no Information, so there are no news compilers," Roz says. "But we need to know what's going on out there. Information offices are sending people out into the streets and then sharing their reports over the intranet."

Ken refrains from asking what they plan to do with these reports. He doubts Information is sending riot police out in Zurich.

"I want you to go check on the situation in Doha. You get the idea from these: a few sentences is all we need, although more details would be great. And don't put yourself in any danger. Okay?"

"Sure," Ken says, wondering what it is about him that

made her think he'd make a good spy, or reporter. Maybe he's just expendable.

He's never been to Doha before, and so he ventures out onto the streets with interest. There are a lot of big office parks right around the Information compound, not many pedestrians and not much to see, which is especially boring when it's ninety-seven degrees and the sun's beating down on your head. (When were these office parks built? What role do they play in the local economy? No way to know.) For a few minutes, he feels dazed and dizzy; he hasn't been outside in two days and has barely eaten or slept. He definitely hasn't hydrated enough. Then he turns onto a street that is shaded and breeze-tunneled, and immediately feels better.

Blinking in the sudden shadow, he makes out rows of small shops; not a souq, exactly, a commercial street. He glances up, curious about how the shades operate and what they're made of, but no helpful Information annotating appears beside the dim shapes blocking the sky above. At least his translators still work.

He ducks into the first store that looks like it might sell bottled water, and gets a nutrition chew while he's at it. There are two clerks behind the counter complaining to each other about the lack of Information, one of them incessantly trying to connect on his handheld, but they don't seem unduly upset. Ken clears his throat. "Can I pay you with an Information chit?"

The clerk with the handheld holds out his hand without looking up, brings the slip of paper that Roz gave Ken up to his eyes, checks the number against something stored in his handheld. "Sure," he says. He glances at Ken's purchases and writes out a double receipt, handing Ken a copy. Ken pockets it, wondering how long it will take for the world to slip irrevocably back into paper currency.

Out on the street, Ken notes a few other people walking: a woman draped in black pushing a climate-controlled stroller, a couple of white-robed men standing in the doorway of a restaurant. (What kind of restaurant? He doesn't know. What are the favorite delicacies here? No idea.) Everyone seems calm enough. He walks for a few more blocks. Most people are going about their business. He thinks he hears an anxious undercurrent, but maybe he's imagining it. It's so quiet and normal that his antennae haven't jumped once, and the contrast with how strange it feels working without Information's net is unnerving.

Ken turns down another side street, thinking he can make a big loop in the covered area of the city, maybe even sit down and get a meal as part of his snooping before he heads back. The change is gradual, but a block or two down this street, he realizes he's in what could be an entirely different country, which would make perfect sense if Doha had different centenals like everywhere else. The people here are skinny and browner and dressed differently, the smells are spicier, and when he turns off his visual translator for a moment to check, the lettering on shop signs is different.

The mood is different too. People—mainly men, a few women in saris or waitress or nanny uniforms—mill around or stand whispering in small groups. It's not a mob, not even moblike, but Ken thinks it might qualify as "minor unrest" or "growing concern." He wanders through, trying to look like he has somewhere to be on the other side of this block, and listens.

"They are voting without us, malli."

"I can't reach anyone back home."

"Do you think the Qatari have news?"

"There must be a way to call."

"What if there's rioting there?"

"Go inside, nangi. I'll come in and tell you what I find out."

"I heard all the flights are canceled."

"What about boats?"

"Is the connection down everywhere or only here?"

"Do they know we can't vote?"

Ken's translator tells him that they're speaking Sinhala. This is enough, he thinks, he could go back and write it up ("Doha: Qatari population more annoyed than worried; foreign workers from Sri Lanka nearing panic") but he is reluctant to take data without giving some back. He can too easily imagine their situation: far from home with no way of communicating, maybe no safe way of getting back. Anything could be happening there. He circles a few more times, trying to identify someone to approach. There aren't many older people here, and there isn't a clear leader. They are bunched into clusters, maybe by workplace or by home cantenal or village. Ken picks one of the larger groups, eyes it for a few minutes, then taps the shoulder of a young guy who people listen to.

"Hi," he says.

"Hi," the young man says, and then, "Who are you?" It is not unfriendly but puzzled.

"My name is Ken. I . . ." He hesitates. Technically, he doesn't work for Information, and he doesn't want to lie. Besides, he's not sure being from Information is a good thing in this context. He doesn't want to become a scapegoat for an organization he doesn't even work for, doesn't fully trust.

He falls back on the truth: government workers might not be any more welcome than Information workers, but if he's going to get mobbed, he'd rather have earned it. If this turns out well, he might even win a few more votes for his (old?) team. "I work for Policy1st. I just happened to be here. . . ."

"Oh, yeah, Policy1st, I've heard of that government," the kid says. It sounds more polite than true.

Ken remembers belatedly that they don't have a single centenal on Sri Lanka. "Anyway, I'm visiting in the Information office, and they have a little bit of news from their offices in other places. If you want, I can go see what I can find out about your hometowns."

"Oh, really?" The youth's eyes go wide and happy, and he turns to his friends to explain. In a few minutes, most of the crowd is focused on Ken. He ends up with a list of improbably long city and town names and a couple of centenal numbers for rural areas, and promises to be back as soon as he can.

"It won't be much," he warns them. "There's only a trickle of data getting through."

"That's okay, that's okay," his new contact, Sandika, assures him. "We'll be happy to hear whatever you find out."

"Think about a way to post it or something so a lot of people can see," Ken says, and heads back toward Information.

About a hundred miles outside of Tokyo, they lose connection. Panning the camera as they fly over, Mishima can't identify any new, postearthquake damage. Crows are designed to fly at the lowest altitude possible that enables a straight line between the origin and destination, and Mishima uses cached maps to generate a flight path that brings them in over major arteries, keeping them low and for the most part hidden behind buildings. When they're in range of the Information building, she deploys the Lumper.

Small arms seemed an entrenched problem during the early twenty-first century. The invention of the Lumper changed that. The backpack-sized device uses precisely targeted magnetic force to permanently disable all metal firearms within its effective radius. It took some time to catch up with the surplus of guns in the world, but since the technology was cheaper than an AK, readily accessible, and safe (with the exception of some unconfirmed reports of bad interactions with old-model pacemakers), it eventually rendered metal firearms all but obsolete. It is still standard practice to deploy one before any security operation.

Some people say that it is the Lumper, along with improvements in body armor, that made the pax democratica of the election system possible, more than the sudden sweep of political technology or the vast Information bureaucracy. Others point out that vicious inter- and intrastate war existed long before guns came into use, and that nations still can (and do) use a multitude of other explosives against each other.

There is still concern about printed plastic weapons, although they remain far less common. For that eventuality, Mishima carries a thermal-intensity flamethrower slung across her back. Her stiletto is tucked against her body as usual, but in her right hand is a larger fighting knife, and she carries a lightweight, three-pronged sai strapped to her right leg. For distance work, she has ten shuriken, with which she is adept though not expert, tucked into a strip on the left forearm of her navy blue body armor.

. . .

Domaine is a person of resources. Normally, he would be able to reach out to contacts on five continents, some of the same people who set up the interviews for that damn vid in the first place, and find out who's after him. Now he's running blind. He was tearing northward through the park, trying not to get lost on the twisting paths, when it occurred to him to wonder how the cop found him. Under normal circumstances, this wouldn't even be a question, which is why it takes him so long to think of it. Domaine tries to fly under the radar, but if anyone wanted to figure out where he was, it wouldn't be difficult, especially if they knew what he looked like. There are vid feeds almost everywhere, as well as data on purchases, hotels, transport, comms. Except none of that is available now. Assuming SecureNation hasn't managed to reach Information when it's down everywhere else, how could they know where he was? He slows to a walk, and when he comes to the next turn, he aims himself west. That meeting at the Museo del Barrio isn't worth it, not if they know he's going to be there.

Despite the chilly temperatures, there are people in the park. Mostly runners, bicyclists, and uniwheelers, and a few families bundled in heater jackets. Domaine keeps turning to check over his shoulder, and whenever he's alone on a stretch of path, he quickens his pace. The Information vacuum works both ways: he's halfway through his revenge plan when he realizes he doesn't know the cop's name or what government he's contracted to. With no Information, the encounter wasn't recorded, there was no tracking, there's no way he can lodge a complaint or take care of it in a less formal way. And if it wasn't random, and there's no accountability, they're going to try again. He has to find some safe place to wait it out.

Ken talks his report out quickly as he walks back, and has a version ready to project for Roz by the time he arrives. He fidgets while she reads it; he can't access the Information intranet himself, and so he needs her help to comply with his promise. When he explains the situation to Roz, she listens, nods, and generates a password for Ken to access the intranet. He spends some time sorting—for a monolithic global bureaucracy, Information has a pretty crappy search algorithm—and then prints out a list, alphabetical from Anuradhapura to Vavuniya, on the old flash-printer. He can't find any information for the rural centenals; apparently, Information offices are not sending their staff that far from home.

"You don't mind if I take it to them now?" he asks Roz.

"Consider it part of your job," Roz says. "And get something to eat while you're out."

He keeps his eyes and ears open on his way there. The Qataris still seem calm, although he does hear one shopkeeper cursing Information, with a fist-shake in the direction of their compound; he doesn't know when his resupply will come in or what his prices should be.

The Sri Lankan street is mostly empty, and for a moment, Ken wonders whether he managed to navigate correctly without his Information map. But then a skinny kid, twelve or fourteen at most (is he a foreign worker, Ken wonders? Or somehow along with his family?), runs up to him and guides him to a shop with a thatched awning and a sign overhead that says (according to his visual translator) HOME TASTE.

Within the restaurant, the air is dim and rushing with overworked ceiling fans. All of the light in the place comes in through the plate window at the front, bounced off the bright pavement outside. People are packed in, sitting at tables or standing against the walls. As Ken's eyes adjust, he makes out Sandika coming toward him, hand outstretched in greeting.

"Hello, hello, you came!" Sandika says, taking Ken's hand in both of his.

"Yeah," Ken says. "So, I guess everyone's ready to hear the news? I told you, it's not much . . ."

"No problem! Everybody's happy with whatever you have." Ken hands him the printout. Sandika looks surprised to see paper but quickly recovers, taking a picture of it with his handheld and then fiddling with the projection. "Have something to eat," he suggests to Ken, motioning toward a row of earthenware amphorae in the back of the room.

Ken grabs a plate and works his way along the smorgasbord while the shreds of Information scroll slowly up the wall, improved by Sandika into a variety of fonts and colors. He can't find a seat, so he leans up against the wall with his plate as, at the tables around him, tiny cries of relief and busy hushed conversations greet the news from town after town. Ken scanned the bulletins before he came; there isn't a lot of news, but none of it is particularly bad, either. He wondered whether he should censor it if there was, and was leaning against it, but he was glad not to have to make the choice.

Satisfied, he turns his attention to his plate, heaped with rice, dhal, chicken curry, slithery fried eggs, cashew curry, mutton curry, okra curry, coconut sambal, and fried pappadam. Having just come from Chennai, he feels utterly comfortable digging his fingers into the lukewarm morass and shoveling it into his mouth. His tongue is on fire, but it's a vibrant, deep-flavored fire. Sandika appears out of the dimness and hands him a cool glass bottle. Ken downs half the ginger beer in the first swallow. It's almost as spicy as the food, but the peppering of its carbonation does something to quiet the chili sting. Sandika grins and comes back with another bottle and a small container of yogurt, which does more than the drink against the burn.

Ken feels exceedingly grateful to Roz (is she his boss now?) for giving him permission to eat. He would have done it anyway, but it's more pleasant without any underlying guilt. Although now that he thinks about it, her words could have had a different meaning. The next time Sandika comes by, Ken asks if he can get another meal to go. He heads back toward the Information compound a few minutes later with a notepaper-wrapped parcel that weighs half a kilo.

The official security people go first, disembarking rapidly from the crow and fanning out across the roof before taking the roof-access door with no resistance. Even though Mishima is not part of their team, she has worked security for Information in the past, so she has the same training and knows their weapons and drills. The team leader, Simone, didn't even question the idea of her joining the foray. Mishima is paired with a young officer named Mazen, and together they bring up the rear; not the safest place, but in this case a lot better than the front. Once they get down the narrow stairwell from the roof, the team fans out, each pair taking a different direction as the corridor branches and crosses. Mazen and Mishima are tasked with clearing a long stretch of hallway to the right of the central corridor, with conference rooms and offices off each side.

The floor has that strange silence of an office on a holiday, when the carefully designed working areas seem random and meaningless. At least there are no bodies yet, Mishima thinks. They each take a side to peer or push in the doors. Mishima berates herself for not having gone through the blueprints more carefully; she hasn't spent much time on this floor.

Mazen is a step or two ahead when she pushes at a door sitting ajar and sees a man on the other side. He's across the room, standing at a workspace, wearing dark body armor. She inhales carefully. The man is holding a katana, and as Mishima registers it, he turns his head and sees her.

For an instant, she feels, in the antiquated but expressive phrase, outgunned. But a katana is only deceptively simple: for someone who doesn't know what they're doing, they can be worse than useless. The room is crowded with servers and computer equipment, a table, and a couple of chairs, which advantages her shorter weapons. This guy is holding the sword in his right hand, perhaps a little too much in the middle of the grip. That, combined with something in his posture, suggests to Mishima that he is not an expert.

At least she hopes so as she rushes him.

As she starts forward, she lets fly a shuriken, then another. The first bounces off his facial armor as she expected—the idea is more to startle and distract him than anything else. His flustery attempt at a parry shows that she was right, that he doesn't know what he's doing. As he raises his sword, she gets lucky, and the second sharp-edged star catches him in the underarm seam of his body armor. He winces and twists to the side, and Mishima charges in.

He recovers faster than she thought he would, and has the sword in the air ready to strike. He's still swinging one-handed, but it's a katana and even a glancing blow will do some damage. By now Mishima has her sai out and ready. She doesn't feel confident enough to block and trap the sword, but she sidesteps the arc and slams the long tine of the sai down on the back of the blade, pressing it to the ground. She swipes her combat knife across the inner elbow of his body armor, opening it up and gashing the flesh beneath, then steps away, flipping the sai and slamming the stubby handle into the side of the guy's head. She keeps moving, getting some distance before she pauses, poised, to check the results. The sword is lying where he dropped it, still clattering against the tile. His body hits the floor beside it in an ungainly pile.

Mishima sheathes her sai on her leg, wipes the big knife on the guy's body armor and then slides it back into the holster on her hip, checks his stats, and slaps elasties on his wrists and ankles. Mazen pokes his head in the room.

"That was fast!" he whispers.

Mishima grins at him. "Big sword, small brain," she says, pointing at the unconscious man. She collects her shuriken, wiping down the one that nicked him in the armpit, and folds them away. Mazen is looking around the room. "You think he was guarding this?" he murmurs.

Mishima takes it in more carefully, seeing the surroundings not as obstacles but as equipment. "Could be the comms," she says. She pushes every on switch she sees, and is rewarded by a reassuring hum, but neither of them wants to stick around to see if the machines reboot themselves. Not yet.

Mishima picks up the katana, considering whether to use it or stow it. Odds are the other baddies have the same weapon (unless they're doing a ninja-turtle thing). She wastes ten seconds thinking about whether she wants to meet them on their own terms or whether there's more advantage to facing off with her own idiosyncratic combination of weaponry. But she can't leave the katana here. She doesn't know how many are in this group or where they are, and she can't risk this guy rearming if someone comes along to free him. In the end, she takes it, holding it in front of her in a mid-level guard posture, and edges out into the hallway again.

They've only checked a few more doors when they hear a crashing sound back the way they came in, and then yelling. Mazen breaks away first, and Mishima follows him and the shouting back to the main corridor, a hard right, and another hundred feet down a short passage to the right and through an open door with a melted lock. Mishima leaves some space between herself and Mazen as he charges into the room; she's still leading with the sword and doesn't want to impale him if he stops or jumps back suddenly. She shuffles into the room in a toe-to-heel formal stance, then hears the *whoosh* and *hiss* of a flamethrower and speeds up.

She finds herself in a large space, with a couple of desks facing each other in the middle and a row of doors along the back wall. Her attention is immediately grabbed by the combat. The Information security team wears dark blue body armor with complicated iridescent armbands that are near impossible to forge, so the strategic situation is obvious at a glance: four baddies against a pair of InfoSec, now joined by Mazen. Three of the bad guys brandish katanas against an Information fighter who has gotten his own flamethrower out and is waving it between them, holding them off as he backs toward the door. The other Information officer is on the floor as if he's thrown himself out of the way, right hand gripping his left arm, where the body armor appears singed. The fourth assailant stands over him with a flamethrower, a tiny wisp of steam curling from its multiorifice mouth. Mazen has paused ahead of her, and the attacker with the flamethrower is lining up to blast the security officer on the floor again.

Mishima's dojo training kicks in and she lets out a guttural yell. That's normally a stupid move in this kind of situation but now works nicely to let Mazen know she is charging past him, sword above her head. Her cry startles flamethrower guy into looking up right before she brings the katana down on his forearms. The folded steel slices through body armor, skin, muscle, and bone with a sharp squelch that is horrible and satisfying, and bites into the burning metal of the flamethrower with a thunk. The man screams.

Mishima wrenches the sword away from him. The blade pulls a spurt of blood from the deep cut in his arm, and yanks the flamethrower along with it, the sword firmly notched into the barrel. She pivots so that she's facing everyone in the room and backs away.

One of the other attackers is trundling toward her, sword raised. Mishima shakes the unbalanced monstrosity in her hands, but the katana won't come free. She is trying to figure out how to defend herself with the ugly flamethrower-katana hybrid she's holding when Mazen roasts the bad guy with his flamethrower. Body armor offers a fair amount of protection from a thermal-intensity flamethrower, but a direct hit like that is still going to burn, and the force of it knocks her assailant off his feet.

Since both the katana and the flamethrower she's holding are now essentially useless, Mishima throws the whole lot toward an unoccupied corner and pulls out her knife.

By this time, the downed Information officer—Mishima didn't bother to learn all their names; she thinks he's the tall one—is back on his feet and pressing the singed man hard, knife slashing at his arms. Mishima sees him lunge forward for a vicious stab to the thigh and then knock the katana out of the baddie's hands. Mazen has gone back to the other side of the room, but during the fighting, another pair from the Information team has charged in, and the remaining opponents are hemmed in.

Mishima drops down next to the man she disarmed, who has fallen to the floor and is trying to use his less-injured right hand to hold together the bleeding gap in his left arm, sliced almost all the way through. She pats him quickly for other weapons, tosses the knives she finds over to join the flamethrower, and starts working on a tourniquet for his bad arm.

Mazen joins her before the guy has completely passed out. "How many more?" he yells. The guy just glares at him through his body armor mask and lets his eyes roll up in his head.

"The other one said there are five of them," Mazen tells Mishima. Glancing up, she sees that all the intruders have been disarmed and are unconscious, fettered, or both.

"Which means the one in the server room," Mishima says. "Can that be right? To take this huge place?"

"They took it a while ago," Mazen offers. "These goons must be a rear guard. Although it's strange, they must have known someone would come eventually. We'll do a sweep to make sure. Once we free the prisoners, they can tell us more."

"Prisoners?" Mishima looks up, and it clicks: the doors along the back wall lead to holding cells. She had known, somewhere in the back of her mind, that the Tokyo hub had detention facilities, but they are so rarely used that she had forgotten until now. Two of the Information security officers are fiddling with the locks. She turns her focus back to stabilizing the man she maimed. They want all the intel they can get out of these guys.

CHAPTER 23

The main Information hub for New York City is in the heart of the Bronx, which seemed inconvenient for many years until seawater started to eat away at the edges of Manhattan, and then seemed prescient. Domaine gets out there on a public transportation crow, walks in, and tells the man at the front desk, "I want to see Mishima."

"Who?"

"Mishima."

A long pause while the expressionless, heavyset man blinks and swivels his eyes, presumably scrolling through an eyeball-projection of a directory. Domaine takes this as a promising sign. He's betting that Information still has some kind of internal connection going on, and the time it's taking him to search suggests this directory includes more than the New York office.

The receptionist's eyes refocus on Domaine. "Can I ask what this is regarding?" He's not expressionless, Domaine decides; the perfectly calibrated blankness is actually an expression of disdain.

"Tell her it's about . . . about what we talked about, about her team."

The guy's eyebrows go up, while the rest of his face remains frozen at disdainful.

"About the moles."

Not even an eyebrow flicker this time.

Domaine gets frustrated. "Just tell her I did it! This, this whole thing—it was me."

That, at least, gets a reaction. Turns out New York is one of the Information hubs that has holding cells. Two for one, Domaine thinks, settling into the safety of captivity.

A receptionist and a comms agent were killed in the initial assault, which, according to those in the holding cells, involved a lot more than five assailants. Everyone else is alive. Most of the upper management is crammed into the five holding cells, cramped and hungry and bruised. In their sweep of the building, the Information security team finds all the translators and grunt-work analysts locked in the translator bay, the doors fused by flamethrower.

As soon as they are out of the cells, a small squadron of techies and comms agents heads for the server rooms. Simone, the security team leader, wants them to have a medical diagnostic first, but there's a queue for that and these people have been biting their nails for the last eighteen hours, desperate to restore connection.

"That must be why they attacked here," Yelinka Korbin, pale and smelly but calm, tells Mishima. "Uplinks were still limited, since the earthquake, and there was a bottleneck here. We were hosting the municipal coalition uplink until they could get back on their feet. When they knocked our comms out here, Tokyo went dark."

"The whole world went dark," one of the security officers puts in.

Startled, Korbin glances at Mishima, who nods. "In the middle of voting. We're working on it."

"Everywhere? Then how . . ."

"The intranet is up. You guys were the only big hub that wasn't on it. Also, someone managed to program the telegraph with an alert." She pauses, looks back at the cells. "So, why did they stay? They must have known we'd get here eventually. Did they want to get caught?" Mishima wants to know how carefully she has to sift through their statements. Could they be decoys?

Korbin is still processing the news that Information is out. She seems more shaken by that than by a day of captivity, but she pulls herself back to answer. "Couldn't tell much from inside those cells. But it was silent for a long time. My feeling is, the main group left, and then this bunch came back."

"What about our security guards?" Mishima asks, but Korbin only shakes her head.

That question doesn't get answered until Simone repeats it in the formal, closed-door debriefing an hour or two later. The techies have gotten the intranet up, so the debriefing is live, although the thin connection means they're keeping it audio only. Mishima probably wouldn't even be in on the call if she weren't there in person, with the battle smell still thick on her.

It is LaForge who has to answer, and Mishima has to admit, he does it with impressive dispassion. "Due to the high costs, hiring challenges, and the prohibitive lack of capacity involved in running our own security program, we made the decision about two years ago to outsource to SecureNation."

That raises a deep murmur. The smart people are wondering whether SecureNation acted alone or was subcontracted for the attack. Mishima hears someone mangle the quis custodiet quote. Everyone's much less erudite without Information constantly at the tip of their tongues. She sees Korbin shut her eyes briefly, but whether in pain at the poor

Latin or because she's spent a day in a tiny holding cell because some idiot cut the wrong corner, Mishima can't tell. She has a call coming in on her handheld. She stands up, says, "Even a narrative disorder couldn't dream this up," just loudly enough for LaForge to hear, and walks out of the room. That was even better than rescuing him, she decides.

Ken is back to work on the ballots. Most of the thrill has faded by this point, and he is sorting mechanically, barely even registering the Policy1st votes, when Roz stands. She hasn't changed her clothes since he got to Doha, but the salwar kameez is weathering it better than his decidedly crumpled trousers and button-down.

"There's a meeting on what we're going to do with this mess," she says, waving a hand at her cluttered workspace. "Are you coming?"

Ken jumps up and follows her. He's starting to learn the building, but they are headed for a higher floor than he's been to since he came down from the roof when he arrived. He's guessing this is an important meeting.

"Um," Ken says, catching up at the coffee machine. "You do know that I don't actually work for Information, right?"

Roz takes her coffee. "Do you really think that I don't know exactly who you are?"

Ken, falling behind again, reflects that the communications drop has significantly diminished the awe in which he held Information.

"Mishima vouches for you," Roz says, turning to push the door of the conference room open with her shoulder. "That's enough for me."

Digesting that, Ken misses the first five minutes of the

meeting and looks up to realize he has no idea who the people in the room are. There are two older men, an older woman, and five people around Roz and Mishima's age, along with half a dozen projections of people teleconferencing in. The whole scene is not at all how he would have pictured a high-level meeting in the inner bowels of the menacing Information bureaucracy: ominously dim, the speakers' faces angled with shadows, the surfaces hard and polished to a high gloss. Rather, it is a conference room awash in the latest thinking on productivity and harmonious consensus. Classical Arabic music plays at the edge of hearing to promote complex thought, and the lighting is soft and variable, designed to suggest that they're sitting under a broad, spreading tree. There is even a faint breeze from time to time, bringing a hint of sea smell. Of course, it must have been ridiculously expensive, but right now, Ken is the beneficiary of this pleasant space, and it makes it hard for him to believe that the people around him are conspiring against the world. He feels instead like he's been included in benevolent discussions of global significance.

"We think we can get it back up in the next twelve to twenty-four hours," a young woman is saying. Ken perks up. He can't wait to get back on Information; this is worse than after the earthquake.

"Everything?" a projected head asks.

"Everything, but not all at once. Service will be restored in layers, and probably with geographic lags as well."

A current of resigned dissatisfaction.

"Voting?" the older woman at the table asks.

"Along with the rest of it," answers the woman. She is wearing a black tunic and loosely woven head wrap, and must be some super techie.

Ken has a sudden urge to take notes but quells it; nobody told him he was the damn intern here. He focuses on the conversation.

"Where are we on the counting?" This from a projection of a middle-aged woman with bangs who speaks with authority. She is looking at Roz, and Ken feels his face prickle with heat even though no one expects him to say anything.

"We're at about seventy percent of what we have," Roz says. "But that doesn't include what we're about to receive from Tokyo, where most of Asia's ballots were tracked for tallying. Obviously, they got held up there; in fact, that may have been part of the rationale for the attack, and for the return of a small group of assailants."

Ken, who has heard nothing about an attack on Tokyo, is drinking this in, baffled.

"That will add some time," Roz continues, "but we'll also have help from their staff. With a push, we could finish in the twelve- to twenty-four-hour timeframe. But I question whether that is the best use of our resources."

Ken can't help nodding, although he tries to do it thoughtfully rather than emphatically.

"For the moment," Roz goes on, "the results are of limited usefulness to us. We have few if any complete centenals. Incomplete centenals range from zero to ninety percent participation. We could make predictions on a few of them at the latter extreme, but not enough to get any sort of sense of the Supermajority."

"So, we throw those votes out?" asks a projection.

"Not yet," Roz says. "We're still checking through them and considering other analytical approaches to see if they can tell us anything about the methods of the attack itself. It's possible we may find something of interest. What are we going to do about restarting voting?"

It's exactly the question Ken would have asked, and he's hanging on the answer. But from the first tentative responses (". . . we could restart completely, but invalidating the previous votes seems premature . . ." "Is it necessary to restart everywhere at the same time?"), the debate is so convoluted and so far from resolution that he loses the thread again. He wonders about Policy1st's chances, and what will happen to him in the aftermath; whether Suzuki will forgive him for going AWOL, or even know about it; whether he wants to go back to Policy1st, and whether that answer would change if by some amazing chance they win the Supermajority. He surfaces when he hears someone mention territorial aggression.

"I'm just saying we don't know what's going on out there," a grizzled projection is complaining. "Other than these ridiculous bulletins, that is. Is there any way we can turn on Information for the security of the election process without making it more widely available?"

"Information is a public good," one of the older men says with finality. "It may fail for technical reasons, and we may strategize about the best technical approach to get it back up, but we will not withhold Information once it is in our power to make it available. We cannot give ourselves the power to see and leave everyone else blind."

A brief silence, and then the same projection says, "Well, then, we bring it up for everyone. I need to know what's happening so that we can respond! Centenals could already be fighting each other."

"The problem with that," another projection answers, "is that as soon as we turn Information back on, the campaigning will start again. There's no way to stop it."

Ken pulls out his notebook and pen and starts scribbling. The breeze and all are nice, but pen to paper is the only way he's going to stay focused, and he wants to catch all of this.

"It's not only the campaigning," a projected woman answers. "This act in itself, the reality that Information has been down and that we have to restart voting, will affect people's decisions."

"After a shock like this, everyone will run to SecureNation if we let them—"

"SecureNation won't be on the ballot," the woman with bangs says definitively. Ken feels his eyebrows jolt up in surprise and busies himself with his notepad.

"Well, then, Heritage. Stability, safety, trust."

"Heritage could be behind this."

"They might have won anyway; we don't know that."

"We can't delay the voting until we conduct a full investigation, it would be anarchy."

"People can't stick with their current governments for another two months?"

"We can't postpone the vote that long," Roz puts in with authority. "The most important assets for the election systems are trust and routine. Both are badly damaged already; we've got to salvage to what little is left."

"The only solution I see," says the older woman in the room, the one with blunt-cut silver hair who has said little so far, "is to restart voting without making the rest of Information available. To anyone," she adds, glaring at the unshaven projection who asked for private Information access.

There's a brief silence.

"Can it be done?" someone asks.

"Maryam?" asks the silver-haired woman, and everyone turns to look at the lead techie.

"Sure. Not instantly; we want to make sure the voting is ironclad and goes live simultaneously all over the world, but I would say we can do that within the next, say, twenty hours. Fifteen if we make it our priority."

"And then shift efforts to bringing other services online while people are voting?"

The techie nods. "That would work for us. Although of course, we'll want to keep a close eye on the voting as it goes on, in case of any further attacks, so we'll need to keep some resources for that."

"This will affect people's votes," the woman with the bangs says. "But then, I don't suppose there's any way we can avoid that."

"Not without a time machine," someone else says, and there are guffaws around the room.

"In that case," one of the projections says, "we should consider whether to use the existing votes."

Silence again. "Use them for what?" asks the woman with the bangs.

"For data. Let everyone vote this time—if we tell people not to vote if they already did, lots of other people won't get around to it either. But we'll keep the old votes and use them as a basis for comparison. We can see how many people changed their votes."

Murmuring and consternation.

"Which set do we use, though?" someone asks. "We need to decide that before the voting restarts. We can't wait to see how they're different and then decide which one we like better."

"If we use the initial votes, we have essentially two voter groups with different sets of Information."

"That's not true," a tall man answers. "Or rather, it's

always true. Voters in different places or voting at different times during the twenty-four-hour period always have different sets of Information."

"The initial votes are purer," someone else says. Ken feels, rather than sees, Roz roll her eyes.

"Purer, bullshit," the grizzled projection says. "The votes we use should all come from the same batch."

"Roz," says the woman with the short silver hair, "in your opinion, is the initial voting set uncorrupted? Could it be used, either as data, for comparison purposes and so forth, or as actual votes?"

"We haven't found any evidence that the attack on the Information servers affected the votes that were cast," Roz says. "Although I will add that's another reason not to suggest people who voted last time shouldn't revote. We can't say for sure that nothing was lost, particularly at the precise moment the comms went down. We can certainly use the initial set, although I would ask that they be run through the compiler. I don't want my team to be the only ones checking live votes." Ken is pleased to hear himself referred to as a team.

"Interesting." There is some general muttering. Ken can feel the discussion edging toward stability. His face grows hot in anticipation, but he can't let this go.

"Excuse me," he says, and immediately feels like an idiot. Everyone else jumped into the conversation so smoothly, and he practically raises his hand and waits for the teacher to call on him. They're all looking at him now, probably staring at the space next to his head where his public Information should state, at the very least, his title and name. International man of mystery, Ken thinks, and plunges on. "You can't—that is, I don't think you can keep people off Information for an extra day when you have the technical ability to give it to them. There are people out there who are away from their homes, their families, and have no way of getting in touch with them or finding out anything."

"He has a point," Roz says after a pause. "We need to consider humanitarian principles."

"We are not humanitarians," snaps the woman with the bangs. "We are bureaucrats. That said," she adds more gently, "he's not wrong. People are bound to realize that if we can manage voting, we can manage comms, and it could lead to backlash."

"We can probably get comms up and running at the same time as voting," the super techie offers. "Person-to-person calls. No news compilers, no global vision. All that is going to take more work, anyway."

Ken thinks about mentioning weather predictors for the fishermen but decides not to push his luck.

There's a what?" Mishima says into her earpiece.

"Someone here who says he wants to see you." It's the New York hub, over the intranet. Mishima tries to figure out who's speaking or picture the office, but she can't remember the last time she was there. All she can be sure of is that it was in the Bronx. "He says . . . he says he did it."

"Did what?" But she's starting to get an inkling. Mishima is tired, she's wearing someone else's blood spatter, and all she wants is to go back to Doha, ideally with a shower along the way, and see if she can figure out how to apologize to Ken. Except that there is one thing she wants more than that, which is to fix this mess. "Can you describe him?"

CHAPTER 24

Suzuki is camped outside the Information hub in Paris.

He spent the first day trying not to go crazy, checking whether Information was back up approximately every thirty seconds. The thought that he wasn't going to be able to vote was making him ill, visible hives and a pounding headache. Then the rumors started flying and he began to suspect, and then believe (although there was no way to confirm it, of course; how could he confirm it?), that Information was down everywhere.

Down everywhere. On Election Day. Years of planning, and they have technical difficulties. That makes him want to curl up in his hotel room with the lights out and his handheld set to alert him when the world is connected again and not before. He could sleep until then. Or, and the thought is seductive, he could go see the sights. Stroll the Louvre, climb the Tower, take a boat down the Seine. He could go shopping! He desperately needs a new raincoat (particularly if he's going to be stuck in Paris for any length of time) and wouldn't mind some new dress shoes, either.

Once he's had a chance to recover from the shock and set his well-oiled, slightly oily mind to work, he sees that the Information hub is the key to it all. They will get the election, and everything else, back online. They are too well-funded, too respectable, too incredibly capable not to. It is only a matter of time. And once they manage the technical hitches, they will need to come up with a new set of rules. In all probability, those rules will be designed to exclude campaigning, but in reality, they will define a new form of campaigning, one with a very short time frame. Suzuki doesn't see the powers-that-be pushing the election off for a month, three months. If they didn't do it after the earthquake, they won't do it now. It would mean admission of defeat, not to mention incredible added expense. No, they will want whatever happens to happen fast. And whoever learns the rules first will have an advantage.

So, he waits. At first he tried to see someone in the hub, but politely, not insistently, and when he was just as politely rebuffed, he left his contact details, which at this point are reduced to "the restaurant across the way," and went there to wait. At least he's getting a leisurely meal, the first in quite a few months. It looks like there's a shoe store on the corner; maybe he'll get some shopping done after all. He doesn't think so, though. This is the closest restaurant to Information, their staff must eat here sometimes, and who knows? Maybe he'll overhear something useful.

In any case, he wants them to be able to find him when they're ready.

D omaine, I don't need to fly all the way to New York for you to tell me something. Just say what you have to say."

Mishima's voice is a growl. Domaine wishes he didn't like it so much, because she's obviously not interested in him. "Two reasons I can't: one, this call is not secured, and what I have to say is highly sensitive, and two, they're not going to let me out of this holding cell unless you make them, in person. And I'd like to get out."

"You're in there for a reason," Mishima says. "Why should I get you out?"

"I'm in here because I confessed to something I didn't do. It was the only way I could get them to put me in touch with you. It's not so easy for us plebs to communicate these days, you know."

"What did you confess to?" Mishima asks, distracted. She's got the debrief audio in her other ear as she talks to him.

"This! This whole thing. Obviously, it wasn't me."

"How do I know you didn't do it?" Mishima asks, although it's a ridiculous question. "You would love to disrupt Election Day like this."

"Yes, I would love to, but first of all, I can't, and secondly, I won't love what's coming next. Neither will you. So get over here and listen to what I have to say! Come on, it's not like you're paying for the flight."

"I'm paying with my time," Mishima says. His constant digs at supposed Information privilege are starting to grate. But she already knows what she's going to do. At least she can rest on her crow. "If whatever you have to say doesn't pan out, I'm going to tell them to throw away the key."

"Accepted," he says. "And if it is good, can a man get a dinner date?"

She signs off.

The observations culled by hardworking Information lackeys all over the world keep trickling in over the intranet. Ken keeps an eye on them, and when he's seen enough substantive reports come in from Sri Lanka, he asks Roz if he can take another walk out to share it with the migrant workers.

268 · MALKA OLDER

"No problem," Roz says. "Bring back more of that take-away, okay?"

Ken lingers. "Are you sure? I know we're on a tight schedule for finishing the ballot count." It's hard to slack in the face of Roz's unrelenting work ethic.

She flaps her hand at him. "We're fine. Although I may have something else for you when you come back . . ."

Ken is preoccupied. "We can finish everything, including that new stuff from Tokyo, in the next fifteen hours?"

"They've kicked it out to twenty-four," Roz says, "to let the techies make sure that everything is absolutely as robust as possible before restarting. Also, Mishima is helping. She's traveling and apparently bored, so she offered to take some on."

That gives Ken something to think about while he walks out to Lankaland. He's relieved Mishima is alive, because he had been hearing hints that she was involved in something gnarly, maybe that attack on Tokyo they were talking about. But then it hits him that she contacted Roz, is probably chatting away as they sort ballots to keep their brains from numbing over. She's *bored*. And she still hasn't gotten in touch with Ken.

He thought he was being all adult, telling her to call him after she stabbed him, but who is he kidding? He's a sucker.

True, calling him would not be so easy right now. She probably doesn't know he's up on the Information intranet. He could send her a message.

No. He shuts that idea down right there.

At the restaurant, which is noticeably quieter now that the first rush of news has been digested, Ken sits with Sandika and some of his friends. Most of them work at hotels or other tourist-trade facilities, and they tell him about the difficulties in sending money home. Some of them love working abroad. Sandika, for one, still finds it thrilling. He meets people from all over the world, makes enough money to have spending cash after he sends some home to his parents, and he goes to a lot of parties on his off time. But for others, it has become a grind, and one that they are increasingly convinced is not fair.

"You know, Policy1st has really strong protections for citizens who work abroad," Ken starts, and then stops abruptly, embarrassed to be shilling for his government. Campaigning, in fact. He remembers, guiltily, the conversation during the meeting about campaigning during this strange interim between voting and voting.

But Sandika and the other guys seem so interested, and he can't find a good way to avoid telling them now. He tries to state policy as plainly and clearly as he can, as if he were the Information annotations alongside Suzuki's beautifully turned statements during a debate.

"So, what do you guys think about Information?" he asks as soon as he can work in a change of subject.

They look at each other. "I mean . . ."

"It's fine."

"Normal, right?"

"When it works."

They laugh.

Once en route to New York, Mishima does a mental-emotional scan. Domaine will be trying to manipulate her; she's better off knowing her weaknesses, unpleasant though that may be. She runs the diagnostic and takes a look.

Mishima's mental state appears, according to her preferences, represented as shaded, color-coded, overlapping line graphs. There's the sound the sword made slicing into the arm, a red spike; her feelings about it are a deeper, more complicated purple, wider and shallower around the red peak. The jagged cluster of sensations around the attack on the second debate is already fading into the background. Her general low-level ambivalence about Information work, on the other hand, has heightened to a strident orange-yellow color, and her anxiety about the possibility of global war is a looming grey bluff. There is a pale blue hump of sadness over the two people killed in Tokyo, both of whom she knew slightly. A small bile-colored triangle represents her gloating over LaForge's dishonor. The most dramatic peak, however, is the green of her guilt about stabbing Ken, which shades into the pulsing yellow serration of mistrust toward almost everyone. Her narrative disorder is the background palette, a bright but 85 percent transparent pink faintly patterned with lightning bolts, ninjas, flowers, sailing ships, smoking guns, and horses.

What a mess. She looks at the recommendations. A long unburdening to a close friend is at the top, but impractical for a number of reasons. Exercise is up there too, but also difficult in the close constraints of the crow. She is aware that this is the logical sequence she follows almost every time she undertakes this exercise. One of the reasons she does it as often as she does is that reliably, never first but always somewhere in the top five, she finds "unwind with premade content." License to feed the addiction. She has used this as an excuse often enough, dived into films or soaps or series or novels. Today, though—or tonight; she can't keep track anymore—she doesn't desire unreality. She wants to be busy.

She sends a message to Roz, asks if there's anything she can do to help with the vote analysis.

When Ken gets back, Roz is ready for him. She unwraps the parcel he brought, delicately avoiding the fragrant stains that have seeped through the notepaper (someone's high school math homework, apparently) as she explains what she wants.

"I've been thinking about what else we can find out from this data. How are you at analytics?"

Ken puffs slightly. "Before I hit the campaign trail, I was doing a lot of poll dissection, working alongside some of Policy1st's best analysts—"

"Okay," Roz cuts him off through a mouthful of string hoppers and brinjal curry. "This shouldn't be too challenging, at least initially. I want you to work on crunching some of the ancillary data from these votes. Start with time—the exact time, as close as we can get it—place, and government, and we'll go from there."

Ken raises an eyebrow. "Looking particularly at the votes around the time of the outage?"

Roz nods. "You can start there and work your way back. It might not tell us anything, but I think it's worth checking, since we have the person-hours."

Ken is so pleased at the thought that his presence is helpful, and so busy trying to hide his glow and stay professional, that it isn't until he's started working through the analytics that he catches the other implication of what she said, the slight emphasis: "*I* think it's worth checking." Maybe this is a private initiative, something best not mentioned to the higher-ups, at least until it's proven worthwhile.

Speaking of gossip. Ken has been hesitant about asking Roz anything, since she's so laconic and hardworking herself. But with the vote count under control and Roz contentedly munching on the last few pappadam, this seems like a good moment. "So, what did SecureNation do, exactly? I mean, why are they barred from the election?"

Roz looks up from the few remaining morsels on the notepaper, surprised. "You don't know? They were the ones who attacked the Tokyo office."

"How was the Tokyo office attacked?" Ken is careful to ask in a neutral, nonpanicked tone.

Roz leans back, thinks. "Of course. That was when Mishima left. I suppose nobody else would have told you."

Roz may not talk much, but when she sets out to tell a story, she does it properly. As she finishes eating and drinks the ginger beer he brought back for her, she lays it out for him: the anachronistic SOS call; Mishima's rapid departure with the security team on the expectation some other assistance would reach the office first; a reasonably exciting rendition of the events once they arrived.

"The men they captured haven't talked much, but everything they've said supports the hypothesis that Tokyo was attacked because of its vulnerable state after the earthquake. Also, as a regional vote collection station, it offered them the option to steal or corrupt some votes, but they may not have realized that at first. They sent a smaller group back for the votes, and our security team surprised them."

"And they were from SecureNation?" Ken asks.

"They had SecureNation badges and training, but they have all claimed to have acted without the knowledge of the larger organization. That's pretty much all they'll say. What is damning is that the security personnel in the office, who were subcontracted from SecureNation, aided or at least did not prevent the attack."

"So, there was some kind of conspiracy," Ken says. "What does SecureNation say?"

"That a group of their staff acted completely without their knowledge or approval in a heinous act that they disavow entirely. Since it will take some time to reach any conclusion in this investigation, the compromise is that SecureNation will only be able to compete for centenals it already holds. In all other centenals, they won't even appear on the ballot."

"So, they're getting away with it?" Ken's brain is filled with images of sword-wielding militiamen attacking Mishima.

"They may not have done it," Roz points out. "In the worst case, those at the top will have maintained a plausible deniability. But as you know, most SecureNation centenals— and there aren't that many; they've never been in the running for Supermajority—are made up almost entirely of military personnel and their families. What do you think would happen if we were to tell those well-armed soldiers, who incidentally control most of the remaining nukes we can account for, that on Election Day they can't vote for the only government they've ever known because of some incident most of them have never heard of?"

Ken frowns. He doesn't like to hear Information's famous neutrality being watered down for practical reasons in the face of military strength.

"Don't worry," Roz tells him. "The investigation and trial will happen, just after the election. Besides, the censure SecureNation is worried about is economic, not political."

"What do you mean?"

"SecureNation is quite small as a government, correct? Most of their influence comes from contracting their services out to other governments. So, what do you think happens if word gets around that their employees are unreliable and have a penchant for attacking the governments they're supposed to be protecting?"

"Everyone will switch to their competitors," Ken says.

Roz smiles. "Information is very good at getting word around."

Mishima finally gets a few hours' sleep and wakes up in time to eat and take a little care over her appearance. It's not that she wants to look good for Domaine; what she wants is not to look harried, desperate, or otherwise off her game. She pulls her hair into a chignon using a capilliphelic gel that draws the strands smoothly together on the outside even when the inside is a tangled knot, and puts on loose grey silk trousers with a tight matching jacket that has a million self-adhesive buttons. A light spray of oxygen and she gets off the crow looking as fresh as possible. She doesn't want to go into this feeling rushed, so she spends a little while catching up with Nakia, her closest friend in the New York hub, over coffee. Then they go to see Domaine.

The holding cell here is slightly larger than the ones in Tokyo, and nicer, although in fairness, she saw the ones in Tokyo only after eighteen hours way beyond maximum capacity. She asks for an office or small conference room, and Nakia leads them to a room with a round, plastic-finish table, four chairs, and a bleak view, and leaves them to it.

"Okay, Domaine," Mishima says. "I'm here. Spit it out."

He takes his time, looking her over. He's lost some of his brashness; being without Information has been hard on him too, especially while locked up. On the other hand, he exudes a kind of righteousness, the conscious nobility of a bad boy who's stepping away from his persona to consider the greater good, a little Judd Nelson in *The Breakfast Club*. It's cloying. She half-expects him to break into a riff about how this is a far, far better thing he's doing now.

"I don't have too many details, and maybe you won't think it's worth your while to have come. But I couldn't take the chance. Being in the business I'm in, you hear things."

"Hear them where?"

Domaine shifts. "Look, I'm piecing stuff together here. There have been . . . hints, shall we say, in the circles in which I move. People laughing when they shouldn't be, or making 'offhand' comments that didn't make any sense until now. But"—he puts his hands up as Mishima prepares to stand—"I do have something more concrete, okay? I'm just telling you that there have been multiple indications."

"Where does this concrete something come from, then?" Mishima asks when Domaine doesn't go on.

"In this case, from funders. A funder." He hesitates, then names a music star. He's already got half a dozen warlords after him; no point in worrying about a pop singer.

"And?"

"And this funder, among others, supports my cause but also other, rather more, um, opportunistic ones."

Mishima refrains from commenting. She supposes Domaine does see himself as selfless, and it's true he probably wouldn't get much directly from toppling the global order.

"So, I hear things. Now, I don't know what's happened in the last thirty-six hours, I have no way of knowing, right?" Mishima is not ready to concede that. There may be open comms that she doesn't know about. But she nods to keep him talking. "But I'm fairly sure there's been an attack on one or more Information hubs. They would be places where regional votes are compiled. The attackers would have disabled the comms, maybe stolen or corrupted votes, and disappeared. Not many casualties, if any, because they don't want you to focus on finding them but to keep reacting to what they're doing."

"Go on," Mishima says.

Domaine leans forward. "It was an inside job," he says. She doesn't react. "Some Information offices have been outsourcing their security, and that security is compromised."

"So?" Mishima says.

"So, what? Am I right?"

"Whether or not you are," Mishima shifts her position, as if impatient, "you're still talking about the past. How does this help me?"

He eyes her. "Knowing that it's an inside job? I would think that would be very helpful."

"Very," Mishima says, standing up. "And we already knew it."

"All right," Domaine drawls. "So, you are aware that SecureNation is not reliable. Do you know who hired them?"

"Why don't you tell me what you think you know, and then we'll see how useful I think it is?"

Domaine blows air through his nose. "Fine. Since you came all this way . . . the funder I'm talking about, she didn't put any money toward this. But she likes to think she's a radical, hangs out with geeks and mercs, you know what I mean? When we talked last week, she said that we had one more reason to try to crash the election system, because if we didn't, they would do it for us."

"They who?" Mishima is getting impatient.

Domaine clears his throat, looks down at the table, up at the corner of the room, plays coy. "A major government." Mishima glares at him. He sighs dramatically: can't she figure anything out herself? "Heritage."

Mishima shakes her head with more conviction than she feels. "That makes no sense. They have the most power. They were likely to win again. Why would they take that kind of risk?"

"Maybe they would win, maybe they wouldn't," Domaine says. "But after the earthquake, their numbers went shaky and they panicked, started putting out feelers to the kind of people who could do this kind of thing. And some faction of SecureNation was willing."

"Still risky," Mishima says skeptically.

Domaine shrugs. "Power corrupts, and once you get cozy with the Supermajority, you don't want to let it go. Anyway, I made much the same argument in casual hypothetical conversation to said donor, and she told me that it's not only the SecureNation subcontractors: they have someone at Information facilitating things."

"Which, let me guess, is why you have to topple Information, the evil oppressor, blah blah blah," Mishima finishes for him.

"It's true; I would take it with a grain of salt," he admits. "Especially because she did go into a long and borderline narrative-disorder rant at that point. Also, as I think I may have expressed to you before, a Heritage win is Information's worst nightmare. Which is what I said to her."

"I take it there's more?" Mishima asks when he pauses.

"I'm trying to help you here; just let me tell the story. So, she says I'm right. Information doesn't want Heritage to win; they're trying to boost their competitors, or shield them, or somehow tilt the oh-so-fair playing field. Certain individuals within Information think this is wrong and are willing to do something about it."

Mishima doesn't want to show anything, any surprise or interest, but it takes her a fraction of a second to file that statement next to Korbin's analysis of her Liberty report before she goes on. "So what are they doing about it? Comms down in mid-election, an attack on an Information office—what's the endgame?"

Domaine rolls his eyes. "Winning the election, of course. Knocking comms out gives them the opportunity to manipulate votes. Or so I understand it."

"How?"

"I have no idea, Mishima. It's not my plot. I heard someone famous talking about it, and I'm cobbling that together with hints and impressions and cackling self-congratulatory cryptic messages that I've been a party to over the last few weeks. That's all."

Mishima studies him. "Why are you telling me all this? You should be dancing for joy that the election was disrupted."

"I hate your stupid pseudodemocratic infomocracy, true," Domaine agrees. "But I would hate a corporate dictatorship manipulated by the military-industrial complex even more." A pause. "So. How about dinner?"

She stands up, this time without pretense. "You're lucky I'm not telling them to throw away the key."

Mishima enjoys the faint panic in his eyes at that and adds that to the bile-green peak of self-disgust. "You're going to leave me in here? I told you I didn't do this."

"I'm going to check out your intel. If it's good, we'll see about letting you out." She pauses at the door. "I'm also having them do a cross-ref in case there's anything else you should be in here for." She pauses to watch him consider the possibilities. "Like the debate attack."

Domaine leans back, relaxed again. "I had nothing to do with that. I don't run with Anarchy."

"We'll see," Mishima says.

"An onsen full of witnesses will put me in a hot spring during the entire debate. No tech on me at all."

"Very convenient."

Domaine shrugs. "What would you do with a night off in Kansai? You can check it out as soon as Information comes back on." Which is about when he wants to get out of here, anyway.

Mishima is continually amazed by the faith people seem to have that Information is coming back on, any second now. She hopes they're right. She walks out, and a security guard slides in the door before it falls closed to escort Domaine back to the holding cell. In that brief interim between Mishima turning her back and the guard appearing, Domaine manages to palm a coin-sized metallic disk out from under the table, where it has been clinging magnetically since he slapped it on at the beginning of the conversation.

CHAPTER 25

Mishima thanks Nakia for her invitation to dinner but refuses. She leaves the building and walks, directionless. The neighborhood around the Information office is windswept and grey, long roads and difficult intersections lined with garages and parking lots and little of interest. It's built for cars, not pedestrians, and she should take her crow and find a restaurant with moorings, but she keeps walking. She needs time to think.

When Domaine talked about vote manipulation, she couldn't help seeing Roz at her workspace, sorting votes as though with a fine-tooth comb. After a little due diligence, she is happy to discard that suspicion. Her role in analyzing the early votes was an ad hoc decision, not something anyone could have planned for. Mishima saw most of the process on the intranet while she was flying from the Adapted Maldives. It was not surprising, because she's good at that type of work, but not guaranteed. And she didn't volunteer for it. Besides, she knows Roz. Not enough to swear she wouldn't betray them, but enough so that when combined with circumstantial evidence, she can feel comfortable trusting her.

Even so, she hesitates to go to her first. Go to anyone in Information first. There are too many overlapping alliances. Which leaves one perfect (too perfect?) option.

. . .

Ken is working next to Roz when his intranet screen blinks and shows him nine blank spaces. He scrambles up and mumbles something to Roz and takes his handheld into the bathroom. No one else is in there, but he immediately realizes it's a stupid place to talk anyway, so he leaves and goes to the only other place he can think of: right outside the front door of the building. It's not that people never enter or leave, but you can see them in either direction for a few seconds before they arrive, and he's pretty sure no one can manually eavesdrop without him noticing. He types in Mishima's code.

"Hey. Can you talk?" is the message. It's in English this time, not kanji, and Ken wonders if she's realized that he doesn't read Japanese and his visual translator's default setting is off. Whatever. He initiates the call.

"Hi," Mishima says. She looks kind of pale, but maybe it's the lighting. A streetlamp, he thinks. She's wearing a scarf and a knit hat, her ruddy hair loose beneath it. It's winter wherever she is, and night. Good, he's narrowed it down to about a quarter of the globe. "How are you?"

"Fine," Ken says. "How are you?"

"Okay," she says, but as though it's a placeholder rather than an actual word with meaning attached. "How's it going with Roz?"

"Fine," Ken says again, but more warily this time: Mishima's been talking to Roz, after all.

She hesitates, and there's a kind of motion that Ken interprets as her stamping her feet against the cold.

"Are you outside the Information office doors somewhere?" he asks her.

"Yeah," she says. "You, too?"

"Yeah." He stretches his arm out to show her. "Hot out here. At least the overhang gives me a little shade."

She makes a sound in her throat; he can't tell over the crappy connection whether she's laughing or growling at his taunt.

"So?" he says. "What's up?"

She hesitates again. "I've just gotten some intel," she says finally. "The source is . . . a little doubtful, understand? But he says that there's a double agent within Information."

"A double agent?" Ken is intrigued. That would imply that there are single agents.

"Someone who's working against the election process." She sighs. "For whatever reasons."

"So, they knocked the comms out, and the voting . . ."

"This is part one, apparently."

"You mean this whole crisis of communications, the technical issues, all of it—"

"Are a way in. A way to open up a little space to maneuver, maybe have a window of greater authority, or to cast some confusion around the voting, let it be manipulated."

"So, they're working for a government," Ken says.

She looks at him questioningly.

"I mean, not trying to overthrow the system, which is what this kind of looked like at first, but trying to decide the outcome."

"Yeah," Mishima says. "Something like that." Of course that's why Domaine was willing to pass on the intel: their goal is not his goal.

"Who are they working for?" Ken asks.

Mishima hesitates again. "The thing is," she says, "I don't know whom I can trust within intel."

Ken feels a sudden sinking in his guts. "You don't think . . . Roz . . ." He wants to reject this idea himself, immediately, but he makes himself consider it.

"I don't think so," Mishima says quickly. "I'm almost sure not. But . . . what do you think?"

"I agree," Ken says. "She seems solid. And cares about her work."

"Yeah." Mishima sounds relieved. "But still, before I went to her, I wanted to check with you. And . . . I thought maybe you could help me try to figure out who it is. The double agent."

This is almost as good as rescuing her. Ken doesn't want to sound too eager, though. But then, before he can stop himself, he starts to laugh. "So, what you're saying is, two and a half days ago, you stabbed me in the leg because you couldn't trust me, and now I'm the only one you can trust?"

Mishima doesn't join his laughter. "That's about the size of it," she says. Then, with a flash of anger directed somewhere off in the direction of the streetlamp: "Why do people always expect you to trust them? With all the shit that goes on in this world, I don't know why anyone expects my trust just because they are unverifiably, according to themselves, a nice guy. Who the hell defaults to trust?" Then she brings herself back and meets his eyes again, across the thousands of miles of distance and unreliable stream of encrypted-then-decrypted data packets. "About the stabbing, though. Ken, I'm really sorry about that."

"It's okay," he says, and this time he means it. "I've thought about it, and I see why you were suspicious. I'm not saying I would have acted the same way, but—you know, it's okay."

"It's not okay," she says. "But thank you."

"It is okay," he says. "You didn't hurt me. Not, um, for more than a few minutes, anyway. My leg is fine. I'm fine. Someday, we'll joke about it."

She doesn't believe the last bit, but even so, she feels the bright green mountain of guilt inside her subside a little. "So, I do have sort of a plan. It has to do with those votes."

"Oh!" Ken says. "You know, in the meeting about restarting voting—"

"You were in that meeting?" He must have seriously impressed Roz.

"Yeah, well, Roz brought me along." Ken is tempted to tell her about his contribution to world peace through restored communication but restrains himself. "Anyway, there was someone who talked about keeping the initial votes, for data and comparison purposes."

"Who?" Mishima asks, suddenly sharp.

"I don't know," Ken says. "They weren't showing any public Information. I guess no one is these days. Roz will know."

"Yeah," Mishima is thoughtful. "Okay, here's what I'm thinking. We'll doctor up a batch of fake votes to replace the initial votes, keep careful track of the exact distributions, then leave that in place of the real ones for the duration of the election. If anyone switches them in, we will be able to prove it's a fake quickly and, hopefully, nail whoever switched them."

"Okay," Ken says. He has no idea how to create fake votes.

"I'll get started and then I'll send some samples to you and Roz to build on. At the same time, I'm going to try to track this person, whoever it was who said that in the meeting, see if they're a likely mole and what I can find out."

Ken wants to tell her to be careful but bites his tongue in time.

"I'm going to need you to lend Roz your handheld," Mishima goes on, "so we can use this secure connection."

Creating those encryptions is complicated, and she doesn't feel like giving this one out to another person right now, even someone she trusts.

"Hey, Mishima," Ken says, and instantly feels awkward. This may be the first time he's said her name to her face. "You said that you were working on Liberty too, right? You still don't think they have anything to do with this?"

"Not this," Mishima says, "but that doesn't mean that they're not plotting something. I'm working on that, too. In fact . . . if you have time, we need to map out existing Liberty centenals and highlight the ones that might be, um, aggressive. That will give us a head start on where to look, because when Information comes back on it's going to be . . ."

"Overwhelming," Ken says, caught up in the sudden image of once again having real-time access to the sum of the world's knowledge.

"Exactly. But don't take too much time on that. The election is the priority. I don't know how we're going to figure this out before the voting starts again."

"Why before the voting starts again?"

"The fake votes are a last resort, although we'll need to have them ready. It would be better to figure out what government is messing with us before anyone votes again. We can't disqualify a government once the election has reopened and people have voted for them. I don't know how many times we can restart the whole thing before we lose credibility." She sighs. "I wanted to get back to Doha, but with the timing, there's just no point. We're going to have to do it by secure calls and hope no one notices and manages to decrypt them."

She does look pale, Ken decides. And sad. "We don't necessarily have to figure it out before the election starts," he says. "Look, they're only going to try to change the outcome if they're losing. If we can stop them from changing it, they still lose. If they are going to win anyway . . ."

"It's going to be tough to deal with a Supermajority government that planned to but didn't have to sabotage the vote," Mishima finishes.

Roz is quiet for a few moments after Mishima tells her what Domaine said, withholding, as she did with Ken, any mention of Heritage. "I've been working on something here too," she says finally. "Analyzing the last votes that were cast—Ken's been very helpful, actually. Slicing down to the picosecond, we've found a couple of interesting things. First, the origin point for the virus is the Tokyo hub."

Mishima digests that. "Could it be because the infrastructure there was weakened by the earthquake?"

"Possibly," Roz answers. "I passed it on to Maryam—you know she's leading the restoration work? She says the data is too corrupted to be sure, but she is going to recommend that the investigation start there."

The investigation to find the spy inside Information. There is an uncomfortable silence, Mishima thinking back to the absorbed, companionable days and nights after the earthquake. "There's something else, though," Roz goes on at last. "The virus started in an Information hub. But that hub going blank shouldn't affect voting, right? Almost immediately after Tokyo is knocked out, voting goes dark in the Heritage centenals several hundred picoseconds, almost half a nanosecond, before it is cut off in other governments. Once it gets into government systems, it is the Heritage repeaters that go out first and spread it fastest."

"Meaning?"

"Again, Maryam says it's suggestive but inconclusive. It

could be that the virus was designed to spread through Heritage centenals, that someone was trying to shut down the Heritage centenals to knock them out of incumbency, but when that many repeaters went out, it crashed the whole system."

"Or?"

"Or Heritage engineered the outage and purposely lowered the defenses on their systems to let it spread faster."

"Your instinct says that's what happened?" Mishima asks.

Roz nods. "Maryam thinks so too, though she doesn't have anything to prove it."

"My informant also pointed to Heritage."

They are silent for a moment. "So, about the votes . . ." Mishima starts.

"You know," Roz says, "at the meeting on voting, someone talked about keeping the votes. It bothered me because it wasn't one of the initial strategies, and it puts me in a complicated position."

"Ken mentioned that," Mishima says. "Who was it?"

Roz is silent again, replaying the meeting in her head. "Drestle. Do you know him? He works in the Paris hub."

"I know who he is." Mishima thinks. "He worked for a government once, didn't he?"

"Public affairs officer with Heritage. Left a while ago, seven or eight years, maybe."

"Maybe not long enough," Mishima says. "I'm heading to Paris."

Mishima is glad to leave New York. It's a big office, but in terms of the election, it's a backwater. Still, she finds herself unusually reluctant to climb back into her crow. Another seven hours of spotty connection and fretting. At least it gives her time to prepare their play with the votes. And think up a reason for being in Paris. Still, it's almost enough to make her wish the mantle tunnels were already running.

The mantle tunnels. Not quite approved before the election. Would that make the risk worth it to Heritage? Another thing to think about during the trip.

After talking to Mishima, Roz goes back upstairs and beckons Maryam from her tech lair.

"How's it going?" she asks when they're alone in the corridor. Roz and Maryam have been friends since Maryam moved back to the Doha office a year ago, and usually manage to go out for dinner or karaoke at least once a month.

Maryam is wearing a knee-length black tunic, black trousers, and a loose-woven black silk head wrap, all of which have held up well in the three days of nonstop work since the election was interrupted. The strain is starting to show in her face, though. "We will make the deadline, but it'll be close. Japan's still not pulling its weight—not their fault; they're reeling—and I think everyone in Sydney has decided to go home and get some sleep—" She stops, shaking her head. "Sorry. It's just— People keep asking us how this is possible: 'Why are there security gaps?' 'We thought you made everything more robust after the earthquake!' I don't understand how these high-level officials can still believe it's possible to make technology fail-safe!" She throws up her hands. "Anyway. We'll be fine. And you? How's the vote counting?"

"Oh, we're done with that," Roz says, and hesitates.

"So, you're preparing for the crazy possibility of using them?" Maryam snorts, and Roz nods with a grimace. "By the way, who's that guy you brought to the meeting? Is he a specialist from another office?"

Roz smiles. "No, not a specialist at all. Someone Mishima brought in. Not even Information. He works for Policy1st. But he's good, and he's around. He works hard and doesn't ask too many questions."

"Qualities worth having," Maryam agrees. "So, what's up, habibti?"

Roz lowers her voice. "I've gotten more intel that points at Heritage. A dodgy source but pretty specific. What are you finding?"

Maryam shrugs. "Nothing since we talked. We'll see. The forensic team is still looking for something conclusive."

"I'm curious," Roz says, her eyes on the open door of the tech lair, "what is going on in Heritage centenals right now." She leaves a brief space, but Maryam doesn't say anything. "In the meeting yesterday, they were clear about not limiting Information access to ourselves."

"They were," Maryam agrees.

"But I was thinking, for technical reasons, to enable you to do your job in there, you would probably have to . . . I don't know, test it."

"We are," Maryam confirms in a low voice. "It's still very weak. Right now, we're only looking at some patchy stuff here on the peninsula, and with the focus on getting voting back up, it's going to take a while. But yes, we will have Information access before anyone else. It's not that we're intentionally keeping it to ourselves; it's just part of the process of bringing it back up."

290 · MALKA OLDER

"Will you keep an eye on Heritage centenals for me?"

Maryam nods sharply. "Although if they did sabotage their centenals on purpose, they may take longer to come back on line."

"Understood," Roz says. She sighs, shifts to a more personal register. "How are you holding up?" Long distance is hard enough, but without private comms, it must be awful.

Maryam looks down at her hands. "I am too busy to think about it much, but . . . we're both under a lot of pressure, so it's not exactly going well. How are you doing?"

Roz stretches, sniffs at her underarm. "I think I'm going to take an hour or two and go home to change. Can I bring you anything from the outside world?"

Maryam's laugh turns into a sigh. "We have plenty of caffeine and calories, so no, I can't think of anything. I'll sleep when the voting is over."

Mishima works on the votes for a while in her crow, occasionally looking down at the cold Atlantic skimming under the camera. She's building a program to generate and tabulate the false votes. It's a simple program, but she tests it carefully with a number of different small-scale scenarios. They don't want any glitches.

When she can't stare at fake votes any longer, she looks at the Liberty centenal map Ken sent her within an hour of their conversation. It is sobering. Stealing the election seems awful, an affront to micro-democracy and Information and everything her life has stood for over the past five years. But—as visible in that undulating ambivalence line in her emotional profile—she knows that a change in Supermajority wouldn't make that much difference to the lives of most people. She knows that neither elections nor Information are neutral, that subtle changes in where centenal boundaries are drawn would lead to completely different outcomes, and that as much as they try to balance it, Information workers end up transmitting their most minute preferences and prejudices through the subjective choices of their work. And she casts her lot with them anyway, because she can't think of anything better. If she were the one to choose the quote that is found above the entrances of Information offices worldwide, it would be the one that says democracy is the worst system, except for all the other ones.

Information can get so overwrought that sometimes, she wants to take the whole organization and shake it, shake everyone in it and all of their huge, locally contextualized, beautifully designed buildings. Yes, they are right on principle, but democracy is of limited usefulness when there are no good choices, or when the good choices become bad as soon as you've chosen them, or when all the Information access in the world can't make people use it.

Thinking about war puts it in a whole new perspective, though. That would destroy the system, bring the pax democratica crashing down, open the door to every opportunist and violent nutcase and wealthy megalomaniac out there.

And even before accomplishing that, war would destroy everyone in its way. The people whose centenals are highlighted in turquoise on the globe Ken sent her, and the people in the centenals next to them. She skims it quickly, highlights a few that Ken missed, possibly not aware of the political tensions in those regions. She hesitates over two that he highlighted in Naha, because there is so much distance and ocean between them and the Japanese nationalist centenals and territory that would be their target, but Ken left a note that the rhetoric has been high there.

Then she leans back and watches the globe projection spin slowly, superimposed over the screen image of rushing ocean below her. She's been to many of these places—if not the Liberty centenal itself, then the city or the general area—and she tries to visualize them, put herself in each, briefly. What will they do?

She wonders if SecureNation made a deal with both Liberty and Heritage, hedging their bets, taking all they can get. Or maybe Liberty has hired one of the other purveyors of force, YourArmy or LesProfessionnels or a smaller, more specialized one. It's difficult to imagine them transporting a sufficient quantity of soldiers and weapons into each of these far-flung centenals. That logistical difficulty, along with the reduced importance of landmass in geopolitical power dynamics, has always been one of the safeguards of the system. On the other hand, maybe this comms blackout is letting them do exactly that. And most centenals have little or no military readiness other than a contract with one of the armies, which won't do much good if that army is the one attacking them.

There is one thing that has always bothered her about this problem. Liberty hinted at aggression against nation-states, an anachronistic idea that, within the election system at least, no longer exists. She wants to think that this is a sign that it is an empty threat, that they are targeting older voters for whom those old associations still ring strong. But then, those may be exactly the people who pose the greatest threat to the system: the people who can still remember, with rancor and longing and the inevitable distortions of time, what things were like before.

CHAPTER 26

The Paris Information hub has, against all economic sense, clung to a place in the city itself. Although Mishima has been there several times, without the benefit of Information navigation she still has to circle twice before she finds the right rooftop, tucked into the densely packed, finely aged buildings in the fifth arrondissement.

Of course, the first person she sees coming down the carpeted, gilded stairwell from the roof, while she is still rubbing her eyes and worrying the knots in her plan, is Drestle. He is a tall man with an unhealthily large gut and thinning, glossy blond hair that he lets wave down to his chin.

"Mishima! To what do we owe the pleasure?"

"Drestle, hi," she says. "I'm following up on a lead from one of my informants about some Preelection Day campaigning. Figured I'd take care of it during this enforced hiatus."

"Wow, I thought they'd have you busy with more important things," he says. His tone is pleasant.

"Oh, they do," Mishima says, with as much wryness as she can manage, "but all of that I can do anywhere. I'll tell you a secret: traveling without Information access is actually great for productivity."

He chuckles and walks on.

. . .

R oz is aware from the general timbre of the building's hum and from overheard conversations that the techies are losing their voices and straining their sanity to finish new security measures before voting restarts, so she is surprised when she looks up from the fake votes to see Maryam gesturing to her. Roz's workspace isn't sound-shielded, so she follows Maryam up to the roof. She had forgotten the time of day, and when they step out onto the terrace, she blinks her eyes at the low sun and has to remember which way is east before she can decide that it's mid-morning rather than late afternoon. It's already hot enough to ensure no one else will come up there, but Maryam brought a parasol with a solar-powered fan attachment, and standing under that in the narrow shade of the arbor the temperature is bearable.

"How's it going?" Roz asks.

Maryam nods. "We are flat out, but we'll make it. The team is doing amazing stuff." Her voice is hoarse from talking out commands and code. Roz has heard that some members of the team are switching back to typing interfaces to give their raw throats a rest.

She must have something significant if she has taken time out to come by. "What are you seeing?"

Maryam fidgets. "As I thought, Heritage centenals are the hardest to bring back online. Something happened to a large number of Heritage repeaters, and we—I, really—suspect that it's hardware-related. But hard to say without at least a virtual inspection. And we should really be on the ground."

"Have you asked for a security team?"

"In process," Maryam answers. "As I was saying, Heritage is hard to bring back up, so we don't have much intel from their centenals. But I wanted to tell you what we are seeing." From her voice, it's already clear that it is nothing good. "There's a fair amount of unrest out there, across a range of governments. We've seen five or six riots, and at least a dozen places where people are preparing for violence—gathering weapons, organizing militia. And that's only in the limited areas where we have eyes and ears—maybe fifteen percent."

"Have you reported that up?" Roz asks, uncomfortable at the thought of deciding what to do about this.

"I told Nejime," Maryam says. "She can handle al-Derbi." The man who was so forceful about Information for all. "She understands it's a technical issue."

"I wonder if Heritage could be liable for damages," Roz muses. "If we prove they were behind the outage, I mean."

Maryam laughs. "I'm just a coder, habibti; I have no idea about the law. But speaking of Heritage, Nejime agrees that we need to know what is going on in their centenals and so, erm . . . we were wondering if we could borrow your intern."

Ken is working on the fake vote database, expanding, embellishing, and keeping careful track of what the correct computer analysis should show. "We have to have enough Heritage wins so that it's worth their while to take votes from here," Mishima cautioned. "So, we need a smattering of additional centenals going their way, not enough to make it too obvious." He's also running further analytics on the real votes, trying to dredge out further intel about exactly how the voting ended.

With the increased volume of work, Ken has reduced his Lankaland visits. Instead, he takes his brief breaks within the Information building, frequenting the common spaces where people go to take time off or hold informal meetings.

There are coffee machines, a fridge full of artificial beers and a couple of off-brand sodas not affiliated with any government (running low at this point, with deliveries complicated by the Information outage and everyone too busy to go out to get more), teakettles (nuclear-powered, so Ken's put his tea habit on hold), marijuana infusions, and a vending machine with energy chews and packaged snacks. Ken prefers the fried foods and sweets sold by a Lebanese woman in the lobby.

Hanging out around the building has also helped him plug in to the Information community. The partitioned canteen doesn't promote mingling, and people are much more social in the break areas. It is from listening to this chatter that Ken is aware of at least three other individuals or groups who are also playing with the votes, trying to figure out what went wrong, or fail-testing the new model, or trying to find the perpetrator, like he is. Most of them still view him with suspicion, glancing sidelong at him when they meet him in the corridor or when they come to Roz for raw data.

Thinking about what Mishima said, he can't blame them for not trusting him. He came out of nowhere, he doesn't work for Information—he doesn't even know if he's getting paid for his time; probably not—and here he is, working next to Roz, accompanying her to the scary meetings. But as the staff get increasingly overworked and caffeinated, they are getting more gregarious too, and Ken has probably introduced himself or been introduced to a dozen people. He is sitting on the fringes of a group in the third-floor lounge, muttering to his vote database while he listens in on gossip, when Roz and Maryam find him and take him to Nejime's office to tell him about his next assignment.

. . .

Suzuki is rationing the last drops of his sixth coffee—two crèmes, and then four espressos when the milk started to weigh on him—when he sees someone come out of the Information hub front door. He'd been starting to think that they had some kind of underground tunnel system to get food in and out.

It's a slim woman wearing a silver grey rain cloak with a voluminous hood. It hits tailored and flowing in all the right places, and manages to look dramatic and understated at the same time, as if she stepped out of a century, past or future, where this is everyday wear. Suzuki is half-rising in his seat, wondering whether to follow her, when she turns into the overhung entrance of the restaurant. He settles back down and watches her push back her hood, revealing shining dark-red hair. She pulls off the gloves magnetized to her sleeves and removes her cloak, revealing first the left side, then the whole of a peacock green dress in tight, shining panels. She hangs the cloak and perches herself gracefully on a seat at the bar, orders a glass of Bergerac.

Suzuki knows her; he's seen her before around the election way. He doesn't know her name, and he's not sure exactly what she does. He tips the last of his coffee into his mouth.

Mishima waits. When she found Suzuki's note languishing on the Paris hub message space, she had to wonder whether it was a coincidence that he was in Paris. But why would he be waiting in a restaurant, leaving messages at the reception, if he's already on the inside? She goes to the restaurant dressed to be noticed: if he avoids her, he's already got his in. But she's barely touched her wine before he's sliding in beside her.

"Nice evening," he starts, though it isn't.

She looks him in the eye. "What are you doing here, Todry?"

He's slick enough to laugh. "Stuck here like everyone else, I guess," he says, genial, all politician. "I was here for an event, and—well, you can imagine."

"There are still some flights running," Mishima points out. "And Policy1st must have a crow you could use."

"What's the point in going somewhere when I have no Information about what's going on anywhere?" Suzuki motions to the waiter, indicates that he would like one of whatever Mishima's drinking.

"True enough," Mishima is trying to see him without thinking about the way Ken sees him, looks up to him. A mentor, a patron. She has to work hard to look at him without wanting to poke every hole she can in that pedestal. "And what would you be doing if you did go somewhere?"

"Oh, just preparing the ground, you know." Suzuki gestures airily. "It's frustrating; we should be governing already. Instead, our centenals are all on their own."

The restaurant, which was almost empty during the afternoon, is starting to gather clientele and fill up with expansive French phrases and expansive French people leaning back in their chairs, arms spread. From here, it's hard to see the global economic crash that some predict as a certain consequence of this Information outage. "And you were thinking you might be on the cusp of winning the Supermajority," Mishima says, her voice low.

Even with the alcohol hitting his caffeinated veins, Suzuki knows he has to be careful here. "We assumed nothing," he says. "Of course, we were pleased with the way things looked, but it would have been an amazing development. Amazing."

"Indeed," Mishima says. "Revolutionary."

"But this thing has happened," Suzuki says, and he bangs his hand on the bar, but with a muted thump. "We know, we all know that things cannot pick up where they left off. Voters don't work that way. We are losing voters every second as their courage to do something different fades. We were already at a disadvantage. And you? What will you do to fix this?" He has forgotten himself, and he turns his glowing eyes to meet hers, so righteously furious that she feels the shock of it across the dim air between them.

She doesn't blink. "Is that why you kept campaigning— illegally—after the campaign ended?" Mishima touches her handheld, and the projection of his anti-Liberty advid animates, tiny and silent, on the bar.

He deflates so suddenly, she puts a hand out behind him in case he slumps off his stool. "We had to get it out there. We had to get it out in time."

One of the advantages of people thinking Information is all-knowing, Mishima reflects, is that they rarely ask you how you got your intel or suspect your informant. "You could have given it to us."

He shrugs, mutters, "Didn't think you would do enough with it."

"Your illegal advid didn't make much difference either," Mishima comments.

He looks up, suddenly eager again. "How do you know? Do you have the results?" Then: "You're not going to disqualify Policy1st, are you?"

Mishima finishes off her glass of wine. "No, we don't have the results, but that advid didn't get picked up by any compilers. We have the last-minute polls and there are no noticeable changes in the constituencies where that advid played. And no, we're not going to disqualify a major government because one of its operatives did something stupid and unethical." Mainly stupid.

"And me?" Suzuki has his eyes on his wine now, looks like he's about to add a tear to the glass.

"We'll be in touch," Mishima says, getting up to go. It's unorthodox, but she has a little bit of latitude here, and until she knows how things are going to fall out in this election, she'd rather keep Suzuki on a leash.

The crow is the same size and model as Mishima's but decidedly more impersonal. Six narrow, stacked bunks in the cabin instead of a futon, and in the main room a light partition separating the controls from a group workspace. Right now Ken is the only passenger, so he can spread the map projections as large as he wants as he prepares for his mission. (Mission: their word, not his. The excitement drums through him every time he thinks it.) The maps are, necessarily, a few weeks old. There shouldn't be any major changes, but of course, they can't know for sure.

"If you do come up against something serious and unforeseen—if, I don't know, Heritage is building moats around their centenals and raising the drawbridge to keep noncitizens out—get back here as soon as possible. That in itself will be enough intel for now," Nejime had assured him.

Ken had tried not to show how nervous he was in her office. He recognized her as the woman with the short silver hair from the meeting, but since he started listening in on break-room conversations, he's heard her name spoken in awed tones; she is one of the originals who has worked for Information since its founding. Even without that, the fact that she has a corner office on the eighth floor would have been enough to tell him she was important.

"We need to get a sense for what's going on in Heritage centenals right now," Nejime told him with little preamble. "We'd rather not send anyone they can recognize as Information."

"And I only showed up after the comms went down," Ken finishes. No one who hasn't physically seen him here would know he's in Doha at all, let alone helping out.

"Exactly. Beyond that, you seem to possess the necessary skills." She looked at him archly, and Ken felt himself flush, imagining how transparent his little act for Policy1st must seem to these Information mavens. Nejime went on: "We've selected a location in Beirut, only a few hours away, where a Policy1st centenal adjoins a Heritage centenal. With Information down, it will be easy for you to stumble across the border unintentionally."

"And what exactly am I looking for?" Ken asked, trying to sound professional.

"Anything that tells us what that government is doing during this outage. You can compare with the vids from three weeks ago and see if there are new banners, pop-ups, unusual activity . . ."

Maryam jumped in as Nejime trailed off. "If you happen to hear anything about the state of their repeaters or hubs, pay close attention."

Ken nodded, although he didn't see how he could get anywhere near that. Maryam was in that early meeting too, so it's easy for him to identify her as the hotshot head of tech. Everyone says she's on her way up, although she's relatively new in the Doha office and left her previous posting in Paris suddenly.

"Just a little reconnaissance," Roz told him, almost protectively. "Get a sense for it. Then get back into the Policy1st centenal before you hail the pilot on the intranet."

"Don't take too long," Nejime added. "We are in a situation where speed matters more than comprehensiveness. If we don't hear from you within two hours, we will assume something has gone wrong."

Two hours doesn't give him a lot of time to wander from the Policy1st centenal into Heritage, look around, and wander back, Ken thinks, studying the map. The plan is that he will get dropped off at the American University of Beirut Medical Center, where the arrival of a crow is not such a remarkable event. It's a ten-minute walk from there to the border, more if he loses himself convincingly. That shouldn't be hard, he thinks, looking at the maze of tiny streets. The scarier part is figuring out a route that takes him into Heritage and out again. How far in should he go? Where should he look for evidence of "unusual activity?" He supposes he should go by the centenal government building if he can. He glares at the map, trying to memorize all the streets leading to the Policy1st centenal. In the worst case, he supposes, he can aim for the coast and follow that back around.

It is then that he notices the centenal, contiguous both with Heritage and Policy1st, that belongs to Liberty.

After her encounter with Suzuki, Mishima goes up to her crow to change into something more discreet, and returns her focus to her primary target. She laid the groundwork while en route, and she can now look at his schedule without leaving a trail, has mapped where his office is in the building, and, by using oblique search terms, has a pretty good record of his activities from six months to three weeks ago, which is as close as the crashed servers let her get.

Now that she's on the ground, she takes her spying to the next level. She finds reasons to walk by his office several times to check the layout and how he uses it: an old-fashioned keyboard on a standing desk, a leather chair comfortably appointed in the trappings of erudite power facing a larger-than-standard projection area. The third time, after she has visually confirmed that he is in his scheduled meeting on exit polling, she slips inside and sticks a magnetic disk to the underside of his standing desk. Since Information is so well defended against spyware, and since hacking is not Mishima's expertise, much of her spying career has involved analog devices. This one is a powerful audio sensor that will capture any commands he issues to his handheld or desktop, however softly he whispers them, to say nothing of conversations. It can recognize keystrokes by the minute differences in sound between the different keys and translate typing into text. She doubts it will be very useful; most of the talk must be already done, and whatever handheld work is left he has probably masked under anodyne macros. But it's worth a try.

She reminds herself that they may be completely on the wrong track. Using the initial votes for comparison data is not a terrible idea, nor a necessarily nefarious one; Mishima can imagine suggesting it herself if her interests tipped more toward data than reality and if she were several shades more naïve about the way Information works. He may be innocent.

But the more she looks into him, the more she's convinced. She doesn't have time to do a full-immersion background on him the way she'd like to, but she sets up a tightly configured workspace near the espresso machine with one of the latest pre-crash globes on the minimalist projection, and starts unobtrusive conversations with everyone who comes by over the next couple of hours. When she asks, sympathetically, about who seems to be under the most stress, Drestle's name never comes up; rather, he's been supporting people with his calm manner and pleasant jokes. Without approaching the subject directly, she learns that Drestle, like many other staff, had planned to stay over the night of the election and has not left since the crash; she saw seven suits in his office, four of them clearly used. Many people keep one or two extra suits for emergencies, and it's possible that he's extra cautious, or that he sent out for them or printed them, but she suspects he knew he'd be staying longer.

She gets Korbin, who has refused to take time off to recover from her ordeal until after the election has been settled, to reach out to her counterpart Heritage monitor in the Paris office. She learns that Drestle maintains a lively interest in Heritage and often takes the Heritage specialist out for long lunches. He normally works in news compilation oversight, but his election assignment has been poll analysis and predictor supervision. He's well positioned to figure out where minor tweaks can lead to the desired outcome.

When she thinks she's gotten as much intel as she can without attracting attention, she walks down to the river and along the Quai d'Austerlitz to the old national library in the thirteenth. It's well after midnight, the fluoron lamps along the bridges reflecting in the Seine, but the library, no longer staffed by people, is permanently open and has almost as good connectivity as the Information hub. She sends her circumstantial evidence to Ken, just in case, and then, because voting will restart in a few hours at most, she shifts her energies to where she has more of an advantage. Hunched in a small carrel on the ground floor (since the earthquake, she is leery of higher stories), facing her reflection over the darkness of the garden still grey with winter, she opens globes and polls and predictions, overlapping projections crowding the space in front of her eyes. She keeps the data feed from the audio sensor in Drestle's office open in a corner and lets her mind flow over the glowing estimations of the world's political leanings, probing for the weak point, the point she would pressure if she wanted to steal an election.

CHAPTER 27

Ken wanders into the Heritage centenal without any difficulties. No moat, no roadblocks, no SecureNation uniforms. The border would be hard to miss, with a bright
Heritage banner projection across the street (he wonders if
that could count as late campaigning?), but he makes a show
of looking down into his handheld as he passes under it. In
any case, there are plenty of pedestrians and vehicles moving in both directions.

Once he's in Heritage and nobody's looking at him funny,
Ken starts to enjoy himself. It's a beautiful day in Beirut,
chilly but sunny, and it's been a long time since he's taken a
leisurely stroll in a pleasant climate. A few blocks in, he spots
a crowded manakish stand on the side of the road and goes
over to order one with za'atar. "By the way," he says as he's
waiting, "can you tell me how to get to Alameddine Street?
I think I got turned around."

Three men immediately start offering him directions, and
the subsequent argument soon draws in two more. Ken
catches the eye of the manakish seller. "Terrible not having
Information," he says.

"You said it," the man agrees. "Can't understand how
they'd let that happen."

"I heard it was another attack on the election process, like
the debate," someone else says.

"Eh, attack nothing. All those votes overloaded the system."

"Do you think they'll put off the election?"

"It's already been put off, hasn't it?"

"Do you think it will change the result?" Ken asks.

"Here? Nah," answers the vendor, wrapping up his manakish and handing it to him. "Why would we change our votes over a few days' delay?"

"You would think that with the Supermajority, we could get our Information back faster," someone grumbles, but nobody seems to take that as a reason to abandon ship. Ken transmits his details with line-of-sight for eventual billing, thanks the vendor, and raises his manakish in salute to the rest before ambling on.

Four conversations later, Ken has a full stomach but no new intel. The centenal government, housed in a former embassy building, looks so normal that Ken dares to stick his head in the front door. Staff are power walking the corridors, and there's a long line in front of the centenal services desk, but that seems a normal response to the sudden lack of Information.

Ken checks the time. An hour and a quarter since he was dropped off. He turns toward the border with Liberty.

Ken doesn't notice a marked shift in the neighborhood when he crosses into the Liberty centenal. Liberty and Heritage both appeal to broad demographics: in this case, both seem to have focused on populations that are not super rich, not terribly poor. The centenals contain professional, working, and creative classes living in a mix of modern efficiency-contoured apartment buildings, crumbling ce-

ment tenements a hundred years old, sleek white stone mul-
tistories from the beginning of the century, and the occasional
protected church, mosque, or palace.

But if the backdrop looks the same, the atmosphere is
completely different. In the Liberty centenal there are clumps
of men standing around in the street, talking and gesturing.
Advids pop up at eyeball level, individual cries for attention:
**Who do you trust? What is Information telling you? Stand with
Liberty!** Down a side street Ken glimpses a more public bit
of street theater. Half a dozen people—women as well as
men—are watching a large projection of Johnny Fabré sitting
opposite an equally groomed but much younger woman.
". . . believe that Liberty won the election?" she is asking.
"It's not a question of believing; I know it!" Fabré answers,
banging a fist on the arm of his chair. "We *have* the data. But
don't take my word for it. Why would they shut everything
down unless we had won?" The woman nods as if that made
sense.

Spooked, Ken brushes away the pop-ups and ducks into
a pastry shop, thinking he can run his lost routine one more
time and then make for the rendezvous point. The shop,
too, is crowded, although few people seem to be eating or
ordering. A few hold tiny coffees, and all are loud. When
Ken approaches the counter, the shopkeeper looks at him
suspiciously. "Are you a citizen?" he asks.

Ken hears echoes of a French revolution drama he used
to watch. "Um . . . not a Liberty citizen, no . . ."

"Then you won't be able to pay," the vendor says. "Sorry."

"I see. Uh, what I've been doing in most other shops is
giving my verified details through line-of-sight. As soon as
Information comes on, I'll pay the—"

"So, I won't get the money until Information is back up?

Which could be in weeks, or months, or never! Sorry, kid, but I can't run my business that way. How would I pay my suppliers?"

The same way, Ken supposes. But he sees the guy's point. "How do citizens pay?"

The shopkeeper grins and shows Ken a small device on the counter. "They set it all up for us! As soon as they realized that Information wasn't going to come back on immediately, they gave us these thingamajigs, and then they had everyone come in to get an attachment on their handhelds—see, look." With no embarrassment, the man grabs the wrist of a passing client and twists it to show Ken an iridescent bauble stuck to his handheld. The client looks at Ken with mild curiosity, says something to the shopkeeper that Ken's translator finds incomprehensible, and goes off to his cluster of comrades, chuckling loudly. "That works for payment and communications. We have intranet now!" The shopkeeper goes on with pride.

"Very impressive," Ken admits. "But it's a shame people from the next centenal over can't shop here anymore."

"Eh, we get along," the shopkeeper says. He's losing interest in Ken now, his eyes following the give-and-take of a raucous conversation farther down the counter. "What were you going to order, anyway? Here, have this." He gathers a kunafi, a piece of halva, and a square of baklava into a small box and hands it to Ken.

"Oh, I couldn't—at least let me give you my details, and I'll pay you later?" But the shopkeeper is already waving him off, and Ken exits back onto the street, looking down at the sticky sweets in his hands and wondering how that happened. He had been planning to take the next left to head back toward Policy1st, but he is intrigued by this intranet thing,

and he walks farther into the centenal. Now that he's looking for them, he notices the shiny blue-green tokens on
every handheld he sees, and on a couple of earpieces. The
pop-up advids continue, creepier and creepier: **The Information Outage was planned! Make sure your vote counts! Defend
Liberty borders!** Ken wonders if everyone sees them, or if
they are targeting him because he doesn't have the intranet
doohickey yet. Sure enough, a few steps later he gets **Come
by the centenal government for your handheld adaptor. Liberty
is helping YOU stay CONNECTED!** Ken wonders if it's worth going by to see if they will give him one, although he decides
they would check his identification first. He's looking down
at his handheld to consider his options when he realizes he's
about to walk into something and stops short.

Not something, someone. A large man in a cotton shirt
and trousers, grizzled chin, not much hair on top, stands in
his path. "You're not a citizen, are you?"

Ken has a pungent flashback to the early years of high
school, when his strange Brazilian accent and un-Japanese
mannerisms got him beat up more than once. It's about to
happen again, and he opens his mouth with the hopelessness
of the inevitable. "I'm not, no," he says, trying for a smile.
"I was trying to find my way back to Policy1st. It's—this
way, right?"

The man guffaws, his laughter echoed by two men leaning against a building to the left. Ken can't believe he didn't
see this coming. "Well, we can escort you to Policy1st. Make
sure you get there okay." The man nods to his friends and
they fall into formation around Ken, each of them at least
half again Ken's weight.

"Work for Policy1st, do you?" asks one, his hair a stiff
bristle and his denim shirt unbuttoned to the breastbone.

Ken has barely opened his mouth when the third man, slender but hard, speaks up. "I bet he's a spy from that 888 group they were talking about."

This wild leap catches Ken so by surprise that he responds. "What? No, I don't know anything about—"

"That's the Chinese one?" asks the first man, running his eyes up and down Ken. "Sounds about right."

"I'm not even Chinese," Ken protests, although he knows perfectly well that 888 has plenty of staff who are not Han Chinese. "I work for Policy1st. Our centenal is right next door. Look"—he flicks to the ID view in his handheld. "Policy1st. Campaign staff. See?"

The first man takes the handheld from Ken and peers at it as if it were a greasy playing card. "Anyone could have doctored this," he says, passing it to his companions. Ken realizes he's made a tactical error.

"Hey, this handheld doesn't have the Liberty intranet adaptor," the slim man says. "Maybe instead of taking him to Policy1st, we should bring him to HQ so he can get one."

"I'm not a Liberty citizen," Ken explains, trying one last time for dignity. "I'm surprised that you would treat a guest . . ."

They're already laughing, such loose and relaxed laughs that the heavy blow to the gut takes Ken entirely by surprise. He folds over, gasping for breath. He didn't even see which one hit him—maybe the image was pulverized by the impact. He's still wheezing desperately when the next punch comes, right across his cheekbone. He stumbles down onto one knee. If he stays up at all, it's not from misplaced valor, but because he's too confused to figure out what to do. There is a slight breather, long enough for his thoughts to gather

and his hearing to coalesce on the laughter and taunts surrounding him. The side of his face feels huge, and he reaches
up to run his hand along his cheek. He hears a trill, then another. When nothing hits him immediately, he risks looking
up. The men are staring at their handhelds. The guy with
the denim shirt is looking back and forth between his own
handheld and Ken's, mouth ajar.

Ken wants to ask what's going on, but he doesn't dare. He
watches them, wondering if he should run. They're distracted; he might get a good start. But he's nauseous and he
still can't fill his lungs all the way. And they have his handheld.

"So, Information's back up?" the slim man asks.

"Can't you read?" the first guy, the leader, responds.
"Information's not up, but it will be soon."

"But we can vote," the slim man says uncertainly.

"Voting and personal communications," denim shirt says.
A pause. "So, I guess we can call people?"

"How long do you think it will take to get full service?"

"What do I look like to you, an Information grunt?"

Ken tries to swallow, pushes at the ground until he's on
his feet. "Look, gentlemen," he starts.

They look over but don't seem to care that he's gotten up.
"Hey," says the slim man. "We can call people. Let's call
Policy1st and see if this guy is who he says he is."

"Use his handheld," the leader orders.

Denim shirt hands it over and the thin guy looks for the
Policy1st office details. "Kinda funny you don't have it in
saved in here," he sneers.

"It's there," Ken blurts. "Let me find it!" He holds his
hand out. The Beirut office number *is* there, as part of his

mission prep, but he's not sure anyone briefed them about his mission. If they give him the phone, he can call an office in another country; they'll vouch for him . . .

"Nah, I got it." The man is staring at Ken's handheld, waiting for the call to go through. Ken remembers himself in that Information meeting, fighting for communication for the masses. Very noble, and he's about to get screwed for his troubles.

"Nothing," the slim guy says. "No one's answering."

"Must be an overload," Ken suggests. He's trying to edge away from these guys without them noticing.

"Call 888," the leader says. "Let's see if they know him."

"You got the number?"

"Why the hell would I have a number for 888?"

Ken takes a deep breath and bolts. He can feel the dust sliding from the road into the air behind him, hear their shouts: "Hey!" "What the—" But they don't sound worried, just surprised. His lungs are already rasping, and a second later, a huge body tackles him, and then he hits the ground, hard. There's a weight on his back and the sharp pain of a boot striking his ribs. A heavy fist slams into his ear. Ken coughs; his fingertips rake at the dusty pavement. His head is ringing, and everything he hears is garbled.

There's another voice now, a woman's voice, but he can't understand what she's saying. Something angry. The weight lifts off of him, an incredible relief. He cradles his head in his arms, concentrates on breathing and on listening for the next blow.

Ken's not sure how much time passes before he looks up, but it feels like coming out of a fever dream. He lifts his head slightly; no one is standing over him. A foot or two away, there's a woman in a white dress yelling at his attackers, but he still can't make out what she's saying; all he hears are random syllables, harsh tones with no meaning. Could he be brain-damaged? He whispers, "I'm okay," and it makes sense, at least to him. As he climbs to his feet, he realizes that they must have broken the translator slotted inside his right ear. He groans.

The woman turns her attention to him. She addresses him in a very different tone from the one she used with his assailants—apologetic and warm. She hands him his handheld. The three men, meanwhile, are slinking away, not without some grim glances his way. Ken clears his throat, tastes blood.

"I can't understand you," he says, as loudly as he can. "I think they broke my translator." He says it in Portuguese, just to make sure he still can.

The woman's face shows consternation, then thought. "English?" she asks. Ken nods in relief and immediately regrets it. His head is splitting. He glances after the retreating men to make sure they're gone—even moving his eyes hurts—and then focuses on her. She's very attractive: long dark hair threaded through with gold filaments, big dark eyes, and a lovely curve from waist to hips. Her dress is simple cotton but with a herringbone pattern done in microcutouts. "I'm so sorry about that," she says, in smooth but accented English. Nice to hear accents for a change, Ken thinks. "They got a little carried away. Everyone is so nervous, stressed because of these problems."

"Yeah," Ken says, running his tongue around the inside of his mouth to check for loose teeth. "Uh, thanks for your help."

She smiles at him. "The least I could do for a colleague."

Ken has never felt so confused. "Um . . ."

"They didn't believe you work for Policy1st, but I told them it's true. I've seen you before."

Ken can't remember ever meeting her. "Really? Where?" He remembers the vid that caught him in the Tokyo office after the earthquake. It seemed like such a big deal back then.

She is squinting. "Ah. Where? Kiev? Budapest?" He shakes his head. "No, it was warmer . . . wait, I know! Lima." She is nodding. "You visited that funny woman, the profesora."

Ken's jaw drops, painfully. "You were the Liberty . . . scout?"

She laughs. "Yes." Holds out a hand. "Camille Saad. I went back to the woman a few days after my first visit and she told me you had been there and that you were very persuasive." She wags a finger at him teasingly. She's beyond attractive. Ken wonders if she would stab him in the leg.

"Small world," he croaks. He decides she probably would. Maybe better not to ask her about all those weird pop-ups and the intranet devices.

She's started walking, and he follows her a few steps before he realizes it's the wrong direction.

"Where are we going?" he asks. "I need to get back to Policy1st." And maybe a clinic. At least a bed.

"Oh, I was going to take you to the government headquarters so you can make a complaint about those men." It seems like a very reasonable idea when she says it.

"No I—I have to get back." He backs away.

She seems about to argue, then nods and follows him. "I understand. I'll walk you out." A dazzling smile. Ken is feeling more and more nervous, but maybe it's leftover adrenaline from getting beat up. "So, this is your home centenal?" he asks.

"For now, yes," Camille says. "What are you doing here?"

"I came in to do some election monitoring for Policy1st, got stuck here." He tries a disarming look, but he's pretty sure it doesn't make it through the bruises. "I was going stir-crazy, so I came out for a walk. Didn't think I'd end up taking such a beating." He leaves a pause. "Is this sort of thing happening a lot?"

"Oh, they are just . . . as you said, stir-crazy? Everyone is worried. What will happen next? Will Information ever come back or are we back in the forties, you know?" She shivers. "It's scary."

The shiver is a little much. Ken's left eye is swelling shut, and he falls back to put her on his right where he can see her. "I'm sure it will come back on," he says, trying to sound more comforting than confident. "Especially now that the voting is up. So, this intranet thing—did that come from the Liberty global government?"

"Of course not! We haven't had any contact with the global government since Information went out." She peers at him. "Have you?"

"No, no," Ken says. "I thought maybe it was a contingency plan. You got it up so fast."

"We have some good people here. You should consider making the switch," she says, and winks. Ken is glad his black eye prevents him from any temptation of winking back.

"Yeah, heh heh, maybe next election." They have reached the border with Policy1st. "Okay, well, thank you again. How crazy to meet you in person after all that campaigning." He laughs nervously again. "So, I think I'm going to go get myself an icepack or something." He can't quite wish her good luck. "Take care!"

"Okay, you too!" she says cheerfully. "Maybe we can get together sometime after all this smoothes out."

"Sure, yeah." Ken turns away and tells himself not to look back. He is feeling nauseous and every breath is painful, but he makes himself walk straight for three blocks before he turns. As soon as he is sure he is out of sight, he calls in the crow.

CHAPTER 28

The powers-that-be at Information have decided that there's no point (other than tradition) in waiting for midnight on the international date line to roll around, and within half an hour of the techies' declaring the voting system unbreakable, they open it up. Messages go out to every handheld and tablet in the world: Welcome back! Voting has reopened as of [local time to the second]. You have twenty-four hours to make your choice! We are happy to Inform you that personal communications are now functioning, and we are working to bring all Information back at your disposal as soon as possible! The text is adorned with animations of fireworks and culturally appropriate celebratory motifs; there was a small team of techies dedicated to preparing that. In centenals without one hundred percent handheld and tablet penetration, the message is projected in town squares and displayed on public billboards.

The ballots do not immediately pour in; it seems most people want to make use of the personal comms before bothering to vote. About an hour in, however, the numbers start to climb, and by the end of the third hour, the totals are close to what they were four days earlier. Mishima, like most analysts, is tasked with watching for discrepancies as they come in. It's a far more difficult job now, with no Information about what's going on in the centenals.

"How can we know if something is unusual when we don't

know what people have been doing for the past hundred hours?" "Sure, this jump in the incumbent's numbers could be a discrepancy, or it could be that they've been campaigning nonstop ever since they realized we couldn't police them." Mishima, back at her post by the espresso machine in the Information office, watches the complaints in the analysts' section of the intranet. She doesn't disagree with them, but she's too busy to join in. She's tracking a different dataset: as the votes come in, she's comparing them with the initial votes from the abortive election four days ago. It's a difficult problem: she sees totals by centenal but has no way of knowing which vote comes from which person. Different percentages now may mean that a lot of voters have changed allegiances, or that different people are voting. For the moment, she doesn't see any huge shifts, but it's too early to tell.

When the comms went out, Yoriko thought it was only on Amami Ōshima and spent twelve hours cursing the backwardness of the tiny island before finally realizing that the problem might be broader. This was partially because she knew almost no one on the island. If she turned her translator off, she even had some trouble understanding the dialect, especially when the locals spoke quickly. In her efforts to keep her kids (and, incidentally, herself) occupied without recourse to Information, she ended up interacting with more people than she would have otherwise. Amami is quite old-fashioned in that a lot of the service jobs are still done by people. Yoriko was at first annoyed to have to deal with humans at the ice cream parlor, the beach chair rental, and the projection arcade. But once she got used to it, she found she enjoyed the quaintness. It also meant that she eventually heard the rumors that people getting off the ferry hadn't been able to access Information at their points of origin, either.

She can't help worrying about her friends on Okinawa. She had called almost no one to tell them about her sudden move. When she finally gets the message about Information coming online, her first thought is to call her friends and let them know she's alive. She only considers voting once her need for long-distance interaction has been slaked. She is no less angry with Suzuki than before; if anything, more so. She almost doesn't vote at all. If she is going to vote, she needs to choose a new party; after talking to the locals, she has decided 1China is too frightening to vote for, even as a meaningless gesture. She thinks about voting for SecureNation, to prevent any recurrence of this ridiculousness with the communications, but for some reason, she can't find them on the ballot. Finally, she taps YourStory and closes the program in disgust.

Nobody told them to let Domaine out of the holding cell, so he is still there. However, voting rights are inviolable, and once the system is online again, a guard comes down and gives him his handheld and ten minutes of privacy. Domaine has no intention of voting, but he uses the time to doctor the data from the autothief he used on Mishima's handheld and the sensor he had recording their conversation, and sends it out to a couple of key people.

What were you even doing in the Liberty centenal?" Nejime asks. Ken starts to explain: the initial message from Amuru, the hints during the debates . . . "The short

322 · MALKA OLDER

version," Nejime cuts in, glancing at her handheld. Five hours into the election, there are a lot of demands on her time; the fact that she is personally debriefing Ken is an indication of how worried they are about Heritage.

"Heritage was fine," Ken says again. "I don't know if they had anything to do with the outage, but the centenal felt completely normal. But you should be worried about Liberty. We've been tracking them for weeks because of those vague threats, and now they're going berserk. I don't know what you can do, but you better do something."

"Could it be confined to that centenal? Maybe something to do with the centenal government or localized conflicts with their neighbors?" Roz asks. Her eyes don't rest on Ken's very long, reminding him that his face is a mess. He got his diagnostics checked and washed off the blood and dust in Beirut, but he still looks pretty bad.

"I don't know; there were all these advids. And that projection of Fabré? That had to be made after the outage happened, and they got it there somehow. Not to mention the crazy handheld attachments. The Liberty spy I met told me that it wasn't centrally coordinated, but I'm sure she was lying."

"Liberty spy?" Roz asks.

Ken waves his hand. "Long story."

"Do you think they could have caused the outage?" Nejime asks. "Are they trying to steal the election?"

"I don't know." Ken looks at Roz with his good eye. "I guess . . . I hope we'll find out by watching the votes."

"All right," Nejime says. "Get me a full report, and we'll deal with it after the election."

"After the election may be too late," Ken says, but she's

already beckoning other people into her office from the corridor, and Roz shepherds Ken out.

"I don't believe it," Ken says as they walk back toward Roz's workspace. "I was assaulted and she's not going to do anything?"

"She'll do something," Roz says. "You should have seen her when the pilot called in to tell us what happened. But the election's already started. We have to get through it." She glances at him and away quickly. "You don't have to stay. Do you want to go get some rest?"

"Only if it makes you feel better," Ken says grumpily.

Roz glares at him. "We have a ton of work to do. Mishima's staking out Drestle, but we have to watch the votes, especially if the threat comes from somewhere else. But the most important thing is for you to get better, so if you need the time . . ."

"No, I want to work," he says. "Let me grab an icepack."

Mishima's still monitoring the audio sensor and Drestle's comms. At about six hours in, she tightens her watch on his uploading and processor usage. At eight hours, she goes to the vending machine on his floor and arranges herself so she can see into his office. The results are still uncertain, but it looks to her like both Liberty and PhilipMorris have a chance at unseating Heritage, with 888 and, incredibly, Policy1st not far behind. He has to be getting nervous.

At twelve hours, Ken pings her using her encryption code. "Hey," he says when she calls him back. He's not sure if anyone told her about the events in Beirut.

Mishima is crouched in a garret-level maintenance room

to be sure that no one can overhear. "Anything?" she whispers.

"Nothing," Ken says, not sure if he's relieved she didn't hear about the beating he took or disappointed to miss out on the sympathy.

"No requests for the original votes?"

"No. And nothing from Drestle at all, certainly no requests of the size that would be necessary to pull this off."

Mishima rubs her forehead. "He may wait until the last moment, to know if it's absolutely necessary."

"It'll be necessary," Ken says with more assurance than he feels.

"Too early to tell," Mishima says gruffly. But it's true; on the most sophisticated projections, it's not looking good for Heritage. She wonders if people are blaming them, along with Information, for the outage. "Could our target be generating the votes rather than using the originals?"

"Roz says that would never stand up to scrutiny. The individual signatures on the votes are too hard to forge, especially at a large scale."

She taps her forehead, taps the floor. She wishes she could pace. "What if it doesn't have to stand up to scrutiny? What if they just need it to hold for a few hours after it's announced? Then they switch the ballots in after voting closes, when no one's looking."

Ken tries to think this through. "How could they do that?"

"Ask Roz if it would work," Mishima says. "And keep a close eye on your packets."

"Are you going to sleep?" Ken asks, and wishes he hadn't.

"Don't forget to vote," Mishima tells him, and hangs up.

. . .

Shamus was one of the few who voted as soon as he got the message, before calling anyone. Voting is a matter of pride and identity, and it's not like he has to think about his decision. Once he's gotten that taken care of, he turns to business. As he expected, his workspace is filling up with messages, another three ticking in as he watches, then two more. All these gonzos who thrive on publicity, press, splashes, cross-referencing, news. They've been starving for days and probably called him before they called their mothers. Shamus wades through it.

Can you please do an ad for me, ASAP?

Can you show me a draft marketing strategy based on the new election results as soon as they're out?

NOW is the moment to hit with our data security device, will pay extra for quick response.

He flags that one and then pauses when he sees a message with Domaine's name on it. With an attachment.

Mishima is still sitting on the floor by the vending machine when Shamus calls her. She hesitates—Drestle has to make his move soon; they're closing in on eighteen hours—then takes the call.

"How's it going?" she asks, without taking her eyes from the vote totals.

"Oh, not bad, myself," Shamus says. "Rolling in requests to help shape the consumer preferences of the new world order. Erm—listen, I've got something here I think you should see."

"I'm a little busy. Is it urgent?"

"It is a bit. At least, I need to know how to respond." He forwards her Domaine's message. "Take a look at the attachment."

Mishima glances at it, plays the attachment. Presses her lips together instead of swearing. Thinks for a minute. She's been awake for thirty-some hours and has drunk the commensurate amount of caffeine. She tries to steady her breathing. "Go with it," she says finally. She deserves it for giving Domaine even that much.

"You sure?" Shamus asks.

"Yeah. We can handle it. And you're too valuable an informant; I don't want him getting suspicious if you don't run it."

"Okay, then; you're the boss," Shamus says. "Anything else I can do for you?"

She gives him a smile. "Enjoy the fat years, Shamus. I'll let you know if we need anything."

Ken has already voted. Not wanting to take any chances, he set his handheld three days ago to auto-vote for Policy1st at any opportunity. He also ordered it to document the vote three different ways, and he checks those now to be sure, then goes back to watching the feeds with Roz.

They are munching on some ugali Roz made for him on the grounds that it is soft enough for him to chew without hurting his jaw, and that it will restore his strength. Ken finds the blandness comforting. He runs his fingers over his swollen cheek. He considers calling Suzuki, but when he tries to imagine how he would explain where he is and what he's doing, he gives up and decides he's too busy to call right now. If he knows Suzuki, he probably is too.

He's trying to be pleased that Policy1st is doing as well as it is, even if the Supermajority looks unlikely. He has separate feeds open to follow certain centenals: Miraflores, a cluster in Jakarta, most of Chennai, and Sri Lanka. The centenal he went through in northern Japan is already 80 percent counted and ready to be called for 河北, a local government. Policy1st is set to snatch a couple of centenals from 1China in the Ryukyus, and actually, Lima is looking pretty good too, so he feels like he contributed something.

He's watching Miraflores when he sees the shift, so small that he thinks maybe he blinked. His handheld twinkles with an incoming call, and he types in the code with shaking hands. "Yeah?" he says.

"Did you see that?" Mishima breathes. She's speaking so softly, it feels as though she's right next to him, lips by his ear.

"I think so," he says. "Are you tracking it?"

"Yes," she whispers. "I think . . ." She is scanning her trackers, running the program she set up, opening the action record at five levels of complexity. "I got him!" And without even bothering to click off from Ken, she springs to her feet and runs.

Mishima careens into the office of Valerie Nougaz, a large corner room with a narrow line-of-sight angle across the Jardin du Luxembourg that offers a glimpse of the Tower.

Although Information prides itself on its flat, consensus-based organization with no single person at the top of the hierarchy, experience has proven it expedient to have one director for each office, as well as functional regional directors for some of the key areas. Mishima has found that each office has its own subculture, some more disciplined than others. In Paris, it is best to go straight to the top. It won't be easy, because Nougaz is skeptical and straightlaced, but she has a lot of pull in the larger organization, and if convinced, she will do most of the pushing to make sure the plan is adopted.

At this late stage of voting, the office is crowded with people. There are two separate projections, one for Nougaz at her workspace and the other for her deputy, Abendou, in the opposite corner. Nougaz, in a crisp white shirt open across the collarbones, a floaty mauve scarf, and a wool pencil skirt, is tapping out her signature code on an aide's handheld and talking into her earpiece while nodding at the staff member running through a presentation. An election countdown clock, the animated numbers huge, bright, and faintly vibrating, hangs in one corner of the room.

Mishima dodges all the associates to get in front of the boss. "Madame—"

"Ah, Mishima." Nougaz, thin of face and body, maintains a calm authority by refusing to raise her voice, or her pulse, to match that of her interlocutor. "One moment, and I'll be right with you."

"Madame, I'm sorry, but this is urgent."

Nougaz looks over at her, one raised eyebrow hidden behind her improbable bangs.

"We need the room." Mishima, who has her own ways of projecting authority, addresses this to those around her. The woman collecting the signature code has already made herself scarce; the others look to Nougaz questioningly.

"Well, then," she says. The projections snap off and their curators exit quickly. Abendou sticks around at a nod from his boss.

"Madame Director," Mishima says swiftly as soon as the door is closed, "the election is being stolen from this office." She mutters a quick order to her handheld, and the projection she has prepared jumps up, slightly larger than normal to convey the urgency and because there is a lot of complicated stuff going on. Mishima moves in front of it, pointing.

"Here and here," she says. Because the vote shifting is so fast and subtle that it's hard to catch, she's arranged a visual that prints the totals in the centenals she has selected every three seconds, line after line down the projection. She scrolls up five and six minutes to show them the shifts she caught. "Now, if you look at these trackers, you will see the corresponding activity on Drestle's processor." She is aware of Nougaz and Abendou exchanging glances when she mentions the name, but doesn't look up.

"These are very small amounts," Abendou says. "Can you be sure this is not a legal correction of some problem in the field or an error, perhaps?"

Mishima takes a deep breath, pulls up her additional visuals. "I can't be sure yet, but it would be a huge coincidence. As you can see here, based on analysis of the original votes four days ago, as well as the latest polls before that—which we no longer have access to, but which I've reconstructed using what was saved in my system—there was a better than 50 percent chance that Heritage would be edged out of the Supermajority. They might have hoped that the stoppage would drive more people toward stability, but as we've seen over the last twenty hours, it didn't. Rather the opposite. Now, these centenals"—she highlights them with a twitch of her finger—"fulfill three conditions: their results today have shown a jump from their trajectory in the polls; they are trending away from Heritage and toward one of the other top five governments; and the margins of victory, one way or the other, are likely to be very small. These are the centenals where a small shift of votes can send them into Heritage's column and, based on the analytics of their recent history, that shift won't ring alarm bells." She pauses, out of breath. Nobody has yet yelled at her for spying on a high-level colleague or told her she's crazy. She didn't expect them to: these are professionals, and she's never had a problem with anyone at the Paris hub. But she is a little surprised that they aren't trying harder to defend one of their own.

"If we watch," Mishima goes on, scrolling down to the present, "we may see another one happen in real time." She wants to have witnesses for this, if possible. She looks quickly across the stats for the centenals. "Probably here," she says, pointing to Miraflores, in Lima, which has seen a surprising swing toward Policy1st. "He already moved one hundred votes, but it looks like that will not be enough."

"And how does he move the votes?" Nougaz asks. "To be honest, we suspected . . . something would happen connected to the outage, but we didn't think this type of manipulation was possible."

"He's using—there!" Mishima points as the Policy1st vote count in Miraflores drops by twenty votes. They wait, silently hovering, and forty-two seconds later, the Heritage vote count jumps by twenty-one. "Probably one legitimate vote in there," Mishima notes. "As I was saying, he's using the votes from four days ago. I'm not sure how he got them; we were trying to trap him with a decoy set, but I'm almost certain that he got access to the originals. They look legal at first glance, especially when used this judiciously. I imagine he'll use the rush of renewed Information after the vote closes to go in and do a little more polishing."

"Very impressive," Nougaz murmurs. Mishima isn't sure whether she's referring to Drestle's plotting or Mishima's deciphering of that plot. "And what do you suggest we do about it?" she asks Mishima.

"Arrest him," Mishima says. "Immediately, before the election ends."

"Of course," Nougaz says, with a flick of her fingers. "But what do you suggest we do about the election? Do we invalidate all Heritage votes? Let Heritage voters choose again? What do we do with legitimate Heritage centenals?"

"Madame, we don't have time to decide these weighty questions at the moment," Mishima says.

"I'm inclined to agree," Abendou puts in.

"If we need a quick solution"—Mishima shoots him a quick nod of thanks—"get the techies and vote-validation experts on it, and see if you can undo all the fraudulent votes before the clock runs out." She glances up: three hours and change to go. It should be enough. "This second-by-second documentation I've done should help." She motions copies of the program, with its data, into their workspaces, and then freezes.

"What is it?" Abendou asks.

"One of my trackers just died," Mishima says, pointing to a gap in the repeating lines in the projection. "He may have found it." A brief, uncomfortable pause. "We should hurry. If he's taken this risk, it's because he and his counterparts over there think that Heritage is going to lose. So, let it. The Supermajority goes to someone else, the election is legitimate, and the transfer of the Supermajority will give you lots of noisy cover for figuring out what sanctions are appropriate for the attempt."

"Very astute," Nougaz says with approval. "Abendou, can you take the lead on implementing that plan?"

As he is nodding, everyone's handhelds trill.

For a vertiginous second, Mishima is back in her crow, vibrating above a collapsing city. She looks down at her handheld.

Thank you for voting! We are pleased to announce that with voting definitive in 86% of centenals, we can now confirm that the winner of the Supermajority for this election cycle is: HERITAGE!

CHAPTER 29

Mishima glances up at the clock, then down at her projections. "It's not true," she blurts. "Even counting the stolen votes, they haven't won yet. Arrgh, but they're going to . . ." People are still voting, and the numbers for Heritage spike as centenals try to join the Supermajority.

"How the hell did he make that announcement?" Nougaz asks. "Stop this! Detain him." Abendou leaves, calling security as he goes, and Mishima bolts after him. As the door swings closed behind her, she hears Nougaz spitting orders to an assistant. "Get me Boubal! And set up a conference with every director. I know; just tell them the announcement came from this shop!"

Shamus glances at the results on his handheld. "Bastards," he says without surprise, and goes back to work.

Ken stares at the announcement for a long moment, trying to make sense of it, then looks around. He expects pandemonium in the Information office, but all he hears is a brief roar, like the audience of a distant fireworks show. Then a slammed door and running feet. Otherwise, all is quiet. "Do they know?" Ken asks, dazed. "Do they know someone stole the election?"

Roz is poring over her numbers. "If they don't now, they will soon," she says. "I'm trying to make sure this came from the Paris hub."

"You mean that it wasn't someone else who stole the election?" Ken asks.

"Yeah, or more than one person working together," she says, fingers dancing around her workspace. "I'm almost positive, but I'm trying to track it. We have a ubiquity program that makes any Information announcement appear to issue from all hubs simultaneously."

"Uh-huh," Ken says. Typical Information creepiness.

"It's to ensure we all speak with one voice," Roz explains, a little defensive. "To prevent retaliation. And to prevent raising the importance of one office or department above the others. Anyway, this announcement was filtered through that, so I have to track how it entered the program, which is non-trivial. What's happening on Mishima's side?"

"Oh." Ken hadn't wanted to hang up, because of the time involved in reconnecting through the secure line, but he muted the call when Mishima got to the director's office, both because it seemed wrong to listen in and because it was distracting. He raises the volume, leaving his side muted. "Running footsteps," he reports grimly.

"Don't distract her," Roz says. "I've almost got it here."

"Did he think no one would notice?" Ken asks.

Roz shakes her head. "He must have felt threatened, known somehow that we were on to him. But it was not such a stupid move. This is going to make everything a lot harder."

"What do you mean? It's obvious now that someone was messing with the election."

"Yes, but we still have to prove how and where. In the meantime, Information has been wrong about an election result." She taps her handheld and a projection comes up, some kind of complicated three-dimensional map he can't parse. "There. It's clear. It was Drestle. At least, it came from his workspace, with his code. But you see the problem, no? If Information is wrong about an election once, they can be again."

Drestle's office is only one flight of stairs and fifty meters of corridor from Nougaz's, but the three permanent security officers of the Paris hub fall into place behind Abendou before he gets there. Mishima brings up the rear, unofficial as always, she thinks. She is wearing partial body armor under her fitted black corduroys and long-sleeved grey T, but next to the security officers, she feels practically unarmed. She has her stiletto, as always, and the shuriken in their leather case have been an awkward lump in her hip pocket since she shoved them in there some twenty hours ago, but she wishes she had worn the large knife.

The door to the office is closed. The security officers fan out to either side as Abendou knocks smartly. "Drestle?" he calls. "Can I speak with you for a moment?"

No answer.

The security team leader signals Abendou to step aside, but he waves him back and pushes the door open himself, although he does at least turn sideways to present a smaller target. From her position against the wall behind a security officer, Mishima watches Abendou lean forward, then step in. A second later, the security team follows, but she already knows the outcome.

"He's not here," Abendou says, coming out. "His workspace is cleared out. He even took that silly keyboard!"

Still leaning against the wall, Mishima sinks to a squat, palms against her forehead. "He can't have gone far," she says, springing up again. "He must have found my tracker when he packed up his computer. That was only a few minutes ago."

"Down to the street," Abendou orders the security team. "Shut down the building, check the immediate area—is the putain d'Information back up yet? Check on every means of transport that's passed by here in the last five—ten minutes. If you can't find him, come back and search this place with a magnifying glass, understand?"

Mishima has another idea and is running for the roof. She bursts out of the access door and stands there, gasping in the chill air. It is dusk, and Paris is grey and blue, fine nets of bare branches stretching along the boulevards, a glimmer of the Seine visible beyond the darkness of the Jardin des Plantes, the travertine chess piece of Sacré-Cœur hovering in the distance. Her crow is gone.

CHAPTER 30

Yoriko sees the results a little late. She was in a projection film with her kids. It kept them quiet for a couple of hours, but they come out cranky. Nonstop vacation is getting to be too much for them. She feels a dull disappointment that Heritage has won. *Again?* Despite it all, she was hoping that Policy1st would somehow pull it off, that her efforts would make a difference.

But then again, the Supermajority doesn't matter much to her here. She checks the results for the Amami Ōshima centenal. The winner is Amami, a local government that doesn't even compete for any other centenals. Going into the details, she sees that there was more dissent than she expected; Amami won 64 percent of the vote, and she wasn't the only person to vote for YourStory. But now the election is over, and nothing has changed. If she were to start a taxi service, she wouldn't need to worry about knowing what centenal she's in to figure out whether she can turn on red or stop to pick up a fare in the bus lane, because the entire city has one government. There are no public transportation crows here, but there are three bus routes. It's very different and sort of retro, but for the moment at least, Yoriko is happy with this low-drama option.

. . .

Domaine isn't going to ask, refuses to show any interest, although from purely professional curiosity, he's dying to know. The guard, or more likely intern, who brings him his meal doesn't mention results, even though voting must be over. She says nothing when she comes to collect the plates. Domaine is telling himself that this is a discipline, like fasting, going without Information so that he knows he can, when the intern comes back, silicon plates still in hand.

"Oh, hey," she says. "Did you want to know who won the election?"

Domaine's discipline won't let him beg, so he shrugs.

"Heritage won the Supermajority," the guard/intern says. "If you tell me what centenal you're from, I can check who won there."

"Don't bother," Domaine has the satisfaction of saying, turning his face toward the wall. Heritage won, huh? "Wait and see," he says, but softly. He doesn't need to give them any more reason to think he was involved in this.

Mishima is still catching her breath after finally finding Abendou in Nougaz's office. She tore all over the building, looking for him, before finally remembering that Information was back on and calling him.

"They'll find it," Abendou is saying as he hands her a cup of water. "He would have done better to take public transportation."

Mishima shakes her head, but she can neither talk nor drink yet. She shouldn't be this out of breath, but at least it keeps her from crying in frustration and anger.

"They'll find it, all right," Nougaz says. "In the nearest Heritage centenal."

"Yeah." Mishima finally manages to stand upright. "And Drestle with it. They'll never extradite him."

Abendou is muttering into his earpiece. "We've got people checking the likely crowflight routes between here and the three closest Heritage centenals, but you're right; he's probably already in their airspace." He touches Mishima's shoulder. "Sorry about that."

Mishima shrugs. "It was never really my crow," she says, managing a grin. "Information property, I'm afraid."

"And your things? Your data?" Nougaz asks.

"I never leave data on the crow," Mishima says. "Well, almost never." She might have gotten a little sloppy during the earthquake response, but fortunately not today. Her bag of essentials is by the espresso machine. "And it has a completely up-to-date security system."

"We're finding that our security is not what it used to be across the board," Nougaz says crisply. "Well. Are you ready to work?"

Mishima nods. She is already feeling better, letting the last twist of regret fade and shucking off the crow she loved so much. Although she does wonder what she would have to do during this debacle to get them to loan her a new one. Save the election? Save Information? Save the world?

"All right, then. I want you with my vote analysts cleaning up this election. We need to be absolutely certain on every single vote, and we need it as soon as possible, before Heritage has a chance to get entrenched. With every minute that the wrong result is out there, we lose credibility. I'll be working with the other directors to see how we can best present the results when we do have them, and have them absolutely verified and verifiable by anyone. Go!"

Mishima goes.

. . .

It takes the team of ten, with assistance from unknown numbers across the Information world, the better part of eight hours. Mishima spends the last couple of hours with two others building the interface for a program that will allow anyone to search, crunch, and individually verify votes using anonymous user codes. When they are finished, really finished, there are no cheers, no invitations to go for a glass of something. The faces around Mishima are drawn and pallid, and when she rubs her hands over her own, it feels the same. Some of the analysts are leaning back in their chairs with their eyes closed, others are talking quietly, and she sees a few who are already deep in Information, sucking in updates or news from wherever home is or catching up on some content or other. She stands up and wanders out of the analysts' subsection into the hallway, lets the timed light go out, and stands in the darkness.

She wants to go back to her crow and be alone and rest, but that's not possible. Next best thing: go somewhere else to be alone and rest. She grabs her handheld and looks for the nearest cheap hotel. Ah, even better: there's a Merita only a couple of blocks away. Yes, there will be more work to do, but they should be able to get along without her for a while, and Information is back up, so it's not like she'll be unreachable. She hits the light and starts down the stairs, feeling each step in her bones.

"Mishima."

It's Ken's voice, in her ear.

"Oh, man," she says. "You're still there."

"Yeah, but don't worry, I haven't been listening this whole

time. We had some other things to do here. Listen, you just got Heritage knocked off the Supermajority."

"Yeah," Mishima says. "They had it coming."

"Did you notice who you let in to take their place?"

She hadn't noticed it, not consciously, but even before she can bring up her handheld to look, she knows. "Liberty."

CHAPTER 31

Mishima ends up going to the Merita anyway. She tells Ken that if anything comes up, he should call her, or call the front desk to bang on her door if necessary, but she's pretty sure she's not going to save the world in the next eight hours. She's going to sleep, and she recommends he do the same.

When she gets there, though, she doesn't immediately get into bed. She knows sleep is not as urgent for her as solitude. This Paris branch of Merita is, inevitably, smaller than the Singapore version and slightly scruffier, but it is still the biggest and cleanest place she's slept since then. No, she forgot about the nights in the Adapted Maldives. Those days don't seem quite real. At least there's a scar to prove they happened.

She lets herself laugh hysterically for a while, then takes a bath, which she intends to be long, but which she finds she is too tired to enjoy. She towels off and falls into bed.

Once there, though, she is too tired to sleep. There are creaks from the floor and walls, and a rushing of water in pipes when someone on another floor takes a shower. The mattress is too soft. Mishima misses her perfectly calibrated futon, misses floating above a city cushioned by the isolation of empty air, misses her crow. She rolls over. How could she have let him get away with her crow? How could she have let him get away at all? She sits up in the not-quite-darkness of the hotel room and opens Information.

Mishima watches passively for a while, letting the kalei-doscopic play of her preferred feeds guide her through her deep exhaustion. They say that watching projections at night is bad for sleeping, that letting them switch around on auto is bad for concentration. *Don't worry.* Bad for everything. But this is Mishima's world and the way she interacts with it; her brain has long since remolded to respond to sensory over-load. So don't worry. She knows she needs the distraction, needs something to occupy the surface of her mind so the rest of it can work. And it works. She becomes aware of a thought, a phrase, tugging at her attention. A memory. *Don't worry, I haven't been listening this whole time.*

Ken. That was what he said. But what if it wasn't true? Mishima feels her psyche sink, can almost see her profile morphing into a new configuration even without running the diagnostic. Ken, listening in on the entire meeting with Nougaz and Abendou. Ken, who knows her crow, can guess how much it means to her. What if . . .

Kicking herself for being so careless with her comms, Mishima considers calling Roz to confirm what Ken was doing during the last few minutes of the vote, but it's even later in Qatar and everyone must be sleeping after the excitement. Besides, there are plenty of ways he could have warned Dres-tle without Roz knowing, even if she was sitting right next to him. And Mishima is already on Information. She checks everything she can find on Ken's activities and comms since Information came back on, and finds nothing remotely suspicious. He voted so immediately it must have been programmed and spent the rest of the time on a bunch of vote-tracking sites. No outward communications other than the ones to her, at least none that she can see.

Somewhat mollified, she wonders if she can find anything

from the Information blackout. Unsurprisingly, cameras with memory storage and people with too much time on their hands have already started filling in the gaps, and Mishima is able to browse a partial, gossip-ridden, patchy history of the past four days. Almost like being back in the early years of Information, she thinks, remembering the quirks and frustrations, the semisecret tricks for getting better intel.

Then an alert comes up, and her nostalgic reverie is cut short. A feed has identified two of her targets on the clandestine campaign workers list. Mishima is skeptical, but when she skims through the feed, the figure leaps out at her at once. He's looking away from the camera, but it's definitely Ken. What was he doing in Beirut yesterday? And what was he doing with Camille Saad, the Liberty spy, her fluttering hands accenting the inaudible words her mouth is forming as they walk through the feed's angle of vision? Mishima searches the surrounding area before and after but finds no other record of them in the patchy coverage. Saad is from Beirut originally, but what was Ken doing there? She cross-refs further back and finds a few days when the two of them overlapped in Lima. But there is no sign that they were ever in the same room together, or of any communication between them. Mishima searches the data, looking for certainty until she falls asleep, the lights of the projections playing over her face for a few minutes before they darken.

Having slept—fitfully and, as he has done for the past week, under his desk—for most of the time that Mishima spent counting votes, Ken does not take her advice. He spends the time prowling the reconstituted Information. He looks at the centenals that voted for Policy1st, learns about the cities in Sri Lanka mentioned in the bulletins he's been transmitting, finds out what companies inhabit the buildings around the Information offices here in Doha. He feels a remembered urge to pick through the demographics of the vote thread by thread but can't quite bring himself to look at any more ballots right now, real or fake. He puts on some music, reads some comedy, checks out the local news compilations from his centenal in Tokyo. He logs on to an interactive serial he follows. It's set in the tense time right before the election system was put in place, when underpaid bureaucrats with launch codes threatened to use long-forgotten nukes, and supposedly stable democratic governments strained at the seams. Ken plays a suave and experienced British spy who is supposed to unravel a number of (mostly) historically accurate conspiracies while avoiding assassination attempts and laying the foundations for the elections. The narrative is beautifully designed, with delicious atmospheric tension and period detail that has clearly been nitpicked by obsessives. Sometimes, though, Ken comes out of character briefly to wonder whether that era was really so much scarier and more nerve-wracking than the ridiculous election he's living through now.

Once he's sated his immediate Information and entertainment needs, he starts focusing in on the anticipated problem. He isn't able to find any evidence of territorial aggression so far, no troops massing on borders or suspicious arms trading, but it's early yet—Johnny Fabré hasn't even given his acceptance speech. He wonders what kind of advids and projections are playing in Liberty centenals now, and checks on the site in Beirut, but from what he can see, they've taken down all the sketchy stuff. While there's a lot of self-congratulation going on, it is all fairly restrained. He has a moment of doubt: did he really see those crazy advids, or was he hallucinating? There is no way to look it up, and his memory seems to become more tenuous with each passing hour.

He could look up the men who assaulted him, and he thinks about doing so but decides it would be an unhealthy way to spend the next several hours. He spins away from the Beirut centenal Information and returns to election news. Heritage is complaining vociferously on every platform it can find that it shouldn't be held accountable for the actions of one deranged individual, but hasn't made any statements indicating it will allow the extradition of said individual. PhilipMorris, which placed a close third for the Supermajority, is calling for a recount, suggesting, as Roz predicted, that if Information was wrong the first time, they might be wrong again. The vote-counter accessibility program Mishima and the others designed is defusing that.

He's researching the legality of centenal annexation when he sees something else. The advid shows up in a Policy1st plaza where he lurks occasionally, to monitor what people are talking about. It's anti-Information, which is not entirely surprising: Policy1stans do as much griping as anyone about the fairness, promptness, and transparency of Information, and probably more about their lack of a coherent policy platform. This, however, claims to be an exposé of malfeasance during the recent voting debacle, and Ken clicks it on with trepidation.

·   ·   ·

Despite her exhaustion, Mishima wakes suddenly and completely the next morning as wintry light spills into the room. She gets up, washes, and puts on the same clothes as the day before. She debates whether or not to check out but decides since she has very little luggage, she might as well. First, though, she goes downstairs to take advantage of the complimentary breakfast.

She calls Ken from the stairwell. "Hey," she says, and hears the wariness in her voice. Not the smoothest approach if she wants to catch him in a lie.

Ken is oblivious. "Hey!" he says. "Did you get some sleep? I've been monitoring all the centenals we highlighted; seems pretty quiet so far."

"Um." Mishima is uncomfortably aware that she could have gotten much more sleep if she hadn't binged on unfounded suspicions, and also that she never sent Ken the adjustments she made to his map of high-risk centenals. "Yeah, okay." Remembering Information is back on and the connection should be reasonable, she snaps on video. "What the hell happened to you?"

Ken had forgotten about his battered face. "Oh. Let's call it an early run-in with Liberty."

"What?"

He gives her an abbreviated version, focusing on the weirdness he saw in the centenal, downplaying the beating, and completely skipping over the beauty of the Liberty spy who came to his rescue. "Anyway, as I was saying, there are no signs of any illegal behavior."

"Other than beating the crap out of you?" Of course there was a reasonable (heroic, even) explanation for Ken being in Beirut.

"I'm fine," Ken says. "And it doesn't feel like it was an official attack. Although the experience does make me think we were right about them. All those insistent messages, and then the intranet thing—they are planning something. Everyone here is so focused on the election itself, they think everything's fine now that the voting is over and verified."

"I wish I shared their confidence," Mishima says, sitting down at the common table. "Hang on." A waiter is hovering. She orders a double espresso, scans the menu, and adds a termite and scrambled egg enchilada, a glass of carrot juice, and a yogurt parfait. After subsisting on energy chews for the last few days, she's starving for strong tastes and authentic protein.

"Sounds delicious," Ken says, his own stomach growling. Might be time to go see how the Sri Lankans are doing. "Listen, there's something else I have to tell you. I came across this vid last night claiming that Information saved the votes from the partial election to use for some sort of nefarious purpose . . ."

"Oh, yeah," says Mishima, remembering.

"And it referenced you, and um . . ." Ken coughs, embarrassed. ". . . some of the chaos going on in Information right after the blackout. It also sounded like it had your voice in it. I mean, it was hard to tell, because there was distortion, but it sounded like you saying something crazy like 'You should be dancing for joy that the election was disrupted' over and over again."

"Yeah, I've seen it," Mishima says. "Don't worry about it." Her food has arrived, and she puts the handheld down on the table and forks up the first bite. That vid reminds her: she should tell New York to let Domaine go. Partly because it was gutsy of him to record her *and* release it while still in custody, but also because, as far as she can figure, he hasn't done anything illegal. At least, not recently. And the Information he gave her did pan out. Not wanting to sign off from Ken yet, she types out the message with her left hand while eating.

Suzuki is finishing his poached egg on croissant when he sees that woman from Information walk in, casually dressed and ordering a big breakfast as if it were all over. He sops up the last of his egg, downs the dregs of his chocolate, and walks around the common table to where she's sitting.

"Excuse me," he says.

Mishima looks up. "I'll call you back," she mutters quickly into her handheld.

"Is that—" Ken's voice disappears as she cuts the connection.

"Suzuki-san," Mishima says in a more leisurely tone. "What can I do for you?" She's glad she decided to check out, if he's staying here.

"Listen," he says. He collapses onto the chair opposite her, as if he can't stay on his feet much longer. Mishima notices that his hands are trembling. "I just got a message from . . . an associate. From Okinawa. He's given us intel in the past, and it's always checked out. He keeps an eye, that is, he has an interest in Liberty." Amuru had reached Suzuki only half an hour earlier, after being unable to get through to Ken. "In any case, some of his contacts within the Liberty centenals in Okinawa told him that even though they had voted for Liberty, they were uneasy about some of the policies they were implementing."

"I didn't know they'd implemented anything yet," Mishima says, taking another forkful of her enchilada.

"That's the thing," Suzuki says. "Nobody did. Except their citizens. My colleague was able to get a copy, a photo, you understand, of the latest globe." He taps his handheld, and the projection, a tiny square of map, shoots up between them, small and intimate. "Look at this." He gestures with a shaking finger, but Mishima already sees it.

"Liberty holding most of southern Kyushu?" She doesn't want to show doubt in front of Suzuki, but she barely saw the final election results last night; she projects them quickly at eyeball level to be sure, then collapses them again. "Nope, not even close."

"That's right," Suzuki says, jabbing his finger at the map again. "Our globes show one thing, and those of Liberty's constituents another."

Mishima frowns, reaches for her coffee. "I'm not sure . . ."

"They have somehow managed to splinter Information." He sighs, runs both hands up through his hair. "You know, we received intel a few weeks ago, a month, saying that Liberty was threatening 'peaceful annexation' of traditional enemies of their citizens. I couldn't understand what this meant, 'peaceful annexation.' I didn't take it seriously, figured it was just a rallying cry for some of the more deluded among their likely constituency. But this . . ."

Mishima's gears have finally shifted into action. "Can you send me that?" she asks, spewing tiny fragments of mostly chewed enchilada. She shovels another couple of bites into her mouth—*so good*—gulps the carrot juice to wash it down. Sadly, she's going to have to leave the yogurt, but she manages another sip of the scalding coffee as she stands up.

"We'll work on this," she tells Suzuki. "Thank you for bringing it to me." And she's out the door.

. . .

Yoriko's kids are finally in school, and she is down by the harbor, flirting with the ice cream man, when the armada pulls in.

The Hidari Gomon Armada is what they call themselves, on the bright vertical banners—cloth, not projections— streaming from their masts. To Yoriko's eye, they are a collection of pleasure ships and fishing boats manned by a bunch of guys with nothing better to do. They jostle into the harbor, accompanied by a lot of yelling in a dialect that, under other circumstances, would be music to Yoriko's ears: they sound like home. Now, though, she finds herself embarrassed as the men—of course they're almost all men—act out a raucous disagreement about whether to stop for a meal or press on for their destination. The majority of the crafts dock, while a handful head back out to sea. A few minutes later, a pub's worth of sun-reddened men in their fifties and sixties straggles up from the marina onto the main street, where they spread out across the pavement as though it were a pedestrian-only area and belonged to them. They start peeling off into the different establishments—food, alcohol, souvenirs—and three of them enter the ice cream shop, the bell on the door clanging.

"Do you have any shaved ice?" one of the men asks.

The ice cream man, a dapper, balding fellow that Yoriko has taken a shine to, gestures toward the freezer. The man wanders over to look. "Only this premade kind?" He leaves in disgust.

"Sorry about him," another of the men says. His hair is combed back in an Elvis-style pompadour, a solid black wave that is probably dyed or genetically modified, because he looks to be in his sixties. His boating clothes are expensive, and there's a metallic flash from the gold chain on his chest. He looks familiar, and Yoriko tries to remember if she's ever driven him in her taxi, or if it's just that he runs true to type. "I think he got sunstroke on the way over."

"Sailed in from Okinawa, did you?" the ice cream man asks reluctantly. One of the things Yoriko likes about him is that he's normally quite reticent, but these guys clearly want to talk.

"Can I have a grilled-squid soft-serve cone, please?" asks the other man.

The ice cream man sets about loading the machine and preparing the cone.

"We left Okinawa right after the election results showed up. Couldn't believe it!" Elvis says, slapping his leg in self-congratulation. The ice cream man, back to the new customers as he winds out the cone, catches Yoriko's eye; this is going to be good.

"Liberty actually did it! Not only did they win the Supermajority, they won Satsuma!" The man is drooling. As the ice cream vendor hands over the cone to his companion, he smacks his lips and orders the Spam and bitter melon twist.

"Headed over there, are you?" the ice cream man asks. Yoriko is frantically checking the election results at eye level. It's not possible, is it? Could Liberty have somehow won Amami Ōshima too, without her knowing? But no, the results are the same as they were last time she looked, and Liberty has only a tiny smattering of centenals across all of Kyushu.

"Gotta go see it," Elvis agrees. "I mean, not to gloat or

anything . . ." He winks, hard, at Yoriko, who's afraid to talk lest they recognize her Okinawan accent. "But it's our government now, so we thought we might as well take a little vacation there."

The ice cream man hands over the second cone in a way that implies amiable agreement, though he says nothing.

"Well," Elvis says. "We'll be seeing you! And you should think about voting Liberty next time. All sorts of benefits!" He winks again, but Yoriko has already turned away to feign interest in the advids along the wall. What if her face is up on wanted posters in Liberty centenals?

She waits in the ice cream parlor until the armada departs. The ice cream man is in stitches over the whole thing—"Can you imagine their faces when they get there? *If* they get there."—which she finds comforting but not entirely convincing. As soon as the last boat has disappeared over the horizon, she walks out onto the street, shaking despite the tropical heat. Yoriko is desperate enough to briefly consider calling Suzuki but discards that idea almost immediately. He's the one who got her on Liberty's radar in the first place! Should she call her local Amami government? But what if they know she didn't vote for them? Besides, why should they care about what Liberty does?

Finally, although Yoriko has never thought of herself as a snitch, she calls Information. Amami Ōshima is too small to have a permanent Information hub, so she calls the one in Naha and tells her story. The man she talks to sounds impressed. "Hey, did you say you're not from there?" Yoriko explains that she just moved. "Listen, it just so happens we're looking for a nonlocal stringer for Amami. Send me your CV, okay? And don't worry about this mix-up with the election results. We're already looking into it."

. . .

"They're doing what?" Nougaz is already in the office when Mishima gets there.

"They're feeding different people different Information. Probably through these intranet adaptors for handhelds that we have intel about. I don't know; is this better or worse than an actual war?"

"It's going to explode into war if it goes on much longer," Nougaz assures her darkly.

"It does explain one thing that always confused me," Mishima says. "They were talking in such anachronistic terms, threatening countries rather than centenals. I couldn't understand how they planned to overrun a dozen centenals with a dozen different governments, so I figured it had to be an empty threat." She shakes her head. "How can people still think like that?"

"Twenty years isn't that long," Nougaz says. "Our job is to make sure Information and the centenal system survive long enough for those attitudes to disappear."

"To be replaced by centenal-to-centenal rivalries?" Mishima asks, one eyebrow arched.

Nougaz sighs. "I suppose we should feel flattered they're using Information rather than bombs for the moment."

Abendou yanks them back on track. "Is fragmenting Information even legal?"

"It's not, actually," Ken chirps into Mishima's ear. She called him back as soon as she was out of Suzuki's earshot to fill him in, and told him to look into any other cases of this.

"Hang on," she tells him, "let me put you on public." She taps the handset and Ken's image springs up in the projection space.

"It's not legal. I've been looking up what Liberty could and couldn't do with the Supermajority, because, well, we expected they'd do something."

"Ken is at the Doha hub," Mishima says by way of explanation to Nougaz, who is looking at her questioningly.

"Oh, this is Ken?" Nougaz tilts her head to look at the other side of his face. "Your face doesn't look as bad as I'd heard. How are you feeling?"

"Uh, fine," Ken says, after a pause. He hadn't realized the Information grapevine ran so quickly between offices, too.

"I was very impressed to hear about your exploits," Nougaz says. "Do go on."

"Right, um, thanks. Diverting, twisting, or otherwise affecting the Information received by citizens is illegal for any government," Ken says. "They can add data but not subtract or change. This holds true for the Supermajority as well, and we have a precedent to prove it."

"A precedent?" Abendou says. "Someone else has tried this craziness?"

"Not exactly the same," Ken says, "but in their first term, Heritage tried to finesse an unfavorable report on a wonder drug developed by one of the companies in their coalition that has since gone bankrupt. There was a cover-up about the chicken used at KFC, and another one about genetically modified corn from Monsanto. It was early in the Information age, and Heritage thought they could get away with blurring results, words, advertising claims, especially if they did it only in their centenals. Information was still trying to assert itself, and they jumped all over it, shut it down. The language in the legal precedent is clear and forceful."

"And we will shut this down just as hard," Nougaz says. "It's too bad this comes directly after the disaster with the election. Unbelievable, these people. But tant pis." She turns to Abendou. "Let's set up a meet with Liberty right away. I want all the director heads looped in, visibly or invisibly."

"You're going to talk to them?" Ken asks.

"That's step one," Nougaz answers.

Liberty stalls the meet for three hours, then sets it up in their own virtual space. "That way, we can't record them," Nougaz tells Mishima, who will watch with Abendou on Nougaz's projection so that they are not registered as separate participants. Nougaz herself is going in as an "along the wall" as opposed to "at the table" participant. As this is the first time that the Supermajority has changed hands, the protocols are still not fully in place, and Information has decided to bring two primary negotiators. Grier is in charge of Supermajority relations, but up till now he's only dealt with Heritage, so they've added Nejime, who spent years as the liaison to Liberty before taking on her current position as Archives Director. Looking at Nejime's back in the projection, Mishima knows that Ken and Roz are watching everything from her viewpoint.

On the Liberty side, Johnny Fabré sits at the end of the table, facing them. Except for a brief greeting, however, he doesn't speak. The main negotiator is a narrow man sitting to his right, around the corner so that his face is visible only in profile. He looks down as though he were reading from notes, although Mishima doesn't think he is. She can't decide whether he's acting self-effacing to comply with some denialist policy about pretending Fabré's in charge, or whether he's avoiding responsibility. Either way, it bothers her. She's used to assuming that the leadership of Liberty is on an ego trip fueled by populism and lucre; seeing someone there uninterested in his own stature unnerves her.

"The people have spoken," he says in a patient tone, as though explaining to children. "We are enacting the mandate they have given us."

"These so-called annexations were hardly a prominent plank in your campaign platform," Nejime says dryly.

The man curls his wrist in a gesture of dismissal. "Based on polling, we are convinced the issue was decisive to our election."

"Whether you have a mandate or not," Grier says, "this aggression is illegal."

"We have not committed aggression," the man says, feigning shock. "No one has been hurt."

"You have committed an aggression against the truth and transparency of Information," Grier says. "Illegal."

"What do you think is going to happen when people start figuring this out?" Nejime says. "When people in Singapore hear that Liberty citizens in Malaysia think they have conquered them, when Turks learn that, in Greek Liberty centenals, Cyprus is entirely Greek, and vice versa?"

"We find that the people who hate each other that much rarely view the same types of Information," the man says. "It seems terribly unlikely that they will ever know. In the meantime, everyone is happy, and the possibility for real aggression is being defused."

"It is, nonetheless, illegal," Grier repeats. "We are ordering you to cease and desist."

"As the Supermajority government, we believe we have some latitude to adjust the laws in minimal ways where necessary," the man says without changing his tone.

"They expected this," Mishima whispers to Nougaz as

Grier goes into the various precedents when Heritage tried to throw around its weight. "They're not going to back down."

"'The Supermajority position,'" Grier quotes, "'allows for smooth decision-making as necessary on rules governing minor elements of inter-government relations. It is not a position that allows for any interference with elections or Information.' Micro-Democracy Charter, section 58.3."

Unexpectedly, Johny Fabré smiles. "Every system must be refreshed from time to time with revolution," he says. And Liberty closes the meet.

CHAPTER 32

Mishima follows Nougaz from the secure comms room in the Paris hub and catches up with her a few yards down the hall. "Listen," she says. "I made a—an error in dealing with an informant a while ago." Was it only a couple of days ago she was in New York? A week? "He was somehow able to get into my data—I think he got a beacon past all my scanners on a previous meeting and then used it to copy some files. He recorded me, too." She takes a breath. "The point is, he made this." She projects Domaine's vid at an intimate size and in two dimensions so only the two of them can easily see it. "Use it," she says when it's finished. "Say the last elections were flawed, call another vote, and blame it on me. Get rid of these people."

Nougaz appraises her. "Very noble," she says, in a way that makes Mishima think she's read her: she's realized that this isn't a sacrifice, that Mishima isn't throwing herself on a grenade so much as grabbing for a parachute. At this moment, Mishima is tired, disillusioned, and ready to be out of this whole mess. "But I think we are still a formidable enough organization to manage this particular problem without recourse to a scapegoat. Besides, we've already admitted to one election miscount; I'd rather not invent another."

Nougaz pauses for Abendou, who has been hovering a few steps back, to catch up to them. "We'll have a strategy within the hour," she says, nodding to him. He nods back and turns

360 · MALKA OLDER

toward his office. Nougaz shifts her attention back to Mishima. "Take a day off," she says. "When you're back, I want you with the analysts' team. We need all the help we can get, and yours particularly."

Mishima opens her mouth to say that she's fine, that she can go straight to work, and then shuts it again. She nods and goes to find a hotel Suzuki is not staying at.

Ken, on the other hand, is immediately drafted, and he takes to the work with gusto. Nejime appropriates him from Roz, and he spends the afternoon finding ways to build the story of Liberty's treachery into every conceivable platform. News compilers are only the most obvious way to tell the world that the new Supermajority is lying to its constituents and promoting territorial aggression. They work it into talk shows, political features, telenovelas, serials, trade shows, cooking classes, tourist brochures, projection games, documentaries, educational programs, celebrity stalking, encyclopedia entries, and dance contests. Ken is particularly enjoying the task of wandering into centenal virtual plazas and spouting propaganda to whomever he meets there.

"It's amazing," he tells Roz when he stops by to get her for dinner. "I think Information is finally getting a grasp of how to do public relations. If you guys could improve your own image half as well as we're destroying Liberty's, people wouldn't hate you so much."

"Hmm," grunts Roz. Ken wonders whether it's the criticism or the fact that his job is suddenly so much more interesting than hers that is making her grumpy.

"I heard that Information is Lumpering every Liberty

centenal," he says to cheer her up. "*And* working on Lump-ering all the places they lied about."

"Hmph," Roz says, a grumpier variation on her first re-sponse. "Doesn't do much for bombs or flamethrowers. Or pointed sticks, for that matter."

"They've contracted LesProfessionnels on contingency to act as peacekeepers," Ken says. He has been caught up in the excitement flowing around Nejime's office, but Roz's skepticism is slowing him down.

Roz stops at the entrance to the cafeteria. "Let's go out for dinner," she says. "I think you need some air."

"So, what have you been doing all day?" Ken asks as they leave the Information building. It is later than he thought, and the air is refreshingly cool.

"I'm on the SVAT team."

Ken struggles with it for a moment. "The what?"

"Specialized Voter Action Tactics team. For those places where the work you're doing is just too subtle."

"Oh. Wow." Roz's voice gives no hint of pride, but the title sounds impressive to Ken, so *wow* seems appropriate.

"I was working centenals along the old India-Pakistan border most of the day," Roz explains. "With LesProfessi-onnels."

"You *what?*" So much for having the cooler job.

"I do get out of the office sometimes, you know."

"So, what you said about the bombs and flamethrow-ers . . ." Ken realizes he is rubbing the slowly diminishing bump on the side of his head, and makes himself stop.

Roz allows herself a smile. "Today was closer to the pointy sticks and thrown rocks end of the spectrum. But there were a few flamethrowers, yes."

"Are you okay?" They turn out of the office park area onto the shopping street. The awnings that shade the street during the day have opened to allow glimpses of the fading sky.

"I'm fine," Roz says. "It looked like the violence might spill over there, and at that point, nobody is bothering to look at Information for anything except tactics and weaknesses— you know one of our indicators for this is the density of searches for *The Art of War* in local translation?" She rolls her eyes. "These people are so predictable. So, we go in and provide face-to-face Information dissemination where we think it is will have the greatest effect."

Ken is silent for a moment, picturing Roz, as calm and centered as always, patiently explaining to a regressive nationalist desperate for blood and relevance how that authentic-sounding Information about the election was actually counterfeit while muscled ex-French legionnaires with flamethrowers guard the perimeter. "So, did it?" he asks at last.

"Did it what?" Roz is studying a display menu, printed on paper and arranged on a small podium in front of a modest restaurant: a holdover from the blackout.

"Have an effect."

"Some." She runs her finger down the menu, as though savoring the tactility. "Not as much as we'd like. They've been given exactly what they've been dreaming about for years, and now we tell them it's not true. It's a hard sell. Of course, when I say 'they,' I mean a tiny fraction of the people in each centenal who are ready to go conquer. The rest are just confused. I think we're going to shift the focus to them tomorrow." She shakes her head. "But we came out here to clear our heads. Shall we try this place? Maryam told me it's pretty good."

. . .

On her day off, Mishima goes for a long walk. She cuts as straight a path as she can to the river, then turns left and follows its long bend through Paris. It's an ugly day, cold and moist and overcast, with a fierce wind along the quais, but she has a fully charged heater jacket, and with that comfort around her core, she almost enjoys the wet bite of the air on her face. She watches the bateaux-mouches and the barges in the river, and the joggers and the dog-walkers along its banks. There aren't many people sitting still in this weather. She gets as far as the Île aux Cygnes before she decides to turn back. Tired, she shortens the return by cutting through the city. She crosses six different centenals on her way, and each border is obvious. Sometimes, it is the litter on the sidewalk coming to a sharp end, or the roads suddenly riddled with potholes, or the cluster of teenagers who have clearly crossed into the next centenal to smoke cigarettes before going back to class. One government—she doesn't even bother to check which—has set up sidewalk heaters along the central strip of the Boulevard Pasteur, and old women and unemployed men sit there, feeding the pigeons and drinking from brown paper bags. She passes through a street fair selling delicacies from sister centenals in the provinces, and detours into the shared territory of the Jardin du Luxembourg, restfully free of advids and animations by common treaty.

She stops at a hotel near the Panthéon that looks pleasant and spacious, and finds that it is both. Pricey, but she decides to expense it, even if Information didn't exactly send her to Paris and require that she stay here, even if it is a day off. After all, an Information employee just crowjacked her apartment. There's enough floor space in the room that she can lie on the spotless parquet and stretch out her arms. Staring at the off-white ceiling, she lets her narrative disorder run wild.

Liberty planted Drestle to ruin Heritage's chances. Heritage has a secret agreement with Liberty, an illegal corporate merger nobody knows about. SecureNation is using them both and getting away with it because of its willingness to be the power behind the Supermajority. Suzuki plotted out the whole thing, down to their supposed chance meeting in the restaurant this morning. Ken . . . but when she thinks about Ken, she diverts into an entirely different type of narrative. She veers back to the outcome she fears most, the worst case she has avoided envisioning until now. Information, fading into irrelevance due to the stable Supermajority, planned the whole thing. Frustrated with the impossibility of getting people to make informed choices, stymied by the name-recognition problem and the celebrity factor and a million other quirks of neurobiology, the people who cared decided to manipulate the people who didn't.

Trite, she thinks. But now that she's looked, she can't look away.

She runs through it again, tests for narrative cohesion, for character motivations, for verisimilitude.

Not the attack on Tokyo, she decides. Everything else, maybe, but not that.

She starts over with that new parameter, and lets the stories swirl through her mind until she falls asleep.

Ken finds his new job far more comfortable than the last one. At first, he attributes it to the convivial atmosphere: the Information compilers under Nejime are young, gregarious to the point of being rowdy, and every scruffy overeducated one of them seems to think they've hit the employment jackpot. Ken had gotten used to and even come to admire Roz's intensity, but it didn't make for what he would call a fun work environment.

It isn't until the second day that he realizes it's not the company that makes him feel at home but the work. He's slid into the groove so easily that he didn't realize how familiar it is. They call it compilation and distribution, or in some cases highlighting and contouring, but he's done it before under a different name: campaigning. As habitual as it is for him, he can't shake the feeling that doing it for Information is somehow amiss.

Curious about the other prong of Information's response, he looks for reports on the SVAT team activities Roz told him about. He's surprised at how difficult it is to find anything. In the end, all he gets is a five-line report telling him there are eight SVAT teams deployed in different areas of the world (one, he notices with interest, on the extreme southern tip of Kyushu). No vids, no manual, no results. He is relieved when he finds some commentary by witnesses or participants, although the fact that most of it is numbingly positive ("so polite and professional . . . I didn't think Information staff would be like that"; "after talking with them, I have a much better understanding of the situation") makes him worry that something is being suppressed.

Partly to test his theory, and partly because he thinks it would make a great addition to their campaign, he floats an idea for how to highlight the SVAT team activities: a new, short-format game focused on diplomacy in high-stress situations, with enough fight sequences to attract subjects with violent proclivities. It is immediately squashed. "We'd rather not put our resources toward promoting Information," Nejime tells him personally. "The story is not about us." It's a reasonable explanation, especially given the budget equivalency policy, but after that, Ken can't quite find the same enthusiasm for highlighting and contouring.

Mishima's job with the analysts, when she gets back to the Paris office early the next morning, is to unpack polls, plaza trends, opinionators, and any other voter intel she can find to identify Liberty's weakness and optimize the timing. Instead, she sets up her workspace and starts looking at data from Tokyo. She tries satellite imagery first but doesn't see what she's looking for, so she starts going through the servers at the office, the last inputs before the comms went down, intel that hasn't been sorted, analyzed, or broadcast.

Even in that relatively short timeframe, it's a lot of material, especially when she's looking for something clandestine. By six in the evening, she has found nothing, and she leaves the office. She gets dinner at the restaurant Suzuki was haunting, sitting at a table by herself with content flashing before her eyes. She plays *Crow Wars V* for a while to distract herself, but the bad guy has been redesigned to resemble Johnny Fabré. She shuts it down in disgust and eats, enjoying the pigeon breast in mirabelle sauce and watching the other patrons, and then walks back to her hotel. She is still exhausted enough to sleep easily, which is unusual and welcome.

The next morning, in the analysts' section, she turns off her translator to listen to the tone of the chatter around her without understanding its content. Subdued, still. Determined, she thinks. Hopeful, but not yet certain. They're not there yet. She turns the translator back on and gets to work, cross-referencing with the data she put together on the recent movements of clandestine operatives from the different governments.

Midafternoon, she finds it. Maybe. Probably. With the clue—a materials shipment to a certain address in a Heritage centenal in Odaiba, on Tokyo Bay—she goes back to the satellite photos, narrowing the window in space and time. The indications are slight, but she sees them.

If she still had a crow, she would go herself, but she doesn't. And, if she's honest with herself, it would probably take too long, anyway. She goes through official channels instead. Not the head of the Tokyo hub, who's too close to it. Not Nougaz, because as simpática as she is, she wields a lot of power and seems comfortable that way, and Mishima can't get that worst-case scenario out of her head.

She goes to the Kansai hub director, Koshino, whom she knows slightly. He listens to her while looking at the data she's sent over (she didn't bother using a secure connection; at this point, the more people who see this, the better).

He stares at it for a while, then mumbles in his deep voice, "You figured this out using your narrative disorder?" sounding awestruck.

Mishima takes a moment to smile at the success of her strategy to turn her disability into a superpower. This means it's time for phase two: modesty. "That wasn't the narrative disorder," she says. "I just took a step back to look at what didn't fit. Hard to do on an emergency schedule."

"The attack on the Tokyo office," Koshino growls.

"We assumed that it was part of the disruption of the election, but that made no sense. The election was already disrupted. So, I looked for something else."

"And you think it's in the bay?" Koshino asks.

"It's the only place they could conceivably hide it. Also because of the location of that property. It makes sense. Easily accessible by existing transportation but right on the water."

"Why would they move ahead before the approvals went through?" Koshino practically spits at the stupidity of the former Supermajority.

Mishima can't answer and barely cares. "The usual, I imagine. Maybe they suspected they wouldn't be able to hold the Supermajority this time and wanted to lock the deal in for their centenals. Maybe something to do with the construction contract. One way or another, it must be the money."

"Korbin hasn't mentioned anything about this," Koshino muses. "Maybe she didn't know."

"Korbin . . ." Mishima feels her confident grasp on the situation evaporate.

"You didn't hear?"

She hadn't. She had been busy taking a step back.

"Korbin turned herself in yesterday. She gave Heritage the access they needed to trigger the Information and comms blackout." He pauses, but Mishima is in no state to say anything yet. "She claims she didn't know exactly what they would use it for, and she is adamant that she had no idea there would be a physical attack on the office. She seems genuinely distraught over contributing to the deaths of her colleagues . . ." He shrugs. "Hard to say whether it's true, but I believe her. In any case, her evidence gives us enough to fully sanction Heritage."

Some superpower, Mishima thinks. A couple of long nights bonding over disaster response and her narrative disorder is lulled into a completely false storyline. She remembers Korbin on the external stairwell: "There's a lot of concern over the possibility of Heritage winning again." She must have thought the deck was stacked too steeply against them; she must have gotten too close . . .

After waiting again for a response that doesn't come, Koshino goes on. "We did think that there was something missing from the story, so if you're right"—up until thirty seconds ago, Mishima was positive that she was—"this could clear a lot up. Let's see what we find."

Koshino moves quickly. A dive team is scrambled with members from the Kansai, Kyushu, and Tokyo offices, and they're in the water almost before that conversation is over. The first dive finds nothing.

Neither does the second. Koshino has linked Mishima in to watch, but she's only glancing at the watery projection occasionally as she works on what she's supposed to be doing: analysis of voter moods. The strategy is working; voters are shocked by Liberty's cavalier management of constituent intel. They wonder what else they might have been lied to about. There is voter's remorse; there are rumblings. Nobody has mentioned the possibility of another election, but in her estimation, most people will probably welcome it. Mishima isn't ready to make the go recommendation, but it's getting close. Tokyo should tip it over the edge, if they find what she expects they will.

Some of the outrage is, naturally, deflecting on to Information. The usual groups and plazas and opinionators are heating up, launching diatribes and petitions for legal changes to weaken the global bureaucracy. Domaine's vid is popular in those circles and is spreading beyond them, but it doesn't look like it will jump to viral status. That creep at the Liberty meeting was right about one thing: despite all the Information available, people tend to look at what they want to see.

The third dive finds a well-hidden gouge in the seabed: the underwater drill site for the first mantle tunnel, planned to stretch from Tokyo to Taipei, begun in secret without approvals or Information coverage.

So, they're going to call an election?" Ken asks Roz. They're at the Persian restaurant they discovered two nights ago, finishing their zulbia with coffee.

"That's the plan," Roz says. She checks updates. "Maybe tonight."

"Are they sure?" Ken asks.

"In theory," Roz says. He thinks she's finished, because she pauses to take a sip of coffee, but then she goes on. "In theory, no one can be sure of the behavior of voters."

"So, they're taking a risk."

Roz sips again. "I suppose we could keep running elections until we get the results we want."

Her voice is as dark as the coffee. This, besides his gratitude, is why he keeps ditching the gung-ho gang of compilers to eat with Roz. Their unquestioning eagerness is starting to grate.

"What they did was illegal," he points out, as much for himself as for Roz. "It's not like Information does this every time."

Roz doesn't answer, even though Ken waits for two sips to be sure. He squirms. "Where were you today?"

"Iran-Iraq border. The centenal in India has calmed down for the moment. But this one . . . Today got violent."

Ken opens his mouth, but she shakes her head. "Not us. LesProfessionnels dealt with it. We weren't the ones who got hurt. But still . . . People are being displaced into neighboring centenals. This is not going to end with the election." She takes a breath. "We're lucky, though. So far, it's only a few spots, a limited number of centenals. And they're isolated from each other; it's not like they can find common cause."

Ken waits, watches while she sips her coffee again, then changes the subject because the idea of war is too terrifying for him. "This mantle tunnel thing . . . Do you think it caused the earthquake?" Ken has found it difficult to relish that development. Yes, it knocks Heritage out of the running for anything above centenal census-taker for the foreseeable future, but every time he thinks about Tokyo, he remembers a dusty arm curling out of a weighty mound of debris. He hates the idea that someone, some group of people, caused all that destruction.

"The truth is, nobody knows," Roz says. She sighs, puts down the check she was fiddling with. "I've been reading everything I can find on the subject, and I haven't found a reputable geologist, seismologist, or engineer who was willing to commit one way or the other. And the disreputable ones are split down the middle. Not that it matters." Information didn't even have to raise the issue. As soon as the fact that Heritage had been illegally drilling in Tokyo Bay came to light, dominating the news compilers, the plazas lit up with the question of whether it led to the earthquake. "We know that it caused at least two deaths: the Information employees killed in the Tokyo attack."

"So, that attack didn't have anything to do with the election?"

"The attack on the election had to do with the mantle

tunnel. That was part of what made Heritage so desperate to ensure they would win. Then, while they were at it, they decided to make sure there was nothing incriminating in the data at the Tokyo office." She frowns. "We're not sure yet, but the attackers are still denying they knew anything about the tunnel, and my guess is that's why they had to come back. They were told to destroy servers and data, but they didn't do the job completely the first time, because they thought it was about keeping the comms down rather than getting rid of specific evidence."

Ken wants to ask about Mishima, but he's embarrassed to admit he hasn't talked to her in a few days, so instead, he grabs the check. "I got this," he says, grinning. "Yasmin told me they've worked out a way to pay me for my time here."

"You've earned it," Roz says. "So, are you sticking around?"

"Um . . . we'll see."

"You've got to stay at least until Mishima gets back. She said she wanted to watch the election results with us."

"Oh, yeah, of course," Ken says, laughing with relief. "I wouldn't miss that."

CHAPTER 33

For the first time in a long time, Mishima flies commercial. It hasn't gotten any better. But at least it's a relatively short hop, Paris to Doha. To complete the experience, she takes a public transportation crow in from the airport, swaying in the bench seating as it follows the shortest route that gets everyone where they want to go.

The Doha hub has set up a viewing party in the canteen, with refreshments of a higher caliber than the free food everyone there has been eating for two weeks. The partitions have been removed and animated banners shimmy across the walls, thanking the staff for all their extra efforts.

By the time Mishima gets there, at twenty hours in, the results are shaping up. The scandals triggered by Heritage and Liberty have hurt corporates across the board, although PhilipMorris is too strong to be completely knocked out of the running, and 888, Sony-Mitsubishi, and other non-Western corporates took less of a hit. Mishima looks for Ken among the crowd of Information workers watching the projections. She spots him next to Roz and Roman, fluted glass in hand. His tense face tells her he's not ready to believe it yet. He's so enthralled, he barely notices her. Or maybe he's playing hard to get. Mishima mingles.

Looking across the crowd, she's surprised to catch a glimpse of Nougaz. The older woman meets her gaze and gives that distant nod that does nothing to reduce the awkwardness of running into someone in an unfamiliar context. Curious, Mishima stares but can't make out much through the crowd and shrugs it off. She gets something to eat and then finds her way back to catch up with Roz.

Mishima keeps an eye on Ken's face, tight-lipped and twitchy as they make the formal announcement—"Hopefully, it'll stick this time!" someone yells—that Policy1st has won the Supermajority. Then he's hugging everyone, forgetting that they're not all on the same team, that not everyone in the Information office shares his enthusiasm.

"Oh, hey," he says to Mishima, even though she'd already said hi to him twice. "You look great!"

She grins as he goes on to hug Roz and then Roman and then Stanislaw the statistician, whom he's never met, and then wobbles toward the dance floor. Mishima and Roz go back to obsessing over the finer grain of the results. Liberty has lost centenals, not just compared to its win a few days ago but even compared to its fourth-place showing ten years before that. "And that's before the legal action," Roz says with some satisfaction.

Glancing up at the dance floor, Mishima notices Nougaz and Maryam making out with the sort of passion that only a long-distance relationship can inspire.

"So that's why Maryam left Paris so suddenly!"

Roz follows her gaze. "Oh, yes," she says, grinning with relief. "It's been tough on Maryam these past few months; hopefully, they can find a way to make it work."

"Looks like they're trying!"

They drop their heads back into the data. Heritage has lost all its centenals in the Kantō area and in Taipei as well; they've dropped a few in other places but not as many as she expected. The upcoming prosecution for election tampering is likely to weaken them further. Interestingly, a sideline poll shows that approval of Information has dropped significantly, but since they never have to get elected, that is more an indicator to factor into future strategy than a loss.

When the party has calmed down a little, Mishima takes Ken up to the roof. There's a garden there, a small plot with chilies, sesame, basil and rosemary, a patch of cosmos, and a young guava tree, surrounded by hanging lanterns and places to sit. He didn't even know about this, but clearly it's a relaxation area for the staff. It's midnight now, and no one is there. Or maybe Mishima had it cleared for them; that's another possibility. Since coming to Doha, most of Ken's outdoor experience has been during the day, skating from one shadow to the next, sweating and burning as the heat pressed him toward the ground. At night, it's entirely different. The air is warm, but there's a breeze that smells of mint and henna, and the sky seems to have opened up above them, vast and embroidered with stars. The office park surrounding them is dark, but out in the city he can see lights on other roofs, distant squares of dun and red hovering in the darkness. Ken hears music from somewhere; live or recorded, it's too faint to tell. Drums and a winding melody, a horn or a reed or a nasal voice drifting on the breeze.

Ken settles into a wood-and-wicker settee; Mishima drapes herself sideways over an armchair of the same materials. He's tempted to make some joke about whether she'd stab him if the power went out, but he's afraid to jostle their détente. Then he does it anyway. He's learned to live dangerously.

Mishima snorts. "No, this time I think I'd just push you off the roof."

Ken hesitates a second before laughing, and that makes Mishima laugh harder, falling into the seat of the chair. When at last Ken manages to stop giggling, his body feels as if it's been through shiatsu, slumped weightlessly against the lounger. He sighs and stares up at the stars.

Mishima passes him a flask. "Congratulations, by the way," she says.

Ken tips the flask in salute and drinks. "Thank you," he says. "Not that I had much to do with it."

"Come on," says Mishima. "That centenal you were working in Chennai went to Policy1st. And I think you had something to do with Miraflores."

She's been tracking him, Ken thinks, flattered. She couldn't follow him while Information was down, so she doesn't know about what he considers his greatest success: the first Policy1st centenal in Sri Lanka, just south of Colombo. "Well." He passes the flask back to her. "It's been a team effort." He cracks up before he can get the whole phrase out, and they both start laughing again. "No, but really," he manages when he can breathe again. "It's been an experience."

That has a note of finality to it. "You're not going to try to find a job with Policy1st? Exciting times." Mishima takes a drink, passes it back.

Ken grimaces. "I don't know. Suzuki was my . . . contact there, and now . . ." Mishima never had to use her intel on Suzuki's illicit campaigning. Once data was restored from the crashed servers, the vid of him pretending to vote went viral. He resigned before he was asked to and is working on his memoirs.

"They'd be lucky to have you," Mishima says. "Someone there must realize that."

It's probably true, and Ken does know most of the major players to some degree, but no one has gotten in touch and he's not in the mood to go begging. It's not pride, or not only pride. He's not sure how much he believes in Policy1st anymore. Working on the campaign stripped away a lot of his loyalty and idealism, and he imagines that with the Supermajority, things will only get worse. Things meaning people, and policies, and principles.

"Ten years is a long time to wait for the next election," is all he says.

"What about Information?" Mishima asks. "You've earned some goodwill there."

Ken drinks. "It's been great here, but I don't think I want to live in Doha."

He doesn't tell her that Nejime has already asked him to work on the restructured image team. "We're rebuilding it from scratch," she promised him. "We could use someone with your unique combination of experience and skills." He was tempted; she had pushed all his buttons with a few neat sentences. Maybe that's why he doesn't think he's going to take it. It is too close to the way Suzuki used to talk, too much highlighting and contouring.

Mishima laughs. "There are other hubs." She takes the flask. "Nougaz offered me a job in Paris."

"Oh? What kind of job?"

"She wants me to be some kind of special advisor and move into deputy when Abendou makes director."

"That sounds good," says Ken, who knows none of these people and still doesn't have a clear understanding of Information office structure. "Are you going to take it?"

"I haven't decided." Mishima drinks. She's been trying to picture herself strolling around Paris as if she belonged there. Maybe wearing heels, an inconvenient luxury her work in the field usually precludes. Or a compromise, heeled boots. Wandering the streets, stopping by her favorite boulangerie. It's pretty but unconvincing. "It's a great opportunity but . . . different, you know?" She yawns. "I don't know; maybe I'm ready for a change."

"Sure," Ken says, taking the flask back. He's thinking about the other possibility within Information: Roz told him that they are going to expand the SVAT team program, try to use it not just for peacekeeping but for better data dissemination in the most underinformed centenals. She must have seen that his imagination was already running away from him, because she immediately warned him that it wouldn't be as good as it sounds. It's certain to get tangled in bureaucracy and unlikely to have much impact even when it goes to the right places to do the right things. More than that, it would be dangerous.

"But you're going to do it?" he had asked.

"I'm already fully inoculated against disappointment in this particular bureaucracy," Roz had answered.

"I know this guy," Mishima says after a pause. She's looking out at the rooftops and doesn't notice Ken tense up. "He's in the . . . antielection movement, I guess you could say. Sometimes, I almost think I could join it."

Ken tips the flask, swallows. He's glad she said "join it" rather than "join him." "If they're antielection," he says at last, "what are they for?"

Mishima laughs, sort of. "Nothing I can name. I guess that's why I never quite decide to join them."

Ken passes the flask back, and Mishima takes a swig. "Did you hear? They're saying next round they're going to try to get down to the ten-thousand-person level," she says. "Instead of centenals, I don't know, decimals. To keep minorities from getting overrun in their centenals, you know? And so that people take more responsibility for their votes and hopefully make more informed choices. *Nano*-democracy, they're calling it."

Ken shakes his head, exhausted just imagining it. "Do they really think that will help?"

Mishima shrugs, and passes the flask. "I suppose someday they'll get down to one, and then we'll all be happy."

Ken grunts out a laugh, drinks, and says, "I'm thinking about getting out of politics for a while."

Mishima looks at him as though he said he wanted to get out of breathing for a while.

"I mean," Ken says, "until the next election. Or something."

Mishima laughs, briefly. "Do you know why they set the elections ten years apart?" Ken shakes his head. "So that there would be time for governing in between bouts of politics."

"It doesn't work," Ken says immediately.

"I know."

"There are the centenal elections—some governments do them as often as every two years. And referendums and policy shifts within that. The last five years are all about positioning."

"Among the big governments," Mishima reminds him.

"True." Ken yawns. He can't help it. "So, yeah, I guess trying to govern, or whatever, in one of the smaller governments would be like doing something different." He remembers the centenal in Jakarta where he watched the first debate, Free2B. He never did look up all their outposts. "Or maybe I'll become a . . . a bartender."

Mishima laughs, a real laugh this time. Bartenders don't exist anymore outside of films and extremely pretentious bars.

Ken laughs too. "Or a game designer, or a crow mechanic."

"You really think you could live like that?" Mishima is trying to imagine what it would take to slow her pulse down, how it would feel. She imagines the problematic mountain range of her psyche smoothing into a gentle, dull plain, the colors overlapping into blah. Even if she survived like that, even if she liked it, she can't imagine it would last. There would be an emergency somewhere. Someone would call her, offer her payment and per diem, tell her she's the only one who can help, and that would be it.

"Sure. For a couple of years, at least. Could you?" He's searching Free2B's centenals. Looks like there are a few good options, climactically speaking: Peru, northern Vietnam, a couple in New Zealand.

"We could try."

ABOUT THE AUTHOR

Malka Older is a writer, humanitarian worker, and PhD candidate at the Centre de Sociologie des Organisations (Sciences Po) studying governance and disasters. Named Senior Fellow for Technology and Risk at the Carnegie Council for Ethics in International Affairs for 2015, she has more than eight years of experience in humanitarian aid and development, and has responded to complex emergencies and natural disasters in Sri Lanka, Uganda, Darfur, Indonesia, Japan, and Mali. *Infomocracy* is her first novel.